Also by the Author

Razorhurst
Liar

MYSISTERROSA

JUSTINE LARBALESTIER

Published in the United States by Soho Teen an imprint of
Soho Press, Inc.
853 Broadway
New York, NY 10003

Library of Congress Cataloging-in-Publication Data

Larbalestier, Justine.
My sister Rosa / Justine Larbalestier.
1. Brothers and sisters—Fiction. 2. Psychopaths—Fiction.
3. Australians—United States—Fiction. 4. New York (N.Y.)—Fiction.
I. Title.
PZ7.L32073 My 2016 [Fic]—dc23 2016006797

ISBN 978-1-61695-674-5
eISBN 978-1-61695-675-2

Interior design by Janine Agro, Soho Press, Inc.

Printed in the United States of America

10 9 8 7 6 5 4 3 2 1

For my agent, Jill Grinberg,
who's always believed in my writing
and had my back when I needed her most.

A Note to American Readers:

While this novel is set in the United States of America its narrator is Australian. Some of the spellings, words and expressions may look wrong to American eyes, but Australians really do say we had *concussion*, not we had *a concussion*. And we truly *down tools* at the end of the day, or on the weekend, or whenever we feel like it. That just means we stopped working.

We decided against Americanizing Che's voice because we wanted readers to be able to experience his story in his own authentic voice.

PART ONE
Keep Rosa under Control

CHAPTER ONE

Rosa is pushing all the buttons.

She makes the seat go backwards and forwards, the leg rest up and down, in and out, lights on, lights off, TV screen up, TV screen down.

We've never been in business class. Rosa has to explore everything and figure out what she's allowed to do and how to get away with what she isn't.

The flight attendants love her. Flight attendants always love Rosa. Most strangers do. She's ten years old with blonde ringlets, big blue eyes, and dimples she can turn on and off like, well, like pushing a button.

Rosa looks like a doll; Rosa is not a doll.

She's in the window seat, which means there's me between her and any potential victims. For the moment she's enjoying the buttons. She can get lost like that, pushing buttons, counting sand, calculating angles, figuring out how things work, how to make them work for her.

I'm hoping she'll be distracted all the way to New York City. It's not a strong hope. The flight is long: Rosa will get bored, she'll look for ways to make trouble without Sally and David, our parents, finding out. That's the game she plays. My job is to stop her.

Business class will keep her occupied longer than economy ever did. It is pretty sweet. I can stretch out. When I reach forward I can barely touch the seat in front. Nothing bangs into my knees. If only there were a gym. If only the plane was headed home to Sydney.

"I wonder how hard it would be to open the emergency exit." Rosa is staring at the safety card.

"For you? Impossible. You're too small. Besides, no one can get them open when a plane is in flight." I don't know if that's true. I'm sure Rosa will look it up later and tell me.

"What about setting the plane on fire?"

She wouldn't be saying any of this if Sally and David could hear. But they're in the row in front of us and the low hum of the engines swallows our words. I can hear everything Rosa says, the click and buzz of the buttons she pushes, the creak of her seat, and she can hear me; but we can't hear anyone else's words and no one can hear ours.

"Che."

"Yes, Rosa?"

Is she going to ask about blowing up the plane?

"I wish we'd stayed in Bangkok."

I doubt that. Rosa never seems to care where in the world the parentals drag us: New Zealand, Indonesia, Thailand, back home to Australia. It's all the same to her.

"Six months wasn't enough for you?" Six months is a long time for us to stay anywhere.

"I'll miss Apinya."

I cut a look at Rosa but say nothing. Apinya is *not* going to miss her. Not after what Rosa made her do. When we said our farewells Apinya clung to her mother, crying, and refusing to let go. Her parents thought she was distraught at losing Rosa. I knew it was because Apinya was scared of her.

Rosa turns back to the buttons, pushing each one over and over. She's waiting for me to tell her to stop. That's not going to happen. I plug my headphones into my phone and start a Flying Fists podcast— I saved five for the plane—while reading through the last few texts from my besties, Jason, Georgie and Nazeem. I tilt the phone so Rosa can't see.

—She set anything on fire yet?

—Funny.

Funnier now that Rosa's asked about it. I wish Georgie were here. Jason and Nazeem too. I miss them. They're the only ones I can talk to about Rosa. Even if only Georgie believes me.

Halfway through the second podcast, a special on Muhammad Ali, Rosa pokes me in the arm.

"Che."

"Yes, Rosa?" I slip the headphones to my neck.

"I've been good and kept my promises."

I snort. Rosa mostly keeps her promises by finding loopholes. She'll be a terrifying lawyer.

"I should get to do one tiny bad thing."

"Being good is not a game, Rosa." Everything is a game to Rosa.

Rosa dimples at me though she knows I'm immune.

"I should get a reward for being good."

"My not telling the parentals is your reward."

"But you *have* told them."

"Not about what you did to Apinya."

I used to tell the parentals everything Rosa did. I've stopped. They're convinced her *acting out*—yes, that's what they call it—is normal for a kid her age. *Besides*, they always say, *she's much better than she was*. No, she's much better at hiding what she is. As far as they're concerned Rosa *had* a problem. They took her to doctors, therapists, specialists, who cured her. Problem solved. Now she's a bit socially awkward and it's our job to help her by not making it a big deal.

"There wasn't anything to tell. *I* didn't do anything."

I'm not going to say for the billionth time that making someone do something awful is as bad as doing it yourself.

"Other people do bad things all the time."

"You're not—" I begin.

"Look at that old man. *He's* being bad."

Across the aisle a middle-aged guy in a business suit is waving to get a flight attendant's attention. He gulps down an amber-coloured drink as if it were water.

"Drinking like that is bad," Rosa says, primly. "That's his seventh one." She crosses her arms as if she's made a brilliant point. "Why aren't they refusing to give him more? Or putting him in plane jail?"

"There is no plane jail."

"He's bothering that woman," Rosa says as if she cares.

The man is now leaning into the woman next to him, which is hard to do. In business class instead of a narrow armrest there's a table between the seats. The woman is leaning as far away as she can. She has headphones on and a book in her hands.

I wonder if I should do something. Maybe the man will be ashamed if a seventeen-year-old boy calls him on his shitty behaviour.

Before I can get up a flight attendant stops next to us. She doesn't turn to the drunk, she turns to Rosa. "You called, young lady?" she asks, leaning forward to turn off the attendant light.

Rosa beams, dimpling, and making her ringlets bounce.

The flight attendant can't help but return the smile.

"I'm fine, but I don't think that woman is." Rosa points past the flight attendant. "That man is annoying her. Is there something you can do? My brother says you don't have plane jail, but if you do you should put him in it. He's a bad man."

The flight attendant turns her palms out apologetically. "No plane jail, I'm sorry, but it's sweet of you to be worried. Let me investigate." She smiles at Rosa again.

"I like your earrings," Rosa says. They're gold-and-red-jewel studs that sit flat against the woman's lobes.

"Thank you." The flight attendant heads up the aisle.

"See?" Rosa says. "I do care about other people. I helped her. What's my reward?"

"Helping someone else *is* your reward."

Rosa rolls her eyes. An expression she saves for me. "I think the flight attendant should give me her earrings."

I lean back in my seat and return to the Muhammad Ali special. He's still Cassius Clay and an amateur.

Rosa watches a movie. I don't angle my head to see what it is. Maybe it'll keep her from pressing buttons for a while. Cassius Clay has just won a gold medal at the Olympics.

The drunk man is swaying in the aisle. He stumbles, grabbing the side of my seat to steady himself. He reeks of alcohol and stale sweat.

"Hey, little girl," he says, staring at Rosa. "Pretty hair. Just like Shirley Temple. I bet you don't know who . . ."

Rosa sticks her tongue out at him.

"She knows who Shirley—" I say, but the drunk has already pushed himself into a stumble towards the toilets. He doesn't seem to be able to hold one thought for long.

The flight attendant Rosa spoke to walks down the other aisle and crouches to talk to the woman the drunk was harassing. We can't hear what she says, but soon the woman gathers her things and follows the attendant to the front of the plane.

"They're putting her in first class," Rosa says. "I did that. I saved her. They should put me in first class too. *That* should be my reward."

My turn to roll my eyes.

"The McBrunights should have put us in first class," Rosa says. "They're rich. I bet they travel first class."

The McBrunights are Sally and David's oldest friends. They've known each other since they were my age. They are flying us to New York City to start a business. My parents have started many businesses. They specialise in it. They start them, then sell them, and walk away.

"They've moved her, but how are they going to punish *him*, Che? I wish there *was* a plane jail."

"They'll probably spit in his coffee."

"That's not enough."

"I was kidding, Rosa. They won't do that."

"They should."

"The world doesn't always work that way, little sister."

"How doesn't the world work?" Sally asks, leaning over me to give Rosa a kiss. "How are my darling children?"

"Business class is the best," Rosa says. "I like rich-people seats. Let's always fly like this."

Sally laughs. "I wish."

"You can get the McBrunights to pay," Rosa says. "Though you should tell them to put us in first class next time."

Sally snorts.

"I want to see it. Imagine how many buttons there must be." Rosa pushes one to straighten the back of her seat, then pushes it to make it go down.

"You've tested all the buttons, I see."

Doesn't she always, I don't say.

"David did the same thing and now he's sound asleep."

Sally and I exchange smiles. David can sleep anywhere.

"I'm going to watch all the movies," Rosa says.

"Do you need to go to the toilet?"

"Sally!" Rosa says. "I'm ten, not two. I can go by myself."

Sally holds her hands up. "Fine. Fine. You can go by yourself." She lowers her voice to whisper in my ear. "Keep an eye on her."

I always do.

Sally leans over to kiss Rosa, then gives me a swift hug. "Get some sleep!"

The reek of alcohol returns.

"He's a very bad man." Rosa watches him stumble into his seat. "He hasn't been punished," she says, before closing her eyes and falling asleep immediately. Just like David.

Across the aisle the drunk man has passed out. His mouth is open. I'm pretty sure he's snoring.

I WORK MY WAY through the fight movies, hoping to fall asleep before I run out. I think about everything I told myself I wouldn't think about. Like how we're heading to New York City, not home. How long it'll be before I can go back to Sydney. How I'm turning seventeen not long after we land. It'll be just me and Rosa and the parentals. Yet another shit birthday. I've had too many.

Mostly I think about how Rosa is never going to understand why I make her keep so many promises. How can I make her see that being good isn't a game?

I can't sit still. The air smells like recycled plastic. I drink the last of my water but my mouth stays dry.

After checking Rosa's asleep I go to the area between business and economy. The curtains are drawn. There's a white plastic bar with white plastic stools that swivel. I pour myself more water, bracing my foot against the base of the stool to stretch my calf. I drink, switch legs, pour myself more. Four glasses later and my tongue still sticks to the roof of my mouth.

I drop to the ground to do some push-ups. Just a quick set of twenty. Someone might try to walk past, Rosa might wake up.

I make a circuit of the business-class cabin. David is sleeping. Sally is reading. She smiles when she sees me, squeezes my hand, turns back to her book. Rosa hasn't shifted position. Her mouth is slightly open, and she's breathing softly and evenly. She looks like an angel.

I walk through economy where everyone is crammed into tiny seats that barely go back, yet most are asleep. I've never been able to sleep here. I've never been able to sit still long enough, and I was always flying with Rosa next to me, making me twitch as I waited for whatever it was she was going to do next.

I stayed up most of the night before the flight talking to Georgie, Jason and Nazeem; not talking about Rosa, but knowing I could if I needed to. We've known each other since we were five. We met in a kids' kickboxing class. Well, Georgie, Jason and I did. Nazeem was Jason's best friend at school back then. Soon we were all best friends.

It's going to be harder staying in touch from New York. Sydney and Bangkok are only a few hours apart, but New York is more than half a day behind.

I do another circuit of business, though I'm worrying I've left Rosa alone too long. My heart beats a little faster, but there she is, sound asleep. Sally's asleep too. Everyone but me.

I watch another movie. There isn't a single fight in it.

We're going to be last off the plane. We always are, because David doesn't believe in rushing. It doesn't matter how close to jumping out of my skin I am, how desperate to stretch my legs, to *run*, we have to go at David's pace.

As we finally step onto the air bridge, the drunken—now hungover—man, red in the face and panting, pushes past us to get back on.

"What a rude man," Sally says.

Rosa laughs.

I almost join her. We've made it all this way without Rosa doing anything.

AFTER AN HOUR OF going through immigration and getting our luggage we're ushered into the biggest car I've ever been in. Rosa and I sit in the back row. There are TV screens and a remote and bottles of water and tissues and bags of nuts. It's almost like being on the plane again. I have an urge to scream.

The parentals sit in the middle row where there's a little fridge and discuss whether wine is a bad idea and decide reluctantly that it is.

Rosa pushes buttons. I stare out the window even though all I can see is the car parked beside us. My eyes burn. Even my toenails are tired.

"More rich-people buttons."

"All cars have buttons for the windows," I mutter without looking at her.

"Not like—"

"Raining out there," the driver calls from the front as he starts the car. "Might want to keep that window up."

Rosa pushes the up button.

Once the car is on the highway all we can hear is the roar of the engine, the traffic, the wind rushing past. I sink back, staring out at grim, wet darkness, punctuated with occasional smears of coloured lights. I doubt I'll be able to see the New York City skyline. I'm not sure I care, which kind of sucks.

It's going to be my seventeenth birthday in a bit over an hour, which sucks worse: turning seventeen far from home, without my friends.

I close my eyes and drift away.

"Want to see something?" Rosa says right into my ear.

I startle. "What?"

Rosa's grinning, which is never good. I am all the way awake.

The window next to her is open a crack, spitting in rain.

"Close the window, Rosa."

She slides a small book out of her backpack, turning it so I can see the front.

An Australian passport. She opens it to the photo page: the horrible drunk from the plane.

I lunge as Rosa pushes it out the window.

"I win," Rosa says.

CHAPTER TWO

Rosa is a ticking bomb.

I don't think it matters what you call it: psychopathy, sociopathy, antisocial personality disorder, evil, or the devil within. What matters is how to prevent the bomb from exploding.

It would be a lot easier if the parentals believed Rosa is a bomb. It would be even easier if she *wasn't* a bomb. I would give anything for her to not be the way she is. Rosa ticks off everything on the Hare Psychopathy Checklist except for promiscuity, driving too fast and other adult sins. Give her time.

The checklists—there are different versions—each have dozens of questions designed to fit into different factors. The four that make sense to me are:

Callousness: Rosa doesn't care about anyone but herself.

Disinhibition: Rosa is an impulsive thrill seeker. Her risk assessment is terrible because she doesn't believe anything can happen to her. If she wants something she takes it.

Fearlessness: Nothing scares her. She's never worried.

Charisma: She has way too much. She can charm most people and get them to do what she wants.

Rosa is a ticking bomb and she's my responsibility.

My sister Rosa was born in our Sydney home when I was seven years old. I watched the whole thing, though David's parents, Nana and Papa, worried it would traumatise me. There was much shouting at David, Papa in the lead as always.

"He's a seven-year-old boy! You'll be paying his psychiatric bills for the rest of his life! Was it not bad enough that you make him call you by your first names? That poor boy doesn't even have his father's surname! This is not what our parents survived the Holocaust for! Making that poor little boy watch his own sister being born! I'll cut you out of my will!"

Rosa's birth didn't traumatise me.

It was beautiful and kind of boring. I fell asleep on a bean bag the midwife brought. When I woke Sally was leaning with her forearms on the bed, with David's hand gripped tightly in hers. On the floor between her feet was a mirror.

The midwife smiled at me. "Do you want to see, Che? She's crowning."

I crept closer, scared of getting in the way. In the mirror I could see something dark and slimy between Sally's legs. It didn't look like a baby's head, it looked like a monster.

"Here she is!"

Rosa shot out so fast she was a blur. The midwife caught her. David and I gasped.

She was so little, so perfect, with the biggest eyes I'd ever seen, looking straight at me. I couldn't stop staring.

The midwife put Rosa on Sally's belly and Sally cradled the tiny baby in her hands. They were almost bigger than Rosa.

David patted Rosa's back. I had this huge tight feeling in my chest. Love. I was full of love for this tiny little creature person.

"She's gorgeous," the midwife said. "Congratulations."

She gave David scissors to cut the umbilical cord, which looked like a pink and blue rope. It pulsed.

Sally smiled at me.

Tears were pouring out of my eyes, but I wasn't sobbing. It felt like the tears had nothing to do with me. "Can I touch her?"

"Of course."

I reached out to touch her tiny hand. Her fingers curled around my index finger. My heart hurt.

"You're going to have to look out for Rosa, you know," Sally told me.

"Protect her from the world," David said. "You're her big brother."

Protect the world from her, he didn't say.

"How patriarchal of you," Sally said, with no heat. She blew David a kiss and bowed her head.

We were all staring at tiny Rosa.

THE NEW YORK APARTMENT is huge. The plans and photos we've seen didn't make it seem so big. The McBrunights picked it out for us, which is fair, since they're paying for it. I don't want to know how much they're paying. It's like the business class of apartments when all our lives we've lived in economy.

Our less than half-empty shipping crate, which we sent off many weeks ago, sits in the middle of the living room. I'm not sure you can call a room this big a living room. It's bigger than any apartment we've lived in. At one end is the kitchen, which gleams, all metal and marble, with a giant island and two stoves.

At the other end are stairs, leading up to mine and Rosa's bedrooms. In between there are two enormous couches, with side tables at each end and a coffee table in between. The giant TV is on the same wall as the entrance to the apartment. Watching it will be like being at the movies. I didn't know TVs came that big. There are four plants in giant pots against the wall of glass overlooking Second Avenue. They're real. I wonder who's going to water them. We've never managed to keep any plants alive.

The shipping crate doesn't belong in this shiny new place. It makes me feel a little better about being here. Every other move we took only what we could carry. This time we haven't had to leave any clothes, or books, or posters, or Rosa's chess sets behind.

I can't remember what else is in the crate, it's so long since we packed it. There's definitely no furniture. That's languishing under David's parents' house in Sydney. Every so often Papa threatens to throw it out if we don't come home. Almost as often as he threatens to cut us out of his will. Papa changes his will like most people change their bed sheets.

In ten minutes it will be midnight in New York City and I'll turn seventeen. I don't have any texts from Nazeem, Georgie, Jason, or the aunts. Normally on my birthday my phone lights up. But we won't have new sim cards until tomorrow. There's no wifi, David tells us balefully, promising it will be operational in the morning. David is a computer genius. Making the tech work is always his job.

"Help me get Rosa to bed," Sally says.

I pick up Rosa and follow Sally up the stairs. It's hard not to love Rosa when she's sleepy like this, both eyelids drooping, her limbs floppy. She looks the way she did when she was a baby.

"I killed a butterfly," Rosa says softly.

"You . . ." I say before I notice her eyes are shut and she's heavier. She's asleep.

Sally opens the door to Rosa's room. "Put her on the bed."

I do.

"Doesn't she look darling?"

Rosa does. Her blonde curls form a fluffy halo. I kiss her forehead. If only she was the way she looks.

We go downstairs. My legs don't feel like part of my body.

"Well, we're here. New York City," David says, sitting on a couch. "For a while there I thought this was never going to happen." He looks at his watch. "Midnight!" He jumps up and pulls me into a hug. "Happy birthday, Che! Seventeen at last."

"Happy birthday. I thought it'd never get here," Sally says, joining the hug. "I can't believe it. You're seventeen."

And a long way from home, I think. Great birthday present. I don't say that. No point in starting a fight. I think about sleeping on the stairs.

"Wow. You look terrible, Che," David says.

"Thanks," I mumble. "Youse aren't exactly looking . . ." But the words dribble away. David looks like he's woken from a restful sleep in his own bed. It's not fair.

"Bed. Sleep," Sally says, kissing me, pushing me towards the stairs.

I drag myself upwards into my room, strip off my clothes, put my phone on charge so it'll be ready for wifi and a new sim card in the morning, unplug the clock radio that glows too bright, and crawl into the bed, realising my backpack is downstairs with my pyjamas and toothbrush and acne cream and books and everything else. Too far. I close my eyes, ready to fall into oblivion.

I don't.

I lie in my new room, staring at the shadows on the ceiling. Light streams in from the wet, brilliantly lit city outside. I left the blinds up. Sirens sound, getting louder and louder, then fade away. I hear the rain against the window again before it's lost in the roar of a helicopter.

I stagger out of bed, pull the blinds down, and the curtains across. The only light now is a thin sliver creeping in under my door. When I lie down I can't see it.

I close my eyes.

More sirens. I wonder what the emergency is.

It's more than two years now since we lived in Sydney. I miss home with a sharpness that feels like appendicitis.

I used every argument to persuade them. That everything since I was twelve has been chaos. Different homes, different cities, different countries. New Zealand, Indonesia, Thailand and now the USA. Which has meant different schools and sometimes haphazard homeschooling.

How am I going to get into medical school without stability? I didn't bother to mention how hard it is to not work with my Sydney boxing trainer, Natalie. My parents aren't thrilled by my boxing.

What about Rosa? I asked. *She only had five years in the one home. You're keeping her away from our extended family, from our aunts and uncles and cousins, grandparents. She needs to be looked after by family, not strangers. How can she make friends when we move so often?*

She's dangerous, I didn't say.

I talked about how much I missed my friends. How much I missed being surrounded by people who sound like me. How sick I was of being a foreigner.

Friends and family make us who we are, I argued. *Everyone needs a community. Rosa especially*, I didn't say.

You can make more friends, they argued. *We're moving to New York to make the world a better place. Sometimes you have to put the greater good first.*

You care more about the world than me and Rosa, I yelled.

Which was when I lost. Sally and David have no respect for anyone who resorts to emotion. You have to be calm and rational to win an argument. You have to be an adult even if you aren't one.

I hate you, I didn't say.

Instead of home: yet another city, another country, another unfamiliar bed, listening to unfamiliar sirens, staring at an unfamiliar ceiling with eyes so tired they feel as if they're melting down my cheeks. My right calf starts to cramp. I flex my foot, a trick Natalie taught me. Then my left calf starts in.

I'm not going to look at what time it is.

Should I have told the parentals? The passport is gone. Rosa will say there was no passport. They know she lies. They know I don't. Yet Sally will ask if I'm sure that's what Rosa threw out the window. After all, I haven't slept in forty-eight hours.

I add it to the list of things I haven't told them. Worst of all being Apinya's guinea pig.

I can't think about any of that.

I do what Natalie had us do at the end of every training session: I run through every muscle, starting with the lumbrical muscles of my foot and working my way up to the galea aponeurotica on the top of my head. Natalie wasn't that specific, but I want to be a doctor, specifically a neurologist or a psychiatrist. I know the names of all the muscles.

I am not asleep.

Should I embrace it? Go on a no-sleeping strike until the parentals agree to go home?

Best birthday ever.

My eyes burn.

An electronic chime rings out, echoing between buildings.

I can hear the *shush* of car tyres on the wet avenue, the squeal of brakes, people yelling. How can I hear them on the seventh floor? Through the rain?

Will my brain shut the fuck up?

My brain provides the answer to the question I didn't know I was pondering: What was Rosa talking about when she said she killed a butterfly? I'm pretty sure it was at Changi Airport in Singapore. Two years ago? The butterfly garden there is gorgeous. Rosa stood quietly with her hands extended until a butterfly rested on her palm, wings pulsing.

She smiled—a genuine smile—crushed the butterfly, then dropped its body into the greenery, wiping her hand on a fern.

Natalie would be disappointed: a fighter is always able to shut out peripheral thoughts.

What if the new boxing gym is nothing like the one back home? What if we never get working wifi? What if it never stops raining?

What if Rosa . . . I don't want to think about the worst she could do.

A police car screams down the avenue. The siren is so loud the windows shake, rotating through a series of increasingly annoying sounds, one of which makes my bed vibrate, one that sounds like a flock of zombie birds being tortured, and another that's close to a normal police siren, followed by a rumbling earthquake sound. An amplified voice calls a car to the kerb. The siren sounds again and the order is repeated.

I've never heard so many sirens. New York, city of angry police and constant emergencies.

Rosa will be delighted.

CHAPTER THREE

At 5 A.M. I give up on sleep. The sun isn't up. I do my morning stretch and workout crappily, with some Muhammad Ali–inspired footwork so lead-footed and inelegant the great man would be horrified.

Then I creep downstairs, not wanting to wake anyone, but the parentals and Rosa are sitting at the island eating muesli and drinking coffee and orange juice, as wide awake as I am.

Sally's red-eyed and haggard.

"Happy birthday, Che," the parentals say in unison, jumping up to hug me. Rosa joins in the hug.

I forgot it was still my birthday.

"Seventeen, eh?" Sally says, hugging me again.

"It's a prime number," Rosa says. "If you add up the first four primes you get seventeen."

"Can't believe it. Seventeen. That's how old we were when we met," David says, kissing Sally's nose.

"Yes, when you were my wild man. Remember the first time I had to bail you—"

I hold up my hand. "My first birthday wish is that you not reminisce about the early days, or any days, of your eternal true love."

David nods. Sally makes a zipping-her-mouth gesture.

"Actually, I think I'm going to make that a birthday week wish."

"Can I offer you some birthday breakfast?" David asks, ignoring me. "Did you know in this city you can buy the essentials and quite a few non-essentials at any hour of the day? Makes me almost forgive the nonstop rain."

"We only just got here," Sally says. "The rain will stop."

"I like the rain," Rosa says.

"Banana?"

I nod and David slices one into a bowl and hands it to me. I add yoghurt and muesli. "Breakfast of the gods," I declare, digging in. The banana manages to be both slimy and mealy at the same time.

"This banana's disgusting."

"Sorry. Tried three different shops. Seems to be the only kind available."

In Bangkok I lost count of how many different kinds of bananas there were—all of them amazing. "This is hell," I mutter, grinning to show I don't mean it. I do mean it.

"Orange juice?" Sally asks.

I nod.

"When can we give Che his presents?" I feel a little ping of pride in Rosa for asking such a normal question.

"You know he can't make any decisions until he's had the first of his million meals of the day," David says.

"It's my birthday. You can't tease me."

"I withdraw my comment. So, when do you want your presents?"

I look at the giant shipping container, at our piles of luggage. "Can you find them?"

"Yes and no."

"I can wait," I say, though I kind of want a present now. Some sign of birthday-ness in the absence of a functioning phone and messages from my friends.

"Can I have internet access for my birthday?"

"I can't fix it until business hours," David says. "But it will happen today or heads will roll."

"I have my present," Rosa says. "Can I give it to Che now?"

"Sure," I say.

She darts up to her room and returns carrying it. "I wrapped it myself."

No, she didn't. It's too well wrapped for Rosa. "Pretty big," I say. "This was in your luggage?"

"Yes."

I undo the elegant black ribbon and carefully remove the silver paper. Inside the plain wooden box is a plastic teaching model of the human brain. I hold it up. "Look, there's even a brain stem."

"It comes apart," Rosa says.

I pull the frontal lobe out, then the parietal, occipital, temporal and limbic lobes.

"Mmmm . . . brains," I say in my best zombie voice.

Rosa smiles. It isn't her real smile. That doesn't matter, I remind myself. It's an appropriate smile. So is this present. More than appropriate, it's perfect. Sally and David have internalised that I want to be a doctor, but Rosa knows that I want to be a neurologist or a psychiatrist.

"Can I hold one?"

I hand her the frontal lobe. "You're holding conscious thought in your hands, Rosa. That's the part of the brain that makes us most human."

She turns it over. I wonder if she thinks as much about her own humanness as I do. Does she ever wonder what parts of her frontal lobe are missing?

"It's so detailed," I say, peering at the parietal lobe. I'm looking at the lateral sulcus. Within it is the anterior insular cortex, where empathy might lie. I put my finger on it. It feels like plastic.

"I love it," I say, smiling at Rosa, then hugging her. "Thank you."

She hugs me back. She's a lot better at that.

"That's going to be hard to top," David says, as if he didn't know what Rosa was getting me. "Is there anything you'd like to do today, birthday boy?"

"Um." I feel wide-awake yet tired. All I want to do is retreat to my bedroom with a functioning phone, tablet or laptop and reconnect with my friends.

"We were talking about going for a bike ride." David's keen to try out the city's bike-sharing program. "If the rain stops." He waves at the windows, which the rain is hitting horizontally.

"It is grim," Sally says. "Plan B is to go to the movies or a play on Broadway."

"We'd fall asleep." It isn't even six. The day sprawls endlessly in front of me. Maybe I can do a class or two at my new boxing gym? I'd planned to take my first one tomorrow.

"Yeah," David says. "It's early. We could play poker."

Sally and I groan.

David is a poker master. Rosa is his avid student. She has the right face for it, except that when she makes herself smile it's expressionless. David has an impressive poker face, especially as it doesn't come naturally like Rosa's.

David says poker is about thinking with your head, not your emotions, which makes no sense. Our emotions, like our thoughts, form in our brain. You can't separate them.

"No way," I say. "Why don't we go somewhere that has wifi? Is there a library nearby?" Libraries always have free wifi.

"They don't open until business hours."

I groan.

ROSA IS CURLED UP next to me on the library couch with the latest issue of *Chess Life* magazine. Sally is sitting in a chair opposite us stabbing at her tablet. I have my laptop balanced on my knees, angled so Rosa can't see it. David is at home solving our connectivity issues.

It took twenty minutes before there was somewhere to sit. The library's packed with teens hanging out and old people hunched over the few available computers. The waiting line is almost out of the building.

Outside, water pours down the windows, almost obscuring the dead-looking trees. It looks like the end of the world.

I respond to the birthday messages. I almost cry when I see how many there are. Being on the verge of tears over stuff you'd never normally cry at is one of the many signs of jetlag.

I write my list. I write this list every time we move to a new place. My goals. They haven't changed in a while. I write the list, then delete it. It's not like I'll forget them. They rule my life.

No, that's not true. The first one does, the others are me hoping.

1. *Keep Rosa under control.*

Always Rosa. I have to stop her from doing something terrible. I have to find a way to do that permanently. Is there a way to do that permanently? *Permanently* sounds ominous, doesn't it? Like I want her dead. I don't. I love her. She's my baby sister—I can't not love her.

Can she learn empathy? The book I'm currently reading on antisocial disorder in children isn't filling me with hope. Too many case studies of kids like Rosa, who say, when asked to change their behaviour, *I just don't care.* When they're not trying to fool the interviewer, that is. When they're being honest. *I don't care.*

Neither does Rosa.

How can I make her care? How can I get a scan of her brain to see if the right parts light up? What happens if they don't? *Yes, she's what you think she is.* Then what?

All I can do is keep writing down every off thing she does, keep recording our conversations.

Here are my unrelated-to-Rosa things:

2. I want to spar.

I'm never going to move up to the next level with my boxing if I don't spar. The promise not to is holding me back. But I can't break my promise.

3. I want a girlfriend.

It looks pathetic written down. All hearts and roses and fluttering eyelashes and bursting out singing, *I want love!*

I *do* want love. I want to meet someone smart and funny and sexy who likes boxing, Muhammad Ali and has seen *Ong-bak* at least twenty times.

It's normal to want a girlfriend. Or a boyfriend. Not that Jason wants a boyfriend. He's all *I'm a player*, which makes us laugh our arses off. Are you a player if you declare you're one? That's definitely more pathetic than wanting to be with only one person.

I get wanting to have lots of sex. I want to have lots of sex. Or, I'll be honest, *any* sex. But Jason talks as though it doesn't matter what the other person—the person you're having sex with—thinks about it. Like they're a number, not a person.

Jason thinks he's like Rosa. Hard, unfeeling. He's a mostly good guy pretending to be awful. (There's me bringing Rosa into it when it has nothing to do with Rosa.)

I want a girlfriend who's smart and funny and strong and fit and cares about other people. (And isn't blonde!) I don't want a number.

4. I want to go home.

AS I PRESS DELETE Rosa tugs at the sleeve of my hoodie. "What are you doing, Che?"

She's been asking me this question since she began to talk.

"What are *you* doing, Rosa?"

I've been answering her that way for as long as she's been asking. I don't think she saw my list.

"Bothering you, Che. What are you doing?"

"Emptying the trash," I say, doing a secure empty-trash. My list is double-deleted now. "What are you going to do when you finish bothering me, Rosa?"

Rosa giggles. "I'm never going to stop bothering you, Che."

CHAPTER FOUR

As soon as Rosa could move she started following me. First with her eyes, then she would do her strange bum-heavy crawl after me, then she progressed to a recognisable walk.

It made my heart swell. I'd turn and there she'd be, gazing at me. I'd pick her up and hold her, inhale her sweet baby smell, press my nose to the back of her head, feel her soft skin, her tiny heartbeat, and be so overwhelmed with love I couldn't speak.

I'd held babies. Both my parents are the oldest in their family. I have many younger cousins. They smelled lovely too. But not like Rosa. I looked into her eyes and wondered if I'd ever love anyone as much.

Rosa would stare back at me, barely blinking.

Like all babies she was studying me, studying us, learning to be human.

Unlike most other humans, almost nothing came naturally.

Rosa learned everything slower than her cousins. Everything that isn't hardwired. She crawled and walked at a regular pace.

It was smiling and laughing and hugging and kissing and crying and pointing that came slowly. All the things humans do with each other, and in response to one another, Rosa was slow to acquire. She put her arms up for us to carry her months after her cousins did the same thing. Though once she realised she could use us as taxis she was into it.

Every time she held out her arms to me my heart beat faster. She was so soft, dependent, tiny. I didn't need to be asked. I would always want to protect her.

For her first two years she barely cried. She was more intrigued than dismayed by cuts or bruises or illnesses. Most babies cry when someone else is crying, especially another baby. Not Rosa.

The not-crying worried the parentals more than anything else. So Rosa started crying. She watched how the cousins did it and copied. Not convincingly at first. She'd make strangled sounds and blink her eyes rapidly to get tears to roll. But Sally and David bought it and after a while she was producing real tears.

She lied with those tears as surely as she did with her words.

I thought about pointing that out to the parentals, but most of the cousins only cried when they fell if an adult was looking. I wasn't sure how to explain that what Rosa did was different.

She wasn't smiling when we smiled at her. She wasn't responding to her name. She was almost two and was yet to say a single word.

"Che was a bit slow too," Sally said. They'd never told me that.

"Nothing wrong with him now. Babies develop at different rates."

"Not *this* slow," David responded.

They took her to a doctor.

Lo and behold, Rosa started smiling. She started talking.

Her first smile was at that first appointment. We all went.

She understood what they were saying about her not smiling. She looked up from the toys she was playing with and stretched her mouth wide, showing her teeth. It didn't look like a real smile, but Sally gasped. David said, "No way. It's an omen. She's okay."

The doctor said that she was a little developmentally delayed and it was probably no big deal.

When they took Rosa home from the second appointment she walked over to me and said her first words, "I want mine."

Now *that* was an omen: *that* is the phrase she lives by.

How like Rosa that her first words be a full sentence, bypassing the usual first words like *mama* and *dada* and *up* and *hi* and *bye* and *ball* and *ta*, not to mention the babbling stage. A baby who doesn't babble is eerie.

No sooner did Rosa start talking than she started lying.

I HEAD TO MY new gym, armed with a functioning phone, and an umbrella borrowed from the guy behind the desk in the lobby, who said his name was John. I can't stay still any longer, not at the library, not at our new home. I have to sweat and move or I'll lose my mind. Time to truly exhaust every muscle in my body.

The wind cuts through my fleecy hoodie and thickest trackpants and hits me with horizontal rain. The umbrella protects my head but not much else. Georgie's going to be disappointed when I tell her New York City looks like a sea of yellow cars swimming through grey, driving rain. I should have worn a raincoat. I should have gone to bed. By the time I walk up the stairs to the front desk of my new gym I'm dripping and shivering so hard my teeth chatter.

I still notice her.

A very dark-skinned girl, shiny with sweat, in the first ring. I wonder if they make sure their best fighters train in that ring, near the top of the stairs, close to the windows, so you can't avoid seeing them as you walk in, can't help thinking, *Her, her right there, is how I want to move. Make me like her.*

The girl is going through her defensive sets at lightning pace. I like the way she ducks and weaves, how she spins.

People think strength is how you win fights but it isn't—speed and agility are. Plenty of fighters win again and again without delivering knockout blows. That girl in the ring is faster than her instructor. I want to watch her in a real fight.

I could stand here all day watching her. But I've come to wake the fuck up. Un-jetlagged me was smart enough to sign up for everything online, filling in permission slips, putting my name down for classes, reserving a locker, paying my yearly membership. Papa paid. I have a credit card from him that I use for boxing expenses.

Papa pays because he wants me to be a real man. He's afraid I'm growing up weakened by the parentals' lack of backbone and grit and whatever other word he's over-using that week. He pays because the parentals refuse to pay. The parentals do not believe in violence. Despite all evidence that violence definitely exists.

They were horrified when Papa taught me how to punch. Even more horrified when he offered to pay for my boxing classes. Sally and David only agreed to it if I promised not to spar until I was fully grown. A promise I've regretted ever since.

I FIND MY DESIGNATED locker, throw myself in a shower, which runs awesomely hot, then change into my dry training gear, wrapping my wet clothes in one of the fluffy warm towels provided. My Sydney gym charges for scratchy, threadbare towels, which aren't left in giant stacks for anyone to help themselves to. There are free deodorants and hand creams as well. Even a hairdryer, which I point at my shoes, trying to dry them.

I warm up on a treadmill, pounding out a fast pace until the shivers are gone.

My first class is in the bag room. A forest of bags hangs from the ceiling. At a distance they look like bodies. Up close they smell of sweat, not decay.

The girl I watched training in the ring is standing in the middle of the bags, talking to another girl, and smiling. She taps a bag to her friend, easy and controlled as if it is an extension of her arm, then she dodges her friend's faster return, spinning out of the way, almost as if she's dancing.

I can't not look at her.

I force myself to sit, to stare at my hands as I put my wraps on, then to look at everyone else in the class. There are only two other guys. I've never been in a class that was mostly women. This gym is excellent.

She and her friend seem to be around my age. The rest of the class is older. I'm used to being the youngest. I wonder if the girl is too. She's about my height, maybe a smidge taller. Her curly hair is scraped back. She's as leanly muscled as I am.

I'm staring again. I force my eyes to the bag in front of me, wondering what it would be like to kiss her.

We bow in turn and the jetlag hits me harder than a cross to the head. A hazy force field descends. I can almost see cartoon stars circling. The instructor's words slow. By the time they reach me everyone else is in motion.

"One, two, three! Your other left, Jose, the one that's not your right. Everyone, if you're confused, watch Soldier."

The instructor is pointing at the gorgeous girl. Her nickname's Soldier? She must be a total badarse.

I stop trying to listen and instead follow Soldier. Half a second behind is better than minutes behind.

My legs are leaden. Where's my muscle memory? Where's my regular memory?

"Beginner, huh?" asks our instructor. "Maybe you should try a less advanced class next time?"

My brain and tongue won't cooperate to explain I just spent months studying Muay Thai *in Thailand*.

He's passed by to the next student before I can get my mouth open. Fuck.

At the end of the class I sink to the mat. All I want is sleep. I'll prove to the stupid instructor at our next class that I'm no beginner.

Soldier nods at me, undoing her wraps. "You were good in your warm-up. What happened?"

"Jetlag," I say after what seems like an hour. I can feel my heart beating too fast even through the muffling force field. Soldier is talking to me.

"I hear that can blow," she says. Her wraps are off and stuffed into her trackpants pocket. She bends to pick up her gloves. "See you next week?" she asks, walking away.

"Sure," I say, though my voice doesn't have much weight and she's already halfway to the change room. I nod too. Not that she's looking.

Even through my jetlag I'm elated. All on their own my lips shape a smile. She noticed me.

In the change room I sink onto the bench nearest my locker and let the jetlag wash over me. I have to get my sweat-soaked clothes off, shower, dress, find my way home. Impossible tasks.

My phone pings. Jason. I try to figure out what time it is in Sydney. I fail.

—Knocked im deader than dead dead deady dead. He gorn.

I can't figure out what Jason's talking about, and not just because of the Jason-spelling he's trained autocorrect to use. I'm used to that.

—Huh? I tap out slowly. My fingers are too fat for the keys.

—Last night! The fight!

—That's great! I can't remember what fight he's talking about.

—Yeh. Killed it. Killed im.

—Wish I'd seen it.

—Me 2. Come home! Lotsa new moves to teach u. U won't recognise Baxter's. Farking squeaky clean and all machines work. Miracle renos they were. Proper sized ring now. Luv it!

I force my fingers to punch out a question.

—How's it going at home?

—Olds goin nuts. As per. Want me 2 cut training, focus on skool. Blah blah blah. As if. Fighter needs HSC why zackly? Morons.

Jason's going to be a fighter. He *is* a fighter. He's already won two junior bouts. His goal is the Commonwealth Games and maybe beyond.

If I were home in Sydney I'd only ever see him at the gym. Back when I lived there we hung out most weekends, but now he trains every day. I probably wouldn't even see much of him at the gym. He doesn't do regular classes anymore.

We both started at five with Natalie teaching us kickboxing. Now his new trainer has convinced him he can represent Australia and go on to earn money. Jason's head exploded with the desire to fight and fight well. He *wants* it.

Back when we trained together I'm not sure he was better than me. But now? He's way ahead of me. It kind of hurts. It shouldn't—I don't want to be a fighter—but it does.

—Ur bday there 2 now. Happy bday!

—Thanks.

"Sojourner's hot," one of the guys who was in my last class says. He's neatly folding up his wet wraps. What the point of that is, I have no idea. Unless he's going to let them dry like that, unwashed. Foul. "Told her and she ignored me. Bitch."

I'm pretty sure he's talking about the girl I like. I don't know his name, Arsehole Turdbrain, maybe, but now I know hers: not Soldier, Sojourner. I like it.

"Huh?" Jose says. He's the one who can't tell his right from his left.

"Whatever. The hottest ones are always bitches."

Jose rolls his eyes and heads to the shower.

Sojourner is not a bitch.

"What are you staring at?" the guy asks me.

I hold up my hands in a sign of peace. "Nothing, man."

He doesn't stop glaring. A muscle in his cheek twitches.

"Feeling spacey, that's all. Only just landed here. Didn't sleep much on the plane."

"Jetlag, huh?" His cheek stops twitching.

I nod.

"You English?"

"No," I say, wishing I wasn't having a conversation with this bone-head. "Australian."

"Huh." Mercifully he says nothing more as he slouches off to the showers.

I yawn so hard my jaw clicks. Can I sleep here? Would that be okay? No, that would not be okay.

I look down at my phone. Multiple texts from Jason. Too tired to look.

I strip off my sweaty gear, stand to open my locker, then realise I have no idea what four digits I programmed into it. Fuck.

I punch in my birthday. Nope. My ATM card password. Not that either. Rosa's birthday. Sally's. David's. No, no, no. Crap.

Why can't I remember setting a password?

Did I set a password?

I have a vague memory of setting something easy so I won't forget.

I punch in 0000. The locker clicks open. Wow. Even for jetlagged me that is pretty bad. I'm amazed all my stuff is still there.

At least the password panic has broken through the fuzz in my head. I cram my sweaty gear into my bag, put it back in the locker with the same code—why confuse myself further?—and head for the shower, grabbing a clean towel on the way. I turn it on without checking the temperature. Ice-cold water hits my head.

It helps. Nothing like cold water pounding into your head.

As I dress my phone buzzes.

—Happy birthday! You awake?

It's Nazeem.

I sit down to reply. I don't trust myself to text and walk.

—Thanks. It's only afternoon here.

—Right. But you're jetlagged. Thought you might be napping.

—I wish I was. Why you awake?

—Couldn't sleep. Gotta tell you something. It's bugging me.

—What?

—Don't get shitted.

I wonder how I could get mad at him when I haven't seen him in ages.

—Why would I?

—It's not like I meant it to happen. But, you know, you've been away.

Anger spills out of my fingers.

—Yes. I do fucking know I've been away. Not like I wanted to leave.

—Right. Yeah. Sorry. It's Georgie.

—What about her?

—We're, you know, together.

I pause, bewildered. Why does Nazeem think that would upset me? My two favourite people going out with each other. Why would I be shitted?

I realise I'm shitted. Why?

—It wasn't on purpose. You still there? Don't be pissed. I know you used to like her.

—When I was ten. She's awesome; you're not too foul. Just don't convert her. Atheism rules!

—Funny. You're really okay with it?

I'm not okay with it. All this stuff happening to them while I'm not there. I'm blindsided. Jason was probably telling them to get a room weeks ago. I didn't get to tease them. Because I don't know anything about their lives except what they remember to tell me. It fucking hurts.

—I thought you might still like her.

—As if.

—Fucking fickle.

—Well, see, now there are these hot NYC women.

—Thought you didn't want to be there. You said NYC's a shithole.

He's mocking me all the way from Australia. Nazeem would never call anything a shithole sight unseen. He takes his time. Like with Georgie. He probably liked her for years before he let her know.

—I was right too. It sucks here. But I haven't gone blind. Anyways youse'll probably be broken up by the time I get home.

—You're lucky I'm not there. I'd punch you.

—I'm rolling my eyes. You? Punch me? I'm also laughing. Nazeem does not box. His thing is cricket.

Nazeem texts a gif of a garish face sticking its tongue out at me.

—Gotta go. Later.

—Later.

I feel like he's punched me. I feel like they both did. Jason on the verge of a career I don't want as a fighter, and Nazeem going out with Georgie, who I don't want to go out with. I love the three of them. I'm happy for them. But I feel gutted.

I don't make any sense.

But that's how I feel. Forgotten in a city I didn't want to move to with no friends and no support. Just me and my demonic younger sister and parents who have no idea what she is.

Happy birthday, Che.

CHAPTER FIVE

I get home wet through. The doorman has to let me into the building. David opens the door to our apartment and hands me a set of keys.

"Happy birthday," he says.

It's still my birthday. The parentals haven't given me a present unless these new keys are it. I try not to care.

"You're wet."

"Yes," I say. *You're so observant.* "Could you get me a towel?"

I bend to get my wet shoes off.

"Right," he says, disappearing into the downstairs bathroom, returning with a towel. "How was the gym?"

"Excellent."

The crate has been opened. Its contents are disgorged across the living room.

"Where's Rosa?"

"In her room. Sally's setting up the office. I've finished getting the wifi up. Usual login. Much drama was involved. You're welcome."

"Thanks. That's great, David."

"I'll get started on dinner soon. I'm aiming for seven."

I nod. Seven is two hours away. I'm hungry now. I take an apple and a handful of nuts.

Rosa sits cross-legged on her bed reading a book on maths. Rosa loves numbers. She's kind of a maths genius. She gets that from David. They can talk numbers and computers for hours.

I'm not any kind of genius.

Her computer is set up and her science and maths books are on the shelves. The US history books and novels the parentals decided we need to read in preparation for going to school here are in a stack behind the computer. Rosa will read cribs online for when the parentals quiz us on them.

"What are you doing, Rosa?" I ask, leaning against the doorway, popping the nuts into my mouth.

"Reading. What are you doing, Che?"

"Chewing, asking you what you're doing. What are you reading about?"

"Prime numbers."

Rosa can recite the first thousand primes, which is how I know the thousandth prime is 7919.

"Sally and David are fighting."

"What about?" I ask sarcastically. Rosa frequently makes that claim. I've rarely seen them fight.

"About the McBrunights. David says we have to be nice to them."

"We should be nice to everyone."

"Yes, but *everyone* doesn't pay for our plane flights and fancy apartment. David wants us to be *super* nice to them. Sally says they shouldn't try too hard. That the McBrunights are their best friends. Do you ever wonder why we haven't met them before?"

I haven't. The parentals have holidayed with them, but never with us kids. I figured it was because our school years were different.

"I can't wait to meet them," Rosa says. "I want to see what rich people look like."

"I'm sure they look pretty much the same as us."

"I'm going to study them. I want to be rich too."

"You study everyone," I say. The thought of a rich Rosa is horrifying.

"I've never met any twins."

The McBrunights have three kids: Leilani, who's about my age, and the twins, Maya and Seimone, who are a bit older than Rosa. "I'm sure they're also pretty much like everyone else."

Rosa shakes her head. "I read that some twins have their own made-up language and they can read each others' minds. If one twin is hurt and far away the other twin will know. Twins are always best friends."

"Sounds likely," I say, meaning the opposite.

Rosa nods. She's not good at sarcasm. "I wish I had telepathy. I wonder if they use it to mess with Leilani? I'll ask them."

"I'm sure they'll tell you all about their twin superpowers."

"People always tell me interesting things."

This is true. Rosa likes to know more about other people than they know about her. Whenever she's in a group of kids her age she becomes the leader. At first because other kids want her approval, want her to love them, because she's dazzlingly pretty, because it's such an impossible desire. But that love morphs into fear. She collects their stories, the things they don't want anyone to know, then she lets those stories slip when they least want her to.

Rosa has way too much charisma.

Not everyone's fooled. There's always one or two kids who think there's something off about Rosa. But those kids are never popular.

She starts at her new dance school soon. I try not to worry about it too much, because there's little I can do.

Papa pays for her dance lessons because Rosa complained it was unfair that I got to box. Why couldn't she box? Papa said, *Girls don't box. Pick something else.* She chose tap dance, which Papa approved. He likes girls to do things he deems to be girlie.

"What are you thinking about, Che?"

"The devil."

Rosa giggles. "There's no such thing."

FROM THE AGE OF roughly two to three, Rosa was a monster.

When her temper tantrums escalated to unbearable levels the parentals took her to the doctor, who referred her to an early childhood development specialist, which was when the tantrums stopped.

I saw her become angry when thwarted. Often. But after those sessions there were no tantrums. Rosa learned they didn't work. Instead of the parentals capitulating and giving her what she wanted they took her to doctors. Rosa did not like that kind of attention.

After seeing the specialist, a monstrous, rageful expression would pass over her face, but briefly. I would tense, waiting for her screams, but they wouldn't come.

No one else noticed those micro-expressions. She dropped tantrums from her armoury, and instead she lied and lied and lied.

One time we were out for breakfast. Rosa was two and a half, sitting in a high chair, drinking a babyccino. David was charming the wait staff while Sally was buried in the weekend paper.

I saw Rosa pinch her own forearm hard and reached across to stop her. She screamed and cried. "Che hurt Rosa," she blurted.

My hand was on her arm, next to the large red mark.

Sally pulled Rosa into her arms. She cried even louder.

"What did you do, Che?" David asked, as Sally gave me her most disapproving glare.

"I didn't do anything. She pinched herself."

Their looks of disbelief were echoed by the people at the table next to us.

"Why would I pinch her?"

"I don't know," David said. "Why *did* you pinch your baby sister?"

"I didn't."

They didn't believe me. But the parentals changed their minds a week later when Rosa told a woman on the street that she didn't want to sleep in the kennel anymore. We didn't even own a dog.

She only did it when we were out in public. When there were witnesses who wouldn't believe that the little blonde curly haired angel could be lying. She did it to embarrass us. She did it because it made her laugh.

Back to the early childhood development specialist.

The diagnosis was that she might have ADHD. Or that it could just be the attention-seeking behaviour of a young child. The specialist explained that's what toddlers are: monsters who think the world revolves around them. The odds were, the specialist said, that she'd grow out of it.

In the meantime, more weekly sessions.

Rosa behaved perfectly with the specialist; monstrously with us. It went on for months and months. She wore the parentals down. Me as well. Whenever we went out she would tell lies, make scenes.

The specialist said that perhaps it was time to try medication. The parentals prevaricated; she was so young. Then they decided, yes, that was what they needed to do.

Rosa would not take the medicine. She screamed and fought and spat it out.

The parentals were exhausted. But the next time they took her out in public Rosa didn't make a scene. Nor the time after that.

It was a phase after all. The parentals were so relieved she'd stopped, that they didn't have to drug their child, that we went away on a holiday. Sun and sand and Rosa, the perfect little child.

She kept on lying, though. She just got more sly.

She lied to everyone, hid who she was from everyone.

Everyone but me.

Me, she used for triangulation. Me, she watched to see if I frowned at her laughter or joined in. Me, she confided in.

"I pinched that baby," she told me. "I liked pinching it."

Me, she exalted to about her trickery. The old man she'd lied to. The medal she'd stolen.

Me, she trusted. Me, I half hoped, she loved.

But only me.

The parentals thought the phase was over. She was their own sweet child forever. I knew better.

"We've done an excellent job with our children, don't you think?" David says to Sally over my birthday dinner, giving her a quick hug.

I groan.

"I'm only ten, Che's only seventeen. I don't think you can decide how well you've raised us until we're older."

They laugh, but Rosa isn't joking.

I wonder how proud they'd be of their parenting if they knew what happened to Apinya's guinea pig. If they knew what happened to that man's passport. If they knew so many things they don't know. The thought makes me tired. Tired*er*.

Finally they give me my birthday present, which is pretty cool: a vintage *Gray's Anatomy of the Human Body*. As I turn the pages, the smell of old paper wafts up, making me feel even more tired.

I go to bed as soon as I can after dinner. It's not quite eight-thirty.

I text with Jason and Georgie and Nazeem, who want to know what I think of New York. I don't think anything about it.

—NYC sucks.

—You can't say that about the Big Apple! Georgie dreams of living here and being a fashion designer.

—Swap you!

—Yeh, me 2. Jason's thinking about the fight scene here, which is much bigger than back home.

—Bloody freezing and wet. Not glamorous. Not cool. Haven't seen anything but the gym and a library and grey, wet streets.

—Then how can you know it sucks? Georgie points out.

—Sunny here. I can imagine Nazeem's grin as he types that. Bastard.

—Of course it is.

—The end-of-season mangoes are delish.

—Shut up! I don't want to hear it.

—But expensive, Nazeem objects.

I don't bother texting that the mangoes in Bangkok were as good as home and cheap. I'm not in Bangkok.

—I hate it here. I can see how pathetic that looks. It's not that I hate NYC. Anywhere we went would be as bad. Even somewhere sunny. I need home.

—Suck it, Che!

—You only just got there. Give it more than a few minutes.

—I'll try. I just wish I was there. Whatever. Gotta sleep. Late here.

—Not even 9. Think we're 2 stupid 2 figure out time?

—I am, **Nazeem texted.** —Way too stupid. Bloody timezones.

—I'm jetlagged and tired and sleepy and knackered. Me go now.

—Wuss.

—Night, Che!

—Happy birthday!

—Yeah, Che, we're all seventeen now!

—Thanks!

I pull out the *History of the Brain* and try to read. It's dense and hard to follow and usually puts me to sleep within minutes. This time I fail to take in a single word, yet I don't fall asleep.

I get out of bed and run through some katas, hoping to wear myself out.

Finally I drift off, but am woken by the sound of sirens. In the end I manage maybe three hours of sleep.

Happy birthday to me, I think, before realising that my birthday is finally over.

Worst. Birthday. Ever.

Well, almost. Sojourner noticed me.

CHAPTER SIX

Today we meet the McBrunights.

The rain has stopped. The sun is making the streets shine. Grey and drab have transformed into a million different colours: from a giant mural of a rat in brown and blacks and reds to neon-bright graffiti tags, to the elaborate window displays in shops and restaurants of robots and dinosaurs and clothes from decades ago, some of which are being worn out on the streets. I see top hats, and pouffy skirts, and hair in every colour, but mostly pink.

It's hard not to smile, and easy to stay awake. We're meeting the McBrunights for brunch at eleven so I know it's morning, but my body isn't convinced.

I walk around the neighbourhood with Rosa and the parentals. There are puddles everywhere. Rosa tromps through them in her gumboots.

We stroll through Tompkins Square Park. It takes up several square blocks. The trees aren't all dead. Some are covered in tiny pink and white and purple buds, and on a few there are green leaves. Spring-time. Squirrels run along their branches, noses twitching, trembling with anxiety not to be prey. Men play chess on stone tables with inlaid chessboards. Rosa is transfixed. The parentals stay with her while I wander. Chess bores me.

"Keep your phone on," Sally says.

There's a dog run at the other end of the park. It's overflowing with mutts in every size and colour—including two dyed-pink poodles—running back and forth, barking their heads off, jumping all over their owners. When Rosa sees the run she'll renew her requests for a dog. She's been asking for years now. She's never getting one.

A gorgeous girl in a black dress dotted with red flowers walks by. It's fitted to show off her waist, and the skirt flares as she walks. She's stunning, and there's something about the sure, athletic way she moves that makes me stare. Then I realise it's the girl from the gym.

I chase after her. "Sojourner?"

She turns. "Yes?"

I can see she doesn't recognise me.

The flowers on her dress are tulips.

"Hi," I say, feeling like an idiot. "We met at the boxing gym. Down on Houston Street?"

"How-sten," she says.

I blush, which makes my acne sting. "That's how you say it? I didn't know. I thought it was like the city." I'm gibbering.

Sojourner smiles. "You're that new guy. With the jetlag. How's that working for you? Still making you mess up?"

I nod. "Well, I said the street wrong, didn't I? I should be okay in a day or two."

Yesterday Sojourner's hair was scraped back from her face; now it forms a halo. Her lips are painted the same colour as the tulips. She wasn't wearing makeup in class. She looks pretty, but somehow not herself.

"I didn't recognise you without your gym clothes," she says, which is polite of her since we've only just met, and not properly. Does she know my name? "Look at your hands. They're unwrapped, and not red and sweaty. Your shirt has a collar."

I look down at my hands. They're a little red around the knuckles. "I was thinking the same about you."

"Yeah. Every time I put on a dress and lipstick I feel like I'm in disguise."

"Not a very effective one. I recognised you straight away." Which probably sounds weird. I barely know her.

"You'd be surprised how many guys from gym don't."

I'm sure I'd recognise her no matter what she wore. She holds herself easily, as if her muscles move unconstricted by tension. Hardly anyone walks like that.

"Where're you headed?" I hope I'm not staring. I'm fairly sure I am.

"Church. You?"

"Exploring." She goes to church? "Just moved here. I'm checking out Alphabet City." I could have told her I was with my family, that we're about to meet Sally and David's oldest friends for the first time, but I don't want to mention Rosa. It's not a lie. I *am* exploring. "Still learning my new neighbourhood."

"Well, you need to know only old people call it Alphabet City. This is Loisaida."

"This is Lois-what?"

Sojourner rolls her eyes but she's smiling.

"How do you spell it?"

She spells it for me and I put it in my phone. I'll look it up.

"I give you a pass because you're so new."

I smile. Probably for too long. I'm thinking about how New York City is a total mystery and this new neighbourhood, Alphabet City, the East Village, Lois-whatever-it-was, is full of streets I haven't walked along. I'd like to walk along them with her.

"There are a lot of squirrels," I say at the same time as she asks, "How long you been boxing?"

"Since I was—"

"Is this your sister?"

My heart beats faster. I turn. Rosa's walking on her toes so that her curls bounce, which makes her look like a kid from a commercial. Blonde hair, blue eyes, rosy cheeks, dimples, big smile. In case anyone doesn't notice, she's carrying her little white handbag with a picture of Shirley Temple on it.

"She looks like you."

Rosa looks nothing like me. We have the same colouring, but that's it. My hair's straight and thick like David's. I have David's nose. Rosa has Sally's. My eyes are a much darker blue, like Sally's.

"I'm Rosa Klein," Rosa says, holding out her hand. Sojourner shakes it. I stand there, realising I should have introduced them.

"Lovely to meet you. I'm Sid."

Sid?

"You're pretty," Rosa says, dimpling. "I like your dress. Red and black look fabulous together."

"Thank you. I like your dress too."

Rosa curtseys. I wonder where that came from. Her dance classes? Do tap dancers curtsey?

"Soj—Sid and I are at the same boxing gym," I say at last.

"Do you like making people bleed?" Rosa asks.

Sojourner laughs.

"Have you broken anyone's nose?"

"Once."

"Was it fun?"

"Fun? No. But I liked winning that bout."

"What if you killed someone?"

I wonder where Sally and David are and why they let Rosa wander off. I wish they'd show up. Rosa will stop asking questions like this when they're within earshot.

"That would be awful. It almost never happens. More people are killed playing football than from boxing."

I wonder if that's true.

"Boxing's not nearly as terrible as people think. It's about learning to control yourself. If you lose your temper or try to hit someone 'cause you're mad, you'll lose. Good fighters aren't angry. I don't want to hurt people. That's not why I box."

I wonder what sense Rosa makes of that answer, given that she always wants to hurt people.

"I like being in control."

Well, *that* is true.

"Don't we all?" Sojourner says. She smiles at Rosa as if she finds her adorable, which makes my heart sink. I love Rosa, but every time someone likes her I feel sad. How do they not see what she is?

"Do you have to defend yourself for liking boxing?" Sojourner asks me. "Or is that just us girls?"

"All the time. My parents hate that I box."

"Are there any other girls at your gym?" Rosa says at the same time.

Sojourner laughs. "Sure. My best friend Jaime and me train there together."

"You have a best friend?" Rosa asks, injecting her words with all the longing she can.

"Please," I mutter. I don't think either of them hear me.

"Sure," Sojourner says. "You don't?"

Which is exactly what Rosa wants her to say.

"Our parents move around a lot and we're homeschooled. It's hard to make friends," Rosa says with the smallest break in her voice.

Sojourner looks at me.

"*Sometimes* we're homeschooled," I say. "Mostly we go to regular school. Rosa likes to exaggerate. Where are Sally and David?" I ask Rosa. "Aren't we going to be late?"

Sojourner looks at her phone. "I gotta go too. You be at the gym Monday?"

I nod. "In the afternoon. You?"

"See you then."

"Bye, Sid," Rosa says. "It was wonderful to meet you."

Sojourner smiles, waves. "See you later."

"Later," I say. I don't watch her go, though I want to.

"Laying it on a bit thick, don't you think?" I say as soon as Sojourner is out of earshot. "Where *are* the parentals? We're supposed to be there in five minutes. David'll freak if we're late."

Instead of answering my question about sucking up to Sojourner, Rosa tells me she should be allowed to play chess with the men in the park. "David says they're hustlers. But I bet they can't play chess as well as I can. I'll hustle *them*."

I don't doubt it.

We find the parentals arguing politics with an old white man handing out anarchist pamphlets on the other side of the park. They haven't even noticed they lost Rosa.

David waves. "Are you two ready?"

They say goodbye to the anarchist, who grunts at them.

"It's this way," Sally says, looking at her phone. "I can't wait for you to finally meet them. Are you excited?"

Rosa declares that she is, dimpling to underline her enthusiasm. I force a smile. I suspect the McBrunight children are going to be spoiled brats. They're growing up getting everything they want. They probably think people who aren't rich are barely worth their attention.

David slips his arm around Sally to pull her out of the way of foot traffic. She's walking on the wrong side. Rosa and I slip behind them.

"You like Sid, don't you?" Rosa says, watching a man with a tiny poodle in his arms push past our parents. "Her skin is shiny."

I grunt in a noncommittal way. "I don't think they're going to let you play chess with those men," I say, as if that matters to me more than Sojourner.

Rosa smiles.

THE MCBRUNIGHTS WERE BORN and bred right here in New York City. Apparently that's rare. Almost as rare as having been a couple since they were teenagers. Like our parents. I hope they're better at keeping their hands off each other than Sally and David are. Having parents who are desperately in love is embarrassing.

Gene and Lisimaya McBrunight and their three daughters are waiting to be seated when we arrive.

Gene and Lisimaya yelp when they see Sally and David, but I would have recognised them anyway. I've seen a million photos of the whole family. Though they don't quite prepare me for how pretty the twins are: big dark eyes, high cheekbones, heart-shaped faces. They're almost as perfect as Rosa. They're also identical, *really* identical. If Seimone didn't have shorter hair, telling them apart would be impossible. Maya's hair is in a ponytail; Seimone's is in a bob.

Gene and Lisimaya let go of each other's hands to hug the parentals. Holding hands in public. Very Sally and David-like.

Rosa puts her hand in mine and gives it a little squeeze. She's excited. I don't want to know what she's thinking. More people to manipulate?

Gene has tears in his eyes as he draws Sally into a hug. She does too. "Thank you," she says fervently.

Then they're wiping their eyes and exclaiming and clogging the narrow entrance to the Greek restaurant.

"She has your exact smile," Lisimaya says to David after hugging Rosa. "Can she get people to do whatever she wants too?"

David smiles, confirming how similar his and Rosa's smiles are, right down to the dimples.

Everyone in the restaurant is staring. My cheeks grow warm. The twins look as embarrassed and awkward as I feel. Leilani looks bored.

A waiter coughs and says, "Excuse me. Sir? Ma'am? Your table is ready." They don't notice. He coughs again. Louder this time. "Excuse me, sir. Excuse me!"

Sally turns, apologises, and we're led to the table. Two women at the table next to us whisper as we sit down.

We kids don't bother introducing ourselves. We know who they are, they know who we are. I know they're the only people in the world with that last name. I know when their birthdays are. I know Seimone is allergic to peanuts. I know Leilani is almost the same age as me. I know—

"Are you going to stare at them all day?" Leilani asks me. "Yes, it's like two little Korean princesses stepped straight out of a manhwa. So exotic! Two gorgeous chips off their Korean daddy's block."

I don't know what a manhwa is. "I wasn't staring. I was—"

"Yes, they're very pretty."

"I'm pretty too," Rosa says.

"Everyone's pretty," Maya says.

Seimone laughs. "We're all very pretty."

Leilani snorts.

It isn't that Leilani is ugly. She's pretty enough, I suppose. I can hear Sally's lecture as if I said that out loud: *Pretty enough for what exactly?*

Leilani's looks are like mine. Nana would use the word *plain*. We're in the same boat, Leilani and I: the least good-looking person in a good-looking family. I wonder if it bothers her? Or is she relieved like me? At least she doesn't have acne.

She's more interesting looking than her sisters. I can see exactly what she's thinking without her saying a word. She's mostly thinking about what a waste of time this is and how uninteresting I am. I wish I thought the same of her, but watching her face is mesmerising.

Leilani and I are seated opposite each other, with the twins on either side of us and Rosa at the end of the table. The four adults are already drinking wine and talking away at each other, waving their arms around, laughing too loud, pointing. Every second sentence begins *It can't be twenty years . . .* or *Do you remember when . . .* They're laughing at David killing them playing poker, at a disastrous skiing trip. They are ridiculously happy.

"Homeschooling, huh?" Leilani says, dragging me back to the kids' end of the table.

This is going to be a long brunch.

"It's so we don't have our brains warped by the capitalist sausage factory," Rosa says, egging Leilani on.

The twins giggle.

"I don't feel like a sausage," Maya says. "Do you feel like a sausage, Seimone?"

"Well, I am kinda hungry."

They giggle some more. Rosa joins in.

"I like your gloves," Rosa says to Seimone. The gloves in question are red and black. Maya isn't wearing gloves. "Do you play poker?"

Seimone shakes her head.

"I'll teach you. Chess?"

"Yes!"

"Is being homeschooled everything good and wise?" Leilani asks me, while Rosa and Seimone squeal about chess.

She manages to make it sound like I'm an idiot if I think it is while at the same time making it clear she doesn't care what my answer is. It has to do with the way she lifts her eyebrows while curling her upper lip. If I explain that I've been taught at school more than at home her eyebrows will just rise higher.

"Do you like your school?" I say instead, fighting her with banality.

Her left eyebrow arcs even higher. I can't raise either of mine that high. It's clear from that one elegant movement that no one in their right mind likes school or asks such a stupid question. This test she is giving me? I'm failing it. My explaining I know it's a stupid question, that I asked it on purpose *because* it's stupid, isn't going to do me any favours with her, either. I itch to text Georgie a running account of this fun, fun brunch.

"Going to ask me what I want to do when I grow up? What colleges I'm applying to? What my career plans are?"

Those questions have occurred to me.

"I'm homeschooled," I say. "My social intercourse is sporadic."

"But your love affair with the thesaurus is for all time." She gives a small smile that says *wanker* as loudly as if she spoke the word.

"You should be an actor," I say. "You have a wonderfully expressive face."

See? I can be bitchy too. But then I remember she goes to a high school for the performing arts. She probably is training to be an actor.

"I think you mean *actress*. Let's not pretend there's no difference in how much the men get paid for doing the exact same thing as the women. Not going to change a thing pretending like I'm an *actor*. Which is why I'm going to make my own movies and television. Acting is for those who want to be exploited by misogynist assholes."

"You sound like Sally," I say.

"And you sound like my dad. It's a joy, isn't it? We only just met and already we're like family."

I'm tempted to tell her that I don't want to be here either, to suggest that we suck it up since our parents want it so much, and not make this brunch any fouler than it already is. I want to ask for a truce. But I can imagine how quick she'll cut me down.

Rosa giggles at something one of the twins says, but I can see that she's listening to every word from Leilani. Rosa's eyes gleam with admiration, and I'm convinced she's deciding that Leilani's someone who can teach her a thing or two about messing with people.

I'm going to have to keep Rosa away from Leilani. It's bad enough that Leilani can give lessons in mean, but what if she's like Rosa and can teach her worse things? Leilani is not exactly giving off empathetic vibes. Callousness—she doesn't care if she hurts my feelings; disinhibition—she says what she wants without fear of consequences; charisma—it's hard not to pay attention to her. Is she a thrill seeker? I'm tempted to ask if she likes driving too fast.

Having Rosa for a sister makes me view people differently. I don't trust charm—not that Leilani is exhibiting any, but I can tell she can when she wants. The only people I instantly trust are the ones who are uneasy around Rosa. I'm disappointed Sojourner didn't respond to Rosa that way.

"I love your agricultural shirt," Leilani says to me.

Rosa laughs loudly. Leilani looks at her appraisingly. "Those dimples work for you, don't they?"

Rosa's eyes narrow. Only briefly, but I see it.

Well. Rosa will not be wrapping Leilani around her finger anytime soon. Like recognising like?

My father has the same easy charm as Rosa. But he also cares. Rosa is too much like Papa and Uncle Saul. Not a gram of empathy between the two of them. Papa is constantly trying to manipulate everyone around him. Putting people in his will when they please him, taking them out when they don't. Every favour he grants has strings attached. Uncle Saul's a chip off the old block.

"How are you all getting along?" Gene McBrunight asks.

Leilani does not hide her eye roll. "Oh, it's fabulous at this end of the table. Che and I are already planning our wedding. There'll be doves. Also penguins."

I blush, not because I think she's cute. The twins laugh and shoot me looks I'm sure mean they're convinced I have a crush.

"That was quick," Gene says.

"Leave us alone, Dad," Leilani says. "We just met. We're not best friends who've known each other since cell phones came in suitcases, okay?"

"Fine, fine," he says, turning to Sally.

"Mobile phones used to come in suitcases?" I ask. Leilani doesn't smile, let alone laugh.

"In case you've gotten any ideas," she says, "and that blush wasn't just your overreactive sympathetic nervous system, I have a girlfriend. I don't go for boys. No, not even whichever movie star you were about to suggest."

I wasn't about to suggest anyone. I'm too busy wondering how she knows what the sympathetic nervous system is. She's studying to be a director, not a doctor.

"If I ever found a guy attractive it wouldn't be a boring, corn-fed farm boy from Australia like yourself."

Rosa and the twins giggle.

"Good to know," I say. I've never been called any of those things. Well, boring maybe and Australian, definitely. But not the others. I've never stepped foot on a farm and I'm not a big fan of corn.

"I might take you shopping, though." Her eyes drop to my shirt. "If we're going to be forced into each other's company as often as I suspect we are, you're going to have to wear clothes that don't make my eyeballs bleed."

"Sorry if mine clothes offend thee," I mutter.

Leilani smiles. I'm surprised she knows how. For a second I'm certain she isn't like Rosa.

CHAPTER SEVEN

After brunch we go to the McBrunights' home, which towers over the street, taking up almost the whole block. It used to be a synagogue. Walking up the steps and in through the huge wooden doors is like walking into the Great Temple in Sydney.

I knew they were rich, but seeing their home, now I *really* know it.

Shafts of light fall from a giant skylight, as if from heaven itself. It's like they live in the Louvre. Only the Louvre is way more cluttered.

Skylight is the wrong word. Two whole sections of the ceiling, and the roof beyond, have been replaced with clear glass.

The ceiling looks like the inside of a whale with ribs that extend down into columns. At night you must be able to see the stars.

"Your mouth is open," Leilani tells me.

I close it.

"Everyone stares. Though you're the first to drool."

I wipe at my mouth before realising I haven't drooled. Anyone else would have laughed at me. Leilani achieves the same effect with a tiny lift of her eyebrow.

"Do you want the tour, or are you happy to stand there and stare? Your mouth's open again, by the way."

It is. I close it again.

They've done what they can to make this giant room more human-scaled. Half the space is occupied by comfortable lounge furniture. Seimone drags Rosa to the largest couch, where they start a bouncing contest. They've been whispering and giggling all the way from the restaurant. Maya hasn't been giggling with them. She stays by her mother.

"Were those the balconies?" I ask, looking up.

Leilani nods. "It's where they exiled the women. We've converted them into rooms—after doing a cleansing ceremony to rid the building of all that misogyny."

I can't decide whether she's being serious.

"Come and see the kitchens," Lisimaya says.

"Ah," Sally says. "Your famed carbon-neutral kitchens."

The parentals and Gene follow her to a door on the other side of the hall.

"It's a kitchen," Leilani says.

"Your mother said *kitchens*. They're carbon neutral?"

"Whatever. It's not like the olds do any cooking. I suppose I should show you the rest of the house."

I'm tempted to say *if it's not too much trouble*. But she clearly thinks it is. "Thank you."

There are two lifts. One for each side of the building, or wings, as Leilani calls them. The east wing and the west wing. "If I were Dad doing this tour, I'd say, *Yes, like the White House*."

I groan, since that's what she wants me to do, but I'm not sure what wings have to do with the White House. I imagine the wings of a giant bird and the whole building taking flight.

"Never been in a house with a lift."

"*Elevator*. I think we've established this is a big house."

"You have four floors," I say idiotically, staring at the panel of buttons. There's an emergency button and a handset like a lift in a regular building.

"Five. You missed the basement. You know, where the swimming pool is."

"Wow," I say and wish I hadn't.

She indicates that she is rolling her eyes with only the barest glance upwards. "I was kidding about the swimming pool."

"Oh." I would have said *of course you're kidding* except that there's no *of course* about it. Why wouldn't this place have a swimming pool? Though there is the matter of only four buttons on the panel. "So I guess that means you don't have a helipad on the roof?"

"Don't be silly. The helipad is over the garage behind the house."

"Seriously?"

"No, not seriously. There are rules about where helicopters can and can't fly. They can't fly here."

"How do you even *know* that?"

No laugh from Leilani, just her raised-eyebrow laugh substitute.

"Have you always lived in this house?"

"I think you mean *mausoleum*. Yes, they've owned this place for twenty years."

I don't make the mistake of saying *wow* again. I can't imagine growing up in a place like this. Mind you, I can't imagine living in one place my whole life. We lived in the same house until I was seven. After that: chaos. Different homes in Sydney until I was twelve, then different places in Australia, then New Zealand for a couple of years, then back to Sydney for a year, then Indonesia, then Thailand and now here.

"You're lucky," I say. The look Leilani gives me says she doesn't agree. "What's it like being rich?"

"What's it like being Australian?"

The lift stops and the doors open onto a room filled with books.

"It's not my money. It's theirs."

"But," I begin. It doesn't matter who's making the money. She's swimming in it. "They're your parents. Doesn't mean you're poor exactly, does it?"

Another scathing look. "I didn't say I was poor. But this is theirs. If it weren't for my parents I wouldn't be living like this."

"Sure. If it weren't for my parents I wouldn't be living in New York. They control us until we're old enough to leave."

"Unfortunately."

"Might as well enjoy it, right?"

I get the are-you-an-idiot look again. "What's to enjoy? They only had us to carry on the family name—the stupid invented family name—and for us to be perfect little mini-thems. That never works, but you'd be surprised by how vain some people are. I wouldn't be. But you're surprised by everything."

"It's all that corn I eat. Makes me credulous. It's the insecticides they use, apparently."

She makes a half-snorting sound.

"You almost laughed!"

"No, I didn't," she says, with her hand over her mouth. "I'm not smiling. This way."

I follow, wondering why she's so caustic about her parents.

"That's Maya and Seimone's room."

The door is closed with a hammer and sickle painted on it. I don't ask.

"Maya's doing. It has something to do with Siberia."

Apparently I don't need to ask.

"They share?"

"They like it. They've always preferred being together. Except Seimone has dance and Maya tennis. It's a twin thing. This is their study."

The door is open. I see two desks, chairs, beanbags, books, tablets, a fish tank, and a mural of underwater creatures. Above one of the desks are posters of beautiful Asian pop stars. Above the other is a horseshoe hanging from a nail.

"Is that Chinese?" On the wall facing us is a large scroll.

"Korean. My dad's Korean. Been there a million times. We have family in Seoul."

I know that. Gene was adopted by a white American family, who made sure he learned Korean, and as much about his two countries as possible. They stayed in contact with his birth mother.

"My room." The door's closed with no sticker on it. Leilani doesn't open it. "This is my study."

The floor is black. It's spongy under my feet as I follow her in. "A training floor. Cool. What martial art do you do?"

"None, not as in going after a black belt. I act, remember? Acting is all body work. So I dabble in all sorts—a little bit of karate, fencing, boxing, gymnastics. It helps to be fit."

"Hence the treadmill."

"I don't always have time to run outside. Treadmills are a vaguely acceptable substitute."

It's on the tip of my tongue to say *let's run together some time*. There are tracks on either side of Manhattan.

"Now the deck."

"If there is a deck," I mutter.

"There's a deck," Maya says from the doorway. We both startle.

"Where are Rosa and Seimone?" I ask, feeling a prickle of worry.

"Dad's doing magic tricks."

Leilani groans. Maya giggles.

"Rosa wanted to see. So Seimone's being nice and sitting through it."

"Poor Seimone. She's too nice."

"Rosa dances," Maya finishes as if that explains everything.

"Ah," Leilani says.

"She's going to McKendrick's too."

That name rings a bell. "Rosa and Seimone are at the same dance school?"

"Uh huh," Maya says. "We're going for a swim after the stupid magic show. I volunteered to get the bathing suits."

"You really do have a swimming pool?"

Leilani puts her hand over her mouth. Maya giggles.

There is a deck.

With views. We can see the tops of other buildings, many water tanks, some rooftop gardens and clotheslines.

"The olds aren't allowed up here," Maya says. "It's all ours. See that church? The roof there? There's a woman who brings her dog to do his business. But she never cleans it up. It must smell nasty over there. We've never seen anyone take the dog outside. Poor thing."

"But how do they get on to the roof?" It's flat with two spires on either side but I don't see how anyone would get access.

Leilani stares at me. "Through the door."

"It's a Catholic church," Maya says as if that explains everything, but I'm still bewildered.

"Is this what you do up here? Watch other people?"

"Everyone does," Maya says. "We've never seen a murder though."

"Maya keeps hoping."

So would Rosa.

"Mr. Smokes Too Much had a heart attack." Maya points to the apartment block next to the church, where a man on the fifth floor sits smoking on his fire escape. "I bet he's not allowed to smoke anymore, but he's always out there. He lights one cigarette with the butt of the last one. So. Gross. We saw the ambulance come. His face was purple. Yani at the bodega says his heart stopped. He was dead. Can you imagine that?"

"Yes," Leilani says.

Maya ignores her. "But there he is smoking like before. Yani says he only ever buys beef jerky, candy and cigarettes. She also says he's forty-three. That's younger than our parents!"

"He looks like our grandparents."

"Great-grandparents."

"Great-grandparents of the mummies in the Natural History Museum."

Maya laughs. "Wanna play hide-and-seek?"

"No," Leilani says. "I'm not five. Nor am I wasted."

"I *like* hide-and-seek." Maya turns to me. "Do you want to?"

"Um," I say. "Why don't you ask Rosa and Seimone?"

Maya shrugs. "They're busy with the magic show."

"Isn't it better with more people?"

"I guess."

"Must be fun playing it here, though," I say. "Lots of places to hide."

Leilani makes a muffled noise.

"What?"

"She's eleven, not five."

"It *is* fun hiding here. You can get up into the ceiling. Why do you hate fun, Leilani?"

Leilani snorts again. "I hate Fun with a capital F for the same reason you hate Seimone's idiot boy bands. Because they're evil and wrong."

Maya laughs. So do I. Leilani cracks a smile. I wonder if she ever laughs.

Leilani's phone buzzes. "The olds. Your parents are heading home. Apparently these brunches are going to be a weekly thing. Joy."

We go downstairs. Goodbyes are exchanged.

"It's ten tomorrow morning, yes? We'll be in touch asap about a date for that party," Gene says.

I've never heard a person say *asap* as if it were a word.

Rosa and Seimone hug each other tight and declare they're best friends. Maya rolls her eyes when none of the adults are looking.

"We'll have to teach you all how to use an auto injector. It's easy. I'll send you a link to the vid," Gene says. "I think they're going to be spending a lot of time together."

"A what?" David asks.

"Auto injector. For if Seimone is exposed to peanuts."

"Look!" Rosa says, pulling something out of her pocket. "Seimone gave me gloves like hers! I don't have to wear them because I'm not allergic. But now we're gloves twins! Aren't they pretty?"

She puts them on and hugs Seimone again.

"Bye, Che," Leilani says. "It was nice to meet you."

"Likewise," I say with none of her sarcasm.

"WHY COULDN'T WE SWIM?" Rosa asks as we walk down the street. "Why don't we have a swimming pool?"

"Another time, Rosa."

"I want to live in the McBrunights' house."

The parentals walk ahead hand in hand. They're laughing together.

As we cross into Tompkins Square Park Rosa takes my hand, like she used to do when she was younger, and says, "I'm going to live in that house someday."

I can tell she wants me to ask how that's going to happen. I don't. "Did you take any souvenirs?"

She pulls a ghostly white Korean doll in a huge dress out of her Shirley Temple bag and holds it out. "The dress is made of silk. She's a lady of the court. I wish I was Korean too."

"You'll return that."

"It's a present. Seimone gave it to me."

"Did she?" I ask.

"Of course. She likes me. We can't be in trouble with the McBrunights. David would get mad."

She's said that before.

"Sally and David aren't going to be together much longer," she says as if she's telling me what time it is.

"What?" I ask before I can stop myself.

She swings our hands back and forth. She'll be skipping in a second. "You'll see."

All I can see is that the parentals are half a block ahead of us. Sally leans into David, his arm around her shoulders. They'll be together forever.

CHAPTER EIGHT

Rosa was a toddler when I first made her promise not to kill.

I didn't care what the doctors said. I knew there was something deeply wrong with her.

I typed *something is wrong with my sister*, which brought up sisters who didn't eat, who ran all the time, who pulled their hair out, scratched at their faces, cut themselves. Rosa didn't do any of those things.

I changed *sister* to *child*.

Oh.

There were other kids who lied and didn't care when they were caught, who felt no affection, who smiled and laughed and hugged only to get what they wanted.

Other kids like Rosa.

Who felt no empathy. That was a new word for me, *empathy*.

Almost all kids start out selfish but then they learn empathy. Why wasn't Rosa learning?

The parentals weren't worried. She wasn't throwing tantrums. She was making direct eye contact. (Too direct, if you asked me.) They would remonstrate with her when they caught her lying. "But kids lie," they said.

Worse, though, was how much she liked killing things. Yes, lots of kids do that, but not like Rosa.

I saw her killing ants.

One by one, methodically following the trail, squishing each one flat with her chubby forefinger. Her gaze by turns intent, satisfied, delighted.

Then she started catching moths and pulling them to pieces.

I was eleven by then. Rosa was four.

Sally and David had told me to protect her. If I told them what she was doing, was I protecting her? She might grow out of it. Almost everything I read said most kids did.

I told the parentals.

They thanked me and talked to Rosa about it. She said I was the one who killed ants and moths, not her. The parentals knew I didn't lie.

They took Rosa to a doctor, who referred her to a child psychiatrist. I don't know what the psychiatrist said, but after that Rosa had weekly sessions for months. She hated those sessions.

She stopped killing insects when she thought someone was looking. I saw her.

I watched her killing ants again. She was too absorbed to notice me.

"What are you doing?"

"Nothing."

Her thumb and forefinger were black.

"Why did you kill those ants?"

"I like the popping sound they make."

They didn't make a popping sound. Not that I could hear.

"I like making them stop moving. I like being the boss."

"Don't," I told her.

She turned to give me her full, disconcerting, unblinking stare.

"Because Sally and David don't like it? That's why they took me to that doctor, isn't it? She keeps asking me about it."

"Because killing is wrong. I don't like when you do it either."

"Uncle Saul paid people to kill ants at his place. I wasn't putting poisons in the environment like he did." She was quoting David.

"Uncle Saul is not an ethical person," I said, also quoting David.

"But Sally lays out traps for the cockroaches. Why is it alright to kill cockroaches?"

"Because they're pests that spread diseases." I hoped that was true and was relieved to find later when I looked it up that it was.

"But those sticky traps also kill ants and sometimes moths and that one time a skink."

"Sally and David were unhappy about that."

"They were unhappy about the skink. They didn't care about the moths or the ants. But they care when *I* kill moths or ants."

"Because it makes you smile." Her genuine smile.

"So they don't like me being happy?"

"Killing things *shouldn't* make you happy, Rosa. *That's* why they're worried."

I could see her storing that piece of information. She put up her arms so I would carry her and hugged me tight. All my love for her flooded back. This little girl who liked killing insects, who might not have any empathy.

"You have to promise me not to kill things."

"But I like it."

"What would happen if Sally or David saw you?"

Rosa didn't say anything.

"What would your psychiatrist say?"

Rosa bit her lower lip. "What about mosquitoes?"

"You can kill mosquitoes."

"Flies?"

"Yes."

"Gnats? Fleas?"

"Yes."

"Worms?"

"No. They're good for the soil."

"Spiders?"

"No. Spiders eat mosquitoes."

"What if the spider's biting me?"

"Put it in a jar so the doctors know what antivenom to give you."

"What about—"

I put my hand up. "No other exceptions."

"Alright. I won't kill anymore."

Not long after our conversation she stopped going to the psychiatrist. Sally and David said she'd made progress. She admitted she'd killed the ants.

I didn't catch her killing anything but mosquitoes after that. Though I sometimes found her with dead things. A rat, a sparrow. They were dead before she poked them with sticks, which was disturbing, but I could tell myself she was being curious.

Then there was Apinya's guinea pig.

Apinya was two years younger than Rosa and lived in the apartment next door to us in Bangkok. She was thrilled a big girl like Rosa would play with her. Even more thrilled when Rosa told her that they were best friends. They were the only kids on our floor. Apinya would do anything Rosa told her to do.

I blamed myself. If I'd made more of an effort to learn Thai . . . but I'm not good at languages. Not like Rosa, who was fluent within minutes. Besides, Thai is ridiculously hard to learn. My tone would go up when it should go down. I didn't learn much beyond hello, goodbye, thank you, and how to press my hands together in prayer position to be respectful.

I heard Rosa call out. It sounded like my name. I walked into her bedroom. Apinya was pushing a pillow into the floor.

"What did you . . ." I began.

Rosa said, "Hi, Che."

Why was Apinya struggling with a pillow?

Rosa murmured something encouraging to her. I took in the empty cage on the floor beside them. Rosa looked directly at me and grinned. I lunged for the pillow.

Too late.

Under the pillow was the supine body of Apinya's guinea pig. It wasn't moving.

The word *monster* slid past my lips before I could stop it. I felt sick. Rosa had promised not to kill. She hadn't; Apinya had.

Apinya's eyes were full of tears. She looked to Rosa for approval and Rosa nodded.

I couldn't speak.

Rosa put the guinea pig back in the cage.

The doorbell rang. Rosa ran to get it. It was Apinya's father, home from work. Apinya burst into tears. Rosa looked sad.

Sally and David emerged from their office. Rosa joined Apinya in tears. The parentals comforted her.

I retreated to my room, sat on my bed, stared at nothing.

They would have cancelled their dinner that night, but they were dining with an investor, and cancelling wouldn't look right. Rosa's tears didn't sway them.

It was just me and Rosa.

I reheated spaghetti bolognese—Rosa's favourite. I needed to extract another promise. One without loopholes.

She'd never made someone else kill. She'd never killed anything as big as a guinea pig. She was scaling up.

"Why did Apinya kill her guinea pig?" I asked, knowing exactly why.

Rosa spooned pasta into her mouth and chewed, making sure she chewed fifty times. Sally taught Rosa to do that when she was little to stop her gulping down her meals. It worked. Rosa likes rules. She likes to use them to mess with others.

I put my fork down.

"Because I wanted to see if she would do it."

"How did you feel when she did it?"

"Good."

"You know it was wrong, Rosa."

"Her parents will buy her another one."

"You made her kill something she loved."

"If she loved it she wouldn't have killed it."

"Maybe she loves you more than she loves her guinea pig."

"Then that's her problem. She should have better priorities." That was something Uncle Saul would have said. "She should value life."

"The way you value life? You're the one who told her to kill it."

"I didn't think she'd do it."

"You're the one with the power, Rosa. Apinya's younger than you. She admires you. You made it hard for her to disobey. You know that's wrong."

Rosa put more spaghetti into her mouth and began her million-chew count.

I knew she didn't care. How could I make her care? I thought about telling Sally and David what I feared. But they only saw sunny Rosa. The minute they walked out the door the smile vanished from her face. Were it not for her eyes she would look blank.

"Her doing what I wanted felt good."

"Did it make you want to do that again?" I asked, half hoping she would lie to me.

"Yes."

"Will you do it again?"

She put more spag bol in her mouth.

She was enjoying dragging this out. She liked telling me the truth. There was no one else she could tell.

"I liked watching Apinya fight her tears. I liked seeing her hands tremble as she put the pillow over it. It took her five goes. She was trying to do it one-handed. Silly, really. Animals fight hard to live. Did you see where it scratched her?"

"Was that what Apinya called her pet? It?"

"No. She called it Kitty. She thought that was funny."

"The way you think it's funny Kitty scratched her?"

"I didn't say it was funny. But it was interesting watching it fight to live."

"I want you to promise not to make anyone kill anything."

The last forkful of spaghetti entered her mouth.

What if she wouldn't promise?

What would I tell Sally and David?

Would I tell them about the research I'd done? Show them my journal? Tell them about typing *Is my sister a psychopath?* into search engines, desperately hoping she wasn't?

If I said *psychopath* out loud, if specialists agreed with me that's what Rosa is, what would happen?

I'd read that some specialists argue labelling a child *psychopath* is saying there's no hope for that kid.

"I promise," she said. "I won't kill and I won't make anyone else kill."

I couldn't see a loophole.

Since Apinya's guinea pig there's been nothing. As far as I know.

PART TWO
I Want to Spar

CHAPTER NINE

On Monday morning our new tutor arrives twenty minutes early. He's a whiter-than-white guy called Geoffrey Honeyman. I can't believe we don't get more of a reprieve before our first class. We've only been in New York City for about ten minutes.

Maths and most sciences are not my thing. Biology, yes. But physics? Uggh. Chemistry, ditto. And maths? The worst of all. But without them I can't get into medical school.

I wish we were going to school but the parentals decided April is too close to the end of the US school year. Real schools open again in September. It's been more than six months since we were at the Australian Independent International School in Jakarta. I loved it. So did Rosa, but for the wrong reasons. It's safer when she's homeschooled.

In the meantime we have Mr. Honeyman for maths and science and a stack of books for everything else.

Sally and David intend to quiz us on the books once a week. This is always their intention, but it rarely works out that way. Since leaving Sydney our education's been, to put it nicely, haphazard.

Rosa and I crouch at the top of the stairs, spying.

"He's bald," Rosa says. "I like it when they hire old tutors."

Of course she does. Old people love Rosa.

His head is remarkably shiny. I wondered if he polishes it.

The parentals shake his hand and lead him to sit on one of the couches, where they explain a little more about Rosa and me. Not that they won't have told him everything he needs to know about us a million times already.

"They're telling him I'm a genius," Rosa whispers.

"Yes, and that I'm quite smart despite my struggles with maths."

"Also science," Rosa adds. "You're not that smart, Che."

"Thanks."

"I want to go to Seimone's school. They get to put on plays."

I wonder if the twins go to different schools or if Rosa has discounted the existence of her less-favourite twin.

"Are you two ready up there?" David calls. "Come down."

We wait about thirty seconds then go down. Geoffrey doesn't look old. Not wrinkly old. He's definitely younger than the parentals.

He tells us to call him Geoff and shakes our hands. His are sweaty. I don't understand how he can be so sweaty when the room is so cool and he's been sitting with the parents for the last twenty minutes.

"We should get going," Sally says. She's pulling at the sleeves of her jacket, making sure they don't overhang her shirt cuffs. Then she undoes the top two buttons of her coat. Then does them up again. They're heading to their first formal meeting with the McBrunights. They'll be meeting their staff for the first time. They want to make a good impression.

"Do I look alright?" she asks David.

"Breathtaking." He kisses Sally's forehead. "Do I?"

Sally nods, plucking a stray bit of lint from his sleeve.

Geoff looks embarrassed.

"You both look great," I say. "For jetlagged people who are nervous."

"It's a big deal," Sally says.

"We're not nervous so much as elated," David says. I wonder if he believes it.

"They love you," Rosa says. "That's what they say in the cards they send."

"You're right, darling," David says. "It'll be fine."

They kiss me and Rosa goodbye, shake Geoff's sweaty hand.

"Don't forget to watch the auto-injector vid again."

"Again?" Rosa says. "We've already watched it four times."

"Again. We'll be back before you leave for boxing, Che."

Then they're gone.

Geoff stands awkwardly next to the couch, looking at something slightly to my left.

"You'll start with a test," Rosa says. "So you can see what you need to teach us. Maths tutors always do that. I hope it's hard. Last time it was boringly easy."

"Brat."

"Um, yes," Geoff says at the same time. "A test."

I wonder if he's tutored before.

"Tutors never believe I'm a genius. Too many parents think their children are geniuses if they count to ten by the time they're two. I am a prodigy, though. I'm already working on proofs. Can we work in the kitchen? I like sitting on the stools."

"Um, sure. We can sit wherever you like."

"Are you English?" Rosa asks. She knows he is. The parentals told us.

"Um, yes, I am."

We sit on the stools. Geoff hands us our tests. Rosa starts answering the questions. I read through the test, my eyes already glazing.

"That's annoying," Rosa says. "Stop it, Che."

"It is a bit annoying, actually," Geoff says.

I don't know what they're talking about.

"You're kicking," Geoff explains.

I look down at my legs. My toes bounce off the island, and my heels off my stool. I stop. "Sorry," I say.

I've never felt less like dealing with numbers. My head hurts. I'm sleepy—well, no, not sleepy, more like I'm not entirely sure I'm awake.

The first section is calculus. I try not to groan. I bet if I were in a normal school I wouldn't have to know any calculus yet. If I were in a normal school I wouldn't be sitting next to my ten-year-old sister who's already working on mathematical proofs.

"Kicking," Rosa says. "Don't."

I stop myself again. My phone vibrates in my pocket. Probably Nazeem or Georgie or Jason. Or all three.

"Can I have a moment before I start?" I ask.

Geoff nods, though I can see he's nonplussed.

I head to the bathroom, close the door, and pace. Four steps to the wall, four steps back. I wish I could go to the gym now.

I look at my phone.

—You awake?

It's Georgie. I sit on the counter next to the sink, my legs swinging.

—I'm typing this, which hints I'm awake. Isn't it ridic late there?

—Yeah. Couldn't sleep. But not enough brain to make anything. Besides can't sew—too noisy.

Georgie often has insomnia. Unlike me—except when I'm jetlagged.

—Naz says you're cool about us.

—Course.

—How's things with Rosa?

Georgie always asks. I always tell. I delete what I was going to say about her and Nazeem and tell her about the passport instead.

—The baby psychopath avenger. Maybe she'll use her powers for good from now on.

I laugh, imagining the expression on Georgie's face.

—I wish. She wants to move into the mansion of these rich friends of the parentals. You should see the flat we're in. It's already fancy. But now Rosa's seen better . . .

—She's going to rule the world some day. Won't be pretty.

"Are you alright in there, Che?" Rosa calls because why should she let me have more than five minutes of respite?

"Yeah. Be out in a second."

—Gotta go.

I slip my phone into my pocket and bounce up and down before going out there. Rosa's bent over the test. Geoff's looking at his tablet.

I slide onto my stool. "Sorry," I say.

Geoff looks up, but doesn't say anything. I can't see what he's reading.

"I've already finished the first section," Rosa announces.

"You shock me."

I turn to the test. Why start with calculus? Why not algebra or geometry or something more jetlag-brain friendly, like colouring in?

"If we were in a real school," I ask, "it would be the end of the year, wouldn't it?"

Geoff nods.

"We wouldn't be doing tests right now, would we?"

"You probably would. Late April and early May are exam time."

I sigh. In Thailand this is the beginning of the school year. In Australia the year is only a few months old. I push my gummy brain into gear, trying to figure out equations with the calculator on my phone.

The stool is the wrong height. I twist to get the crick out of my spine, then twist the other way. What I need is to go for a run. Does Sojourner run?

I keep pushing through the test, wondering why x's. Why not r's or l's? When am I going to need to know how to model change and motion? I slide off the stool and stretch my calves, quads and glutes.

"There," Rosa says, putting her pen down and handing the papers to Geoff. "That was challenging."

Rosa asks Geoff about poly-something or others. I've lost what he's saying within seconds. Rosa is mesmerised. This is about the only time I don't worry about her doing evil. She's too focused.

It doesn't take me long to finish the test, because I can only make a stab at answering about a third of the questions in the last section.

While Geoff goes over our tests I make myself cheese-and-ham sandwiches. When I get to the gym, I'm going to give Sojourner my number. We've connected, haven't we? It wouldn't seem too weird.

Rosa drinks a glass of orange juice and watches Geoff mark our tests. Geoff hands our tests back. Mine is covered in red scrawl. I barely passed. Rosa has two errors. I'm relieved and she's annoyed. She concentrates intently as he explains where she went wrong and why and gives her further examples. I am less attentive.

Sometimes I think the only relationships Rosa's capable of are with people who understand maths and chess better than she does.

My phone buzzes a few times. I want it to be Sojourner, but she doesn't have my number and I can't think of any way she could have gotten it.

Geoff addresses more of his explanations and examples to Rosa. It's like I'm not in the room. I wish I wasn't in the room.

We take another break. The texts are from Jason and Nazeem. I eat the protein I need but the translucent wall has descended over me yet again. Geoff's voice is a million miles away.

Just before two as Geoff is finishing up, Sally texts. —Meeting running long. Be back at five. You mind missing gym? Just this once?

I do mind.

—You know we wouldn't ask if it wasn't important.

I glare at the phone.

"Who's that?" Rosa asks.

"Sally. They won't be back till five."

"But you have gym," Rosa says.

"I *did* have gym."

—Text back so we know you got this.

"Sometimes," I say to my phone, "you shit me."

Geoff continues to pack up.

"Could you stay longer?" Rosa asks Geoff.

He looks at her and blinks. I'm probably blinking too.

"They'll pay you. I'd love extra tutoring."

"Well," Geoff says.

Will he be able to keep Rosa in line? I want to go to the gym. I *need* to go. I need to exhaust myself, then I'll be able to sleep and get past this stupid jetlag. I need to see Sojourner again.

Rosa dimples. "Please, please, please teach me more."

Another text from Sally. —Please answer, Che.

I'm not going to beg Geoff. I want to beg Geoff. Surely it will be fine leaving them together like this? Rosa is obsessed with maths. She respects Geoff's knowledge.

"Pretty please," Rosa says. "We could work on a proof!"

"Alright, Rosa," Geoff says. His forehead is shiny with sweat. Apparently proofs are irresistible. I'm not entirely clear on what a mathematical proof is.

"Thank you," I say, resisting the urge to yell my gratitude. "I am so grateful."

—Geoff is staying to teach Rosa more maths. I'm going to the gym. You'll have to pay him more.

I make myself more sandwiches, pack my gym bag.

"You'll be good, Rosa?"

She dimples again. "I'll be good."

"Don't dimple. I don't trust your dimples."

She clears her expression. "I promise I'll be good."

—Are you sure that's a good idea? Sally texts.

—Too late.

"You'll make sure she's good, Geoff? Don't let her talk you into doing anything that isn't maths-related."

He blinks rapidly. "I'm her maths tutor."

I kiss Rosa on the forehead, grab my bag and bolt.

Behind me I hear her say, "Tell Sid hi from me."

CHAPTER TEN

Sojourner is in my three o'clock class in the bag room. So is the meathead.

"Hey, Outback Steakhouse," he says, punching my arm a little too hard. "How you doing?"

I mutter something that could be mistaken for *fine* and sit next to the nearest bag to Sojourner, putting on my wraps while leaning forward to stretch my hamstrings.

I look up and see Sojourner. I smile. She returns it but stays focused on her warm-up. Her friend is on her other side, saying something about a protest. Sojourner nods and her forehead creases. I want to move over and smooth those lines away.

Our instructor walks in. She's short and lean with clipped blonde hair.

"I'm Dido," she says. "For those of you who don't know me, I'm tough, but fair."

I deduct points because every trainer says some variation of that. I'm waiting for the first one to say, *I'm pissweak and totally unfair.*

"I want to see solid form and hard work. If you're feeling half-assed, try another class. If you don't leave dripping sweat from every part of your body, then I failed. Okay, are we warmed up?"

We agree that we are.

"Gloves on. Show me what you got. Two two-minute rounds. Ten-second break in between. Go all out!"

I do. I give the bag everything: jabs, crosses, hooks, upper cuts, combinations. I bob and weave and duck and feint and parry and dance around the bag, which I'm imagining is a two-metre tall monster built like a brick shithouse. But he's slower than me and is used to getting in the knockout blow early; he doesn't have a lot of stamina. I go at him like a gnat, hitting him dozens of times in the kidneys.

The bell rings for the end of the first round. I'm dripping.

"Ten-second rest."

I grin.

Bell for the second round.

Everything flows. I'm dancing. The two-metre monster goes down. Next up, defence. Dido goes round the class, correcting everyone. She's a stickler for precise, tidy movements. I like her.

At the end I'm exhausted but exhilarated. The whole class is bent over gasping, but most are grinning.

"Sparring's at seven every night. No beginners, but everyone in this class is more than ready to join us. We welcome new faces. Interested?" Dido asks, turning to me.

My heart sinks. "I don't spar," I mutter. Stupid promise. I wonder if this is how Rosa feels keeping her promises to me.

"Well, if you change your mind you're more than welcome."

I nod, wipe the sweat from my face and hands with my towel and peel my wraps off.

"Australia, huh?" Sojourner asks me.

I look up at her and nod. She must have overheard the meathead.

"You don't look Australian," she says.

I stare.

No one's ever said that to me. I have blond hair and blue eyes. Mostly when people ask where I'm from and I say Australia their next question is *do you surf?* Because of the blond hair, blue eyes. They assume every Australian looks like me, which no, and that we all surf, which also no. I've never surfed.

"All the Australians I know have broken noses and messed-up ears."

"We're a pretty people."

She laughs. I shove the wraps in my pocket, grab my towel, water bottle and gloves, and stand. We're the same height, surrounded by a forest of punching bags. I feel myself lean towards her as if I'm trying to absorb some of that laughter. Her eyelashes are crazy long, curving up so high they almost touch her eyebrows. I take a sip of water to distract myself.

"Your little sister's awfully cute," she says.

"Too cute," I say. I don't want to think about Rosa. "It was nice running into you yesterday. I don't know many people here."

She smiles. "How come you don't spar?"

"I promised my parents I wouldn't until I stopped growing," I blurt. My cheeks burn. Why did I say that? *My parents won't let me.* What am I? Five?

I'm sure she's trying not to laugh at pathetic little me doing exactly what my parents tell me. Should I tell her I don't do everything they tell me? That will make me seem even more pathetic. Why am I so honest?

"What if you've already stopped growing?"

I laugh. Way too loud. "That's what *I* said. They said if for three years in a row I haven't grown they'll consider me stopped. I argued them down from five but I think one year would've been fairer."

"Huh."

Too much information. Too much blurting. Jason would piss himself if he overheard this. Georgie too. Even Nazeem. Just as well they're never going to know.

"I'm already a centimetre taller than last year." *Shut up, Che.*

"I like sparring," Sojourner says. She's smiling. I'm hoping she's smiling with me and not *at* me. Does that even make sense, or is the with/at thing only about laughing? "I love it. It's a million times better than any of these classes, and I *love* these classes. Dido's great."

"She's alright, isn't she?" I've decided the initial point deduction for *tough but fair* was a bit rough. Natalie has been known to say the same thing. It is what you want from a good trainer: toughness and fairness.

"I'm Che Taylor, by the way," I say, sticking out my hand. "We never said our names. I mean, I already heard yours."

She offers me her fist. We bump, me feeling like an idiot. Fighters always fist bump.

"Che was a twentieth-century revolutionary," I say automatically. "My parents want to save the world. They approve of revolutionaries."

She laughs again. "You get asked who Che was a lot, huh?"

"Sometimes. Mostly I get people assuming I don't know who I'm named after. I say that before they get a chance to ask me if,"—I put on a posh accent—"*I even know who he was.*" I return to my normal voice. "I mean, it's *my name.* Of course I know who Ernesto 'Che' Guevara was. Class traitor, sexy revolutionary pin-up of the world, executed in Bolivia where they put his head on a stake, blah blah blah."

Sojourner is still laughing. "Me too! I get that all the time. From now on I'm going to tell them first."

For a second I almost say *but your name's not Che*, then I realise. Shit. I have no idea who Sojourner is named after. I'd just thought it was a cool name. It didn't occur to me to look it up.

"Funny us both being named after revolutionaries," she says. "I was named for American ones. I'm Sojourner Ida Davis. But my friends call me Sid. For my initials. We'll see what you get to call me."

I want to tell her how beautiful her name is. *Sojourner.* I want to call her that, not Sid. Sid is a creepy old guy name. But I want to be her friend; if calling her Sid means we're friends, then I'll call her whatever she wants. I think about asking if she's doing anything right now. Will she go for a walk with me? Tell me more about herself? Kiss me?

"Are you . . ." I begin.

"Wassup, Sid." Her friend walks up to us, her hair wet and her bag slung over her shoulder.

"Hey, Jaime," Sojourner says.

"Who's this?" Jaime asks. "You were in Dido's class, weren't you?" I nod.

"This," Sojourner says, "is Che."

"Che?" Jaime laughs. "Seriously?"

I nod again, feeling foolish.

"Don't worry, Jaime. He knows who Che was," Sojourner says. "We gotta go. Nice meeting you, Ernesto."

She shrugs fully into her backpack and walks towards the exit, saying something to Jaime that makes them both laugh. My ears are hot. I hope they aren't laughing at me.

I think about trying to tag along. Maybe they'll take pity on the foreigner? But her *gotta go* was emphatic. I don't want to make a fool of myself. More than I have already. Instead I watch her walking away.

I pull out my phone ready to search on *American revolutionary*, *Ida* and *Sojourner*.

There are many messages: Sally with several different variations on —Meeting still going. Will probably have dinner as well. Please can you get home so Geoff can leave? Four missed calls from her.

I'm about to phone her when another text comes through. This time from David.

—It's okay. We're on our way to pick up Rosa. She'll have dinner with us. Work out for as long as you want.

I punch the air.

The search terms lead me to Sojourner Truth and Ida B. Wells. Turns out the original Sojourner was a former slave who fought for abolition and women's rights. Wells was a journalist and editor as well as a campaigner against lynching and also for women's rights.

Reading about them makes me want to tell Sojourner about my sister being named for Rosa Luxemburg and Rosa Parks. She'll be impressed.

I want to float on having talked to Sojourner again, having been close enough to smell her sweat. It might be the jetlag, but right at that moment it makes me feel invincible. I want to be alone with that feeling, not answering questions from the parentals or worrying about Rosa. She's in her maths heaven. For once I don't have to worry about her.

I fuel up on sandwiches, put my headphones on and slip my phone into my pocket, shutting out the rest of the world. I hit the treadmill running as hard as I can for half an hour before switching to intervals on the rower, then to weights.

Lifting weights is one of the most boring things in the world. Repetitive motions for no reason except to make your muscles grow. Weights can't make you more agile; there's no artistry to it like there is to every martial art; it doesn't do much for your cardio fitness. There's not even much you can do to get better at it. Once you've learned correct technique, all you can do is get stronger and lift heavier weights.

I lift hard and long and think about Sojourner.

I keep lifting until I'm exhausted. It's only at around eight, when I'm ready to collapse, that I pull out my phone.

I see a million increasingly frantic texts from Sally, as well as many missed calls.

Rosa is missing.

CHAPTER ELEVEN

I don't shower. I shove my gear into my locker, head down to the street, and hail one of the millions of yellow taxis.

—Where's David? Why did he say it was okay for me to stay at the gym?

—David lost his phone.

Holy fuck. The text was from Rosa, not David.

The text from David, or rather Rosa, was at 5:15 P.M. Three hours ago. Has she been gone that whole time?

—Do you have any idea where she is? Sally texts.

If this was Sydney there'd be dozens of places she might have gone, dozens of people to call.

—Did you try the McBrunights' place?

—Yes.

That's all I can think of. We don't know anyone else here.

The taxi is barely moving. I throw the rest of my cash—five dollars—at the driver and haul out. I run the rest of the way home, grateful for the numbered and lettered orderliness that makes New York City so easy to navigate. In the lobby of our building I ask the doorman if he's seen Rosa.

"Told your parents. Haven't seen her. Sorry, kid. I'll call if I do."

The lift is on our floor. I can't wait. I run up the stairs. David flings the door open as I put my key in. I stumble, struggling to pull the key out.

He stares at me and says, "Oh." He was hoping for Rosa.

"I'm sorry. I shouldn't have left her with Geoff. I thought the maths would—"

Sally hands me David's phone. "It was in the fruit bowl."

I'm looking at the texts Rosa sent Geoff.

—We're on our way. Thanks so much. We'll transfer the extra money first thing tomorrow.

—Almost there. You can go now. We appreciate you doing these extra hours.

—Are you sure it's okay to leave her alone? Geoff texted back.

—Yes. We'll probably see you in the lobby.

"Devious," I say.

"If you'd been here, Che," David says, "it wouldn't have been a problem."

"It's my fault? If *you*'d been here it wouldn't have been a problem either. You knew I had a class. You know what training means to me."

I can feel my anger building. I want to scream at them that I'm their seventeen-year-old son, not Rosa's co-parent. But I am, even if they'll never admit it.

This isn't the first time they've left me looking after her so I've missed out on a class or hanging with my friends. This *is* the first time I've ignored them. I should have said, *No way. I don't care how important your meeting is, I'm leaving right now and you better get back here to look after Rosa.*

"This is not the time to argue," Sally says as if they didn't start it. "How long since we called the cops?" She looks at her phone. "Thirty minutes. Should I call again?"

"Is anything of Rosa's missing?" I ask.

"Her backpack, raincoat, gumboots. But not her phone."

Without her phone we can't track her. It's eight-thirty. Dark outside.

"I don't think she has any money. But I could be twenty dollars light."

It's the first time I've ever heard Sally admit that Rosa steals.

"What time does the zoo close?" The last time Rosa disappeared she went to Dusit Zoo in Bangkok. She wanted to see the white Bengal tiger, and the parentals had said no. She'd made the mistake of taking her phone.

"Hours ago."

"I'll go look for her," I say. I head for the door before Sally or David can respond, grabbing a jacket hanging by the door to pull over my hoodie.

"I'll go with you," David says.

"No," Sally says. "Keep your phone on," she shouts after me.

MY GYM CLOTHES ARE damp with sweat. It's cold despite the jacket. I should've showered and changed, but I have to find her. My stomach gets colder thinking about what might happen. I can't be sure if I'm worried for Rosa or for what she might have done.

Both, of course, both.

Rosa isn't afraid of anything but being taken to doctors, of being locked away. She isn't scared of vicious dogs, or heights, or strange men.

What she is doesn't matter if she runs into someone who's worse. She's ten years old and unafraid. Would she decide it's funny to get into a stranger's car? Would she say *yes* to an invite to have dinner in a stranger's home?

I walk up the avenue past people out with their dogs, their partners, their friends, or rushing to get home from work in their boring suits and work clothes, but with ties loosened, heels swapped for comfy shoes. I wonder if I should stop people, show them pictures of Rosa. *Have you seen this girl?*

Parks are the natural place for Rosa to go. Especially ones with playgrounds. Rosa loves messing with other kids. The biggest one is Tompkins Square, but there are a couple of community parks on the way. The first one is more of a garden than a park. The second is full of concrete bowls and ramps. Neither has a kids' playground.

—Police are on their way.

—I'm checking parks. Heaps of people out. Someone will have seen her.

It starts to rain lightly, turning the air into mist, making me colder. I pull my hood over my head and zip up my jacket.

There are a lot of people out on the streets, but not many kids. It's probably too late. As I cross Avenue A into Tompkins Square the rain increases, and umbrellas go up. There's a kids' playground near the Ninth Street entrance, but it's empty of everything but squirrels. Next I check the dog run, which is full. I walk the perimeter, but Rosa isn't peering over the fence, plotting to steal a dog.

I cross to the smaller playground on the east side of the park. There's a giggling small boy being pushed by a woman who looks too young to be his mother. They're both in raincoats and gumboots.

"Is it rainy enough now?" she asks him.

The boy laughs harder.

"Excuse me," I call out. The woman turns. "Have you seen a little blonde girl? She's ten."

"Keep pushing," the boy says.

"Rude," the woman tells the boy, shaking her head at me. "Just us here for the last ten minutes. Sorry."

Rosa's probably found an ice-cream shop, or a second-hand store, and is currently attempting to wheedle the staff into giving her a cone or a creepy old porcelain doll. She'll turn up, I tell myself. Most missing people do. I read that somewhere. Or was it that they mostly turn up within the first day? But if they don't . . .

My phone rings. David.

I let it ring a few more times. I'm afraid of bad news. The rain is easing, but it's already soaked through my hood. I turn west along a path at the bottom of the park heading back to Avenue A.

"Yes?" I say, answering at last.

"The cops want you to—"

Then I see Rosa.

Of course. The parentals told her no.

"I see her!" I tell David. "In the park playing chess!"

I run to where she's playing. Her fingers are on the black bishop. She's too intent on the board to notice me. The man she's playing groans. He looks homeless. His long beard is ungroomed. His clothes look dirty.

Rosa, her opponent and all the men watching them are oblivious to the rain.

"Thank God!" David says. The phone muffles as he relays the news.

"Checkmate," Rosa says.

The man shakes his head. "You're a ringer."

Rosa is holding out her hand. Before the man can put money on her palm I put my hand on her shoulder. She startles. The notes land on the table.

"I'll call you back. I'm bringing her home," I tell David, ending the call.

"That's my money, Che!"

"I think he needs it more than you do."

"She won it," the man says. "Fair and square." He stands up.

Rosa grabs the money and slides it into the pocket of her raincoat. "Mine," she says, glaring at me. "Morris says it's mine. You heard him."

One of the men who's been watching slides into the vacant seat. "You gonna beat me, little one?"

"No, she isn't." I grab Rosa's hand and pull her from the seat. She glares harder.

"You come back soon, girlie," the man says. "Looking forward to teaching you some humility."

Rosa glares at him and he laughs.

"I don't want to go," she says to me. "I want to prove I'm the best one here. I've only lost one game and that was because I wasn't warmed up yet. I want to make more money. You made me lose my spot."

My phone rings. David again. "I'm bringing her home," I say. "She's fine."

"Hurry. The police want to talk to her."

"I don't want to," Rosa says.

"We're on our way. Five minutes."

David doesn't ask to speak to Rosa. I put the phone in my pocket.

"We're going. The parentals are freaking out. They thought you'd been kidnapped and murdered."

"As if," Rosa says, calmly certain that nothing like that would ever happen to her.

"You can't take money from strangers."

"They're not strangers. I learned their names. It's not like we were gambling." Rosa points to the sign behind the tables which reads, THESE TABLES ARE FOR CHESS AND CHECKERS ONLY. THERE IS A TWO HOUR LIMIT PER TABLE. TABLES ARE FREE FOR PUBLIC USE. NO GAMBLING OR FEES ALLOWED.

"Brilliant. You broke the law."

"I wasn't gambling."

"He gave you money because you won. That's gambling."

"Morris didn't believe I could beat him. He gave me money because I proved him wrong."

"That's a bet, Rosa. Betting is gambling."

"But I wasn't going to give him anything if *he* won."

"An uneven bet is still a bet."

I look both ways before we cross the road, not trusting myself to remember which way the traffic runs.

"Everyone else was betting. There are cameras. Morris says there are cameras everywhere. Some of them have live feeds. They wouldn't gamble with cameras pointing. I was about to play Isaiah. He's the best player there. I'm going to beat him."

"Didn't anyone ask you where your parents are?"

"They asked. Especially about my parents."

"What did you tell them?"

"I said I ate them."

"Jesus, Rosa."

"They laughed. Isaiah said white girls are vicious and they laughed even more."

CHAPTER TWELVE

There are two police officers, both of them severe and scary.

Rosa isn't fazed. They ask detailed questions about where she's been, what she's done.

She walked to the park. She patted some dogs. She tried to pat a cat but it ran away. At the park she watched the dogs running around—*Can I please have a dog?* she asks—and she went to the playground, but there weren't any kids her age, then she remembered about the chess. She likes chess.

"I'm a chess prodigy," she says. She doesn't smile or dimple.

The expression on the taller cop's face says that she thinks Rosa is a brat. Her hair is tied back in a bun so tight it looks like it could explode. The gun on her hip makes me nervous.

"You need to respect your elders when they tell you to stay at home," the cop says. "You listen and you obey. This is not Australia. New York is a very big and very dangerous city."

"We used to live in Bangkok," Rosa says. "It's much more dangerous."

"I doubt that, kid," the cop says.

"Bangkok has a much higher murder rate than New York." Rosa begins to recite statistics to prove it.

"Rosa!" Sally says. "The police are here to help you, not to hear a lecture on comparative murder rates."

"I didn't do anything wrong," Rosa says, glancing at me. "I was good. I didn't get into any cars with strangers. Playing chess is educational."

"You can play chess," David says. "We're not stopping you from playing chess. I'm sure there are chess clubs for kids your own age here."

Rosa begins to protest.

David holds up his hand and Rosa shuts up, folding her arms across her chest. The look she cuts at David is venomous.

"Thank you, officers," David says. "We'll make sure this doesn't happen again."

"She's a handful, sir," the shorter cop says. He doesn't sound charmed.

"Yes, she is," Sally says. "Thank you so much. We'll be talking to her at length about this. She will not enjoy her punishment."

"That's good, ma'am. You need to get her under control," the taller cop says.

"Thank you," Sally repeats. "We really appreciate it. We're sorry to trouble you unnecessarily."

"Nothing unnecessary about it, ma'am."

David sees the cops out the door. As he closes it I think I hear them laughing. Laughing at the stupid foreigners and their bratty kid.

"You lied to us, Rosa," Sally says. She holds up David's phone. "You lied to your parents and you lied to your brother."

"No, I didn't!"

David holds up his hand of silence again. Rosa looks like she wishes she could cut it off at the wrist.

"You can't lie to us, Rosa. We've discussed that. You've said you wouldn't lie."

"I'm a child," Rosa says. "We're supposed to pretend. I was playing a game, *pretending*. I'm supposed to do that!"

"You were *pretending* to be David so you could get around our rules! It's not the same thing. What were you thinking?" Sally asks. "What's come over you?"

Nothing, I want to tell them. *This is Rosa.*

Sally and David see her every day. They see her sometimes forget to act like she cares when people are hurt or sick. Even when it's one of us. They've seen her complete lack of fear in front of those cops.

Why don't they realise she isn't like other kids?

"What possessed you to go off on your own like that?"

"Anything could have happened!"

"I won," Rosa says. "I beat those men who've been playing chess longer than I've been alive. You should be prou—"

"Proud of you!? We thought you'd been kidnapped! We thought you might be dead!"

Rosa stares. David rarely yells.

"An essay," Sally says. "We want a thousand words explaining what you've learned today. Sent to us by dinner tomorrow."

Rosa hates writing essays. "A thousand words?"

"Yes, Rosa. It's not okay to pretend you're me. There are different kinds of pretending. The kind you did was not childish play. It was not fun. It was deceitful and wrong. You stole my phone. You knew it wasn't okay."

"I borrowed it. I was playacting," Rosa begins, but then her face shifts as she finally realises she's played this wrong, that she should show contrition, that she should have charmed the cops. The parentals don't think she's been clever beating adults at chess, showing that she knows more than the police about which cities are dangerous.

Next time she'll judge better when to be the prodigy and when to be the little girl.

Rosa bursts into tears.

Between the tears she squeezes out fragmented phrases about being sorry and not realising and whatever else it is she thinks the parentals want to hear.

David pulls Rosa into his arms. "Oh, possum, it's okay."

"You frightened us," Sally says, putting her arms around Rosa and David. "You can't wander off like that. Especially not when you don't know anyone. We've been here such a short time. You could have gotten lost."

Rosa turns her head, catches my eye. She smiles.

I have to give it to her. She's turned around a bad situation.

She won't turn me around, though. We're going to talk about what she means by the word *good*.

She promised to be good. She wasn't.

WHEN I GO UPSTAIRS the light seeps out from under Rosa's door. I knock.

"I'm asleep!"

"Yeah, me too," I say loud enough for her to hear. Switching my phone to record, I open the door.

Rosa sits on her bed, her face illuminated by her tablet. Her blonde curls look almost gold.

I close the door and sit on her desk chair.

"You broke your promise," I say.

"You know they love each other more than they love us," Rosa says at the same time.

I do know that. But I try not to think it, let alone say it. I don't want it to be true. They're our parents; Sally and David should love us best. But they don't, which is how I've become the one responsible for Rosa. They don't love us enough to notice what's wrong with her.

"You broke your promise," I repeat. "You said you'd be good."

"I was good. Seimone plays chess. I wanted to practise before I play her. She's won competitions."

"Being good doesn't mean wandering off on your own and gambling with strangers."

"Yes, it does. The parentals want us to explore and be brave. I was exploring and being brave. I was being good."

"Bullshit, Rosa."

"I never promised not to pretend. I never promised not to lie."

"Would you promise not to lie?"

Rosa shakes her head. "Lying is too useful."

"Are you lying when you make promises?"

"No. I didn't break the promise. I *was* good."

"In a way that directly disobeyed what the parentals told you."

"They never told me not to go exploring."

"They said you couldn't play chess in the park and they arranged things so you wouldn't be alone. It was clear they didn't want you to go exploring at night."

"They didn't say not to."

"That's not being good. That's being a weasel looking for loopholes."

"I didn't hurt anything or anyone—not even a spider. I didn't steal. I *borrowed* David's phone," she says quickly before I can dispute her. "I didn't make anyone do anything they didn't want to. I *was* good."

Rosa leans forward and rests her chin on her knees. She looks like she believes every word. "The parentals being mad at me isn't rational."

"How many angels on the head of a pin, Rosa?"

"Huh? I was being good to you, Che. You wanted to go to the gym. You spent hours there!"

"Really? You went and played chess in Tompkins Square Park for me? How kind."

Rosa nods.

"That was sarcasm."

"Sarcasm is stupid. Did you see Sid?"

"Who's Sid?" I ask, forgetting for a moment that it's Sojourner's nickname. Then I blush.

Rosa giggles. "I can concentrate on being good if you like. Though I don't know what *good* means."

"It means doing what you're told, not gambling, not taking other people's stuff without asking, not using someone's phone to pretend to be them—"

"Not even as a joke?"

"It wasn't a joke."

Rosa sighs. "Aren't there times when if you do what you're told you're doing something bad? Like when Apinya did what I told her to and killed Kitty?"

"Talking to you is like talking to . . ." I was going to say *the devil*. "A slippery eel."

"I'm trying to understand. Good is complicated. But I'll try to be it. I don't like it when you're annoyed with me."

"You care what I think about you?" I didn't mean to say that.

"I like that you like me best. I like being liked."

CHAPTER THIRTEEN

The next afternoon I have to duck out of the gym to walk Rosa to her first dance class. The parentals are at yet another meeting with the McBrunights. They spend most of their time over there. The McBrunights' au pair will pick up Rosa and Seimone and take them to the mansion. Sally and David will bring Rosa home. Once I get back to the gym I can train for as long as I want.

I wonder if the parentals have warned the McBrunights or their au pair that Rosa can be a *handful*. Not that I'm worried. It was only yesterday that Rosa tested the limits of *good*, and there's always a lull between incidents.

Rosa takes my hand. If she were some other kid I'd assume she was nervous.

"No cars coming," she says, having looked left and right on the one-way street.

"Cute," I say, meaning the opposite. "We'll wait for the lights."

On the other side of the road she drops my hand to pat a dog that's bigger than she is. The woman holding its leash smiles at Rosa.

"This is Harry. He's an Irish wolfhound."

"He's beautiful," Rosa says.

The woman thanks her and tugs on his leash. The dog trots after his owner.

"I want a dog like that."

"That's not a dog, Rosa. It's a horse." At least she'd find it difficult to kill such an enormous dog.

"Don't be silly, Che. It's a dog."

As we wait for the next set of lights she holds my hand again.

"When are you going to write your essay, Rosa?"

She scowls and drops my hand.

"They said you have to send it to them by tonight."

"They might forget."

"They won't."

"Suzette has a crush on David."

"Who?"

"The McBrunights' au pair."

"Everyone has a crush on David. Don't change the subject."

The lights change and we cross.

"What did you learn from last night?"

"Not to be impatient about getting to checkmate. That game I lost? I would have won if I'd waited a few more moves."

"You're hilarious."

"I wasn't joking."

I know that. The only kind of humour Rosa understands is slapstick.

"What did you learn about behaving like a normal person?"

"I need to lie better. I should have pretended to be sorry straight away. Next time I'll burst into tears as soon as I see the police."

"What about next time you don't trick your tutor into leaving before an adult comes home?"

"You're not an adult."

"How about next time you don't wander off on your own?"

"Nothing happened. I wasn't far from home. I don't see why I wasn't being good."

Here we go. Her latest loophole: *I don't understand what* good *means.* "Why did you leave your phone behind if you thought you were being good?"

"I forgot it."

Rosa never forgets anything. "You're lying."

"Lying isn't bad."

"What?" I stare at her.

"Everyone lies," Rosa says. "Everyone pretends that lying is bad but everyone does it. Telling the truth is ruder than lying. If I told people what I thought, I'd be in trouble all the time. My mistake last night was telling the truth: that I was proud to beat old men at chess. I should have lied."

"I don't lie."

"Yes, you do. You lie by not answering questions you can't answer without making trouble."

"That's not lying, Rosa."

"Yes, it is. You say you're fine when you're sad. When people ask you about me or the parentals you don't tell them you think I'm bad and they're terrible parents."

"I don't think . . ." I can't finish that sentence.

"This is it," Rosa says brightly. "I bet I'm the best dancer in my class."

I was so sucked into our conversation I failed to notice we're surrounded by leotard-garbed girls in sizes varying from tiny to almost as tall as me. I walk Rosa to the reception desk and make sure she's properly enrolled. The dance school smells like my gym: sweat and industrial-strength cleaners. I follow the directions to lead Rosa to her class.

This is something the parentals should have done.

I don't think they're terrible parents. They love us. I think they're *negligent* parents. That's not the same thing.

BACK AT THE GYM I train hard, trying to put Rosa's views about lying out of my head. I'm worried she's right. I worry that the solution is not to teach Rosa to be good—she's never going to understand what good is—but to teach her how to fake being good.

I exchange only a few words with Sojourner. Her friend Jaime is there. I don't ask for her number or give her mine. When the seven o'clock sparring session rolls around I head for the change room. I'm thinking about texting Georgie and Nazeem for their views on lying. I'm pretty sure Jason's will be too close to Rosa's.

Instead I text my Sydney boxing coach:

—Thinking about sparring. Do you think I'm ready?

I'm about to pocket my phone when she answers.

—You've been ready for years.

I stare at my phone. I wasn't expecting a response. Natalie only checks her phone between classes.

—Are you okay?

—Taking a day off.

Natalie does not take days off. —Seriously?

—I'm taking my own advice and learning to chill. You're ready to spar. You'll get a lot out of it.

—You never said that.

—Not saying it now. Texting it.

—Funny. You sure?

—Yes. Did your parents change their mind?

—No.

—Oh.

—Yeah.

—But you've changed your mind about obeying them?

I don't know what to tell her. I won't lie to them. But disobey? I try not to. But they're being unjust and wrong.

—I don't know.

—I'll talk to them if you want. Offer still stands.

"That looks intense," Sojourner says. She's sitting on the bench outside the women's change room, holding ice to her hand.

"You okay?"

"Pinged my wrist. So no sparring."

"Is it bad?"

She shakes her head. "I got a fight coming up. Not taking any risks."

I nod.

"Anything wrong?" Sojourner's looking at my phone. I'm holding it thinking about what Natalie said. Thinking about what it would be like to spar against Sojourner. She's amazing. Would I even land a punch?

"Texting with my trainer back home. I asked her if she thought I was ready to spar."

"And?"

"She thinks I'm ready."

Sojourner gives me a soft punch to my shoulder. "'Cause you are. You trained great today. Jetlag gone?"

"I guess." I wish.

"So are you going to spar?"

"I want to."

"So do it!"

"Wanna get a bite to eat?" I ask, before I can talk myself out of it. "I mean, since neither of us are sparring. I'm starved."

Sojourner looks at me, staring into my eyes like they'll tell her whether I'm worth eating with. I keep my mouth closed so I won't say anything stupid.

"Sure," she says. "You like Mexican?"

I nod. I'll eat anything she wants me to eat. It's all I can do to keep from screaming, *Yes!*

I shower and change lightning-fast, then wait for her, sitting on the same bench, trying not to feel excited about that, or that we've punched the same bags, walked on the same floor, breathed the same air, because it's ridiculous. *I* am ridiculous.

WE WALK ALONG HOUSTON—*HOWSTEN*—TOGETHER and I try to think of what to say. I'd like to ask Sojourner about fighting. Sojourner's had two real fights. Did they push her to another level? But she's asking me why I'm hesitating about sparring. She seems to think all I have to do is explain to the parentals I'm not going to get any better unless I spar and bingo!—they'll change their minds. Instead my choice is between defying them or lying to them. I don't want to do either and I don't want to talk about it.

I think about asking Sojourner where she goes to school. But what if she's already at university? She won't want to hang out with a seventeen-year-old.

"Do you think I should train with Dido?" I ask. "One-on-one?"

Sojourner nods. "She's not a shouter. My first coach used to whack me on the head with his glove whenever I made a mistake. Never stopped screaming. I don't learn much when I'm being yelled at."

"Ditto. My coach back home in Sydney likes to talk about the similarities between boxing and meditation."

"Because you lose yourself?"

I nod.

"I love when that happens. The moment when it clicks and I'm out of my own head."

"We're mere atoms, part of something much bigger than us," I quote Natalie.

"Like at church."

"Um, yeah, I guess."

"You don't go to church, do you?"

"Why do you say that?" Which is stupid, given I just spluttered at the mere mention of the word.

"Because you're named after a Communist guerrilla and you're white. Am I wrong?"

"You're not wrong."

"I didn't think Jesus was in your life. Did you know Sojourner Truth was a preacher? My mom is too. I can't go out with you."

It feels like she punched me. If I were Jason I'd say, *I'm not into you* and imply she was up herself for suggesting it. I'm not Jason.

"Oh," I say, which does not convey how miserable I feel.

"That was kinda harsh, wasn't it? I don't want to mess you around. You seem like a cool guy. I feel like we can be friends. But I can't date someone who doesn't have Jesus in their life."

"So it's not because of the lunar surface that is my face?"

Sojourner stares. "Huh?"

I blush. *Of course* I blush. Every zit on my face burns. "It was a stab at a joke. Sorry."

Her eyebrows go up.

"A really unfunny joke."

"Very unfunny. It's not about anything like that. I like what I know about you. I just think it's fair I tell people straight away. Especially white boys called Che."

"That was you making a joke. I can tell because it was funny."

"I know it's heavy, but it's the most important thing about me."

"I get that. You could try to convert me, couldn't you? I could be converted."

I'm kidding. But for a second there, walking beside her, looking at her profile, those big soft lips, those eyelashes that curl up so high, I'm thinking, *maybe there is a God?* I could worship a God that resembles Sojourner. I realise if I told her she'd freak out. Or maybe she'd expect blasphemous thoughts from a white guy called Che.

"Nah. Converting people is the fast track to letting your beliefs twist into something ugly. You believe what you want to believe, Che. Or don't. Take care of yourself, be good to others. You don't need religion for any of that. I've known plenty without God who are good people. I don't judge."

I nod. That's pretty much my ethics in a nutshell. Along with preventing others from doing harm, particularly younger sisters . . .

"If you ever start to question," Sojourner says, "if you start to think about seeking a different path, then we can talk."

"So you won't talk to me until then?"

Sojourner gently punches my shoulder. "Sure I will. We're talking right now. I'll eat with you too. But I won't talk to you about God, religion or spirituality."

"Or dating?" I smile to show her I'm kidding.

She laughs. "Or dating."

I don't flinch, but it hurts. I try not to think about how much I love the sound of her laugh. Or looking at her lips. Sojourner isn't interested in me. I have to deal. It isn't the first time the girl I want hasn't wanted me. Or the second, or the third.

Though, wait, is that what Sojourner's saying?

"Do you mean," I ask her, "that if I *were* religious you might be interested?"

She looks at me sidelong. "You're not religious."

"But say I was?"

"Are you asking me to tell you if I think you're cute?"

Of course I am. Everything I've said to her is basically an announcement that I think she's gorgeous. "I like you," I say. "I think you're—"

"Hey, girl. You are fiiine."

I turn to see a man leering at her. "Whatcha doing with that nasty-looking white boy?"

"Minding my own business," she says, without turning her head. "Try it."

The man makes a hissing sound but he keeps walking beside her, leaning in like he's about to touch her, then pulling away.

I open my mouth to tell him to piss off as he increases his pace to stride ahead of us.

I close my mouth, deflated. What the hell was that? The man disappears down a subway entrance. I think about chasing after him. How dare he talk to Sojourner like that?

"Are you okay?" I ask.

Sojourner blows air through her teeth. "It's wind."

"Sorry," I blurt.

"For what?"

"I should've said something. Told that guy off. He was out of line."

"What would you have said?"

God. I have no idea what I'd have said. "*Don't?*"

"That'd work," Sojourner says, laughing. "Hell of a comeback. The wit alone would slay him."

I blush more intensely. She doesn't seem bothered. I want to kill that guy. "I'd let him know that wasn't okay."

"He knows. He doesn't give a damn."

"But—"

Sojourner puts her hand on my arm. "It sucks, but you punching him ain't going to change anything. Happens all the time. It's no big deal."

I know that's not true.

I don't know how old I was when Sally first talked to me about harassment. She was determined no son of hers would ever harass anyone. Sally and Georgie both say they're hassled on the street every day. They hate it.

I put my hands in my pocket because they're shaking. I should have done something.

"Listen, yes, Che, it's bad. But if I let it get to me I'd lose my mind, or kill them all, you know?"

I nod. I want to kill every man who's ever harassed Sojourner. Or Sally or Georgie or any other woman.

"Would you come to church with me?"

"I'm sorry?"

"Come to church this Sunday, to the evening service. You say you're interested in me, so come see a big part of my life."

"I thought you weren't trying to convert me?"

Sojourner smiles. "I'm not. But I thought you might be interested in seeing what it's like. Have you been to a church service?"

I haven't. "Sure, I'd like that," I say. Why not?

THAT NIGHT I SLEEP. A deep sleep uninterrupted by New York's cacophony of car horns, sirens, and people shouting.

I dream about Sojourner.

She's wearing that tulip dress, then she *isn't* wearing that dress. We're chest against chest, kissing. I can smell butterflies. They're everywhere, tiny and golden. Sojourner's hair floats around her. Her hands are against my chest, then my belly. I've never felt so happy. There's a light as bright as the sun. It gets brighter and brighter and brighter.

And explodes.

I wake smiling. I'm wet.

I slide out of bed to clean myself, taking a step in the dark towards the bathroom.

"I was good today," Rosa says.

I jump and half yelp, feeling my cheeks burning, though she can't know why I was out of bed.

Rosa is at the foot of my bed. In the dark I didn't see her.

She laughs. A genuine laugh. Though she is getting better at making her fake ones sound real, I can still tell the difference.

"What the fuck, Rosa?"

How long has she been standing there, watching me dream about Sojourner?

"You shouldn't swear in front of me. I'm only little."

The parentals' policy on swearing is that it's okay if we're sure it's not going to upset anyone.

"You scared me."

"I know. You yelled. I'm studying sleep. I've been watching you."

"That's creepy, Rosa. Don't do that."

I've just dreamt about sex with Sojourner. I'm covered in my own jizz and there's my little sister staring at me. "*Never* enter my room again without knocking first. It's beyond creepy."

Rosa shrugs.

"You want to pass for a normal person? Don't tiptoe into people's bedrooms at night! Ever."

"I can be creepy in front of you."

"No, you can't! You need to go now."

"I'll go watch the parentals."

"No, Rosa. You can't watch *anyone* sleep. Okay?"

"If they wake up they'll think I was sleepwalking. People do that. I always know what to tell them."

"Go to bed, Rosa."

She shakes her head and turns the light on.

"Why are your pants wet?"

"I had an accident," I say, which is true.

If Rosa didn't exist would I be okay with lying? Did I lie before Rosa was born? I realise I don't remember much from before then. The thought makes me feel bleak.

"You wet your pants? Like a baby?"

"I wet my pants, yes. So now I'm going to have a shower and change and you are going back to your bedroom."

Rosa doesn't move, so I ask a question calculated to annoy her. "Did you write your essay?"

Rosa nods. "I wrote about how I learned that I'm not allowed to leave the house without you or them accompanying me. Even though I know how to read a map and not to get in a car with a stranger. I learned to not be rude to the police because they can lock you up or kill you if they want to and they won't get in trouble. I concluded that our society doesn't let ten-year-olds be independent and brave and explore even if that's what parents say they want and that's why most ten-year-olds act like babies. I wrote that in the Amazon there are three-year-olds who already know how to skin and gut an animal and sharpen their own knives, who don't act like babies. I concluded that I learned that our society is broken."

"Sounds like a great essay. What did the parentals say?"

"They hadn't read it before I went to bed, which means I also learned that writing the essay was a waste of time. Did you know that when you sleep your legs move like you're trying to run? Did you dream about running?"

"No."

"Do you remember what you dreamed about?"

I don't answer.

"I never remember my dreams. I might not dream. It's another way I'm not like other people. Most people dream."

"How do you know? I'm sure there are other people who don't dream or don't remember their dreams."

Rosa doesn't say anything. She continues to stare at me. I feel cold and so creeped out I'm close to simply picking her up and carrying her to her own room.

"I think you were dreaming about a girl," Rosa says, looking from the wet patch on my pants to my face. "I know which girl, too." She leaves, shutting the door behind her.

I realise I'm sweating.

CHAPTER FOURTEEN

I don't go back to sleep. In the dark, or as dark as New York City gets, I go downstairs to have breakfast. Sally is already there, nursing a cup of coffee.

"You too, huh?"

I nod, grab a bowl and spoon and put my breakfast together. Sally's already cut up some fruit. I pull up a stool opposite her.

On the street people are yelling, and further away are police sirens. Weirdly, that's beginning to seem like quiet. Now's the time to talk to her about Rosa again.

"David's sleeping like a baby. I was tempted to wake him up by asking him if he was asleep. He hates that. Sorry you didn't get the good sleeper genes."

I snort instead of telling Sally that genes don't work like that. I think about the genes Rosa and I share, but who we are isn't genes alone. Thank God. I'll take not sleeping over psychopathy.

"There are worse things," I tell Sally. "Like these bananas, for instance."

"We'll find the good bananas. I promise."

"Rosa," I say. "I'm worried about her. I know you don't think her running off like that was a big deal."

"I didn't say that. I said I don't think she realised the dangers. She's young and thoughtless."

"Right," I say, "but I don't think she gets why she shouldn't do whatever she wants to do. I've been doing a lot of reading. I think—"

"What ten-year-old does?"

"Me," I say. "When I was ten I got it. Rosa doesn't understand why she should follow rules. She doesn't care if she gets caught. How many ten-year-olds do you know like Rosa?"

"More than you'd think," Sally says, but she doesn't name any. None of the cousins or her friends' children are like Rosa. "She's not average, obviously. How many ten-year-olds are doing calculus? Yes, she's not always great in social situations. But Dr. Chu said she's done well, that she's in the spectrum of normal for her age."

Dr. Chu hasn't seen Rosa since she was little. "She's not two anymore. Or three. Or four. She's ten."

"I know, Che. Rosa sees the world differently. We've always encouraged you both to explore—"

"That's *not* what I'm talking about. I'm talking about the fact that she doesn't care what you or anyone else thinks. Rosa doesn't think anything is her fault. Rosa doesn't care. It's more than that. Rosa *can't* care. She doesn't have any empathy. She's like Uncle Saul. I think she has antisocial personality disorder."

"Don't be ridiculous."

"I'm *not* being ridiculous."

"No need to shout, Che."

I'm not shouting, though my fists are clenched. I relax my hands.

"I know she's not a normal ten-year-old. Not many ten-year-olds play chess the way she does. You weren't a normal ten-year-old either, Che. You were obsessed with violence. You wanted to know about guns. Guns! Then Papa taught you how to punch and you wanted to learn kickboxing, you always wanted to see people fighting—"

I've heard all this. "That's not the same thing. *I* never hurt anyone."

"Your father did. When he was young. But he learned not to give in to his violence. It scares me how much you love boxing."

"I'm not David. I'm not violent. I've never even been in a fight."

"Yes, but you *want* to be in fights."

"In a boxing ring. Under controlled circumstances. Wearing protective gear. Why are we talking about me? I'm not the problem. Rosa is."

Sally's face tightens. She takes a deep breath. "I know you worry about her. You two are close. But you have to accept that she's not like you. You were always sensitive."

"For a violence-obsessed thug?"

"I never said you were a thug, Che. You're not. But there's something in you that—"

"Am I sensitive or am I a thug?"

"You're *not* a thug. You've always worried about everyone else. I swear you were ten going on thirty. You were responsible and never selfish. Rosa's not like that. But *most* ten-year-olds aren't. Most are selfish. Do I wish she was less selfish, more sensitive? Yes! Sometimes I wish you were *less* sensitive. You're so easily hurt, Che."

I'm not sure I recognise the Che she's talking about.

• • •

I RUN ALONG THE East River. I wasn't expecting this many other runners. The sun isn't even up, yet there they are: ears stoppered with headphones, not seeing, let alone nodding at, the other runners pounding past them. I half wonder if one of them might be Leilani, but she doesn't strike me as someone who would get up earlier than she has to.

In the pre-dawn darkness the river looks like an oil slick. I imagine aquatic megafauna lurking beneath, all jagged teeth, talons and poisonous tendrils. Creatures Rosa would feel kinship with.

I am not violent.

My strides match the syllables. *I am not vi-o-lent. I am not vi-o-lent. I am not vi-o-lent.*

How can Sally compare me to Rosa? We are nothing alike!

I am not vi-o-lent. I am not vi-o-lent. I am not vi-o-lent.

I am not like Rosa. I am not like Uncle Saul.

He has no empathy, little self-control, he's addicted to thrill-seeking, has serial girlfriends and wives, loves flashy cars and driving too fast. He can fly a helicopter and he parachutes. I suspect there's worse. So many ticks on the Psychopathy Checklist.

I think Papa is like Rosa too.

Papa really is violent. Or, at least, he used to be. He still yells, but he used to beat David and Saul, until they were big enough to stop him. When he was younger Papa had affairs. He did whatever he wanted. Sally says it's a miracle David isn't like his father. I guess that's Saul's job: being exactly like Papa.

Psychopathy can run in families. That's the DNA part, though there's also environment. The two are hard to separate.

When I ask Papa about his parents, my great-grandparents, he says they were smart and ambitious. *They made me what I am.* If that's literally true then they could have been like Rosa too.

David says his grandparents were broken people. That his grandfather never laughed, always criticised. That his grandmother didn't say much. His grandfather beat Papa the same way Papa beat David and Saul. *Being beaten and surviving*, Papa told David, *is what makes you a man.*

It might not mean anything. Back then, parents beating their children was normal.

Papa loves that I like to box.

David says the Nazis broke his grandparents. They lost their parents and brothers and sisters and cousins and uncles and aunts and grandparents and cousins and nieces and nephews and friends and acquaintances and enemies. The rabbis, the matchmakers, the butchers, the tinkers, the tailors. Dead in the Warsaw Uprising. Dead trying to escape. Dead at Treblinka, Sobibór, Auschwitz-Birkenau. Dead of starvation after the war.

Then there were three: my great-grandfather and great-grandmother and their small boy, Papa.

Trauma can kill empathy too but only if you're genetically predisposed.

Papa doesn't tell many stories about his family. But there was a great-great-great grandfather—give or take a few greats—he talks about. A crack shot, excellent horseman, with a reputation for derring-do and success with women.

Papa has a faded photo of him with an absurdly curled moustache and a tankard of beer. He's not smiling and his eyes look cold. But back then everyone with pale eyes looked cold in photos; no one smiled, because you had to sit still for so long.

He could have been like Rosa. Or he could have been full of empathy. Liking to shoot and ride doesn't mean he was a psychopath.

If I become a father, will my child be like Rosa or like me?

There's no way of knowing. It's always both nature *and* nurture. We are the sum of our genes, the morphology of our brain, and our environment. Our genes are not just the DNA we're born with. Genes can be shaped by environment too. Brain morphology is not fixed, brains rewire themselves as we grow and in response to trauma. Our environment is more than the spaces we grow up in, it's everyone we interact with, starting with our parents, our carers, our siblings, our friends.

We can be affected by unusual experiences: being kidnapped or even something as mundane as meeting someone different, even a book or a movie can change us.

Discovering boxing rewired my brain, made me faster and fitter. All the travel we've done, living in Auckland and Wellington in New Zealand, Jakarta in Indonesia, and Bangkok in Thailand—even though I didn't pick up much Bahasa or Thai—those places changed me.

It's dark. I need to sleep. But I'm wired and angry and hungry and I don't have any money, just Papa's credit card. What would he say to paying for my breakfast? I could tell him the parentals forgot to give me pocket money, which is true. David gave me twenty dollars on our first morning and nothing since. I have a handful of change left.

Papa will be happy, I'm sure. He'll love that I'm at odds with the parentals, especially Sally. At the moment Rosa and I are in the will and David isn't. Sally never was. Papa's convinced that without Sally's influence David would be a captain of industry.

I text the parentals that I'm going to spend the day exploring the city. I don't wait for their response.

I keep running.

I am not vi-o-lent. I am not vi-o-lent. I am not vi-o-lent. I am not vi-o-lent. I am not vi-o-lent.

SOJOURNER IS AT THE 5 P.M. class. I was close to falling asleep during my pre-class stretch, but when I see her the tiredness is gone. She's with Jaime.

"Hi," I say.

"You still up for church?"

I nod. Jaime smiles slyly. Sojourner gives me the time and address.

We both have our phones out. Hers is old and crappy like mine. I should ask for her number. But Jaime's right there.

The church is on Second Avenue a few blocks from our apartment. Does that mean she lives close too? The class starts before I can give her my number.

I text the parentals that I'll be late. I'm not ready to face them. Or Rosa.

I hang around to watch the seven o'clock sparring session. My legs feel like lead, but I'm buzzing, ready for anything. I may never sleep again. I don't care anymore. Is this how Rosa feels all the time? Not giving a damn?

The session consists of Sojourner, Jaime, Meathead and four others I recognise but don't have names for, as well as six strangers. Dido runs the session. I think I'm going to ask her if she'll take me on as a one-on-one student.

Then somehow I'm sparring.

I don't decide to do it. It just . . . happens. Dido assumes that's what I'm there for. She asks Sojourner if she'll be my opponent. Sojourner grins.

Then I'm in the ring wearing slimy headgear that smells of a hundred other people's sweat and a hard plastic mouthguard that doesn't fit which Dido keeps as a spare. She assures me it was disinfected. I believe her because it tastes like bleach.

Dido nods. We touch gloves.

Sojourner's first punch lands before I'm ready. I blink and my nose stings.

I don't know if she hit me with her right or left. If it was a jab or a cross or a hook or an upper cut.

Left cheek. Then ribs.

So a jab, then an upper cut. I think. Then another. Then my nose again.

I have to *stop* thinking and start seeing.

I have to look her in the eye.

I move. Her cross glances my chin.

I look straight at her. I see the cross coming.

I shift left, spin, parry the next jab, feint back.

I remember how to defend myself.

She's really hitting me.

With gloves. In my face. On my body.

My nose.

Ow! I don't say. I grunt.

I'm thinking, not seeing. When I look in her eyes I see the punches coming. That cross again. I duck.

Someone's yelling but the headgear muffles it.

Her fist comes at me again. I weave right. She misses. I can do this.

I diamond cut out of her path. I slide backwards, hitting the ropes, then sideways. *A boxer never moves in a straight line.* A boxer doesn't stand still, either. I pivot out of her way.

I weave, I bob. I parry a fraction too late. Right cross to my nose. Again. It throbs.

Liquid pours down my face. Blood? Snot? Or merely sweat? Probably sweat. My eyes are stinging. I can taste salt. Though blood is salty too. Dido will stop us if I'm bleeding.

Too much sweat in my mouth, which is already full of too much saliva. The mouthguard is manufacturing it now. I want it out of my mouth.

I duck again. Almost falling. I spin to the corner of the ring, turn quick, but she comes at me with a flurry of punches I try to block, to parry, to evade. I mostly flinch, my back to the ropes, my gloves held in front of my face.

I force myself off the ropes, away from her punches. I follow Sojourner's eyes, evade her blows.

A bell sounds. *The* bell sounds.

Sojourner stops, lowers her gloves, taps mine. I tap hers. I sink to the floor, back against the ropes, struggling to get my gloves off.

Dido steps into the ring, pulling the velcro on my right glove, undoing my head gear.

"Good first go," she says. "Maybe next time you might want to think about throwing a punch. Offence is a thing, you know?"

I look up at her, sweat running into my eyes, then across at Sojourner. "I didn't punch you?"

"Dude," Sojourner says, wiping her face with a towel, "you didn't even try."

I didn't?

A boxer who doesn't punch. *Great start, Che.* I wish Sally had seen it. Maybe she'd believe I'm not violent.

Dido pats me on the back. "Next time. You used your feet. You remembered your defensive sets. Sid hardly laid a glove on you. Four good hits is all I saw. Not bad."

I thought I landed punches. I thought I'd *thrown* punches.

"So what did you think?" Dido says. "Your first time. It can be intense."

"It was fucking awesome," I say. I hadn't realised until that second but now my exhilaration takes hold. "Nothing like training. I fucking loved it."

She pats my head. "Good boy. Next time: throw a punch! Get some ice on your nose. It'll bruise up big otherwise." She peers at it closely. "Don't think it's broken."

WHEN I GET HOME no one's in the living room. I make a sandwich and quietly eat it over the sink, then slink upstairs and close my bedroom door behind me, wedging my chair under the handle. I don't want another nocturnal encounter with Rosa. My backpack and shoes by the door downstairs will let them know I made it home.

I crawl into bed. I doubt it's even nine yet. I've evaded saying a word to the parentals about sparring. No matter what Rosa says, that's not lying. I've broken a promise but I haven't lied. I'll tell them in the morning.

It was more intense than I imagined. Part of me thought Sojourner was trying to fucking kill me. I'm pretty sure my heart is still beating too fast. I *have* to do that again.

I crash.

When I wake it's the next afternoon. My heart feels like it belongs in my chest for the first time in days.

"He woke up!" Rosa yells as I walk down the stairs.

Sally and David come out of the office.

"Welcome to the land of the living," Sally says. "You beat the jetlag, eh?"

"I think so. I hope so."

"Why is your nose red?" Rosa asks.

"Because," I tell her, "someone punched it."

David stares. "What did you say?"

Sally too. "You promised you wouldn't spar!"

I'm about to tell them that I broke my promise, but Rosa's right there. If I break a promise, why should she keep hers?

"Sometimes the pads slip," I say, which is true, but it's an evasion. What's an evasion but a kind of lie? I'm lying because of Rosa.

I hold my hands up to demonstrate. "We work with pads sometimes. In pairs."

"Sounds dangerous," Sally says. "Maybe you shouldn't do that."

"I've been doing it for years. How often have I come home with a bruised nose?"

Sally bites her lip.

I should tell them about the sparring right now.

But Rosa.

How can I make her see my breaking this promise is not the same as her breaking her promise not to kill?

Sally reaches forward to touch my nose. "It looks swollen."

"I iced it," I tell her. "It'll be fine. Doesn't hurt unless I touch it."

"Ice it again," Sally says.

I do as she says. It hurts.

CHAPTER FIFTEEN

On Sunday I get to the church a bit early, waiting out on the street, feeling like an idiot.

It has a giant rainbow flag hanging above its doors. I'm wearing my one suit, which doesn't quite fit anymore, with a tie I borrowed from David, who thinks it's hilarious I'm going to church.

I didn't know what to wear. The few times I've gone to temple I wore a suit. This is nothing like temple. There's that rainbow flag, shifting in the breeze, and all the guys around my age are wearing jeans and T-shirts. One balances a skateboard between his legs. Oops.

They're all white. I realise I was expecting it to be a black church.

No Sojourner. I've been looking up and down the avenue, willing her to appear. My hands are in my pocket because I don't know what to do with them. I pull my phone out again. No texts.

Someone taps me on the shoulder. I turn and there's Sojourner in a blue dress and shiny black shoes. Her hair's pulled back. I can't help smiling. "Where did you come from?"

She gestures up the church steps. "Helping Mom. She's a minister here."

I nod. She already told me that. It's another reason I'm wearing a suit.

"Look at you," she says. "I'm impressed."

"I wasn't sure what to wear and . . . You look great."

Two men say hello to her, both of them black, and wearing suits.

More people show up. Black, brown, Asian and white. Older women in dresses, a few in giant hats. One woman has feathers. Most of the older men are in suits; most of the people our age are more casually dressed. I don't stick out, though. I'm not the only teenager in a suit.

"What kind of church is this?"

"A welcoming church. An interfaith church. A diverse church. A place of worship and social action."

"You sound like you're reading a brochure."

Sojourner laughs. "I helped my mom write it."

"Oh." I look nervously at the church entrance again.

"You'll be fine, Che. Let's grab a seat."

I follow her in, feeling like an impostor who might get struck by lightning. A white woman in robes is by the door.

"Hello, Sid," she says, hugging Sojourner. "Who's this?"

"This is Che. We train together. He's new in the city." Sojourner turns to me. "This is Alice."

We shake hands, but instead of letting go Alice puts her other hand on mine and holds it firmly, as if she's worried I'll escape. "Welcome to our church and to New York City. Where are you from?"

"Sydney. Australia."

"Wonderful."

"Thanks."

She smiles at me warmly, letting go of my hand. "I hope you'll find a place here."

Everyone waves or says hello to Sojourner. She introduces me as a friend from her gym who's interested in learning more about their church. This leads to many hands on my shoulders, hearty handshakes, and heartfelt wishes that I find what I'm looking for. Almost all of them bless me.

"You know everyone."

"Mom's a minister. Remember? I've been coming here since I was in Mama's womb."

Because of all the greetings we wind up having to squeeze into the last pew. We're pressed against each other, thigh to thigh.

"Sorry about the crowd. Should've warned you. Evening service is popular. We have the best choir."

I don't mind.

The members of the choir wear robes and gather on the stage. The church is buzzing with conversation. Seems like everyone knows each other.

Then the choir sings. Sojourner hasn't lied. They're amazing. Without my realising what I'm doing I'm on my feet, swaying like everyone around me, smiling.

The song makes me want to sing, but once I've picked up the chorus I realise I can't without being a hypocrite, given that I don't love Jesus. I hum and sway instead.

When the song ends we slide into our seats with contented smiles, so the woman who gets up to welcome us is greeted with warmth and joy, because that's what the music gave us, and now we're giving it to her no matter how boring her administrative announcements are.

There are more songs, more singing.

Everyone stands, sways, arms in the air, praising Jesus. I stop feeling like a hypocrite atheist moving to gospel music and I just move. I'm not sure if it's the music making me feel this way so much as it is Sojourner next to me feeling the music.

"I like you too."

At least, that's what I think Sojourner says. Her voice is low and the choir are singing loud.

Her side brushes against mine, our hands graze. We're both smiling hugely, then she whispers it again. "I like you too."

Her breath brushes against my ear. I swallow.

I feel light and giddy and overwhelmed and I shift, then stumble.

"White boy," she says, with laughter. I smile, find the rhythm again, sway with her once more, feel the music travelling through our bodies.

The back of her hand slides past mine. I slip my hand into hers. She doesn't pull away. Our fingers interlock, warm, strong, callused. She squeezes. All the breath goes out of me.

"Yes," I say.

Sojourner nods. "You feel it too."

I do. I more than like her. I more than want her. What I feel for Sojourner is too big for words. What I feel for her makes my whole body, my heart, my mind, my pancreas even, yearn.

We turn at the same time and our mouths are so close that for a split second I know we're going to kiss but then the moment passes. We are in a church, surrounded by her family, her friends—there's no way we can kiss.

The song stops. I stand, blinking, as everyone sits. Sojourner pulls me down. "Che," she whispers. I'm dazed.

I look around. I'm not the only one. Ripples of happiness run through the congregation. Sojourner and I hold hands. Alice, who greeted me, is behind the lectern, talking to us about something, Jesus most likely. All I can hear is the heartbeat in Sojourner's fingers, in her palm.

I'm pretty sure I'm in love.

I feel love for everyone. I look around the church, taking in the smiling faces, a small girl with bouncing blonde curls.

"Oh my God."

Rosa's on the other side of the aisle two pews down. Sally and David are not with her.

"What?" Sojourner whispers.

I point.

"Your sister?"

"What the hell is she doing here?"

A man in front of us turns and puts his finger to his lips.

I lean closer to whisper into her ear. "She does this. Runs away. I should take her home. Parentals will be worried."

"Can't it wait till after the service?" Sojourner's mouth almost touching my ear sends my thoughts away from Rosa.

I shake my head. My sister can't be here. "I'll come straight back."

She squeezes my hand and I ease myself out of the pew, hating letting go of Sojourner's hand. I cross the aisle and crouch down next to Rosa's pew.

"Time to go," I say, keeping my voice low.

The woman on the other side of Rosa looks at me questioningly. She is wearing a large red hat with feathers. I nod, hoping that will reassure her.

Rosa shakes her head. "Don't want to." She doesn't bother to lower her voice.

"You have to." I turn to look at Sojourner, who gives me an encouraging smile. "I'll carry you out if I have to."

"I like it here."

"Up, now."

"I want to stay!" Rosa says loud enough that several rows of people turn to stare. "They beat me at home!"

I force a smile. "She's lying."

"Are you okay, honey?" the woman next to Rosa asks her.

Rosa shakes her head pitifully.

"She's my sister. She's not supposed to be here. She snuck out. I have to get her home."

"Is that true, honey?"

Rosa shakes her head again.

Sojourner's by my side now. "Rosa, what are you doing here?"

"I want to learn about Jesus."

"I'm sure you can come back if you ask your parents for permission, Rosa," Sojourner whispers.

"She says her family beats her," the woman in the red hat says.

"Is that true, Rosa?"

Rosa looks down and blushes, which is a new trick. I've never seen her blush. How do you *make* yourself blush? "No, it's not true. I just wanted to learn about Jesus."

"Jesus does not like children who lie," the red-hatted woman says.

The entire church is looking at us. Alice has stopped talking. I'm sure Rosa is loving that she's the centre of attention. Sojourner takes her hand and Rosa obediently follows her down the aisle. I want to strangle her.

Out on the avenue I glare at Rosa. She's holding Sojourner's hand and looking forlorn. "I want to learn about Jesus. My mum and dad won't let me."

"Bullshit, Rosa. The parentals'll let you learn whatever you want to learn."

"I want to go to church with Sid. I want to learn about Jesus."

"Rosa, if your parents say yes you can come to church with me whenever you want. You can join us at the kids' Bible class. You don't have to tell lies." Sojourner opens her bag and pulls out a battered book. "This was my first Bible. You can borrow it if you like."

Rosa takes the Bible from her and hugs it to her chest. "Thank you," she breathes, letting a few tears slide down her face. "I'll read every word. Will you help me understand?"

Please. Sojourner bends down to give Rosa a hug. "I've gotta get back. See you later?"

"Thanks. I'll be back soon. We only live a few blocks up. Sorry about this."

Sojourner laughs. "You be good now, Rosa. Mind your brother. See you soon," she says to me. I have an urge to kiss her cheek, but she's already up the steps.

"Tears? Seriously?" I pull Rosa up the street. "How the hell did you know where I was? What are you doing? Where are Sally and David?"

"I followed you," she says smugly. "You didn't even notice. I would make a great spy."

"Jesus fucking Christ, Rosa."

"I wanted to see what you were doing." Rosa laughs. "You don't have to pull so hard. I'm coming."

She's holding a long red feather in her other hand. It's the same size and colour as the feathers in the hat of the woman she'd been sitting next to.

"Where did you get that feather?" I ask, though we both know.

"I didn't steal it. I picked it up from the floor. Isn't it pretty? I want a big hat full of feathers. Can we go to church? I like it because of the music and the hats and that lady was saying fascinating things about purity culture. I'm more sincere than you. I was there because it was interesting—you're only there because you like Sid."

I check my phone. Nothing from the parentals.

"They won't have noticed. Sojourner likes me. What if she likes me better than she likes you?" Rosa looks up to gauge my reaction. I'm pretty sure I'm not showing any. "She's going to teach me about the Bible. I'm going to spend lots of time with her. More time than you will."

I don't respond.

"I knew you wouldn't like that. What if we're hanging out together and Sid falls down the stairs?"

"Jesus Christ, Rosa. You're threatening Soj—Sid? She's a skilled fighter—you're a ten-year-old girl. What do you think you could do to her?"

Rosa giggles. "She's going to be my best friend."

"No, she's not." I text the parentals that I'm bringing Rosa home. I text Georgie too. —She's messing with me again.

I KNOCK ON THE study door and David opens it. He has a whiteboard marker in his hand. Sally is bent over her laptop on the couch. The parentals hadn't noticed Rosa was gone. They haven't looked at their phones.

"What—" Sally begins.

"Rosa followed me to church. She told people there that you beat her."

"Again?" David says. "That lie wore thin when you were wee."

"And she stole a feather out of someone's hat."

"No, I didn't," Rosa says. "I found it." She's still holding the feather. "Che said I could go to church with him. But then he wanted to be alone with his girlfriend."

"Stop lying, Rosa," I say, heading towards the door.

"Wait!" Sally calls, chasing after me. "Are you okay?"

When I don't say anything she pulls me into a hug, holding me tight. "I know Rosa's . . . wilful. We'll talk to her. But don't storm out angry. You might trip."

It's a weak joke but I smile, feeling the anger seep away.

"Rosa looks up to you, you know. She wants to be grown up like you."

I imagine Rosa at seventeen. I shudder.

"I'm okay. But I do want to go back. It's not what I was expecting. Nothing like temple."

Sally nods. "You converting?"

"Hardly. The music was great, though." And the hats.

"So it's not about the girl?"

"Well . . ." I'm not sure what to say. It's all about Sojourner.

"Uh huh. I love you, Che."

"Love you too."

WHEN I WALK INTO the church a black woman is in front of the lectern talking about the strength she's drawn from her illness. I wondered if she's Sojourner's mom. I wonder what her illness is.

I sit back in the pew next to Sojourner.

"Rosa in trouble?" she whispers.

I nod.

The pew's not as crowded as it was. There's now space between our thighs. Sojourner does not take my hand. Rosa has what she wanted. All that delicious energy between me and Sojourner, that space of an almost kiss, it's gone.

"I bet she just didn't want to be left out," Sojourner whispers.

When the service is over Sojourner thanks me for coming, hopes that I have a better sense of her faith, of her Jesus. She smiles, takes my hand for a few seconds. I'm dizzy. All I can do is stare. I can't speak.

"I gotta go help my mom," she says, letting go of my hand. "Can you hang around? We could get coffee? I want to hear what you thought."

I nod.

Alice walks over to me. "What did you think?"

"Er," I say, caught in the feeling of Sojourner's hand on mine. "I'm sorry about my sister interrupting you. She was here without permission, so I had to take her home."

Alice smiles. "These things happen," she says as if Rosa were a rain shower. "Why don't you bring her next time? She's most welcome."

I'm not sure there will be a next time. "Thanks. I'm glad I came. The music was wonderful. Everyone seems so warm, so happy. It made me feel good because everyone else seemed so . . . happy," I repeat.

"I'm glad you could attend too."

An older woman comes up to me, takes my hand in both of hers, thanks me for coming, blesses me. This happens over and over again until I feel like I've held hands with everyone there. Despite those other hands, all I can feel are Sojourner's.

"Thank you for joining us today," another woman says. It's the black woman who spoke about illness on the dais. She has a frame to help her walk. She reaches out to take my hands in hers. "I'm Diandra Davis, Sojourner's mother."

"Oh," I say. "Wonderful to meet you. I'm Che. Sojourner and I train together. I liked your . . ." I pause, not sure what to call it. Speech? Talk? "I liked what you said about illness."

The woman nods. She's looking into my eyes with such intensity I feel like I should confess my sins. Though that's Catholics, isn't it?—not whatever kind of church this is.

"You be kind to yourself, child," she says, "and kind to my Sojourner. God bless." She squeezes my hands, then moves on to talk to someone else.

WE WALK. I APOLOGISE for Rosa again and loosen my tie.

"Maybe the sermons will have an impact on her," Sojourner says. "You should bring her again. I'll ask my mom to preach about respect and obedience. She'll laugh her butt off."

"Great. More time spent babysitting my stalker sister." I wish we weren't talking about Rosa. "Does your church offer exorcisms?"

"Funny. Most kids've got some devil in them."

Not like Rosa.

We're in Tompkins Square Park. All paths lead through it.

I think about telling Sojourner about Rosa. It's too much. I barely know her.

We go to a coffee shop a couple of blocks past the park and grab a table by the window. We drink coffee and Sojourner insists I try a delicious red chocolate cake. She doesn't ask me what I thought of the service. I don't ask her what *interfaith* means. I'm thinking about how much I want to kiss her.

"Your parents must be kind of hippy, right?"

"Huh? I wish."

"They called you Che, so they must be about social justice and changing the world, yes?"

"Not really. Well, some. They're all about discipline and working from the inside to make change. They think smashing capitalism is impossible so instead you create businesses that make money but do it by creating things that help people and make the world a better place and by ploughing the money you make into more businesses that do the same and blah blah blah and they're even disciplined about taking time off—once a week they down tools. That's all me quoting them."

"Sounds like they're Puritans."

"Well, except that they drink and dance and don't believe in God."

"You call them by their first names."

"How did you know?"

Sojourner laughs. "Because your name is Che and because of everything you said. So you do call them by their first names?"

"Yes. We always have because, and I'm quoting them again, *we are not gendered roles, we are not a mum and a dad, we are people.* They also believe that children are people and should be allowed to develop at their own pace and not forced to enact the role of *child*."

"So you get to do whatever you want? Give me some of that!"

I laugh harder.

"I wish. Instead of saying *because we told you so* they say *because we are legally bound to look after you and teach you and should you do this thing we do not wish you to do there could be legally sanctioned repercussions. Even if there aren't until you are eighteen you have no legal standing to disobey us*."

"Wow."

"Yeah. Arguing with them is like arguing with the wind. A caring, loving wind that wishes it could help you out. But wind. All wind."

"Do you ever want to punch them?"

I am not vi-o-lent. I could have said, *No, I've never felt like that,* but I don't lie. Them not letting me spar. Them dragging us here. Them . . . There are times I want to punch them. "Maybe."

Sojourner laughs. "I want to punch mine often. It's why I box—so I don't punch anyone outside of the ring. I channel my rage into training to make it disappear. Or not disappear exactly, but turn it into something more useful than rage. I love boxing."

"Yeah. Me too."

"I can't disappoint my moms, you know? Mom has multiple sclerosis and Mama has done everything she can to make sure Mom's life is as much like it was before. I don't want to add any more trouble."

I nod. She's describing my life. Not making trouble because Rosa is nothing but. I think about telling Sojourner. But I don't want to kill whatever fragments are left of what we felt between us in church when we held hands, when we almost kissed.

Sojourner talks about her next fight, how much weight she'll have to cut. Then she has to go. She and Jaime are studying together. They have exams.

We touch fists, not mouths.

CHAPTER SIXTEEN

Monday morning I'm sitting at the island eating breakfast while David drinks coffee. Rosa skips down the stairs in her happy-that-it's-maths-time mood.

"Good morning," she says in her sunniest voice. "How are you both this morning?" You'd almost think she cares how well we are. She's wearing a necklace with a heart on it I haven't seen before.

"Where did you get that?" I ask, touching the red, sparkling heart. I don't think it's glass.

"Seimone gave it to me," she says, pulling herself onto a stool.

"No maths today," David says. "Today you write an essay and read about US history."

"No," Rosa says. "You didn't mean it."

"We did," David says. "You'll work on it in the study with me and Sally. Cheer up, tomorrow you're going to the New York Historical Society with Seimone and Maya and their au pair."

"Suzette," Rosa says.

"Huh?" David says. "Their school's having a curriculum day. You'll be learning history and you'll be writing an essay about your visit."

"You don't even read the essays you make me write."

"We'll read your essay."

"And me?" I ask. "Do you want me to go too?" I'm hoping not.

"You can do whatever you want, Che."

"That's not fair," Rosa says.

"When you sneak out and lie, there are consequences."

Rosa glares at David. "There are never any consequences for you."

"My life is one big consequence. Go work in our office. Quietly. Sally's on the phone."

Rosa stomps away.

Sadly, maths is not cancelled for me. Even the crestfallen look on Geoff's face when he hears he will not teach Rosa again until next week does not reconcile me to the hours of calculus ahead. I start counting

the minutes until I can head to the gym, to Sojourner, to sparring. I'm
definitely going to spar again.

An hour in I get a text and retreat to the loo to read it.

—I'm taking you shopping.

—Who is this?

For a brief moment I think it's Sojourner. But why would Sojourner
take me shopping? Also, she doesn't have my number.

—Leilani McBrunight. Your sartorial savior.

My heart doesn't sink exactly, but it isn't filled with joy.

—I think you have the wrong number. This is Che Taylor's phone. (Also,
it's saviour with a u.)

—Not in this country, farm boy.

—This benighted country, I think you mean. Why would you take me
shopping? You don't like me.

—I like shopping, though. The Olds are going to inflict you on me often. I
refuse to look at your tedious clothing again. It must be fixed.

I'm tempted to text *fuck you.* But I have a feeling that's what she's
going for.

—Wow. Way to win me over. You should be a diplomat when you grow up.

—It's on my list. You free this afternoon?

—No.

I'm not skipping boxing and Sojourner to go shopping with Leilani
McBrunight.

—Tomorrow? This is your final offer.

I love that she thinks she's doing me a favour.

—I'm not into shopping.

—That's evident. I will demonstrate that it does not have to be a dire
exercise in draping tedium about your person.

We're going to see a lot of each other. The parentals are throwing a
party. She will be there. We might as well be friends.

Besides, Leilani McBrunight knows more about her part of the city
than anyone else I'm going to meet. She can teach me about her New
York City, the one that's full of rich people. The parentals' new business venture means we're going to be hanging out with rich people a
lot. I need to learn their ways. Rosa said the same thing. I don't mean
it the way she means it.

—Fine. How about tomorrow morning?

She texts me an address and we agree to meet there at eleven.

—It's on the northwest corner.

—I'll remember to bring a compass. Should I bring an astrolabe too?

—Droll. That's Manhattan northwest.

—Whatever that means.

—Street numbers going up = Manhattan north. Avenue numbers going up = west. You're welcome.

ON THE WAY TO the gym I stop at the sports store Dido recommended, drop her name as instructed, and get a twenty percent discount. I'm going to keep sparring. Papa will be delighted to see those line items.

Sojourner is already on the mats stretching. I haven't seen her since Sunday. Yesterday, but it seems longer. She looks gorgeous. I'm smiling before I realise it.

"Hi." I slide down into a hamstring stretch. "Thanks for inviting me yesterday."

"Hi," she says. "It was a pleasure."

I try to think of something else to say.

"Hi," Jaime says. I haven't noticed her because I can't stop looking at Sojourner. I can tell from her grin that she knows it.

"Hi," I tell her.

"Did Rosa get in trouble?" Sojourner asks.

I nod.

"I'd be happy to talk to her if you think it'd help."

I need to change the topic. Jaime keeps glancing from me to Sojourner and smiling.

"What?" I ask, hoping that Sojourner has told her she likes me.

"Nothing," Jaime says when Sojourner glares at her.

"It's something," I say, though I should probably leave it alone. This is between me and Sojourner. But I need to know. My face burns.

"Well," Jaime begins.

Sojourner shakes her head.

"It's okay," I make myself say, though now my neck is burning too. "You don't have to tell me. Thanks for inviting me to your church, Sid. You were right. The choir is amazing."

"So you liked the music?" Jaime asks.

I nod.

"Did you like anything else? Did you *feel* anything else?"

"You are so dead," Sojourner says. "I told you that in confidence. You said you wouldn't tell."

Jaime giggles. "I know, but I can't resist. How long have you known me, Sid? You wouldn't have told me if you didn't want me to blab."

"I keep thinking one day you'll grow up. One day you, Jaime Maria Abreu de Leon, will earn the trust I have so stupidly placed in you."

"You sound like your mom. FYI."

Sojourner makes a face.

"He likes you," Jaime says. "You like her, don't you, Che?"

I don't know what to say. Should I agree? Sojourner *knows* I like her. "The music was great," I repeat. The words feel like dead fish falling from my tongue.

Are my zits glowing redder than red on top of the red of embarrassment spreading down my neck?

"She thinks you found God," Jaime says.

"She what?"

"I did not say that!"

"Sure you did. You said he looked like the spirit had moved him." Jaime looks at me and raises an eyebrow that's Leilani-like in its power to let me know that she knows *exactly* what part of my anatomy was moved and that it's a long way from my soul. "You didn't find God, did you, Che?"

I shake my head.

I might be (sort of) lying to my parents about sparring but I'm not going to lie to Sojourner. "No. I didn't feel anything spiritual or religious. I liked the music, the energy. I liked how warm and friendly everyone was. They seem like good people. But I still don't think there's a God."

Sojourner flinches.

I was moved, though, I want to tell her. *I realised I might be in love with you.* I thought she was starting to feel something for me. But it wasn't about me; it was about Jesus. *Fuck.*

"I knew that," Sojourner says but she sounds sad. "I'm still glad you came."

I STAY FOR SPARRING. I'm wearing a mouthguard that fits and headgear that doesn't smell like the sweat of a thousand other fighters. This time I'm up against the meathead. I can beat this guy. As I think that, he lands a right cross on my already-bruised nose. I grunt.

"Gotcha, Steakhouse!"

He doesn't think I can beat him. He winds up for a cross. I duck.

Every time I evade, he tries to punch harder, but I can see it coming. His chin goes up, telling me where his punch is aimed. Every time he misses he gets sloppier. He tries to grab me. I sidestep, feinting back. He misses completely. I land a flurry of jabs and crosses.

He lets out a sound that's somewhere between a roar and a wail and tries to tackle me. "Fucker!"

Dido steps in and pushes him away.

"You're sparring, not fighting. Relax. Breathe. Stay in control. Look at me. Are you calm?"

Meathead nods. He isn't looking at Dido. He isn't calm.

"You don't look calm."

"I'm calm!"

Dido puts up her hand. "You're not. Bout's over."

He takes off his gloves, sweat flying out in an arc, throws them over the ropes, tears off his headgear, glares at me, looks like he might throw it at my head.

Dido grabs his chin and makes him face her. "You're not calm. You're nowhere near calm. If you lose control you will never win a fight. Do you want to win? Do you want to be a fighter?"

For a moment I think Meathead is going to punch her but he deflates. "I want to be a fighter," he mumbles. "Sorry."

"Good. You know what to do." She releases him.

Meathead walks over to me and holds out his fist. He touches his wrapped fist to my gloved one.

"Sorry," he mumbles even more indistinctly. "Got anger issues."

"Get some ice on that eye," Dido commands. "On your nose, too, Che. Neither of you should be hitting that hard. I want to see more control. But you're throwing punches now, Che. Good."

We climb out of the ring. Sojourner and Jaimie climb in. Sojourner touches her glove to mine, gives me a half smile.

I sit with ice held to my nose and watch Sojourner school Jaime for blurting out her secrets. She's so fast, so focused. I learn more watching her spar than from a thousand regular lessons.

If only she weren't religious.

If only she didn't care that I'm not.

If only Rosa weren't trying to make trouble between us.

WHEN I GET HOME Rosa and Seimone are working on a jigsaw puzzle on the coffee table. They've taken their gloves off to do it. They look up as I slip off my shoes and slough the backpack. I wonder what Seimone is doing here so late.

"Sleepover?" I ask, wondering if that's a good idea.

Rosa nods. "Leilani was being mean so Seimone's staying here until she can be nice again."

Seimone giggles. "Lei-Lei's the worst. She always takes Maya's side. Hi, Che."

"Your nose is red again," Rosa announces.

"It is kind of red," Seimone says. "Do you have a cold?"

"Hi, Seimone. My nose is fine. Where are Sally and David?"

"Study. Working."

"Did you finish your essay?"

Rosa makes a vomiting noise.

"What essay?" Seimone asks.

"She has to write an essay on why lying is wrong."

Seimone makes an *ooooh* sound. "Did you get caught lying?"

Rosa shrugs. "Everyone lies. *Adults* never get in trouble for lying."

"Yes, they do," I say. "It's called perjury."

"Lying is fun."

I grab some ice, wrap it in a cloth, hold it to my nose.

"Thought you said your nose was fine? Liar."

"It will be soon."

"Someone punched him," Rosa tells Seimone. "He likes punching people."

Seimone shudders.

I sigh. "It's called boxing, Rosa. It's a sport."

"He doesn't spar," Sally says coming into the kitchen, pouring herself some tea. "He learns how to box without actually boxing. It's beneficial for overall fitness. Nose bothering you?"

"I'm being cautious."

Sally nods and pats my shoulder in approval. I feel my face burning and am grateful for the fast-melting ice. Rosa's right. I'm lying.

Rosa smirks as if she knows.

"Finished your essay yet, Rosa?" Sally asks. "You have to give it to us before you go to bed."

Rosa flounces towards her tablet on the couch and taps at it. "How do you spell *hypocrisy*?" she asks.

CHAPTER SEVENTEEN

The address Leilani gave me doesn't look like a shop. There's a black door with a picture of a cotton reel on it. I'm about to press the buzzer when the door opens and a burly guard looks at me disdainfully. As Leilani instructed, I tell him I'm with her and he reluctantly lets me in.

It is a clothes shop, or boutique, I guess. Unless there's an even fancier word. Even I can tell from looking at the elegantly displayed clothes and the art on the walls that this place is ridiculously expensive.

Leilani is chatting with one of shop assistants, who's tall and thin with gold hair that stands out against her brown skin. I have no idea how you turn your hair gold.

"Hi, Che," Maya says, waving at me. She's almost lost in a huge black velvet chair, kicking her feet back and forth.

"I didn't know you were coming."

I sit on a metal stepladder next to her. There's a large sports bag on her other side.

"Your tennis gear?"

Maya nods. "I'm sick."

She doesn't look sick.

"Sick of Seimone. She's being the worst. So Leilani said I didn't have to go to the museum."

"Why isn't Leilani in school?"

"I think she said independent study? Who knows? Leilani makes her own rules."

Maya has the same red heart necklace as Seimone.

"Where'd you get that?"

"Rosa has Seimone's now, doesn't she?"

I nod.

"Our grandmother gave them to us." She holds out the heart for me. "It's a ruby."

"I'll get it back for your sister. I promise."

"Seimone says she gave it to Rosa. But she would never."

The gold-haired shop assistant shows Leilani a dark red dress, fanning the skirt out to demonstrate the contrasting orange pleats. Though she doesn't call it a dress, she calls it a *piece*.

"Hey, Che," Leilani says as if she just noticed me. "The olds are ridiculously thrilled we're hanging out today."

I nod. "While the other littlies go to a museum. They're in heaven."

"Che, this is Deanna."

Deanna holds out her hand. Her fingers are long and elegant, each adorned with a ring. We shake briefly.

"I see what you mean," she says, giving me the same up-and-down look as the man on the door.

I'm wearing tracky dacks and a T-shirt. "I'm not into clothes."

"Evidently. But we can teach you the joy of them, can't we, Leilani?"

"Anything's possible," says Leilani in a tone that implies *anything but teaching Che about clothes*.

"What about this piece?" Deanna holds up green and silver pants. She's asking Leilani, not me.

"Cool," Maya says.

"We don't want to scare him. When Che goes out, everything he wears is a size or two too big. He sticks to jeans and T-shirts or short-sleeved collared shirts."

That description is scarily accurate. "How do you know what I wear?"

"I've seen far too many photos of you, Che. You wear clothes in all of them. No polos, Deanna."

I'm not sure what a polo is.

Deanna holds out a black shirt. Leilani nods and Deanna passes it to me.

I look at the price tag. "How can a shirt cost a thousand dollars?" I ask in a louder voice than I intended. It's a regular black shirt. The buttons aren't made of gold or diamonds. The fabric's soft, I'll give it that, but I have cheap T-shirts that feel as nice.

Maya laughs.

One of the other assistants looks at me as if she's realised a giant cockroach wandered into her shop. She gives Leilani a sympathetic look.

Surprisingly, Leilani doesn't roll her eyes. "Do you know how clothes are made?"

She continues without giving me a chance to answer.

"That shirt was not made in a factory or by piece workers in their own homes, paid well below minimum wage with no coverage if they're sick or injured. The people who cut and sewed that shirt were paid above-union wages in full-time jobs with full benefits. The cloth was woven at a mill where the workers likewise. That shirt was made from cotton grown without pesticides by small-scale farmers. It was designed by one of the most brilliant designers in Japan, who also happens to be one of the most ethical. Not one person was exploited to produce that shirt. Unlike a five-dollar T-shirt, it's being sold at its true cost. A thousand dollars is how much it costs to make a shirt this gorgeous when no one is exploited."

My hand sweats where I'm holding the hanger. Will I have to pay for the shirt if my sweat drips on it?

"Even if you care nothing for ethics,"—Leilani's tone says she expects such hideousness of me—"that shirt is an investment. There are only five in the world. In a year or two, you'll be able to sell it for more than you paid for it. *That* is why the shirt costs one thousand dollars."

"Exactly," Deanna says. "Very well said, Lei-lei."

I blush. Before I landed here I'd've said I'm not a blusher. It would have been true.

So only rich people can afford to be ethical? The T-shirt I'm wearing is fair trade. It's from one of the parentals' previous ventures. I'm tempted to ask Leilani why she doesn't weave her own clothes.

I return the shirt to Deanna and try to find something my parents won't freak out about. The only thing, I mean *piece*, I can find under two hundred dollars is a tie.

"Try these," Leilani says, thrusting two shirts and three pairs of jeans at me. There's no way I can buy any of them. I have two credit cards—one is the parentals', the other is Papa's—they'd all freak if I spent as much as fifty dollars on a shirt.

I push open the heavy wood-and-metal door to the change room. I'll tell them I didn't like anything. The light makes even my skin look okay. Can they get that effect with lights? Or is the mirror distorted? It's ridiculously flattering.

I touch the first shirt. It's scratchy, but the second one fits great and is softer than the thousand-dollar shirt. Maybe it costs a million dollars.

In the dressing-room mirror it's the same blue as my eyes. I know that's a trick of the light, but I can't help liking that about it. The first pair of jeans are so comfortable it's like wearing another skin. They're tighter than I usually wear, narrower too. I like them.

I wonder if Sojourner would like me in them. I imagine us walking together: her in her tulip dress and me in these fancy clothes.

When I walk out Leilani laughs. So it was just the lighting.

"Much better."

I'd expected her to mock me.

"It's almost like you're an actual human being and not a breathing, slightly sentient, gym monkey."

"Fuck you too, Leilani."

Maya looks up from the game she's playing on her phone to laugh.

"He does look better," one of the shop assistants says, sounding surprised. "We have that shirt in other colours. If you're interested."

"Perfect," Deanna says.

I really like the shirt. I wouldn't have thought I'd have such strong feelings, but I feel different wearing it, cooler. I have that I-don't-want-to-take-this-off feeling, which I haven't felt since I was six and evil Uncle Saul gave me a Superman costume for Chanukah 'cause he thought it would piss off the parentals. I wore it till it fell apart.

I follow Deanna, as if under a spell, and then I'm standing in front of a mirror while she and Leilani discuss which colours work best for me.

She brings out shirts in different shades of blue and green. I like them. I sneak a look at the price tags. They're over a thousand dollars. The jeans too.

I go into the change room and put my own clothes on and hand the *pieces* to Deanna.

"Which ones are you taking?"

I shake my head.

Leilani is wearing the red and orange dress. When she turns it sparkles in the light.

"Cool," I say.

Maya nods.

"I'm getting it. Give me a minute. Shoes next."

How much can shoes cost? Though I know how much some trainers cost. They can be pricey, but never a thousand dollars. I'll buy some. If they're as comfortable and amazing as those shirts it'll be worth it.

Maya walks outside with me with her giant tennis bag over her shoulder.

"Want me to carry that?"

"It's okay. Coach says carrying it'll make me stronger."

"That or it'll break your shoulders. Looks heavy."

Maya shrugs. "I'm really strong."

"Here you go," Leilani says a few minutes later, stepping onto the street. She hands me two shopping bags. "I bought you the shirts and the jeans and a jacket."

"You can't—"

Leilani puts up her hand. "Stop! I did. What you mean to say is *thank you*. But not too profusely. I shop here a lot. I don't pay full price. If we're going to be hanging out you have to dress nicely. I have a reputation to uphold."

I don't want to be rude. "I can't take them."

"You should take them," Maya says. "They look good on you."

"Do you not like them?"

"I didn't get to try the jacket, how do I know?"

Leilani waves that point away. "You tried on the shirts. You liked them. I could tell."

"I did. But I can't afford them."

"I can."

"But now I owe you and I can't pay you back. I can't throw money at things to get what I want."

"Don't be mean," Maya says. Her hands are on her hips.

"I'm not being mean. I just—I can't. I can never afford these. Not in a million years. I can't buy Leilani anything like this."

"You don't have to, silly," Maya says. "Leilani has all the clothes she needs."

"I don't," I say. "I don't have money. Not like you two. How can I pay you back?"

"Would you take them as a favour to me?"

"What?"

"You look great in them, Che."

Maya nods.

"It makes me happy to give them to you. What's the point of money if I can't use it to make my friends happy?"

"We're friends?"

"Practically," Leilani says.

"It was his birthday," Maya says. "Rosa told Seimone she gave him a brain."

Leilani stares.

"A plastic model of a brain."

"Can we say they're a birthday present?" Leilani asks.

"Happy birthday, Che," Maya says.

Leilani smiles at me as if she's genuinely delighted to be giving me a birthday present.

"Thank you," I say. Part of me is happy. I'll find out what Sojourner thinks of me in them.

But I also feel, well, manipulated.

It's the feeling I get when Rosa pulls one of her tricks and gets away with it. I know this isn't the same but I can't quite trust it.

LEILANI DRAGS ME INTO a few more shops, but I refuse to let her buy me anything else.

"You sure I can't carry that bag?" I ask Maya.

She shakes her head. "Tennis players carry their own gear. Serena Williams carries her own gear."

"Serena Williams is bigger than you." The bag is almost as big as Maya.

"She wasn't always."

"Don't bother arguing," Leilani says. "She won't budge. Even if carrying that thing is permanently damaging her back."

I buy a pair of black leather shoes that Leilani says can be formal and informal. They're on sale, so they're *only* two hundred dollars. I almost pass out paying for them. I'm not going to enjoy explaining them to the parentals. Maya buys electric blue sequinned sneakers and wears them out of the shop. They sparkle as she walks.

Everywhere we go, people know Leilani.

"What are you, the shopping queen of New York City? How does everyone know you?"

Maya laughs. "Tennis time," she tells Leilani. "Can we take the High Line?"

"Sure." Leilani leads us across the old-looking street of smooth bricks and up a wide flight of stairs. "You been here yet?"

"Nope." I have no idea what they're talking about.

"It's a sky park," Maya says.

"A narrow sky park full of annoying tourists who stop and goggle at everything. But it does mean no cars for four blocks."

At the top of the stairs there's a wide pathway lined with trees and clogged with people.

"It used to be an abandoned railway," Leilani explains, moving in front of me and making a path through the crowd.

The trees look young. I wonder how long this park has existed.

Everything looks pretty new. We're passing the fourth or fifth floors of apartment buildings and offices and hotels. I step sideways to allow a couple who won't let go of each other past.

The next section widens out to allow for a row of seats full of people sitting, enjoying the sun, and not paying much attention to the steady stream of tourists walking by, gawking at everything. I've heard six different languages float past.

The path narrows again as we walk through an archway of trees growing over our heads. It's gorgeous, even if the people walk far too slow and stop far too often to take photos for Leilani's liking.

"You should have seen it before the mobs descended," Leilani says.

"It was almost bare," Maya says. "Tiny trees, and the little plants on the ground hadn't spread out. It's better now."

"Except for the people."

"*I* like people. My tennis school is down there." Maya points west to where there's a glimpse of the Hudson River.

AFTER WE'VE DROPPED MAYA off we head back to the East Village.

"You should grow a beard," Leilani says.

"I'm seventeen. I *can't* grow a beard."

"Half the boys at my school have beards."

I look at Leilani dubiously.

"They do. Not full-on Williamsburg-I-cure-my-own-meats-and-brew-my-own-beer beards—except for Mikal, but he's a six-foot-five freak—but facial hair? There's a lot of it. See?"

She points at a man with a long, black bushranger beard, who's about to walk past us. He smiles at her, but Leilani's already pointing out the next bearded man.

"I know what a beard is, Leilani. You're telling me I should kowtow to the latest fashion in men's grooming?"

"Kowtow? If it's a *good* fashion, sure. You'd look less farmer-boy with a beard."

I sincerely doubt that.

"I'm blond."

"So?"

"How often do you think I shave?"

"I have no idea." Leilani's imperial eyebrows go up. "Boys' shaving habits are not something I give much thought to. Every day?"

I snort.

Leilani touches my cheek, carefully avoiding pimples. "But it's smooth. When's the last time you shaved?"

"A week ago? I haven't shaved since we landed. So ten days? Two weeks?"

"God. You're, like, practically hairless." She grabs my arm, peers at it, then points at her own. "You have no arm hairs! *I* have more arm hairs than you, and I'm not exactly hirsute. Okay, forget about growing a beard. It would take you a thousand years."

"Even then it would be a soft cluster of bum fluff."

"Bum fluff!" A sound like the cackling of a hen that's been attacked by an axe explodes out of her. It takes me a moment to realise she's laughing, not dying. With that ear-curdling sound and her cheeks turning red, for the first time Leilani doesn't look remotely cool. "Bum fluff! What does that even mean? Do you Aussies grow cotton balls on your butts or something?"

She laughs harder, adding snorts to her squawking. People are staring.

I have no idea what's so funny, but her laugh? Leilani's laugh is the most outlandish thing I've ever heard. I'm laughing too.

"Your laugh," I gasp. "Your laugh!"

"I know," she says in between snort-squawking. She's bent over. "Must stop." She wipes tears from her eyes.

"It's spectacular."

She snorts again.

"You have the worst laugh in the world."

She nods while snorting.

"Here was me thinking you were cool." My laughter slows into a grin.

"I am," she manages to say, breathing slower. "No one cooler. I only share my, um, unique laugh with a privileged few."

She uses her no doubt ridiculously expensive sleeve to wipe away the last of the tears. "That's it. I'm taking you to meet Ronnie. You've heard me laugh. I have no secrets left."

"Ronnie?"

"Yes. Ronnie—Veronica—my girlfriend. Come on. Her shift ends in about forty minutes. We're going to this new ramen place with her best friend. We've enough time to drop off these bags at my place, for you to change, and get there. Are you hungry?"

I'm always hungry but the thought of missing a class makes me twitchy. Even when I know Sojourner won't be there. But I can make a later class and sparring isn't till seven. It's not a sin, I tell myself, to have the occasional slower day.

"Sure," I say. "Let's see your girl."

CHAPTER EIGHTEEN

"Her name's Veronica Diaz. We were high-school *sweethearts*," Leilani stresses the last word to mock it but also to dare me to laugh.

"*Were?*"

"She graduated already and now she's working at the Sunshine on Houston," she says. I wonder how long it will take for the How-sten pronunciation to stick in my head. I also wonder what the Sunshine is.

"She acts too. She's been in student films and a couple of ads and one episode of *Law and Order* when she was little. She's done close to a million auditions. She had a part in an Off-Broadway production but the funding fell through."

I try to look impressed, though I'm not sure if I'm meant to be or not.

"It's not enough to make her rent. So she works at the Sunshine and at a shitty cafe on St. Mark's. Coffee Noir. Stupid name."

Leilani's tone sounds almost annoyed. I wonder if she offered to give Veronica money. Leilani has all the money but her girlfriend struggles to pay her rent. None of my friends are massively richer or poorer than me. Well, except Leilani.

I know how I feel having Leilani buy me those clothes without asking. If they've fought about this, I'm on Veronica's side. Then I remember that right now the McBrunights are paying my rent. It didn't worry me before. How do Sally and David feel about it?

"Is it love?" I ask as we cross the street.

"It's certainly lust," Leilani says. "Lots and lots of lust. Wait till you see her."

Sunshine is a cinema. There are signs up for an Iranian film festival.

Even through scratched plexiglass Veronica is good-looking: curly blonde hair and green eyes. She is the big eyes, small nose, full lips picture of beauty. She saves herself from genericness with asymmetrically cropped hair and multiple piercings. She excites no lust in me, but Leilani is grinning as soon as she spots her and speeds up to lean over the counter and kiss her.

"Missed you," I hear her murmur as she pulls away. "This is Che."

"Hi, Che. Heard a lot about you."

None of it good, I'm pretty sure.

She holds out her hand. We shake.

We don't have to wait long for her replacement to show up, then I'm following them down a dark alley to a restaurant that expands out of nowhere. The entrance is small and narrow, yet the restaurant is huge. Behind a long counter chefs toil over giant pots of boiling water and noodles fly through the air. The staff chant a greeting in Japanese. Veronica and Leilani bow and return the greeting. We're given the last table.

"Elon's always late," Veronica says. "We should start."

"I heard that," says a black guy, who's a bit shorter than me with a goatee and shoulder-length, too-shiny hair. He looks like Prince Valiant. "God, Elon, take that stuff off. You look ridiculous."

Elon slides the wig from his head and the beard from his face, and stuffs them into his pocket, where they look like feral creatures ready to leap out and attack us. Without the fake hair he looks like a girl.

"Much better," Veronica says, reaching up to stroke his smooth, but red from the false beard, chin. Maybe Elon is a she?

"I look divine," Elon says in a voice that's too deep for a girl, sliding into a seat. Maybe he *is* a boy? My own cheeks aren't much rougher than his. Hers?

Elon's hair is flattened. He pats at it and frowns. "I'll order then go fix this mess. I'm starving. But I must look dreadful without my princely accoutrements."

"This is Che," Veronica says.

"Oh, this is the dweeby son of your parents' best friends. Did I get that right, Lei-Lei? Wasn't that the word you decided on after scouring Ye Olde Slang Dot Com?"

"Elon!" Veronica says. Leilani doesn't even roll her eyes at him.

"That would be me," I say and hold out my hand.

"Oh," Elon says. "A hand-shaker. That *is* dweebish." He or she proceeds to air kiss me. "You don't exude rich. Do rich Australians not like to show off their wealth?"

"I'm not rich."

"He's not rich," Leilani says at the same time. "Not all my parents' friends are rich, you know."

"Is that how you developed your taste for slumming?" Elon turns to me and lowers his voice. "Veronica and me were *scholarship* kids and we share a rent-controlled sublet. Tell no one." He stands up. "Tonkotsu for me. With an egg."

I watch Elon walk towards the toilets. Slim hips, but a small waist. He walks with a sway. Doesn't help me figure out if he's a boy or a girl and I'm pretty sure I better not ask.

"You're not Elon's type," Leilani says.

I blush. "I wasn't checking—"

They laugh at me.

"Elon's not my type either," I say, trying for arch but landing on sullen.

"Oooh," Veronica says, "so what is your type?"

My phone chimes. I look down. — Fucked her yet? A text from Jason. I groan.

Leilani leans over my shoulder. I click the phone off.

"Fucked whom?" she inquires delicately as the waiter arrives to take our orders. He raises his eyebrows but says nothing. "So?" Leilani prompts when the waiter leaves. "Who's the fuckee?"

"No one. He's joking. Crap joke, obviously. He's not really a dick." Which isn't true. Jason can be a total dick and he probably isn't joking. I wish I hadn't told him about liking Sojourner. At least my brain was on enough to not tell him her name.

Veronica nudges Leilani. "What did the text say? Tell me."

"What text?" Elon asks, sitting down.

"Nothing," I say at the same time as Leilani says, "*Fucked her yet?*"

"That's what the text said," she clarifies. "I wasn't asking a question."

"He was kidding," I say. "It wasn't about anyone."

"Was it about Leilani?" Elon asks. "I think you've got a shot with her." Elon leans forward and says in a theatrical whisper, "Just between you and me I think she's ready for a change. She and Veronica have been together since the dawn of time."

Veronica punches him.

"Ow!"

Our noodles arrive.

"Soothe your pain with tonkotsu."

The noodles are amazing.

"Good, huh?" Elon asks, broth dripping down her/his chin. "Oh, Lei, did I tell you I didn't get the part?"

Veronica rolls her eyes. "You don't know that's why, Elon."

Elon makes a snorting sound. "Ah, yes, I do. Apparently I don't have the right *look* for Peter Pan."

"They're calling being black a look? How progressive of them." Leilani blows a raspberry. "You'd be perfect."

"Do we have to talk about this?" Veronica asks.

My phone buzzes. I risk a look. It's Rosa.

—Miss you! We had such fun at the museum.

WE WANDER AROUND WHAT my phone tells me is the Lower East Side while Leilani, Veronica and Elon gossip about people they know and debate clothes, shops and restaurants and some new hotel as if they were as old as the parentals. Elon keeps asking Leilani about her website.

"You have a website?" I ask. It seems kind of old-fashioned to me.

The three of them laugh. "Yes, Leilani McBrunight has a website," Elon says. "It's called Neophyte?" He's staring at me as if I should know what that means.

"Never mind," Leilani says. "Che's not much into fashion."

"Really?" Veronica says. "That shirt is divine."

"*I* made him buy it."

My phone buzzes. Sally telling me that Rosa is having a sleepover with Seimone and Maya at the McBrunights' and that she and David are having dinner there. I doubt Maya's a willing party.

"I should head," I say.

"You got somewhere to be?"

"Gym," I say.

"It's not even dark yet," Elon protests. "I haven't ferreted out your secrets."

"What makes you think I have secrets?"

"Yes," Leilani says. "Stick around. You can skip gym, surely? You're new to New York. We can teach you the secret passwords."

"Where the dragons' lairs are," Veronica says.

"How to slay them," Elon adds.

I'm curious about Leilani and her friends. They're nothing like my mob at home. Nazeem and Jason and Georgie do not talk clothes the way these guys do. Or pretty much anything they're talking about.

I kind of want to know how Leilani and Co. amuse themselves, and the parentals will be thrilled I was hanging out with her. That might balance out how not-thrilled they're going to be when I tell them about sparring.

"Fine," I say. "You can teach me your ways."

Elon mock hugs me and makes I-am-giddy-with-joy noises. "Let the lessons begin!"

I text Sally to let her know I'm with Leilani and her friends. —Have fun, she texts back.

"Step one," Leilani says. "We visit Ronnie and Elon's."

"Wasn't step one eating ramen?" I ask.

"No, step one was retrieving me from the job of total boredom," Veronica says.

"Just open the door, Ronnie."

Veronica opens a graffiti-splattered door and leads us up four flights of stairs.

"I love walkups," Leilani says.

"It's humble but it's home," Elon says, grinning. "We're getting an elevator installed in our apartment any day now."

The stairs are filthy. I can smell dust and years of crud walked into the fraying carpet. My shoes stick a little with each step. The walls are all scuff marks. On each floor at least one apartment has a pile of garbage leaning next to the door. The first floor has only one bag and it doesn't smell too terrible. The second floor is much worse.

"They think elves will take the garbage down for them," Elon says as we reach the fourth floor and their apartment. Outside the door are two bags of garbage. "Veronica! It was your turn."

Veronica has the grace to mutter an apology, but then follows Elon into the apartment.

"Veronica!" Elon yells. "Take the garbage down."

"Oh. Right."

"Now!"

Veronica sheepishly goes out, dragging the garbage behind her.

"Ronnie is the worst," Elon says, dropping onto one of the couches. "It's like filth is invisible to her. If Veronica wasn't such a great cook I'd be looking for a new roomie like this." Elon snaps his or her fingers.

"And if she hadn't been your best friend since you were both five," Leilani says.

"Six. Yeah, there is that. She's such a slob, though. I don't mind untidy, but filth? She doesn't even clean the toilet after—"

Leilani holds up her hand. "We don't want to know!"

"Sit down already," Elon commands.

Leilani sits on the couch opposite as I sink down next to Elon. The couch has a lot of give, my arse is almost touching the ground, my knees are near my eyes.

"Welcome to our palace."

I laugh. "Very palatial."

It's about as far as you can get from Leilani's. The room is crowded with two couches, table and chairs, shelves groaning with books and DVDs, and speakers, screens, computers, routers and wires. The kitchen is against the wall. One tall, narrow window next to it leads out onto a fire escape.

"It would be tidier, but we had to let the butler go." Elon lowers his voice to whisper theatrically, "He was raiding the liquor cabinet."

Leilani taps away at her phone. I don't know for sure, but I have a feeling the McBrunights have a butler. Possibly more than one.

When Veronica comes back up Elon produces a joint, lights it, takes a drag, and hands it to Veronica, who drags on it and passes it to Leilani, who takes a toke so long I think the whole joint is going to disappear.

Leilani hands it to me before I've opened my mouth to explain that I don't do drugs. Then I think about what they'll say. How tedious the teasing will be.

Leilani already thinks I'm a—what was the word she used?—*dweeb*, that's right. I'm used to that. Most of my peers think I'm weird: sometimes homeschooled, use too many big words, blah blah blah. I don't care what they think, but not taking the joint will start the how-weird-is-he convo too soon. I don't want to listen to them going on about my being straight-edged for the next few hours. Or days. Or, God, for as long as I live here.

I pretend to take a toke, then pass it to Elon. None of them notice.

How does stoned feel? I don't even know what tipsy or drunk feels like. I'm always good. I try not to make trouble, because I'm acutely aware of what hell Rosa can, and probably will, bring down upon our heads some day.

Why can't I just this once do something I shouldn't?

Because I'm too scared of being out of it at the exact moment Rosa decides to—I don't know—push Sojourner down a flight of stairs.

I won't see Rosa until tomorrow. She's with Seimone and Maya and they have adult supervision. If I'm going to try, now's the time.

When Leilani hands me the joint again, I inhale and hold my breath.

I don't cough, though it makes my throat tickle. I hand it to Elon. My eyes sting.

We do two more rounds until the joint's too small to hold. The smoke tastes sweet, almost like basil. I breathe in as little as I can. I don't want to overdo it. I wonder when I'll feel something. Soon, surely. But the others seem normal. In the bathroom mirror my eyes are pink.

"I would be the best Peter Pan ever," Elon says.

"Elon!" Veronica says. "Let it go!"

"Don't worry, Ronnie. We know you don't see colour."

"That's not what I said," Veronica mutters.

"Your sister," Leilani says, when I sit down on the couch, "doesn't like me."

"Of course she doesn't. You don't think she's adorable. She's used to charming everyone."

"She's not adorable. She weirds me out."

My heart beats faster. *Leilani noticed*. I also feel sick. I can't escape Rosa. She's not here and yet she is. Is Leilani bringing her up a bad omen? I almost have an urge to call the McBrunight home and see if the twins are all right.

"Her eyes are a bit *too* big. She's almost *too* perfect. Those blonde curls. It's almost like she's in the uncanny valley."

She just means Rosa looks like a doll. I hope my disappointment doesn't show.

"The what now? Uncaring alley? *Down in the alley*," Elon sings, "*we having fuuuun*."

"Shhhh! Un-can-ny valley," Leilani repeats more slowly. "It comes from robotics. When something looks almost, but not quite, human it makes our skin crawl. But up until that point we think it's cute. Like putting eyes on a rice cooker. Or teddy bears, or basically everything we find cute. Until it gets that little bit too close, then it's—"

"*Polar Express!*" Elon shouts.

"Oh. My. God!" Veronica screams. "The olds made me and Saskia watch that when we were little. Nightmares. For months. Years! I am *still* traumatised. What were they thinking? What was anyone involved with that nightmare monstrosity thinking?"

"What's *Polar Express*?"

"He's homeschooled," Leilani faux whispers.

"*Sometimes* I'm homeschooled—I'm not from the Middle Ages."

"Aren't homeschoolers basically Amish?" Veronica wants to know.

"Do I *look* Amish?" I have only the vaguest notion of what Amish is.

"Not without a beard," Leilani says, then puts her hand over her mouth to keep her insane laugh from slipping out.

"Also they have much worse clothes," Veronica says, glancing at Leilani, clearly wondering what's so funny.

"I told you. I made him buy that shirt." Leilani's hand being over her mouth makes her sound marginally less smug. "Also the jeans and shoes. He was a sad little gym rat before I fixed him."

"I'm not homeschooled or Amish. I have computers. A phone. A tablet." I would like to shout that I've had sex and done drugs but I haven't, well, not until a few seconds ago, or minutes, or whatever amount of time has passed, and only the drugs part. "I'm an atheist who believes in social justice and equality for everyone whatever their colour or gender or sexuality or anything else. I just haven't heard of *Polar Express*! What is it?!"

They're laughing. For a moment I want to yell at them, but then I can feel their laughter enter my pores, and tickle me from the inside, until I'm laughing too. We laugh so hard we gasp.

"Movie," Veronica says at last, wiping tears away. "Really horrible animated movie."

"So what," I ask when the laughter finally floats away, "does the uncanny valley have to do with Rosa?"

I regret it at once. I was having fun.

"Ah," Leilani says. "Yes. Well, she lives in the uncanny valley. It's like she's learning to be human, but isn't there yet. Her skin doesn't look like it has pores and those creepy, creepy eyes. Then there's the way she smiles and laughs, always a fraction of a second behind everyone else. I gotta be honest, Che, she gives me the fucking creeps."

"Wow," Veronica says. "I have to meet this kid."

"Yeah, me too."

"If I pressed a button on her back," Leilani says, "she'd dance."

I laugh. "She does. She dances! She started learning tap after seeing a Shirley Temple movie. People kept telling her she looks like her." Then I remember Leilani knows that. Seimone and Rosa are at the same dance school.

"Shirley Temple has to be the creepiest white child ever." Leilani shudders.

"Who's Shirley Temple?" Veronica whispers.

"Stage actors, man. They know nothing. How," Elon asks, "did you get a job in a movie house, Ronnie? Have you ever even seen a movie?"

Veronica rolls her eyes. "We theatre people are too good for your plebeian arts."

"Says the girl who was on *Law and Order*."

"I was a kid! Besides, every actor in the history of the universe has been on that show!"

"Not anymore," Elon says. "Moment of silence for the passing of NYC's great employer of under-utilised actors."

"Oh, for fuck's sake, Elon, it was cancelled years ago."

"Maya doesn't like Rosa either," I say. "But Seimone does. Have they always had different friends?"

"No. Rosa's the first friend they haven't shared. Maya doesn't like being in the same room as Rosa. She told Seimone there's something wrong with Rosa, that she should stay away from her. Seimone said she wished Maya was dead. When I called her on it she said she wished I was dead too."

Elon makes scary noises and giggles.

It's not funny.

"That's heavy," Veronica says. "How old is Rosa?"

"Ten," I say. I'm staring at Leilani. She's staring back. For a long, long, long moment, it might have been hours, we are locked in that stare and I'm on the verge of telling her everything, all my fears about Rosa.

Leilani seems to understand the way Georgie does. It would be such a relief to tell her.

"I have to have a lobster roll," Leilani declares. "Who is with me?"

The moment is gone.

CHAPTER NINETEEN

I don't get home until four in the morning. Instead of falling into bed I write in my journal. Words pour out of me. I wonder if I'm still stoned. Or am I just drunk? When did we start drinking? Does my wondering prove I'm not drunk or does it prove I am?

I slide off my chair and towards my bed, shoes off, jacket off, under sheets, eyes closed.

Morning.

My eyes are glued shut with sleep. My tongue sticks to the roof of my mouth. For a moment I think I'm on a plane again.

I guzzle water. My tongue unsticks, but now I have an awful aftertaste from everything I drank and smoked and ate last night. I drag myself to the bathroom. I floss, I brush. I go through half the mouthwash, rinsing and spitting. I wash my face, towel it dry, put acne cream on, drink more water.

I pull out my phone. Too many messages.

I make my way downstairs, wincing at the creaking of the stairs. I hadn't noticed they creaked.

"You got in late last night," David says.

He's sitting at the kitchen island drinking coffee.

"Where're Sally and Rosa?" I ask, pulling myself onto a stool opposite him.

"Breakfasting with the twins and Lisimaya and Gene and their au pair. Can't remember her name."

"Did you know *au pair* means *equal to*?" my mouth says before my brain registers the thought. Not very equal if David can't remember her name.

"Huh," David says. "They'll be back after breakfast. You look like you died."

"Leilani's a terrible influence." The coffee tastes awful. I hope that's because my mouth is coated with mouthwash.

"So I see."

"Is this an intervention?"

David laughs. "After your first night of typical teenager behaviour?"

"I wanted to see how drugs and alcohol would affect me. You know, the way teenagers have done since time immemorial."

"Teenagers are a recent invention," David says, smiling because that's something Sally likes to say. "What did you think of drugs and alcohol?"

"Last night or now?"

"Last night."

"Last night it was fun and weird and I had strange conversations and I ate more food than I think I've ever eaten."

"*That* I find hard to believe."

"Bad-for-me food. Now I feel awful. Inhaling smoke into your lungs is foul. I can't think straight and I want to go back to bed."

"You didn't get much sleep."

"Felt like anti-sleep. I'm going to the gym to see how badly buggered my reflexes are."

"A lot, probably. You're such a finely tuned machine I'm sure some of your pistons frayed."

"You sound pleased." I have to concentrate hard to keep up with what David's saying and spit out a reply.

David breaks out his full-wattage smile, dimples and all. "I'm enjoying seeing you behave like the teenager I was and that Sally was. Your lack of experimentation makes us nervous."

David's eyes seem bigger. Also they seem to be moving independently of his face, which can't be right.

"Sorry for not wanting to smoke and drink poison. I blame you for not letting me stay in any school long enough to have to resort to drugs to cope."

"You're welcome. We're proud to have produced two kids whose minds are unfettered by the noxious bullshit that would have been pumped into them if you'd spent all your time at a regular school."

It sounds like he's reciting the words. For a moment I wonder if David actually thinks that, or if he's repeating Sally. I must still be stoned. The room is slightly tilted. I *am* still out of it. I hate it.

"I don't want you to get into drugs or alcohol. They lead too many people to bad places. But I don't trust extremism. Teetotallers make me as nervous as alcoholics."

"That's silly. Not drinking *isn't* extreme. It's not doing something everyone else does. As of last night, or rather this morning, I now know

why I avoided alcohol and drugs and why I'll continue to avoid them."
I sip my coffee. It makes me feel worse. "That's like saying atheism is
extreme."

David is too close to me. Except that he probably isn't. I'm not sure.
"Atheism," I continue. What am I saying? "Atheism it's, well, it's
not, really. I mean there's nothing to it except not believing in God."

I grope for my point. "The only thing you learn about someone if
they're an atheist is that they don't believe in God. It's only extreme
if atheists are trying to stop everyone else from believing whatever it
is they want to believe. If they're doing that they've missed the point
of not believing in God." Not drinking, *that's* what we were talking
about. "I don't know anyone who doesn't drink or do drugs who's
trying to stop anyone else from doing the same."

"Remind me to teach you about Prohibition sometime." David
holds up his hands in mock surrender before I can say anything. "You're
pretty articulate for a teenager who's hungover. I blame your excellent
parenting for that."

"Self-praise is no praise."

"So what are you going to do today?"

"I told you, gym. I guess I'll catch up too. Read those history books
you're never going to ask me about. Are there eggs?"

David nods. "Bacon too. Want me to make us a fry-up?"

"Sure. Though you know it's weird parenting to reward me for a
night of drugs and alcohol, right?"

"We've always been weird parents."

The smell of the eggs frying sends me running to the bathroom.

I RETREAT TO MY room. I should do the problems Geoff has set me but, well,
my head. I open one of the Studs Terkel books, but I can't concentrate.
I turn to my journal instead. Through the nausea there's a persistent
drum of Rosa.

Leilani noticed Rosa's weirdness.

I read my notes on Rosa, trying to think how they would look from
a stranger's point of view. What would Leilani think?

I should have tried to talk to David. He was in such a mellow mood,
making me breakfast, being proud I smoked a joint. But I'm not ready
for a repeat of the conversation with Sally.

I read through my account of Rosa making Apinya kill her guinea pig.
There, right in the middle: *Set it on fire, watch it burn.*

I don't remember writing that.

Could I have written it last night? I don't remember getting home. I know I opened up my journal and wrote something. I don't remember what.

The most recent notes are a disjointed rambling journal entry about my evening with Leilani and her friends. Nothing weird in there, except I'm more obsessed with knowing whether Elon is a girl or a boy than I realised. Elon could be neither. There are people who are neither.

I'm as obsessed with Sojourner as I thought I was. I delete those parts. I crap on about how much I love sparring even though I'm shit at it. I imagine what it'd be like to truly land a punch. Apparently I think it will be like coming. Ewww. I don't think that. I'm definitely not drinking or getting stoned again. It turned me into an idiot.

I turn back to the Apinya entry.

Set it on fire, watch it burn.

That's not the kind of thing I'd write. Did Rosa?

Rosa giggles.

I turn. She's in the doorway.

"Sally and David say I can have a dog if I take care of this fake dog without killing it for two months." She holds out her tablet to show the dog app.

"Congrats."

She couldn't have accessed the journal, could she? I'm vigilant about changing passwords. The files are buried deep. I quit out of the journal, put the computer to sleep, switch my phone to record.

"I want you to give Seimone's necklace back. Her grandmother gave it to her."

"I gave it back already. It was a loan. See?" Rosa pulls her collar open to show that there's no necklace.

I pull out my phone.

"What are you doing, Che?"

"Texting Leilani to make sure Seimone got her necklace back."

Rosa pouts. "Well, she did. Seimone and I danced last night. Though she does ballet, not tap. We taught each other some steps." She pirouettes to demonstrate.

"What was Maya doing?"

Rosa shrugs. "How should I know? I asked Seimone lots of questions. She answered them all. I showed an interest. I know all sorts of things about her now."

"That's great," I say, though I'm not sure it is. "But you two didn't play with Maya?"

"Of course not. She doesn't like me and she's mean."

I believe the first bit, not the second.

My phone pings. It's Leilani. —She was wearing it this morning. Why?

Rosa smirks though she can't see the phone. "I'm going to get a dog, Che. When I get it I won't hurt it. You'll see. I keep my promises."

"I'm glad."

Rosa hugs me, tablet in her hand. I think about asking her if she'd hug me while holding a puppy. But she's warm and clings to me like she did as a littlie. That soft, fresh baby smell is long gone, and she's done and said many awful things, but I want to believe that hug.

I love Rosa. I don't think I'll ever be able to stop.

"Hugging is nice," Rosa says and it's on the tip of my tongue to tell her she's laying it on too thick.

Set it on fire, watch it burn.

Is that what she's trying to do to me?

PART THREE
I Want a Girlfriend

CHAPTER TWENTY

Four weeks after landing in New York City I type out, then delete, my list again.

1. Keep Rosa under control.

Rosa, Rosa, Rosa, Rosa.

The good news is she hasn't done anything worse than sneak out of the apartment, be rude to cops, and steal: that feather from the woman at church and the Korean doll and necklace she claims Seimone gave her. Oh, and lie, an endless string of lies. All of which is Rosa status quo. But no more dead guinea pigs. No dead anything. No new weird entries in my journal.

The bad news is Rosa threatened Sojourner. She's been to the kids' Bible class Sojourner teaches twice, and won't tell me about it. She says Sojourner is her friend now, too. Georgie says she's trying to do my head in. That I shouldn't let her.

I'm no closer to talking to Sally and David seriously about her. What will it take?

2. I want to spar.

I sparred! I spar! I am sparring!

I'm addicted.

Even more than training I can lose myself in it. I don't think about anything but defending, attacking, counter-attacking. I see only my opponent, their eyes, their gloved fists.

Rosa is not in my head for a nanosecond.

Everything that went before is nothing compared to being in the ring. To exchanging blows. Defending. All of it. Now I know what fighting is. How little, and how much, control I have over my body. I don't have to consciously think to throw a punch. It's automatic. I've learned. I'm a fighter.

Dido is impressed with my progress. I'm impressed with my progress. Jason can't wait to spar with me.

I haven't told the parentals, which kind of makes me a liar too. I have to tell the parentals.

3. I want a girlfriend.

Sojourner is my friend. She's fucking incredible. Great fighter, smart, funny. Not Leilani funny, quieter than that. I feel chill around her. Well, except for when I'm thinking about what it'd be like to hold her, to be skin to skin, to . . . Yeah.

I'm trying not to think about how to get us from friendship to boyfriend and girlfriend. It's not going to happen. I don't believe in God; I'm not going to pretend I do.

4. I want to go home.

Not as much as I did. This city's kinda cool, but it's not home, and it's been too long.

TONIGHT'S MY SECOND BOUT with Meathead. He's been avoiding sparring with me. Embarrassed, I guess.

One round of three minutes.

He's in control of himself this time, but still slow. I see his eyes flick and his shoulder move long before his punches land. It's easy to duck. He tries to move faster, which makes him sloppier.

"Watch the eyes, not the gloves!" Dido calls out.

All I see are Meathead's eyes, bloodshot and blinking too fast, to keep the sweat out.

Then the bell, stopping, touching gloves, stepping back, gloves off, headgear off.

"Good work," Dido says to us, pulling Meathead aside for detailed critique.

I'm elated. That was easy. Meathead didn't lose it. I didn't get sloppy when he got sloppy. Both of us are better than that first session. I'm breathing hard. It doesn't feel like three minutes passed. I want to fight again. Preferably against Sojourner. She isn't slow. She doesn't telegraph her punches.

"Che," someone says as I climb out of the ring.

It sounds a lot like Sally. I turn.

It is Sally.

Christ. My entire family are standing in my gym staring at me. Sally and David and Rosa, and with them the McBrunights. Seimone is wearing green gloves. Maya gives me a little wave. Matter out of place. My face is already hot from exertion, but now it's hotter. My pimples are in danger of erupting like mini volcanoes.

Rosa grins.

"We thought you might like to join us for dinner," Sally says with as little warmth as she's ever used towards me. "We've a table in fifteen minutes around the corner."

David doesn't say anything. His lips are pressed together.

"One of our favourite restaurants," Gene says as if I haven't just been busted doing something I promised I wouldn't. Maybe he doesn't know. Maybe me stepping out of the ring is what he expects to see here in a boxing gym.

"Sounds great," I say.

"Well done," Dido says, patting my shoulder. "Especially your cross. Left hand's dropping and chin comes up on your hook. But much, much better."

"These are my parents," I say because it would be weird not to intro duce her. "Dido's my trainer here. She's great."

"You have a lot of parents." She smiles at the four adults and holds out her hand to David, who unleashes his full smile.

"I'm Dido," she says, blushing as they shake hands.

"I'm David, Che's dad. A pleasure to meet you."

"I'm Sally." Sally holds out her hand and Dido blinks, remembering to let go of David's hand and to stop staring at him. Sally introduces everyone else, warmth returning to her voice.

"I'm Rosa," Rosa announces before Sally can. She does her little curtsey. "Was Che sparring? Did he win? It looked like he won."

"Yes, he was sparring. He didn't win because it's not a contest, just a way to test skills," Dido says. "He did well. Che's a natural fighter but a cerebral one. Great combination. You should be proud. If you'll excuse me."

"You're very dedicated, Che," Gene says. "Working out on a Friday night."

I smile, not sure what to say to that in front of the parentals.

"Nice gym," Lisimaya says. "Not what I was expecting. It's so clean, and so many women."

"Yeah," I say. "It's not old-school. I don't like the old-school gyms. Too much testosterone."

Sally and David are silent.

"Ah, um, I should get changed."

"We'll wait out front," Sally says, walking away with David.

I stand there dripping.

Rosa and the twins are watching training in the other ring. Judo. They're down on the ground grappling. Seimone giggles.

"Hello," Sojourner says, walking over to Rosa. "Now do you believe I'm not the only girl?"

She peels off her wraps and smiles.

I realise I still have mine on. They're soaked with sweat.

Rosa nods. "Now I want to learn how to fight too."

Sojourner laughs. "I'll give you self-defence tips any time you want."

"Yes, please!"

"Me too?" Seimone asks. "I'm Seimone."

"She's my best friend," Rosa says.

"Nice to meet you," Sojourner says. "I'm happy to give you tips."

"This is Maya," I say.

Maya says, "Hi."

"Nice to meet you too," Sojourner says. "Are you—"

"I've got questions," Rosa says, leaning closer to Sojourner. "About Hebrews 4:13. About most of Hebrews, actually."

Bible questions? Please.

"Can you have dinner with us?" she asks, raising her voice, looking at Gene and Lisimaya who say, "Of course, how lovely, the more the merrier."

Say no, say no, say no, I will Sojourner.

"I'd love to," Sojourner says. "Just gotta get changed."

"Me too," I say. Fuck. Surely she's got better things to do. "Won't be long."

"We'll text you the address," Lisimaya says. "It's on Clinton. Leilani's meeting us there."

Awesome, I think.

We head to the change rooms.

"You don't have to come," I say. "Rosa can be kind of a bully."

"I want to. It's what friends do. Find out more about their friend's family so they can use it to embarrass them later."

"Great. Look, this won't be exactly typical. You know how I promised them I wouldn't spar?"

Sojourner nods.

"Well, I didn't tell them—"

"You lied?"

"Not directly. I didn't mention it . . . But it's the same thing. I know that. It's going to be a fucking awkward dinner."

Sojourner grins. "Now I really want to go. See how searing your folks' cold eye is."

"Perfect," I mutter. I turn towards the men's change room.

"Che," Sojourner calls out. "I won't go if you don't want me to."

"Really?"

"Sure."

I think about telling her not to but I can't. It's more time with Sojourner.

"Nah, it's fine. But you have to invite me to dinner with your family, and it better be nightmarish for you."

Sojourner laughs.

WHEN WE GET TO the restaurant it's packed. The floors and walls are tiled, amplifying the clatter of dishes, conversations, and the crack of heels against the floor. We have to squeeze past tables packed with diners and waiters toting huge trays. When we get to ours only two seats are empty: one on the adult side of the table and one on the kids'.

"This is Sojourner," I announce. "We train together. Rosa invited her."

Everyone says their hellos. Sojourner calls the adults *ma'am* and *sir*. They tell her to call them by their first names.

Sally nods to me, indicating the seat between her and David. *Great.* Leilani raises her eyebrows as if to say *bummer*.

Sojourner sits between Rosa and Leilani. My phone buzzes in my pocket.

Gene orders for us in Korean with Leilani and Maya chiming in. All the staff seem to know them.

"Is that the girl who took you to church?" Sally asks, lowering her voice. Even though she's next to me I have to lean closer to hear. "The one who's teaching Rosa about the Bible?"

"Yes." Across from me Leilani says something to Sojourner, looks across at me, then quarter raises her eyebrow. Sojourner laughs. My cheeks feel hot.

"She's very striking."

"A boxer has to be," I say. "Good at striking, I mean."

Sally doesn't laugh.

Seimone is seated on Rosa's other side and Maya next to her. Seimone's turned towards Rosa, shutting Maya off. Maya leans against Lisimaya, who has an arm around her.

Rosa and Seimone laugh when Gene asks them a question, and exchange a look.

Leilani and Sojourner are talking. I think I hear them say something about running, but it's so noisy I'm not sure. Sojourner shifts in her seat. Dinners like this are torture.

"How long have you been boxing, Che?" Gene asks. His voice is naturally loud.

"Since he was five, though it was supposed to be self-defence," David says. "Turned into kickboxing quickly, then boxing. What about you, Sojourner?"

The question has to be repeated before Sojourner hears.

"My Aunt Susan," she says, having to almost shout. "She's a trainer in Jersey. I learned to box along with my cousins. I was the only one who was into it."

"I learned from my dad," Gene says. "Lucky us, eh?"

Sojourner nods.

"Main thing I learned from boxing is that defence is always key." Gene chuckles. "Also never skip a meal. Man, was I hungry when I used to box."

"Yes," I say, exchanging a nod with Gene. I dig into the pickles and pancakes laid out in front of us.

Everyone's eating. Leilani's talking to Sojourner. Rosa and Seimone are giggling. No matter how much I strain I can't hear more than a word or two that any of them says.

Maya looks up and I smile, rolling my eyes in Rosa's direction. Maya returns the smile.

The adults talk business. Under the table I text Jason. —Shit has hit the fan. Parentals know I'm sparring. They're not happy.

As soon as we've emptied one plate they bring another. I'm grateful I can keep my head down and eat. Sally and David don't say anything to me.

I look across at Rosa. I'm pretty sure this is her doing. She's the one who suggested they drop in on me at the gym. Since when does my family not text first?

I watch Sojourner laughing with the girls. She includes Maya. Leilani is bent over her phone. I keep eating, glad to be left out of the conversations.

"Leilani," Gene booms. "No phones at the table."

Leilani doesn't look up. It's unlikely she didn't hear.

"No phones at the table, Lei," Gene repeats even louder.

This time she can't pretend not to hear him. "It's time sensitive, Dad. Has to be up by midnight."

"Midnight on a Friday night? The deadest time for a press release?"

"Fine." Leilani slides her phone onto her lap.

"We'll be home long before midnight," Gene says. "If it really is time sensitive."

The noise in the restaurant drops. The huge party next to us has finished and their large table is cleared and broken into smaller ones. Rosa asks Sojourner loudly, "Is Che your boyfriend?"

Sojourner laughs. "No, we're gym buddies."

Leilani arches an eyebrow. I wish I could say something funny that would crack the tension. I can't think of a thing.

"Oh," Rosa says, putting as much disappointment into her voice as she can. "Che's never had a girlfriend. I think you'd be perfect together."

"Er, thank you," Sojourner says. She gives me a look I hope is meant to be sympathetic rather than pitying. Her face isn't as easy to read as Leilani's.

Leilani's eyebrow stays up. I can see her repeating the conversation to Veronica and Elon. She'll probably make sure I'm there when she does it.

"Really?" Gene asks. "A good-looking boy like you?"

Lisimaya nudges him.

Sally asks Gene about a potential investor who's been invited to the party. I tune them out and hoe into the pork that lands on the table.

"What do you think, Che?" Sally asks.

I look up. "Of what?"

"We've invited your friend here, Sid, and her best friend—what's her name, Sid?"

"Jaime."

"We've invited them to come to the housewarming party as well as those friends of Leilani's you were out with the other night. What were their names?"

"Veronica and Elon," Leilani says, grinning.

"Sounds fantastic," I say.

SALLY, DAVID AND ROSA walk ahead of me on Clinton. Rosa chatters to them about Seimone: *Can she go to dance camp too?* There are lots of *Can I?*s and *Gimme*s. Neither of them try to talk to me, let alone deliver the lecture I'm expecting about my sparring. I guess that will happen at home.

It's much quieter than Second Avenue. The stores with their roller doors pulled down and padlocked look abandoned. Most of the doors are splattered with messy tags and more random graffiti. If it weren't for the bars and restaurants the street would look abandoned.

I pull out my phone. Texts from Leilani wanting to know why my parents were so grim and this, of course: —No girlfriend? Ever? That means our group is now the complete set. We've been missing a virgin for ages.

I quickly text back. —Fuck you. Also no girlfriend doesn't mean I'm a virgin.

—Are you a virgin?

—Wait. You included me in your group. I'm in! I feel so honoured. Do I get a tiara? Should I give a speech?

I've never been naked with a girl. I've kissed, and touched breasts and arses through clothes. Is that even second base? I'll have to look it up. I'm the only one who's ever touched my dick. Pretty pathetic.

The phone buzzes again. I pull it out.

Rosa drops back to walk beside me. "You'll fall over. Did you know it's against the law to walk and text here?"

I shoot her a look. "No, it's not."

"Yes, it is."

"That's ridiculous."

"No, it's not. Look, you almost tripped. What if there'd been a hole in the footpath?"

"There isn't a hole, and texting doesn't make my peripheral vision disappear."

"There are cameras everywhere so they can see when people are breaking laws and arrest you."

"For texting and walking?"

"Though some of the cameras are broken and they're not on every corner."

"How do you know that?"

Rosa shrugs. "I like knowing things. They might not have filmed you. This time."

"Why are you such a brat?"

"Because it's fun."

"Why did you make sure the parentals found out I was sparring?"

"You don't know I did," she says, confirming it. She looks both sly and smug. "It's fun having you be the bad one. I think you should stay the bad one. I'll be good from now on."

She looks up at me. It feels like she's waiting for me to ask why she told. I'm not going to.

I know why. Because she could.

"If I wanted to get you into trouble," Rosa says quietly as we cross to our block, "I could get you into worse trouble than this."

Once we're home I take my gym clothes to the laundry and put a load on. The parentals still haven't said anything.

I hear Rosa asking if she can have ice cream and the door of the parentals' office closing.

When I finish in the laundry Rosa is sitting at the kitchen island eating ice cream and leaning over her tablet. Playing chess, most likely, or plotting world destruction, or sitting conveniently close to the office so she can listen at the door when the parentals call me in. *If* they call me in. They might let me stew overnight.

I realise I have no idea what they'll do because I'm never in trouble.

I pour myself a glass of milk.

Rosa doesn't look up.

I walk over to the windows. In the apartments opposite the lights are either out or the blinds down. I can't spy on the people living opposite like Leilani and her sisters do. I sit down on a couch, pull out my phone. I text Natalie first —Am loving sparring. Thanks for the advice.

I text Jason again —Parentals found out I started sparring. Am so busted. How's with you?

To Nazeem —How're you doing in the land of love?

Lastly to Georgie I text —One of my friends here is really into fashion. You'd like her. She took me to this ridiculously expensive shop full of the kind of clothes I think you'd drool over.

I wish I could text Sojourner, but I don't have her number. I've been too chicken shit to ask. I could have asked tonight, but not in front of everyone else. At the gym Jaime's always around.

A reply comes through from Georgie —Cool. What's the boutique called?

—Dunno. It had a picture of a spool of thread on the door. It was weird. They keep the door locked. I guess you have to do that here. But you'd think a shop would want people to get in.

—That's Spool. OMG! You're describing Spool?! You're kidding! You can't have gone to Spool.

—Huh?

—Spool's only like the most exclusive boutique on the planet. The curator has to check you out online before they'll let you in and you have to make an appointment and you would not believe the people they haven't let in. Like famous, rich, whatever.

—Sounds mean.

—OMFG how did you get in?! What were you wearing? You weren't wearing tracky dacks, were you? Jesus, Che!

I don't tell her I was.

—Well, Leilani seemed to know everyone. She goes there a lot.

—Your friend's name is Leilani? As in Leilani McBrunight?! You can't be serious?! Holy fucking Jesus, Che! How do you know Leilani McBrunight!?

Sally comes out of the office. "Che?"

I turn the sound off on my phone and slide it into my pocket, follow her, and close their door behind me.

I haven't been in their office since they crammed it with their crap and turned it into the same messy but somehow organised place it is wherever we live. Their corkboard is covered in notes, a timeline. For their new business with the McBrunights probably. There's always a corkboard or whiteboard in their office. Always at least one timeline, sometimes many.

Offence is the best defence. Clichéd but sometimes true.

"I broke my promise," I say. "I sparred and I loved it and I want to keep doing it."

Both Sally and David try to break in, but I keep talking.

"Everything I've been studying, the drills, it makes sense now. When you drop your hands, you leave yourself open. When your chin's up, likewise. When you move backwards in a straight line, you get stuck against the ropes.

"Not sparring is like learning a language by studying the alphabet, the rules of grammar, how to spell, but not being allowed to say anything. I can't not spar. It was an unfair promise," I say, speaking even louder to drown out David.

"I always do everything you ask. I kept this promise for years! But I couldn't anymore. Who knows when I'll stop growing? It wasn't fair of you to make me make that promise."

I sit down. Sally sits beside me and takes my right hand in hers. "Are you finished?"

I nod, leaning back and closing my eyes.

Sally lets go of my hand. "You lied, Che."

I start to respond but David holds up his hand like it has the power to stop speech. "We let you have your say."

I don't remember him using his let's-all-be-calm voice on me. On Rosa, yes. Occasionally on Sally. On every other member of his family, especially Uncle Saul, but never me.

"You lied to us, Che," Sally continues. "You promised you wouldn't spar. You sparred without telling us. It doesn't matter if you didn't directly say words that were untrue. You broke your promise, then hid it from us. Lying by omission is still lying."

I can't help but think of how Rosa agrees with her.

"Che, if there's one thing I've always been certain about in this family—other than how much we love each other—it's that we don't lie. But now you have."

I don't know what to say. I'm not going to point out that Rosa isn't capable of loving anyone. Neither of Sally's certainties are certain. "I was going to tell you. I planned to tonight, but then you showed up at my gym. Why didn't you text first?"

Neither of them answer my question.

"Now I don't trust you," Sally says.

I wait for them to tell me what my punishment is. They don't. David turns to his computer, Sally to her phone.

"That's it? I'm dismissed?"

"This isn't the army, Che. It's a family."

"We're thinking about how to punish you," David says. "We're shocked. You've never lied to us. You've never broken a promise."

I get up, walk to the door. As I close it behind me I think I hear Sally crying. I hate that I made her cry. I go upstairs and lie down. Rosa says something as I go up the stairs, but mercifully I don't hear it.

This one thing? And now they don't trust me.

I glance at my phone. There are a tonne of messages. Georgie squealing about Leilani, Jason sympathising and sharing parental woes, Nazeem telling me to fuck off, Natalie congratulating me.

I don't know what to say to any of them.

To distract myself I google Leilani to see what Georgie is going on about.

Oh.

Leilani is kind of famous.

There are thousands of photos of her at fashion shows. She started her own fashion website for teens when she was twelve, which was mostly her blogging about clothes and music and the fashion industry and politics. Now it's a huge online magazine with lots of other writers and an insane number of people reading it. It's called Neophyte, like Elon said, and her fans are called Neos. She's interviewed some of the most famous women in the world.

Of course they know her at that fancy clothes shop.

Why didn't Leilani mention that she's famous?

Though what would she say? *Oh, by the way, I'm a big deal?* I can't quite believe it. From what I'm reading she could be rich in her own right. At the age of seventeen. Jesus.

It makes me feel a lot better about her buying those clothes for me. Though I have no idea why. It's still being controlling, isn't it?

I text Georgie. —Just looked up Leilani. I had no idea. Woah.

I get out of bed. Go through some katas, focus on moving fluidly, correct form over speed. I wear my body out, fall into bed, sleep.

When I wake the sun is coming up and Rosa is curled up in a ball on my bedroom floor.

Her face is relaxed, her mouth a little open. She looks like the baby she once was, the one whose tiny fingers curled around mine, who smiled up at me. It's hard to believe this is a child with no heart.

She opens her eyes and smiles as if she is pleased to see me. For a second I believe it.

"Still studying sleep, are you?"

"I wanted to make sure we're friends."

"I'm the only one who understands you," I say, knowing how slim her understanding of sarcasm is. "How can we not be friends?"

CHAPTER TWENTY-ONE

Our weekly Sunday brunch with the McBrunights is in their mansion. Their giant table is spread with enough food to feed twice our number. I pile my plate with salmon and tiny quiches and sausage.

I wish Leilani was here but she's too busy with Neophyte. The parentals and Gene and Lisimaya talk business. Rosa and Seimone whisper to each other. Which leaves me and Maya.

"I didn't know Leilani was famous."

Maya screws up her nose and goes cross-eyed. "She's not *famous* famous. She's a little bit clothes famous."

"Do people stop her in the street and ask for her autograph?"

Maya shakes her head. "Not really. Once a girl wanted a selfie with her. We were at the bodega on the corner. Lei-Lei did a duckface." She lowers her chin and purses her lips, making her eyes big.

I pull out my phone and take a photo of her, then we do a double duckface selfie.

"Let me see," Maya says and we look at the photo. Our eyes are twice their normal size and our lips ditto. We both laugh.

"I'm sending it to Leilani."

"Send it to me too," Maya says, taking my phone and adding her number. She hands it back and I add her duckface to her contact.

"Are you in trouble?" Maya asks quietly. Leilani must have told her.

I nod. "They're disappointed in me and don't trust me anymore."

Maya's eyes cut to Rosa. "Do they trust her?"

"She's ten. Apparently ten-year-old-ness excuses everything."

Maya snorts. "I'm eleven. Are they making you quit boxing? Rosa says when she does something bad they make her write essays then don't read them. She says she cut and pasted the same sentence over and over in the middle of her last essay to see if they'd notice, but they didn't."

"Sounds like something she'd do. They haven't said no more gym."

"If they did, would you stop?"

I shake my head.

"I don't see what the big deal is. It's exercise! I'd like to learn boxing," Maya says. "Looks like fun."

"It is. What about tennis, though? Don't you do that practically every day?"

Maya nods. "I'm going to tennis camp too. Two whole weeks!"

"Can we be excused?" Seimone asks. "Rosa wants to teach me a chess problem."

"You'll show it to me later?" Gene asks.

They agree that they will.

"I hate chess," Maya says when they're gone.

"Me, too. David tried to teach me, but ugh. Rosa's been playing since she was four."

"Seimone never used to like it."

"I'm sorry. About Rosa and Seimone."

"Me too," Maya says.

WE'RE WALKING THROUGH TOMPKINS Square Park, Sally talking about how much greener it is now than when we first arrived, how much fatter the squirrels are looking. Some of the trees are still in blossom, but most have replaced their flowers with green leaves. May in New York City has been a lot less miserable than April.

"Isn't that Sid?" Rosa asks, waving.

It is. She's walking towards us wearing her red-tulip dress. She's with her mom, Diandra, who's in a wheelchair being pushed by another woman. I assume she's Sojourner's other mother.

Sojourner returns the wave, smiles.

She looks beautiful. That's the dress she was wearing then *not* wearing in my dream. I blush, scared that somehow she'll know from looking at me what I dreamed about her.

"Your face is red," Rosa says loudly. "Not just your nose."

"Yes," I say softly. "It's called acne."

"No, redder than usual. Like you're embarrassed."

"Well, I wasn't, but I am now that you've drawn everyone's attention to the acne on my face."

"As if they wouldn't notice. Especially when you're blushing," Rosa says. "Hello, Sid!" She gives Sojourner a huge hug.

"Hi," I say. "Hello, Diandra." I bend to shake Diandra's hand. "Funny running into you here."

"Not really. This is where everyone runs into each other. The very heart of the neighbourhood. Sid, honey," Diandra says, smiling at me and Rosa, "are you going to introduce us?"

I blush harder. I should have started the introductions.

"These are my moms," Sojourner says. "Diandra and Elisabeta Davis. This is Che—"

"Oh," Elisabeta says. "You're from Sid's gym. The Australian boy. She told us about you."

My face burns.

"Nice to meet you," I say, shaking Elisabeta's hand. "These are my parents, Sally Taylor and David Klein, and my sister Rosa."

"Isn't she a little cherub?" It isn't clear from Diandra's tone whether that's a good thing. "Are those curls for real?"

Rosa nods. She's pretending to be shy. Why she's bothering after loudly drawing attention to my hideous skin I've no idea.

There are handshakes all round. Rosa eases herself next to Sojourner and starts whispering.

"We're on our way home from church," Diandra says. "Over on Second Avenue. Che joined us recently for the evening service. Have you found a church you like? I know you only just moved here. Why not join us? We're open to all faiths."

Elisabeta says something softly that sounds like, "Now, Dee."

"We don't go to church," David says. "We're not Christian."

"Oh," Diandra says. "What faith are you? We have some non-Christians at our services: Jews, Muslims, Buddhists."

"Secular humanist," Sally says.

"Hmmm," Diandra says. "Well, those are prettier words than *atheist*."

"Mom," Sojourner says.

I can't imagine how this could be more awkward. I look at Rosa, waiting for her to announce that *God is dead* or *Only idiots believe in God*, which neither Sally nor David has ever said. Instead she whispers in Sojourner's ear again.

"We all find our own way in the darkness," Diandra says. "There are as many atheists walking in the light as believers. They just don't know it."

Sally doesn't say anything.

"How do you feel about your boy fighting?" Diandra asks.

"Mom! I told you how Che's parents feel!"

"That's why I'm asking. I want them to know they're not the only ones conflicted. Boxing isn't a regular sport. It's not like you're running track or basketball—"

"Yes, Mom, because basketball is so injury-free and non-violent."

"Are you sassing me, Sid?"

"I'm disagreeing with you."

Diandra shakes her head. "Yes, you are, and now you're letting me say my piece." She reaches up to touch Sally's hand and draw it between hers. "We weren't sure about Sid learning to box. Violence is wrong. Standing in a ring with a referee or your trainer doesn't make it any less wrong."

Sally nods.

"But my girl loves boxing and it keeps her healthy and strong. Neither of us have the heart to stop her. They tell us she's very good."

"Sojourner is," I blurt. "Sid, I mean." I turn to her. "You're amazing." *God.* There go my cheeks again. Neck too.

"Her trainer thinks so too, Che. But fighting. Well, I'm proud of her and I want her to be happy, but I can't help wishing it was something else."

"Yes," David says. "There's something so brutal about it. We watched Che in the ring last night. It was ugly."

He sounds exactly like Sally. I glare at him, itching to point out his hypocrisy. When he was my age he was expelled from his school for breaking another student's jaw. How do you hit hard enough to break a *jaw*? I've never broken anyone's anything.

"Yes," Sally says. "Che promised us he wouldn't spar until he stopped growing. Last night we discovered he's been lying to us."

Diandra nods her head and looks sympathetic. I think I'll die a million deaths as I hope to God—the God I don't believe in—that Sojourner isn't listening to my humiliation, caught as she is in the web of Rosa's sticky whispers.

But, no, she turns her head.

"There's nothing wrong with sparring," she says.

"Sojourner," Diandra says. "This is not your business. It's between Che and his parents."

"It is my business, Mom. His parents don't understand what they were asking." She turns to Sally and David and says almost apologetically, "Che wasn't getting anywhere, you see. He's got talent and it wasn't being used. Sparring's not dangerous. We wear padded headgear. It's safer than getting in a car!"

"Sojourner Ida Davis!"

Sojourner shakes her head but she doesn't say anything else. Sally's staring at her.

"I understand you feel passionately," David says. "But we have to protect our child."

"I apologise for my daughter," Diandra says. "She has strong opinions."

"No need to apologise. Our children are not our possessions," Sally says, and I suppress the urge to snort. "Of course they'll disagree with us and disobey if they think we are unjust. It's not easy being a child or a parent."

"Amen," Diandra says.

"How did you reconcile yourself to Sojourner boxing?"

"They haven't," Sojourner says. She squeezes Diandra's shoulder and kisses Elisabeta's cheek.

"No, we have not. But what can we do? I pray. I remember that the Good Lord rewards love and patience and understanding. As you say, our children's paths are not our paths."

"Thank you," Sally says. She leans down and takes Diandra's hand. "I'm glad to talk to someone who understands."

"You're welcome. You'll find the right thing to do. I'm sure of it."

"Are the two of you doing anything tomorrow night? We're having a party. A housewarming party. We'd love it if you could join us. Sojourner's already said she'd come."

"A Monday night?"

"I know it's a bit odd, but that was the only night that worked for some dear friends of ours and we didn't want to put off having the party for much longer."

"Elisabeta?"

Sojourner's quiet mama nods.

"We'd love to," Diandra says.

They swap numbers and addresses and discuss wheelchair accessibility. Great, the parentals have Sojourner's parents' numbers before I have Sojourner's.

"I don't have your number," Sojourner says and I grin. "Jaime and I run together. Want to join us?"

I nod.

Sojourner and I swap numbers as Rosa watches.

"You ready for Sunday school?" Sojourner asks.

Rosa nods.

Rosa goes with Sojourner and her moms, turning to smile at me, to let me know that she's with Sojourner and I'm stuck with Sally and David. I hope there are no stairs where they're going. Not that I'm seriously worried Rosa would do that. I resist the urge to run after them.

"It's a beautiful day," Sally says.

It's true: the sun's out, it's warm, people are dressed as if it's already summer, but it's not the kind of thing Sally usually says. It's hard to appreciate it when I can see her deciding what to say to me. Sally does not have a poker face.

We walk past where the chess is being played. There's a game at every table. A few men are crowded watching one table. As we pass I see that it's Isaiah taking on another challenger. How much money does he make from chess? Judging from his clothes, not a lot. All the chess players are men. Their audience too. How did Rosa waltz in and start playing? I couldn't have done that at ten. Or now. What's it like having no fear?

"We're not going to punish you," David says.

"I can keep sparring?"

Sally nods. "We can't stop you, can we?"

They *did* stop me. If this is my punishment I should have disobeyed sooner.

"It scares me that you're violent. You could kill someone if you lost your temper." She glances at David, but he doesn't say anything.

Outside of boxing, I have never hit anyone. I've never even come close. Who does Sally think I am?

"Whose idea was it for me to join you for dinner? You know I spend my evenings at the gym. Why didn't you text?"

"Rosa was keen that you join us and we were only a couple of blocks away."

"I thought so. She wanted you to catch me sparring."

"Come on, Che," Sally says. "Rosa didn't *know* you were sparring. This is not about her, this is about you."

"Every time I try to talk about Rosa you change the subject. *You* don't want to talk about her. You don't want to recognise there's something deeply wrong with her."

"Seriously, Che? Deeply wrong? We know she had developmental issues. Yes, she can be socially awkward. She's ten years old. She's behaving like a ten-year-old. Stop seeing—"

"I know how old my sister is."

"Rosa worships you," Sally says. She's about to cry. "Do you know how long she saved up the money to buy your birthday present?"

"Do you know how Apinya's guinea pig died? Rosa—"

David puts up his hand. I'm close to screaming at them both. But I can't, can I? That would be violent.

"Che," David says in his let's-be-calm voice. "I know you didn't want to come here. We know you'd rather be in Sydney. But acting out like this isn't helping anyone, least of all yourself."

"I'm not acting out! I was telling you what Rosa did in—"

The hand goes up again. I have a strong urge to punch it.

"How can we trust you when you won't accept responsibility? When you try to blame Rosa for everything?"

I stare at Sally. I've never blamed Rosa for anything she didn't do, let alone for *everything*.

"I give up," I say. "One day you're going to see what Rosa is and you're going to wish you'd listened to me. I'm going to the gym."

"Che!" Sally says.

"No, let him," I hear David say as I stride away angrier than I've ever been. They're never going to listen to me.

I WORK OUT AS hard as I can, not caring that it's my day off, that I should be giving my muscles a rest. It's three hours before the anger is out of my system, before I can think about the parentals, especially Sally, without wanting to destroy every punching bag in the gym.

I can't go back there. I'll get angry again. I can't stand to see either of them. Or Rosa. Bloody Rosa, who is with Sojourner. Would she think it weird if I texted her to see if Rosa's behaving herself? Probably.

I pull my phone out. There are a million texts. None from Sojourner. But several from Rosa.

—I asked the smartest questions. Again. Sid likes me best now.

I text the parentals. —I'll come home when I'm less— I hesitate: I can't type *angry* because Sally thinks I'm a rage monster —upset.

I sit on the bench outside the change room staring at Sojourner's number. I could ask her out. In a friend way. We could hang out. Maybe if I suggest Jaime join us?

I start to type —Wanna see a movie? I stop. I don't want to see a movie. I could ask if she wants to go for a run. She's already suggested that. I've been wanting to do the track as far around the island as you can go.

—What are you doing?

God. That's shit.

—Thinking of going for a run, I add. —Wanna join me? Jaime too?

Ugh. I put my phone in my pocket and decide against showering. I go to the mirrors and shadow box, focusing on defence, bobbing, weaving, ducking, getting out of the way of my imaginary foe who is ten centimetres taller than me.

My phone does not buzz.

I get on the treadmill, run for twenty minutes. Towel myself down. Check my phone. Nothing. It's almost half an hour since I texted Sojourner. I do not want to go home. I do not want to work out anymore. I want to see someone I'm not related to.

I text Leilani. —What are you doing?

Then I shower, change and check my phone.

—It's supposed to be What are you wearing? Also, eww, don't sext me.

—Funny. I wish to rebel against my parents by not going home. Can you assist me in my rebellion?

—I'm heading to a private showing with a new designer, who you won't have heard of since you haven't heard of any of the established designers. I doubt you're dressed for it.

—I'll have you know my tracky dacks and T-shirt are clean.

—You don't get extra points for your hideous attire being unstained.

—I didn't say it wasn't stained. I said it was clean.

—I communicate with you why exactly?

—My charm. Showing of what?

—Droll. Clothes. What else?

I think about sending her a list. Turnips? Wallaroos? Dandruff?

—What's up with your olds, Che? Why are they pissed? Does your virginity embarrass them?

—Funny. I promised I wouldn't spar. Then they busted me sparring.

—Ah.

—Yup.

—At least you didn't kill a man in Reno.

—They're pretty sure that's next.

—Have they met you?

—Doubtful.

—Your punishment is?

—They don't trust me anymore.

—That's their terrible punishment? I'm underwhelmed. I thought they'd whip you or something.

—Violence is wrong, Leilani.

A text from Rosa:

—They're cranky with you. I told them that you're mostly good and they shouldn't be so mad. Did you know that Sid is scared of heights?

CHAPTER TWENTY-TWO

I decide to do that run even without Sojourner, and head to the East River Parkway. It's what Georgie calls the golden hour, with long, soft shadows. Georgie's been bugging me for photos. I stop to photograph the side of an old building. It's the kind of thing she would appreciate. The building next to it has been demolished, but somehow the remaining building has a metal fire escape dangling from its side, leading to nowhere. I send it to Georgie. She dreams of living in this city.

I take more photos for her, including one of a giant inflatable rat outside a clothing store. I should ask Leilani what that's about. I kind of like the randomness of it.

My phone pings. I have the sound up loud, hoping to hear from Sojourner. Instead there's another text from Rosa.

—You better come home. They're getting crankier.

I'm tempted to text her back. But that'll only bring a cascade of even more annoying texts.

Then the parentals:

—When are you coming home?

—I'm not sure. Going for a run.

—Let us know.

—Ok.

Rosa texts again:

—Did you know fear of heights has a fancy name? Vertigo.

My phone pings again. Rosa is succeeding in getting to me. I'm tempted not to look.

—You want to run? Sojourner texts. —I gotta get out. Feeling too restless to study.

—Sure.

WE MEET ON THE park side of the Sixth Street pedestrian bridge over the FDR Drive. Sojourner takes off before I have a chance to say hi.

"So who's shitting you?" I ask as I catch up with her.

She shoots me a sidelong look. "Who's shitting on me?"

"Who in your life is annoying you at this time?"

"Do all Australians talk as weird as you?"

"Every single one."

She grins. "Mom. Mama too. They've been at me for disrespecting your parents."

"Sorry."

"Not your fault."

"You were defending me."

"Nah. Yeah. Some. Mostly what I said was aimed at my moms. Not that I thought they'd listen. Adults don't. They're *always* right."

I laugh. "So fuckin' true. Whatcha gunna do?"

"If I said that in front of my moms they would wash my mouth out with soap."

"Metaphorically?"

"*Actually*. I haven't used a swear in front of them since I was five years old."

"They sound tough."

"Mom more than Mama. Though it's not like I'd ever sass Mama either. Mama's more quiet disappointment. Sometimes that's worse."

That I understand. "You don't argue with them?"

Sojourner laughs. "All the time. But, you know, *respectfully*."

"Jesus. How do you manage that?"

Sojourner comes to a dead stop. I overrun and have to walk back to her.

"Che, don't ever *ever* blaspheme in front of my moms. I'm serious. They won't think much of you if you say *any* swear. But if you use the Lord's name in vain they will be done with you. Done."

"Because I said *Jesus*?"

Sojourner nods. "Mom's ordained. You heard her preach. She takes blasphemy seriously."

I don't know what to say. *Jesus* and *God* are what I say when I'm trying *not* to swear in front of someone who might be offended. I've always thought of them as the least offensive swear words. Along with *damn* and *blast* and *crap* and *bother*.

"You don't swear, do you?" I realise I haven't heard her say so much as *crap* since we met.

She shakes her head and starts running again.

I catch up. "I've never met anyone who doesn't swear."

"Really?"

I try to think of someone. Even my grandmothers swear. "Really. Australians must swear a lot, I guess. I never thought about it."

"Seems like. Not in front of my moms okay?"

"I'll try," I say.

"Don't blaspheme in front of them. Seriously."

"I won't."

"What about your little sister? I haven't heard her swear."

"She swears." I itch to ask her about Rosa at Bible study, but I'm also desperate not to. Rosa eats up too much of my life.

"Wow. You Australians are potty-mouthed monsters."

She laughs and runs a little faster. I keep pace.

We run without saying anything, heading north. The path narrows. The park and the river disappear and we're running in between buildings and highways with only room for two abreast. We have to fall in behind or in front of each other to let the occasional other joggers pass.

I can hear her every breath. I can smell her sweat.

I want to kiss her.

I've wanted to kiss other girls. I *have* kissed other girls.

I've never wanted to kiss anyone as much as I want to kiss Sojourner.

Her mouth. I try hard not to stare. The upper lip and bottom lip are almost the same thickness, with the bottom one only slightly fuller. The indentation of her upper lip makes me want to place my finger there, like that's what the dent is shaped for. Sweat is forming there. I think of licking it away, running my tongue along her lips, sliding my tongue inside her mouth.

I lose my footing on nothing.

"Fuck!"

I almost fall before I stutter-step my way into stride.

Sojourner turns. "You okay?"

I nod, picking up my pace.

"Track runs out fairly soon."

"It does?" I'm blushing because I was thinking about her mouth. She can't tell, I'm sure. I'm sweating. It's dark. The Manhattan lights are a strange orange colour.

"We can turn around. Go all the way south then around to the Hudson."

"Sure," I say.

We turn.

"I'm not ready to face my moms."

"I'm not ready for the parentals."

"*That's* what you call them? Is that an Australian thing?"

"Nah. It's a me-and-Rosa thing."

"You two close?"

"I guess." I do not want to talk about Rosa. "You don't have any sisters or brothers?"

"Nope. Just millions of cousins."

"Me too. Well, not millions. But a bunch."

We keep running. Feet hitting the ground in unison. We're soon beside the East River again.

"It's a lot more fun running with someone. I don't love running."

Sojourner laughs. "Me either. But Dido insists. Good for cardio. Good for making me last more than three rounds in the ring."

"I guess, but Jesus it's boring."

"Why don't you practise not blaspheming in front of my moms by not blaspheming in front of me?"

"Fuck. Sorry."

She laughs. "Let's see how long you can go without swearing." She looks at her watch.

"Are you timing me?"

"Of course."

"Shall we make it a bet?"

"Wow. So Australians swear too much and they gamble. No wonder you're not a Christian!"

"The Bible doesn't say anything about gambling."

"How do you know that?"

"I've read the Bible. Just because I don't believe it doesn't mean I haven't read it. I've read the Koran too."

"You're full of surprises."

"I like to know things."

"The Bible *does* condemn love of money. Gambling is about loving money. So it indirectly condemns gambling."

"But gambling's not a recent invention. It could have been on the forbidden list. Must not have been considered that bad."

"Maybe. It sure does ruin lives."

"I wasn't going to suggest a money bet."

She runs faster. I keep up with her, but I'm feeling it.

"You trying to lose me?"

She increases her pace again. I run faster, overtaking her.

We continue chasing and overtaking each other until we're on the other side of the island, running beside the Hudson River. It's a dark expanse reflecting more lights than the East River. My legs burn, my lungs too, but I'm buggered if I'll stop first.

There are more people to dodge on this side. Fewer runners and more people hanging out. There are long piers for them to hang out on. I prefer the darker, quieter east side.

I'm panting. I'm sure she is too. I can't hear over my own ragged breathing. I don't know how far north the track goes on this side.

I let Sojourner set the pace. She hasn't sped up for at least two piers now. I think she's slowing. I haven't run like this in ages.

"Sid! Sid!"

Sojourner doesn't slow.

A good-looking black guy runs up beside us. "Sid!" he shouts again. He touches her shoulder.

Sojourner stops. So do I, leaning forward, resting my hands on my thighs, breathing hard.

"You got a fight coming up or something? Pretty late to be out running. Who's the white boy?"

Sojourner's bent over too. She puts up her hand so he'll give her a second.

I pull my water bottle out of my pack, take a swig, hand it to Sojourner.

I stand up, offer my fist. "I'm Che."

He touches his knuckles to mine briefly. He's frowning. It doesn't make him less handsome. Or less tall. There isn't a single blemish on his face.

"He's—" Sojourner begins, handing me back my water bottle.

"We—"

We both stop, look at each other. I have an urge to laugh, but I have no idea who this guy is.

"Che's a friend," Sojourner says. "This is my ex, Daniel."

Oh, I think.

"Pleased to meet you, Daniel."

"Likewise," he says, sounding no more pleased than I am. He jerks his thumb behind him. "Friends're back there. Just wanted to see if you're okay."

"I am."

"You look good," he says. "Sweaty, but good."

"Sweat is good. You look healthy too."

"It's great to see you, Sid. I, ah . . ." He trails off and shoots another look at me, like he's willing me to step back, but Sojourner doesn't look comfortable.

I stand my ground, drink more water. If Sojourner asks me to give them space I will.

"Tell your moms I said hi. Jaime too."

"Will do."

He walks backwards a few steps, eyes on Sojourner, gives a half wave, not bumping into anyone or tripping over. He shoots me another glare before finally turning and walking away.

I hand Sojourner the water. My legs ache, and my feet. I need a massage, a sauna, and a bath.

Sojourner takes a giant swig. "You up for another race?"

I stare at her. I'm pretty sure my eyes are popping.

She punches my shoulder. "Kidding! I'm beat. Kinda hungry too."

"I'm starving."

We walk and drip sweat and empty the water bottle. I wonder how long she went out with Daniel and why they broke up. Seems like she broke up with him, but I could be reading that wrong. He definitely has feelings. Why does he have to be so good-looking *and* taller than me?

He would look good walking beside Sojourner in a way I never will. They fit together. Both beautiful. But I'm here and he's not. I can smell her sweat and he can't. The smell of Sojourner is making my brain melt, not his.

It makes everything melt.

"There's a decent diner a few blocks in."

I nod.

"You're paying, rich boy."

"Rich boy? I wish."

She looks at me sideways but doesn't say anything.

I'll have to use Papa's credit card. The parentals haven't given me any more cash. I'll have to explain to Papa. I wouldn't put it past him to cancel the credit card if he thinks I'm misusing it.

We cross the highway.

I try not to think about how Sojourner makes me feel. I'm grateful when we reach the diner. I order my first American hamburger: a bacon cheeseburger with a ridiculous amount of toppings, a large side of fries, and a malted milkshake. I want carbs and proteins and lots of them.

Maybe food will make me stop thinking about Sojourner's lips, about her skin, about how amazing she smells.

Sojourner orders as much food as me. "Gotta enjoy it while I can. Cutting starts next week. It's the worst."

"Can be dangerous too." Sally sends me every article she finds that outlines the many dangers of fighting. There are many on how dangerous rapid weight loss is. No amount of my telling her that I don't want to be a fighter gets through to her. If I'm not a fighter I'll never have to cut to make the right weight division.

"Yes, Daddy. I train with Dido. I don't cut recklessly."

"Uh huh." I'm not sure how you can cut without being reckless. Most of our weight is water. The main thing fighters do is not drink water, which is reckless.

The milkshakes come first. Mine tastes like chocolate. I thought *malted* would be more exotic.

Sojourner sips and laughs. "You're really not going to ask about Daniel, are you?"

I blush. "I didn't want to pry."

"Sure you do."

"Well, yeah, but I don't know you that well and it's not my business. If you want to tell me you will."

"He broke up with me. He was starting college. I was in high school. It was going to be long distance." She shrugs. "But then he tried to get back with me over Christmas and it turns out he has a college girlfriend. I wasn't pleased. Hadn't seen him since, till tonight. He's a jerk."

"Does *jerk* count as swearing? 'Cause if so you just swore."

She takes a half-hearted swipe at me. Her stomach growls loudly. Mine echoes hers.

"Doesn't that mean you lost the bet, Soj—Sid?"

"*Jerk* is not swearing. I did not lose the bet. We did not have a bet."

"Noted. I'm allowed to say *jerk*. We do have a bet. We just didn't say what we were betting."

Our hamburgers are placed in front of us.

We hoe in. Mine's great. About halfway through I slow down, eating a fry in two bites instead of one.

"So, why do you always go to call me Sojourner, not Sid?"

"I like it," I mumble.

"What?"

"I like your name. Sojourner. I like the sound of it. It's how I think of you." I take a bite of my burger.

"I like the way you say it."

"Thanks."

"It's your accent, makes everything sound cuter."

"You think I'm cute?"

"I think your *accent* is cute."

"So I don't have to call you Sid?"

She nods. "You can call me Sojourner. But not in front of Jaime. I'll never hear the end of it."

We walk home.

"How much trouble are you going to be in?" I ask as we cross Lafayette Street and I recognise where we are.

"No more than I was already in. I told them I'd be out late. I told them I was running with you. They trust me. Even when they're mad. They'd tell me if they wanted me home."

I flinch a little when she says *they trust me.*

"What?"

"Mine say they don't trust me. Because of sparring. I've never broken a promise to them before."

"Thought so. I knew it cost you to go against them. I'm sorry they don't see that."

"You and me both. They want me to be like them. Or rather, *not* like them. My dad was wild when he was young. He broke a guy's jaw once."

Beside me, Sojourner tenses. I wonder if I've hit on a sore point. She's never mentioned her dad. I'd assumed there wasn't one.

I look up. "What?"

"Nothing," she says softly. "Don't look."

I look, of course. Two guys in leather jackets with a million tats walk towards us.

If they say one word to Sojourner I am going to say something. Three police officers overtake them. One looks at me. I nod. He nods in return.

Sojourner lets out a breath.

I wonder if those guys would have said something if I wasn't there. I shouldn't be relieved that I'm not a girl, but I am.

At Tompkins Square Park Sojourner starts to walk around it rather than through.

"Is it closed?" The gate is open and lots of people are walking through.

"Kind of. Cops lock it around midnight, so it's best to walk around rather than have to argue our way out if the gates are locked."

It's after midnight. The lights are still on in the park, but I follow Sojourner. "Seems weird not walking through."

"Cause we keep running into each other there?"

I smile. I think of it as our park.

"It's the centre of the neighbourhood. Everyone walks through, hangs out here. Did you know there was a riot here in the old days?"

I didn't.

"My mom says the new rich residents put up their own signs saying the park was closed at midnight when it wasn't. They didn't like people sleeping in there. The old neighbourhood fought back. Mom included. She was a kid. They lost. Now there's way more rich people than poor."

Near the gate we pass a group of people sitting on a blanket inside. One of them strums a guitar. I try to imagine a riot. I can't.

"Mom's always talking about how different it used to be. She can't make up her mind about whether it was worse back then or better. It changes by the minute."

"You've lived here all your life?"

"I was born here. Mom was too. Never lived anywhere else."

I try to imagine that. I can't.

"I like how alive this city is." Some of the restaurants and all of the bars we pass are full. It's a lot like Bangkok that way. We pass other couples. Or, rather, couples. It's not like Sojourner and I are a couple.

"City that never sleeps." Sojourner screws up her face at the cliché. "Though that just means Manhattan. Staten Island and Queens are sound asleep right now."

"Nothing can stay awake all the time." A tall man with a tiny dog passes us. "Though I've never seen so many people walking their dogs this late at night."

"Guess he can't afford a dog walker." Sojourner slows. "This is it."

The front of her building doesn't look much different than the other buildings on the block, or on my block for that matter. It's just narrower: brown brick, single-fronted, with a hardware store at the bottom and a door with four buzzers.

"Night, Che."

"Night," I mumble. Keeping my eyes open hurts, but I don't want to go. I reach out my hand to touch hers, unthinking, and am about to pull away, but Sojourner takes it in hers, squeezes lightly. I feel it everywhere. She hasn't let go. I don't either.

She leans forward, kisses me lightly on the lips, lets go of my hand, pulls out her keys, opens the door, looks back at me.

"You didn't swear," she says. Then she's up the stairs, the door clicking locked behind her before I can respond.

I stand there with my lips buzzing, wishing I'd slipped a hand around her waist, pulled her to me, kissed her back. Instead I almost forgot how to breathe.

WHEN I GET HOME I'm exhausted. I don't shower or change out of my sweats. I fall into bed, thinking about Sojourner, touching my lips where hers were. That kiss didn't have anything to do with God or Jesus. If I weren't exhausted I'd masturbate.

Instead I pass out wanting her.

I wake to the feeling that someone is in my room. I open my eyes a sliver.

Rosa, of course. She's bent over my phone.

I close my eyes. I'm so tired. I don't want to deal with Rosa. But what if she's texting Sojourner something?

I don't want to confront her. I don't want to hear what she's thinking. I don't want her to tell me I'm the only one who understands her. I don't want to know what's going on in that empathy-free brain of hers.

"Rosa," I say, sitting up. "What are you doing?"

"Nothing." She doesn't even look guilty.

"What are you doing in my room with my phone?"

Rosa puts the phone down. She shrugs.

"Rosa?"

"I was bored and you weren't awake."

"So you decided to break into my phone?"

"It's not broken. See?"

She hands it to me. It's almost four in the morning. I would give anything to be asleep.

"How did you get into my phone?"

"It's the same code as your ATM card."

"How do you know that?"

She shrugs again. "I watch."

"Don't!"

"I wanted to know if you were mad at me."

"I'm always mad at you. Take it as read."

Rosa sits on the bed next to me. "But you're my best friend."

"I thought Sid was your best friend."

She doesn't notice the sarcasm. "You'll always be my best friend. I only want to be friends with Sid because you like her. I want you to like me best."

I check my messages, my sent emails. I can't find any sign that she's done anything. Just spying. Just spying?

God. My head hurts.

"You don't talk to me anymore," Rosa says without a trace of petulance.

"We talk all the time."

"But you don't tell me what you're feeling."

"Because you don't care what anyone's feeling."

"I do. I will. I'm learning how. I've been asking Seimone questions and listening to her answers. I asked Sojourner if she likes you. She said she did. Though I could already tell. See? I'm learning about people. I told her you're the best brother in the world."

"Great."

"If Sid were gone, would you like me best again?"

"What do you mean, *if Sid were gone?*"

"I told Sid you might learn to love God if she explained God to you the way she explains God to me."

"So you believe in God now, do you?"

"No. Don't be silly, Che. God's like Santa Claus. But she wants me to believe, so I'm being how she wants me to be. That's what normal people do. I'm being normal. Like you want me to be."

Her logic is so twisted I don't know where to start.

"I'm changing my passcodes. You need to stay out of my phone and out of my room." And out of my head.

"You know I'll figure out what your new one is. David taught me how."

I groan. David is way too smart with computers and way too fond of teaching Rosa what he knows. Just because David doesn't use his knowledge for evil, it doesn't occur to him that she will.

"Did David tell you it was okay to break into other people's phones?"

She nods solemnly.

"Rosa! David would never say that."

"Yes, he would. David says all sorts of things. Did you know he has an escape kit?"

"A what?"

"A kit with the things he needs if he has to leave a country in a hurry."

I shake my head. "Why would you even say that? Stop lying."

Rosa shakes her head. "I told you I can't promise that. Lying's too useful. Besides, you lie. You said your nose was fine when it wasn't. You said you weren't sparring when you were."

"Can you promise not to break into my phone?"

"Okay."

"Say it."

"I promise not to break into your phone."

"Or anyone else's."

Now it's Rosa's turn to groan. "Or anyone else's."

"Go to bed."

"I'm not sleepy."

"Go and be not sleepy in your own room. I am sleepy." I point at the door.

Rosa pouts, then leaves. I try to stop thinking about what she said about Sojourner being gone.

In the morning I'll put a lock on my door.

CHAPTER TWENTY-THREE

At breakfast the parentals and I barely exchange words. So much for this being a loving, open, communicative family. Rosa smirks.

It's like they're conspiring to wipe last night with Sojourner from my mind. It won't work. My lips buzz faintly. Sojourner kissed me.

I don't talk to them about Rosa going through my phone. Even if they listen and deign to respond, what's the point? Rosa is only ten years old and capable of no evil and, hey, how precocious of her to be hacking already.

I overhear Sally on the phone saying something that sounds like "delayed teenage acting out." I think she means for me to hear. I feel my fists clench.

I go to the nearest hardware store and pick the cheapest electric drill and a sliding bolt. That will keep her out of my room. At the counter I hand over the parentals' only-for-emergencies credit card.

"I'm sorry," the clerk says. "That card's been declined. Do you have another one?"

"It's been declined? I don't understand."

"You can't buy anything with this card. It doesn't work."

He must think I'm an idiot. I know what *declined* means. Should I use Papa's card? Will he freak out? I'll have to call him and explain. Again. It's probably some temporary glitch. I hand over his card. It works.

When I get home Sally and David are out and Geoff and Rosa are downstairs geeking out about fractals.

"Morning," I say.

Geoff nods and returns the greeting.

I hand him my homework, more calculus, because I don't get it. He goes over it with me while Rosa plays with fractals on her tablet. I try to concentrate. I want to go upstairs and install the lock.

Geoff's brow is furrowed. He wants me to understand.

He makes a small noise halfway between a squeak and a sigh. "Che, what is calculus?"

"Huh?"

"How would you describe what calculus is if someone asked you?"

"Torture? A series of formulas that I don't understand?"

Now he looks like he's in pain. "What's algebra, then?"

"I'm not Rosa. I have to memorise this stuff. I have no hope of understanding it. You know what, Geoff? I'm out of here."

Geoff stares at me and opens his mouth, but no words come out.

"You can't go, Che," Rosa says. "You're not allowed."

I go upstairs. Rosa follows me. She watches as I throw fresh wraps and my water bottle into my backpack.

"You can't skip maths. Your brain will atrophy. You're already behind."

I ignore her.

"You won't get to be a neurologist if you fail maths."

"Like you care."

"You're not being good," Rosa says. "Why should I be good if you're not good?"

"Because . . ." I pause, drop the backpack and sit on the floor.

"You might not have to do any more maths," Rosa says. "The parentals haven't paid Geoff. They're broke."

"How do you know?"

Rosa smiles.

She's probably broken into their phones too.

"That's why they went to Thailand. They ran out of money. Then when the business there failed too they—"

"Failed? They sold it. How could they sell it if it was a failure?"

"They sold at a loss."

"How do you know?"

"How do you *not* know? The McBrunights are paying for everything here."

I know that, but I hadn't thought it through. It's not normal. "I tried to buy something with the parentals' credit card."

"They're skint," Rosa said. "I looked up all the words that mean no money: impecunious, empty, strapped, hard up, penniless, poor, flyblown, stony, stumped, broken, silverless, ruined, bust—"

"I get it."

Was Rosa making a joke? Did she think it was funny?

"I like *skint* best."

"Their credit cards stopped working when we were first in Thailand. They just forgot to tell their bank we were going there."

"The McBrunights are the parentals' last chance. If this business isn't a success, then David will have to work IT again, and you know how bad he is at holding down a job."

I don't know any such thing. What's she talking about?

"We'll probably have to live with Nana and Papa. They'll send us to a rich school. Like they did with David."

"He was expelled."

"We're much gooder than David was when he was our age. Besides, I'll get a scholarship. I'm a genius."

I don't like this horrible fantasy she's spinning. *I'm* not a genius. Will Papa pay for me to go to school and university? He likes to get something for his money. His paying for my boxing annoys the parentals. Will he pay for our education to spite them too? *You failed, here's me stepping in and saving the day.*

I don't want to live with Nana and Papa. I certainly don't want Rosa to live with them. They play their children off against each other, buying them, selling them. Spending more than an hour or two with David's parents makes me squirm.

One of the aunts would take me in, but if they did there'd be no help from Nana and Papa, who are the only ones with money. Them and Uncle Saul, who would never take us in, and even if he did, it would be worse than Nana and Papa.

"Broke," I repeat. "Why didn't they say anything? They haven't told us to be careful with money."

"Because we always are. That's how they raised us."

I can't make sense of what Rosa's saying. "How can they afford this party, then?"

Rosa looks at me like I'm stupid.

"The McBrunights are paying?"

Rosa nods. How does my ten-year-old sister know more about what's going on than I do? Because she likes to spy. She must be exaggerating.

"All they care about is impressing the McBrunights. I told you they don't care about us." She slips her hand into mine. "Let's do some more maths before Geoff realises they can't pay him."

She tugs my hand and I stand. We go downstairs.

"Sorry," I say to Geoff. "Been a bit stressed."

Geoff makes a sound that could be sympathetic. He looks slightly past my left ear.

Rosa smirks. "Let's explain fractals to Che."

CHAPTER TWENTY-FOUR

When Leilani arrives at the housewarming party with Maya, Veronica and Elon, Rosa and Seimone are giggling in the kitchen as David puts together another tray of nibblies to be handed out to the guests. He doesn't look like a man who's on the verge of losing everything. But then David has his poker face on most of the time.

I greet them at the door. Veronica and Elon are dying to meet my creepy sister.

"Hi, Seimone," Elon says.

Seimone waves and walks over with Rosa. Maya stands behind Leilani.

Rosa is in her favourite dress, white with a blue satin ribbon at the waist and blue gloves to match. Her hair's in two ponytails, one above each ear, and her corkscrew curls bounce when she moves. Her shoes are black, patent leather. She could be a little girl from a century ago. Everyone's been *ooohing* and *ahhing* at her cuteness, which makes Rosa shine.

She never seems as human as when she basks in admiration.

"Quite a dress," Leilani says.

Rosa pauses a second before she smiles.

Elon gasps. "You *do* look like Shirley Temple! Aren't you gorgeous?"

No pause with her smile for Elon. Rosa does her little curtsey. "So are you," she says. "I like your hair."

It's cut into alternating purple and black squares.

"I like your shirt, too. It's shiny." Elon's shirt looks like it's made out of silver. Rosa reaches out to touch it.

"This is Elon," I say. "And Veronica."

Rosa curtseys again and they air kiss.

"Are you a girl or a boy?"

I wish I'd asked that.

Elon laughs. "Neither. Both. Something like that."

Rosa looks at Elon quizzically for a moment. "You don't know?"

"Oh, *I* know. It's the world that struggles."

"Can I have your shirt?"

Elon laughs again. "It's a bit big for you, moppet. I'll have to find you one just like it."

"Yes, please!" Rosa turns to Veronica. "You're beautiful."

"We curly haired beauties should stick together," Veronica says. "You look like Shirley Temple!"

"We'll have to teach her to tap, won't we, Ronnie?"

"She taps," I say, but they don't hear me or remember I told them that already. Leilani grins.

Rosa dimples and does some steps for Elon. Elon copies her, then Veronica joins in.

"How festive," Leilani says. I can almost hear the eye roll.

Leilani and I move towards the stairs as the couches are pushed back to create a dance floor. Conversations die as almost everyone's attention is turned to watching and cheering and taking photos and vids as Elon and Rosa and Veronica dance hand in hand.

Rosa looks like an adorable blonde doll.

"C'mon," Leilani whispers. We sit at the top of the stairs. Seimone stands next to Gene, part of the crowd, watching Rosa showing off. Maya has retreated behind the island to help David with the food.

"You look good," Leilani says. She pats the sleeve of my Spool shirt. "I'm glad I bought the green one for you too."

"Thanks," I say, but thinking about how Sally and David owe the McBrunights everything makes me feel weird about it. If I piss off Leilani, would it change things for the parentals? How precarious is this setup?

Sally and David didn't notice what I was wearing, which isn't surprising. Rosa said, "Nice shirt." She notices everything.

"I am unfond of your sister."

Unfond? I wonder if that's an Americanism or a Leilani-ism. Probably the latter.

"Did you know the twins aren't talking to each other? For a few days now." She's watching Rosa. "They've *never* not talked to each other."

"Rosa . . ." I don't know how to finish the sentence.

"Most people don't see it, do they?"

I shake my head.

"She flatters mercilessly, then there's her adorable-little-girl schtick."

"Well, she is only ten." Why do I want to defend her?

"With tap dancing, no less. I wonder if Shirley Temple was

the same way. Terrorising everyone around her when the camera wasn't rolling. We'd've heard by now, wouldn't we? We know how awful Joan Crawford and Bing Crosby were. Jesus. How do you stand it?"

"Sometimes I can't. But she's my sister."

"What's she going to use when she's too old for this Shirley Temple schtick?"

"She'll find something."

"She doesn't have to try that hard, does she? Most people crave praise. They can't even tell when it's insincere. Elon and Ronnie lapped that treacle right up."

"You're studying acting. Aren't all performers like that?"

"Most are. Elon lives for praise and attention. Not me. I've always known my worth. Elon doesn't."

I guess you have to in order to start your own fashion industry blog when you're twelve years old. I know my own worth too. I never craved praise as much as other kids.

Rosa doesn't need it either. She just thinks she deserves it.

"Is Veronica like you or like Elon?"

"She's somewhere in the middle. No, that's not true. I think she craves praise every bit as much as Elon, but Elon is more open about it. Elon feels no shame, but Ronnie knows she shouldn't want it as much as she does."

The three of them are now bowing. I should feel happy for my little sister having so much fun. But Veronica and Elon strike me as people who'd be easy to manipulate.

"Isn't acting about being the centre of attention? Don't you like being the centre of attention?"

"I do, but I don't crave it. I can act without an audience. Those two need the devotion an audience gives. If I said this to either of them they wouldn't believe it. I've never said this out loud." She looks at me from the corner of her eyes. "You're not what I expected."

"Thanks, I guess. Rosa doesn't either," I say. "Need attention. Need people. She likes it, but it has zero effect on how she feels about herself."

"The thought of her grown up is terrifying."

"Yes."

"Rosa has Seimone wrapped around her finger. They leave Maya out of everything. Not that she wants to have anything to do with Rosa, but it still hurts." Maya's carrying a tray of cut-up vegetables and dips. It's almost bigger than she is.

"Che," David calls. "Your friends Sid and Jaime are here."

There Sojourner is by the door, wearing a red dress with a black belt and her hair in a halo. My heart probably does skip a beat.

Leilani nudges me. "Sid scrubs up well."

I'm already standing, my eyes locked on Sojourner.

"Is it love?" Leilani asks as I head down the stairs. Sojourner smiles and there's my heart again not beating the way it's meant to.

"Hey, Soj—Sid," I say. "I'm glad you came."

I'm glad you kissed me last night.

I'm not sure whether to offer my hand or to kiss her cheek. So I stand there grinning at her for what feels like hours.

She holds out her fist and I touch it with mine. Skin to skin.

"Where are your moms?" I say, pronouncing it the way she does.

"Mom's having a bad day. So Mama is staying with her. They send their apologies."

"I'm sorry."

"It happens." She shrugs.

"Hi," Jaime says. I've forgotten she's standing there. She grins in a way that says she knows and thinks it's hilarious. "Hey. Is that Elon?"

"You know Elon?"

"Sure. Elon's club famous. Elon doesn't know me, though. I'm going to go fix that. Catch you later, Sid. Oh, and I'm definitely staying at Dad's tonight. I forgot to tell your moms."

Sojourner nods. "I'll tell them."

I wonder why Sojourner's moms need to know Jaime's movements. My confusion must show, because Sojourner says, "Jaime lives with us most of the time. Her parents split. Her mom's in Queens, out past the last F stop. Her dad's in New Jersey. She moved in with us so she could keep going to our school. Nice shirt." She briefly touches the collar. "Soft. Makes your eyes almost look green."

"Thanks. Nice dress. You look amazing."

"Thank you." She smiles and my heart speeds up again.

This is ridiculous. "Do you want something to drink?"

"Sure," she says as I lead her over to the kitchen island. "Got any bourbon?"

"Um . . ." I glance at my parents, wondering if it's okay to give booze to someone underage.

She punches me. "I'm kidding! I don't drink. Juice would be great."

"We have pineapple, orange, mango, pear and strawberry."

"Is that one flavour or five?"

"Five," I say. "My dad thinks it's an abomination when juices are blended. But that doesn't stop us."

"Pineapple and mango then," Sojourner says. "In the spirit of rebellion."

Sally is talking to two women I don't recognise. She's giving her speech about beauty. The women are nodding. "Beauty is a cudgel to make us buy things we don't need," she tells them, "to make us feel that we are never as beautiful as we could be. Did you know that skin-whitening creams are a billion-dollar business worldwide?"

"Funny to hear your mom talking about beauty like that when she could be on a magazine cover."

"Only for mature ladies," I say. It's something Sally says. How beauty for women is deemed to be over at thirty—or forty if you have money. "She says stuff like that a lot."

"My moms too."

"Right," I say. "The evils of capitalism."

"Consumerist culture. Mom sure does love to preach that one."

Sojourner sips her juice, looks around. There are a lot of beautiful people here wearing expensive clothes. I wonder what she sees.

"I didn't realise your folks were rich."

"They're not." I'm suddenly very conscious that I'm wearing a thousand-dollar shirt.

Her lips twitch. "Really? This is the biggest apartment I've ever seen."

I wonder how she'd react if I took her to the McBrunights' place.

"It's rented." I almost tell her we're not paying, but that fact makes me feel ashamed.

"Well, okay, that proves you're not rich." She laughs. "*Of course* you rent. Everyone in New York rents. But I bet your parents are paying more for this place per month than my moms pay for our place in a year."

I have no idea what the rent is. I wonder if the parentals know. Do they feel like children having the McBrunights pay?

"Our rent is four-eighty a month. That's rent control, sure. There are five rooms—that includes kitchen and bathroom. Our whole apartment would fit in this one room."

"I'm sorry," I say, though I'm not sure what I'm apologising for. I'm itching to tell her that none of this is ours. That we're skint. Rosa's right. That is the best word.

"Why? We've got a nice apartment. I mean, it doesn't gleam like this place but that's not your fault. All you need to do is get yourself a T-shirt that says Rich White Boy so you don't surprise any of your regular friends."

"You didn't realise I'm white?"

"Funny."

"I'll get going on that T-shirt. Sorry if I offended you."

Sojourner laughs. "You're going to have to try way harder than that. I mean, you've already told me believing in God is silly, and that didn't offend me."

"I didn't say that!"

She grins.

"This place only has seven rooms," I say thinking of how many rooms the McBrunights have.

"There's a tap dance show in your living room! You can't even shimmy in mine." She laughs again. "Don't get me wrong we've got a nice place and we're on the fifth floor. Basement and first floor apartments've been flooded twice in the last few years. What zone is this?"

I have no idea what Sojourner's talking about. Why's she talking so much? Is she thinking about that kiss last night?

"When there's a storm coming you need to know what zone you're in. Zone one's the worst. Last storm you couldn't get out of our building for days. We were happy to be over at Cousin Isa's in Jersey City. You're probably not zoned, which means no evacuation, and no flooding. Doesn't protect you from the blackouts."

"Blackouts?" I repeat. I thought we left blackouts behind in Bangkok.

Sojourner laughs. "You don't know a thing about this city, do you?"

"I don't. It's the movie city. Where smoke comes out of the streets."

"That's not smoke, it's steam."

"Really? It isn't a special effect?"

More laughter. "It's how the city is heated. Steam heat running through pipes. Let me show you."

Sojourner grabs my hand and pulls me through the knots of people. Her hand is warm and dry and callused. I can feel the light pressure of it all the way to my groin.

The tap dancing stops. Everyone claps. I join in half-heartedly and Sojourner more enthusiastically.

We stop at a heater under one of the windows. She lets go of my hand, and I have to stop myself from grabbing it back. She leans in close to me. I can smell the mango and pineapple on her breath.

"So this is a fancy new one," she says.

Her mouth is close to mine.

"But it's the same design as the one in our apartment. The steam comes from that pipe and fills up the heater so both heater and pipes are heating the apartment."

"Huh," I say. I'm looking at the nape of her neck.

"Cause this is a new one you can turn it off. See?"

She's looking at me again. I do see. Her eyes have every colour of brown in them from almost yellow to almost black.

"The only way to regulate ours is to open the window. Sometimes it gets so hot we have to do that even when there's a blizzard outside."

"Sounds annoying," I say because I need to say something.

"What exactly do your parents do? To afford a place like this and pay for you to go to a million gym classes? I mean, I teach there, I get a break on my classes, and I can barely cover costs. But you practically live there."

I don't know what to say.

"So what do they do?"

"They start businesses. The most successful one was SunPow. Silly name." I'm no longer sure this is true. Had it been successful when the parentals sold it? Or did that come after? If it was successful, why are they broke now? "It's a cheap solar-generated power source. People use them camping. Every time you buy one you're paying for another one to be sent to people who live in remote areas around the world and can't afford their own. Another of their businesses was a condensation unit for collecting water in even the most arid areas. They've done heaps of stuff like that."

"They sound like good people."

"They are. They're not rich. Most of the money goes into whatever the latest business is, and funding other organisations, ones for literacy, fighting malaria . . ." I trail off. Is that why they're broke now? "Renting an apartment like this and throwing this party is to raise money. See how David's circulating? He's working the room trying to win over as many people as he can."

We watch David talking to an older couple. They're both rapt.

"Your dad can turn on the charm, can't he?"

I nod. "He has to. There are people here who are the real deal. Super rich."

"Like that couple your dad's charming?"

"Yup. Why," I begin, "did you ki—"

"Does Sid dance?" Rosa asks, and I almost jump.

"Of course."

"Will you dance with me?" Rosa asks, slipping her hand into Sojourner's.

Rosa turns to smile at me as she leads Sojourner away, and for a split second I think of what my life would be like if she didn't exist. I've never wished for it so fiercely.

Whatever she's planning, I'm not going to let it happen. I try yet again to think of a way to warn people about Rosa without saying, *I think my sister is a psychopath.*

Sojourner moves as beautifully dancing as she does boxing. Elon and Veronica are dancing as well, goofily, but it's easy to tell they're good dancers too. Then Sally and Lisimaya join them.

I make my way towards the stairs, nodding and smiling as I thread past people I've never met. Someone puts their hand on my elbow.

"Dance with me?"

I know it's Sojourner before I turn. I smile, because I don't want to risk words. We ease our way to the dance floor. I follow her movements like it's a drill, a kata.

Sojourner's all I can see and it fills me with such lightness that if this is how believing in God makes people feel I'd be in church with her every Sunday.

CHAPTER TWENTY-FIVE

Leilani, Veronica, Elon, me and Jaime go to Coffee Noir, where Veronica and Elon work. All the staff know them. The bartender is plying Jaime, Elon and Veronica with free shots of something green. Leilani sticks to tap water like me.

Elon and Jaime argue about who is more of a real New Yorker.

"I can only afford to live here because it's a sublet from my uncle!" Elon says. "It's rent controlled!"

"Our rent control was bulldozed! Now my mom lives in the part of Queens that's barely on the fucking map!"

"Keep it down." Leilani rolls her eyes. "You're giving me a headache."

Elon and Jaime lower their voices and lean closer. They're close enough to kiss.

"They'll be going on like that all night," Leilani says in a stage whisper. "True love."

"You sure you don't want a shot?" Veronica asks us. "These are awesome."

I shake my head. Leilani says no.

"Leilani doesn't drink in public," Veronica whispers loudly. "In case someone takes a picture and gets her in trouble."

It's weird remembering that Leilani is kind of famous.

"You like that Sid girl a lot, don't you?" Veronica asks, leaning too close to me. Her breath smells cloyingly sweet.

"Um."

"They train together," Leilani says. "Sid's a fighter. She's already had two amateur bouts."

I wonder how Leilani knows that, then remember they sat next to each other at the Korean restaurant.

"Fighting," Elon says, shuddering.

"Did she win her fights?" Veronica asks.

"Both of them," Jaime says.

"That explains those gorgeous shoulders," Veronica says. "I should start boxing lessons, get myself cut like her." She throws some punches. "Is that why you like her, Che? Because she's a fighter?"

I don't want to talk about Sojourner. Talking about it could destroy whatever fragile thing there is between us. We kissed once, held hands a little, danced. And her best friend is sitting right there.

"I think you like her because she's so dark. You think she's exotic, don't you?" Leilani says. She's smiling like she's teasing, but I feel slapped.

"Of course not," I say.

I've never called Sojourner exotic. I've only talked about her with Georgie. Did I think it? Sojourner's darker than any other girl I've liked. She's darker than anyone I've ever *met*.

"Do you get a thrill from the contrast of your pasty-ass skin against her eboniness?" Elon asks.

"No," I say. They're looking at me. Jaime too. She's staring like she's trying to see into my soul, to work out whether I'm going to hurt her best friend.

We've barely touched, and yes, I did get a thrill. How could I not? It's Sojourner.

"You're a mean drunk, Elon," Veronica says.

I have the feeling I'm standing on a pre-existing fracture line with Leilani and Elon on one side, and Veronica on the other.

"I'm not drunk!"

Veronica laughs. "Ha! So you're not denying you're mean. Che likes her. People like each other." She looks from Jaime to Elon and back again. She downs the rest of her shot and waves to her friend for another one.

Their questions do feel mean. But I'm worried there's some truth in them. Do I think Sojourner's gorgeous because she doesn't look like other girls I've liked? But she *does* look a lot like them. Georgie pointed that out. I'm always attracted to girls who are tall, strong and muscled.

"Sometimes people like each other."

"Says the white girl," Leilani says. "Plenty of people are into me because they think my being Korean makes me all demure and innocent and shit." She rolls her eyes. "One girl wanted me to wear my national costume. Seriously?"

"Who are these people?" Elon says. "Demure? You?"

"You don't even look Korean," Veronica says. "You're *not* Korean; you were born here. Your mom's white."

"This again? Ronnie, could you be any whiter?"

"Wait. Are you saying you see *me* as white and not as, not as a . . ." Veronica gropes for the word. "Individual?" She sounds triumphant, like she's made a devastating point.

Elon looks sad. Veronica probably thinks that means Elon agrees with her, but I'm pretty sure Elon doesn't. Jaime is rolling her eyes.

"If you were truly into me," Veronica says, downing the next shot, "you wouldn't notice the colour of my skin!"

Elon and Leilani exchange a look. Jaime snorts.

"I *must* have a white-girl fetish to put up with you." Leilani turns to Elon and Jaime. "I can't deal with this right now. Let's go."

They get up. Elon stumbles and Jaime steadies him. I half rise from my seat.

"See you later, Che," Jaime says. "You need to school her."

I sink down again as they walk out, feeling whiter than I've ever felt.

"What?" Veronica asks. She half rises from her seat, then sits down again. "God. Why does Leilani have to make everything about race? It's not like she's *really* Korean."

"You said that." My cheeks are burning. I hate that Leilani thinks I'm the same as Veronica. At least Jaime doesn't. But the last thing in the world I want to do is *school* Veronica.

"Well, she's not."

"Leilani looks like a mixture of her parents. There's a lot of her dad in her. She speaks Korean. She's spent a lot of time there. Korea means a lot to her."

Veronica waves my words away. "Most people think she's white. She has to tell them she's not. If she didn't go on about being Korean no one would know."

"If Leilani says she's Korean-American, that means it's important to her. Put yourself in her shoes." Show some empathy.

Veronica stares at me. "How long have you known Leilani? Three minutes? Let me tell you something about Leilani McBrunight: she is drama. There's more drama if she goes on about the Korean thing. Like her storming off right now. Her dad wasn't even raised Korean. He was adopted! By a regular American family. He didn't go to Korea for the first time until he was like twelve. Elon is *my* best friend, not hers. Why'd he go off with her? Why do they always stick together?"

I wish she'd shut up.

She downs another shot and it occurs to me that we've been stuck with the bill. Fuck.

"Not everything is about race. People can just be people, you know."

"What about Elon?" I ask.

"What about Elon?"

"Do you think Elon's really a boy?"

"What? No. Of course not. Elon's Elon."

"What about people who insist Elon's a boy or a girl?"

"They're stupid."

"So Elon gets to say what Elon is?"

"Uh huh."

"We're the only ones who know who we are, right? Not other people?"

Veronica nods. But I'm not sure. I feel like I'm on shaky ground. If I declared I was a cowboy that wouldn't make me a cowboy. This is different—I grope for the reason why.

"Leilani says she's Korean-American so that means she's Korean-American."

Veronica downs another shot.

"If Leilani let people assume she's white, wouldn't that be *less* of a hassle for her?"

"I told you: she likes drama. She likes feeling special."

"Is that why Elon says Elon's not a boy or a girl?"

"That's different."

"Is it? Don't you think having people question who you are would make you feel more annoyed than special?"

Veronica deflates. Maybe she's getting what I'm saying or maybe she's about to pass out.

"Leilani *is* special, though," Veronica says, as though it's a bad thing. "She's smarter, more together, more *everything*. She started Neophyte when she was, like, seven. Whatever she does, she's the best. I never realised how, I don't know, *dumb* I am until I met her. I just want to win an argument. Just once. I didn't win that one, did I?"

I shake my head. Why has Leilani stayed with Veronica for so long?

"I fuck everything up. She's going to dump me."

Veronica's face turns red. She's crying. I hand her a napkin. "She's sexier than I am too," she says between sobs. "I think about her all the time!"

The bartender brings over a glass of water.

I was starting to think Veronica is like Rosa, but she's not. Rosa never thinks anyone's better than her.

"There's nothing weird about your sister," Veronica says out of nowhere.

I can't help shivering. It's as if thinking about Rosa brought her into the conversation.

"You and Leilani said those things about her because you were stoned, right? 'Cause she's a sweet little girl. You shouldn't diss her like that. She's a great dancer too. We're gonna busk together."

"You're drunk."

Veronica laughs. "Little bit. We only fight when we're drinking."

"Leilani wasn't drinking."

"When *one* of us is drinking. God. You're right. I only ever try to be smart when I'm drinking. Elon's going to be mad at me when I get home. Elon's going to tell me everything I did wrong and why it was wrong and ugh and I'll be wondering why Elon can't be fun all the time. I'm a terrible person."

She wipes at her face with the already wet napkin.

"No one's fun all the time. You're no fun right now."

"Rude!" Veronica says, but she's smiling at me. "That's true. They like to get deep and shit about *everything* and I . . . I don't. Thinking about that stuff makes me squirm. Do you fancy white girls, too? Or only black ones? Do you think I'm pretty?"

She cares what I think. Rosa doesn't. Why does that make me think less of her? Veronica would probably be less annoying if she were more like Rosa. God forbid.

CHAPTER TWENTY-SIX

When I get home, only a handful of guests are left, including Gene and Lisimaya. They're sitting on the couch with the parentals, clutching glasses of wine and waving their hands around.

They greet me briefly before returning to their important conversations.

I open the door to my bedroom and there's Rosa, cross-legged on my bed, wearing her party dress.

Even if I'd already installed it, the sliding bolt would not have kept her out. I need a lock with a key.

I turn my back on her, act like I'm checking something on my computer, and set my phone to record. Then I turn my chair around.

"Where's Seimone?"

"Suzette took the twins home."

"The twins? Seimone doesn't act like they're twins anymore."

"That's silly, Che. You can't stop being a twin."

"Why isn't Seimone talking to Maya?"

Rosa shrugs. "I guess they're having a fight. Sisters do, you know. I liked the party. I like Elon and Veronica. Especially Elon. I like that Elon's not a girl or a boy. I've never met anyone like that. It's not the same as the ladyboys in Bangkok. They like to be called *she*. Elon said, *Elon is Elon and not a she or a he or a they and definitely not an it. Because no one is an it.* Elon says mostly people assume, then get angry when they're wrong. No one ever guesses that Elon's not a girl *or* a boy. It didn't make me angry. Does it make you angry?"

"That Elon's not a boy or a girl? No. It just confuses me."

"Elon told me Elon's parents don't care. When Elon was five Elon's mom gave Elon nail polish and a tiara because that's what Elon wanted. Elon's dad paid for Elon's dance lessons. They told Elon that Elon didn't have to be a boy or a girl if Elon didn't want to be."

"They sound like great parents."

"You don't think Elon's weird because Elon's different?"

I feel a prickle. When she asks questions like this . . . I can't fall for it. I can't say anything that will let her wriggle out of her promises: *But you said*, she'll say later, all innocence, *I thought that meant* . . .

"Everyone's different in one way or another," I say.

Rosa is looking at me as if there's something in the alignment of my facial muscles she can use.

"I'm different too," she whispers. "Almost as different as Elon."

I say nothing. They are not different in the same way. Elon is not a monster.

"I'm definitely a girl," she says, making her curls bounce, talking in the voice she deploys for the parentals and the rest of the world. Bright and girlish and harmless. "I'm definitely a she. Do you think you're a boy?"

I nod.

"But I'm not like other girls. Or other boys. I have something most other people don't have."

She waits for me to ask her what that is. I'm not going to.

"Are you mad at me?"

"Yes. All you do is mess with me. After you killed Apinya's guinea pig you promised you'd stop."

"I didn't kill Apin—"

"What do you want, Rosa?"

"I want us to be friends again. You don't tell me things. You know my secrets. I want to know some of yours."

"I don't know *all* your secrets."

Rosa smiles and the hairs on my body stand up. "That's true. But you don't tell me *any* of yours. It's not fair."

"I don't trust you, Rosa. You trick your friends into doing things they don't want to do. You're doing whatever you can to turn Seimone against Maya."

"Maya's mean. It would be a lot easier if she was dead. Seimone wishes she was dead."

"Jesus, Rosa, you can't kill Maya."

Rosa doesn't say anything.

"If you kill Maya you'll be locked up."

Still not a word.

"You're clever. But even the smartest killers get caught. Read up on them."

"I have. Those are the ones who were caught. There are lots of unsolved murders."

My turn to not say anything.

Rosa stays expressionless. No dimples. No smiling. No frowning. Bile fills my mouth. I've never believed she'd kill anyone. She's ten years old.

"You want to live in this world with as few restrictions on you as possible, yes?"

Rosa nods.

"If you kill Maya, what do you think will happen? You're different. You already have to work hard to hide that from people, and even then some of them don't want to be near you."

"Like Maya." Rosa frowns. "I'm getting better at being the same as everyone else, though. You saw me at the party. I talked to everyone and they liked me. They told Sally and David how talented I am."

"They could just be being polite. I bet some of them were thinking that you're a show-off and couldn't wait till you stopped tap dancing already. To some you smell wrong. You make the tiny hairs on their arms stand on end."

"Do I do that to you?"

Yes, I want to tell her. *Especially right now when you're calmly talking about killing people and your voice and face have as much emotion as a robot's. You scare the shit out of me.*

Instead I say, "I've known you all my life."

"Do you think I'm the devil?"

I laugh as if to say, *How absurd.* It isn't. Too often I'm scared that some people are born evil, bad seeds, and there's nothing to be done but burn them.

"You don't have much empathy. There are a million theories why some people have little empathy. Given your environment—"

"I was born like this," she says, stating a fact. "But not because I lack anything—because I'm smarter than everyone else. Empathy stops you from understanding the world. Empathy gets in the way."

"No," I whisper. "It doesn't." It feels melodramatic to say that her eyes are cold. But they are. Blue ice. Like those of our great-great-great-whatever grandfather in the photo. "Your anterior insular cortex is damaged or underdeveloped. You're not smarter than everyone else. You're colder."

"I'm different. I think I'm better. You think I'm not. But we agree I'm different."

"Yes."

"Maybe if I killed someone I wouldn't enjoy it."

I have no idea what to say to that.

"Or I would enjoy it, but then I'd have done that and I wouldn't need to do it again. I get bored quickly, you know."

"I've seen you sit and kill ants for hours."

She shrugs. "That was fun. Fun isn't boring."

"You find the wrong things fun."

"You think it's fun to hit people."

"That's different. Fighters want to fight. They consent to it."

"You're the one who says there's something wrong with me because I like violence, but you like violence too."

"There's something wrong with you because you don't care. I care. I've looked after you all your life. I changed your nappy when you were little. I held you and cared for you and protected you and taught you. I love you. Even knowing everything I know about you, I love you. Do you love me?"

I want to know if she feels anything for me or for Sally and David. Have our years of loving her had any effect?

"You're useful to me. You're much more interesting than Sally and David. They just bring in the money. Or they used to. So I needed them. When the McBrunights stop supporting them and they're broke, then it will be Nana and Papa's money. Until I can make my own. You can't exist without money."

I can only think of how ardently Uncle Saul would agree with that statement.

"Do you love anyone?"

"I'm not sure I understand what love is. It's like *good*. No one's explained it clearly. I love ice cream. I love chess and mathematics. I love getting what I want. I love getting away with things. But not people. They're either useful or they're not. You're useful, Che. But I don't think that's love."

"It's not."

"Do you love Sid?"

I'm not answering that.

Rosa smirks. "I like that other people love me. I like being loved. It makes it easier to get them to do what I want."

Now she smiles, as warm and charming as David. Both dimples pop out. Her eyes don't seem cold. I feel myself smile in response and press my lips together.

Her smile widens. *See how easily I can charm? As easy as popping out these dimples.*

"What do you want, Rosa?"

"I want to be able to do whatever I want. But there are too many things I want that aren't allowed. I like it when people are scared or in pain or drunk or angry. It amuses me."

"Why?"

She shrugs.

"Because you don't feel pain?"

"I feel pain! If you cut me I bleed and it hurts."

"Shylock? Really? I thought you hated Shakespeare."

Rosa shrugs. "Other people like him. It's useful to know things. Even boring, stupid things."

"I wasn't talking about that kind of pain, Rosa. Emotional pain. If I told you I don't love you and don't want anything to do with you it wouldn't hurt."

"Yes, it would. Who would I ask real questions? Who would help me? You're the only one who understands."

"You just told me you only care about my usefulness. Why should I do anything for you?"

"I'd be lost without you," Rosa says. Her eyes glisten.

Even though I know she can cry at will, I'm glad. *"Now,* you need me. But you won't always. Why shouldn't I stop helping you now?"

"Then I'd have to find someone else to help me. I bet Sid would. She likes me. But she doesn't *have* to. She's not my sister. You have to help me and explain the rules. Because they don't make any sense."

"I'll keep helping you, Rosa, if you stop messing with me."

"How do I know when I'm messing with you?"

"You can start by not wishing anyone was dead."

"That's not fair. I wish Leilani was dead too. I get to wish whatever I want. Everyone wishes someone was dead."

I wish *Rosa* were dead.

"Stop trying to cosy up to Sojourner—"

"She's teaching me about Jesus. It's all about love and empathy. You should want me to learn that stuff."

"No more Bible study." I don't want her whispering poison in Sojourner's ears.

"I tell her you and she should be together."

"I don't care. Stay away from Elon and Veronica."

Her bottom lip sticks out. "But we were going to dance! For money!"

I shake my head.

"My friends are off limits."

"What else?"

"Stop trying to turn the parentals against me."

"You're no fun."

"That's right, I'm not. No one's here to be *fun* for you."

Rosa doesn't respond, but I know that's exactly what she thinks everyone is here for.

"If I promise not to mess with your friends or the parentals, will you promise to stay with me?"

I stare at her. "Stay with you?"

"I need you to keep answering my questions and help me be normal. I'd be lost without you."

"You already said that."

"Will you stay with me until you finish university?"

"No, that's too long."

"Until I finish high school? It won't take me eight years," Rosa says confidently. "I need you to help me through school. There are two girls whispering about me at dance school. I don't know how to make that stop."

"I promise I'll keep helping you. I'll always answer your questions."

Rosa puts out her hand and we shake. I feel queasy.

"You promise not to mess with my friends, not to turn Sally and David against me?"

"I promise."

"You won't hurt anyone?"

"I can't promise that. I don't know what will hurt people. They have feelings, I don't. I promise I won't physically hurt anyone. On purpose."

I nod. "And killing?"

"I already promised I wouldn't and I promised I wouldn't encourage anyone else to kill. I haven't broken either of those promises."

"Promise again."

"Fine. I won't kill anyone. Not unless I'm sure I can get away with it."

She grins as if to say, *See? I do have a sense of humour.*

"That's not a promise."

Rosa shrugs. "I was joking. I already promised I won't kill Maya. I won't kill Sid or Leilani or the parentals or anyone you care about."

"Or anyone I *don't* care about."

"Fine. Besides, I'm so little. How could I kill anyone?" Rosa rolls her eyes at my stupidity and slides off my bed. "Goodnight, Che."

She kisses my cheek and slips out the door. I try to make sense of our conversation. I can't. I feel like I've barely survived a beating.

What has she promised me?

Not to mess with my friends. Too vague. She'll claim not to think she was messing with anyone. She'll claim she didn't realise whoever she messed with *was* a friend of mine.

Not to turn Sally and David against me. Also vague. *How was I to know*, she'll say, *they'd react like that?*

She's also promised not to physically hurt anyone. On purpose. She'll claim she didn't mean to. What about her not-killing promise? *Not unless I'm sure I can get away with it.*

I won't be able to sleep.

I pull out my phone. It's all messages. From Leilani asking me to another showing as if she hadn't accused me of only liking Sojourner because she's black. Jason updating me on his parent wars. Georgie wanting to know if I escaped the drunk girl, and Nazeem telling me he misses me because I'm the only one who'll appreciate how he got one up on Georgie and he has to tell me about it. I'm about to text Georgie to see if she can talk—I have to talk about what happened—when one comes through from Sojourner.

—Dancing with you was fun.

I stare at it. Touch the screen as if that's somehow touching her.

—Yeah. Me too. I liked it too.

I hold my breath. I type something I'm afraid to send, then before I can stop myself I press send.

—I'm glad you kissed me.

I stare at my phone, willing her to respond, my hands sweating. What if she doesn't respond?

A text comes through from Naz, another from Georgie. I don't look at them.

Why isn't Sojourner responding? Is it too much? Should I not have mentioned the kiss? Are we supposed to pretend it didn't happen? She's the one who said dancing with me was fun. Surely that means something. I didn't say I wanted us to kiss again. I didn't say I can't stop thinking about her. That I'll go to church every Sunday to be with her. That all I want right now is for us to kiss again. Her mouth against my mouth, our fingers touching. Our . . .

—Yes. Goodnight, Che.

Yes, she's glad too? Or, yes, she's glad I'm glad she kissed me? Or, *yes, I know you're glad I kissed you*, which could mean anything, including that she's laughing at me.

I don't think she's laughing at me.

I turn my phone off, put it onto charge, crawl into bed, close my eyes and sleep, dreaming about Sojourner.

WHEN I WAKE SOJOURNER is my first thought. I turn my phone on to check the messages are real. They are.

Downstairs, Rosa is eating breakfast. David is leaning on the island drinking coffee. Rosa's tablet is between them and they're discussing something intensely. Some computery, mathsy thing I won't understand.

Rosa looks up and waves at me, her dimples popping, as if last night she didn't say *I won't kill unless I'm sure I can get away with it*.

"No more maths tutor," Rosa says. "I told you." She slides from her stool to give me a hug. "Skint," she whispers.

David frowns. "You're both on holidays now. In September you'll start at a local school."

Rosa gives me an *I told you so* look. "*If* we're here in September."

David shoots her a look.

"Which school are you sending me to, David?" Rosa asks. "Seimone said most of the schools here are hard to get into. You have to apply ages ahead of time."

David says nothing.

"I'm going to coach Seimone today. Her chess is much better already."

"Isn't she in school?" I ask.

Rosa shakes her head. "It's a private school. They're already on holiday."

"That's why," David tells me, "we called off your tutoring. Neither of you've had a holiday in a while and we thought Rosa and the twins would enjoy being on holidays together."

"And Che would enjoy spending all day and night punching people," Rosa adds, dimpling.

CHAPTER TWENTY-SEVEN

On the way to the gym I text Georgie that I need to talk to her. It's the wee hours over there, but she's often up late.

Sojourner and Jaime are in school. Not that I would talk to either of them about Rosa. I don't want to scare Sojourner away and I don't know Jaime.

All I can think about on the treadmill is Rosa. My brain spirals. Rosa has kept her promises. She's proud of keeping her promises. Why does it feel like when she says she won't hurt people I care about that she's saying the opposite?

I stretch, then force myself into defensive sets. They're a staccato mess. I text Georgie again. It's hours till she wakes up.

I ring Leilani. Her message is typical Leilani: *Don't leave a message. Or do. But don't expect a response. Voicemail? Seriously? What is your problem?*

I hang up and text her —Can we talk? It's important.

I stand up, shaking myself out. I can get a grip. I can work out properly. My phone rings. Leilani.

"What's so important?"

"Rosa."

"The twins still aren't talking."

"I'm sorry."

"Meet me in Tompkins Square. Near the chess. I can be there in fifteen minutes."

"See you," I say as the phone goes dead in my ear.

I wonder why Leilani picked the chess tables. Does she know about Rosa's adventure there?

When I get there Leilani's sitting on a bench, tapping away at her tablet.

"Hey," she says, sliding the tablet into her bag. "Sorry about the thing with Ronnie. She can be a shit. Didn't mean to hit you too."

I sit down next to her. An apology? I'll take it. "It's okay."

"Your new girlfriend dump you? You look like shit."

"She's not my girlfriend."

"Oh." Leilani pushes her hair back from her eyes. "She rejected you. Bummer, dude. But you're not really in her league, are you?"

"They have leagues for everyone here? No one told me."

"Yup. Everyone's enrolled at birth and you get tested every six months to see if you've gotten any hotter. There's a huge amount of movement between leagues as puberty hits, then they're pretty static until people hit the unfortunate forties, then it's the slow slide into the bottom league more commonly known as death."

She's not looking at me.

"Good to know. Very glad to have been spared that system in Australia."

"Australia has it too," Leilani says. "They have the older, ruder system of not telling you about it."

"Harsh."

"Well, it's a big, crocodile-and-poisonous-spider-and-snake-infested horror show, isn't it? Why make anything easy?"

I think about giving her my Australian-snakes-aren't-actually-that-poisonous spiel. "True," I say instead.

"So?" she says, hands resting on her bag.

"So."

"You had something you wanted to tell me?"

"I was hoping for somewhere a little bit more private."

"Can't go back to my place. Too . . ." She doesn't elaborate. "Let's walk. We could walk along the river. I don't feel like sitting around."

There's something a bit off about Leilani. Her voice is higher than usual. Her hands aren't still. She keeps messing with her hair.

She's walking before I've finished saying, "Sure." Only my longer legs save me from having to break into a run.

"Talk," she barks as we take the Sixth Street bridge over the FDR Highway to the stretch of land beside the river. Two joggers overtake us. One pulls a dog in her wake.

"What's up?" I ask, instead of telling her about Rosa.

Her pace increases until she's on the verge of running.

"What makes you think—Fucking Ronnie." She comes to a stop. I stutter-step as I turn to her. "Fuck," she says. "I don't want to talk about it." She hits her thighs with her fists. "I don't want to be *in* it. *Fuck!*"

She walks again, then shifts into a run. I keep pace with her. She runs faster. So do I. I can't help thinking about my run with Sojourner, though Leilani isn't running anywhere near as fast as Sojourner. We come to a stop at the tip of the island where you can catch the ferry to the Statue of Liberty. I haven't seen any of the New York sights. I haven't even gone to the top of the Empire State Building.

Leilani flops down on a bench. I sit next to her. "At least pant a little. Asshole."

I pant like a dog. She punches my shoulder half-heartedly.

"I should be fitter. I used to run all the time. Veronica cheated on me."

"I'm sorry. That sucks. How'd you find out?"

"She drunkenly told me about it last night when I rescued her sodden ass from Coffee Noir. I should've left her there. I mean, Jesus, Che. She's a dolt. You know who she slept with? The director of an Off-Broadway thing. She didn't even get the part! Veronica's all, *It's no big thing.* So I acted like it *was* no big thing. But I feel like . . ."—she taps her heart—"it is a big thing. I thought *we* were a big thing."

"Even though she's a dolt?"

"We all have our faults. Okay, fine, being a dolt is a big fault. I'll dump her. It's just that I thought we were maybe an always thing. Like the olds. High-school sweethearts. It's stupid, isn't it?"

I shake my head. I've gone through moments of hoping for the same thing. The parentals are in love. What would it be like to be with the same person for decades, loving them more each day?

"They may be shitty parents, but they're great for each other. Still in love. I'd like that. Though *I* will not be a shitty parent."

I haven't noticed the McBrunights being shitty parents.

"They're terrible, Che. They barely remember they have children. If we have problems they throw money at them, but they barely spend any time with us. They never have. We were raised by Grandma. When she died it was bad. The twins were broken. I had to put them back together. Now I'm the one raising them. When they can't sleep? It's my bed they crawl into. I'm the one who adjudicates their fights. I'm the one loving them 'cause the olds certainly don't do it."

"I'm sure that's not—"

"What if you can only have one kind of love? If you're completely in love with your partner, then you can't be a good parent. But if you're a good parent, maybe it means you can't be in love? Because you put your kids first, not your partner. Your olds are sloppy in love, too, aren't they? Do they actually love you? Because I know ours don't love us."

She's asking me one of my biggest fears. I don't want to answer because, no, I don't think they love me, not the way they love each other.

"Fuck. This is not me. I do not tell strangers my woes. Not ever." I'm surprised that I'm hurt. We've only known each other a few weeks, but it feels longer. It feels like we trust each other. "I'm not a *total* stranger. More of a *partial* stranger."

Leilani lets out a snort of her awful laugh and covers her mouth.

"I don't laugh in front of *partial* strangers either. Why do I trust you, Che?"

"Is it my honest, farm-boy, wheat-fed, acne-ridden face?"

"Shut up. I never said anything about your acne! You're going to hold everything I say against me?"

"I thought it was funny. I've never even been on a farm."

"God. I have. Horrible places."

"I trust you, too, Leilani. I consider you a friend."

"You *are* a farm boy. All relaxed and friendship-having. Of course you think we're friends. *Shit,*" she says. "*You* called *me*. Rosa. You wanted to talk about your creepy little sister."

"Psychopathic little sister," I say.

"That's a bit extreme." There's a smile in Leilani's voice. "She doesn't look like the serial killer type. You know, being a kid and all."

"Psychopath doesn't mean serial killer. Most psychopaths don't kill."

Leilani's staring at me. "You're serious?" She sits forward, her hands gripping the bag on her lap as I tell her all about Rosa.

"Seimone worships Rosa."

"She likes being worshipped." I've never had this conversation with anyone who believed me. When I first told Georgie she laughed. She thought I was joking. Even now Georgie thinks it's a joke. Leilani understands.

"Seimone can't see it."

I nod. "But you do. Maya does. Most people don't. All they see is the charm."

"Like your dad."

"Right. But with no heart. I swear she copied David's smile. Charm's on the list."

"List?"

I tell Leilani about the psychopath checklist.

"She's not scared of anything?"

"Nope. Except being locked up. She doesn't want people to realise what she is. But she likes to talk about what she does, how she thinks. That's why she likes me. She can tell me anything."

"Fun for you," Leilani says, patting my shoulder. I guess that's her version of a hug. "A psychopath. Couldn't she be more of a sociopath? They don't kill, do they?"

"It's a different name for the same thing. The DSM calls what Rosa has antisocial personality disorder."

"DSM?"

"The Diagnostic and Statistical Manual of Mental Disorders."

"Woah. On the bright side, she's only ten."

I laugh. "You wouldn't believe how often the parentals say that. Jeffrey Dahmer was impaling dogs' heads on stakes before he was ten. Children do all sorts of terrible things."

"No details! Thanks! Do you think she'll kill someone?" Leilani lowers her voice. "Seimone wishes we were dead, me and Maya. She's said it more than once. She never used to talk like that."

"Rosa's always wishing people were dead." I shake my head slowly. "It's only in movies that all psychopaths are killers. In real life they mostly manipulate and lie and treat people like shit."

"Well, that's alright then." Leilani pulls her knees up and rests her head on them. "When I said she was creepy I was thinking she was a spoiled brat. I figured she was a regular narcissist. Except my therapist says we unqualified people should not be making diagnoses."

"Your therapist is right. But Rosa isn't normal."

"I wish I could get Seimone to see what a little shit Rosa is. Can I tell her what you told me? Also Suzette?"

"Sure," I say. "I should have told you sooner. But I haven't had much luck with that."

"People don't believe you," she says. It's not a question.

"Nope. Except for my friend Georgie. But she doesn't realise how bad it is."

"Rosa's gorgeous. That can't help. You need to tell someone who can do something, Che. A shrink, a therapist, a social worker. Someone else in your family. You have aunts, right?"

"That's what Georgie says. I've tried. I really have. But we move around so much. No one else sees what Rosa does. You have to see it to believe it. You've been watching her make the twins hate each other."

"Maya doesn't hate Seimone. She's just sad."

"I'm sorry."

"It's not your fault."

I don't say anything. I'm not sure that's true.

"You need to talk to someone about this."

My eyes sting. I will not cry in front of Leilani. I can't quite believe I told her everything, but I'm glad.

"I know now." Leilani slips her hand into mine. "We're friends."

"Phew," I say. "'Cause I'm not sure partial friends are allowed to confide in each other about cheating girlfriends and psychopathic sisters."

CHAPTER TWENTY-EIGHT

Leilani promises to keep a closer eye on Rosa and Seimone. She's sure Suzette, the au pair, will too. If Leilani can convince her Rosa's a problem.

I won't hold my breath.

I head back to the gym. The parentals text to ask if I'm joining them for dinner. Seimone will be there. She's sleeping over. I tell them no, that I'm sparring at seven.

—Ok, Sally texts, though I know she doesn't think it is.

This time I'm able to forget Rosa and lose myself, running through defensive sets, katas, punching bags.

Sojourner doesn't show up for any of the classes. I know she has exams, but I'd been hoping to see her, depending on it.

Georgie finally texts me. In between classes I tell her a bit about what Rosa said. It doesn't feel as urgent. Talking to Leilani has made me feel like it's going to be okay. That we can deal with Rosa.

Georgie's been reading a book on psychopaths in the workplace.

—They're everywhere. Pity you can't report Rosa to Human Resources.

—Funny.

I've yet to read anything that tells me how to deal with one in your family when your family doesn't believe you.

Sojourner arrives fifteen minutes into sparring. Dido's showing me how not to telegraph my hook and something else I don't hear because I'm watching Sojourner walk in, sink to the mat, and put on her wraps.

Dido waves her hand in front of my eyes.

"Right," I say, switching my attention to her.

"Nope," Dido says. "You can't pay attention. I'll work with someone who can."

She turns to the next two to spar.

I sink down next to Sojourner.

"Who were you up against?" she asks.

I point. "I think her name's Tina?"

"Tanya. How'd it go?"

"Alright. I gotta stop moving in a straight line."

"Keep your hands up and your shoulders in and your chin down."

"Stop telegraphing. Especially my left hook. But other than that I'm good."

"It goes out the window in a fight. Real question is, did you land any punches? More than you took?"

"We were maybe even. Where's Jaime?" I ask, though I'm glad she's not here, that it's just me and Sojourner. "Studying?"

"Ha! That girl? Study? Nuh uh. She's out with Elon on what she swears is not a date. I think she wants it to be a date."

Much like I want this to be a date.

We walk home together, side by side. A couple passes and we shift closer. The back of my hand grazes hers. It's cool out, but the back of my hand is warm.

"I'm starving," Sojourner says. She takes my hand and pulls me towards a pizza place. There's a window around the side where you can buy pizza to go. She lets go of my hand. I wish she hadn't.

"I thought you had to study?"

Sojourner's at a public school. They have classes and exams for another week or so.

"I do. We'll grab a couple of slices. We can walk and eat. My treat."

We go to the window and she buys two pieces—slices—of pizza. It's only two dollars. Even if I wanted to pay I couldn't. They only take cash.

The slices are handed to us on paper plates with a wad of paper napkins. They're piping hot and the grease is starting to soak through.

"Pepperoni. I always buy whatever just came out of the oven."

"Good choice," I say, taking a bite and almost burning the roof of my mouth. I wave my hand at it futilely. Sojourner grins.

We wolf the pizza down. It's all salt and oil and I don't care. It tastes amazing.

"There's grease on your chin." I ditch the paper plate and wipe her chin with a napkin.

"Your parents forgive you? For sparring?"

We're almost at her place. I'm not sure what to say. I don't want to talk about parents. I want to talk about Sojourner. I want to kiss her.

"I like you." My cheeks grow warm.

"Yeah," she says.

God. No *I like you too.* Just *yeah, I heard what you said.* She's not even looking at me.

"I know you said you couldn't date me."

"I did. This is it," Sojourner says.

We stand in front of the door to her apartment.

"I should study," she says.

"Right," I say. I slip my hand into hers. "Goodnight."

"Night," she says. She doesn't let go of my hand.

"I'm sorry that I don't believe in—"

Sojourner puts a finger to my lips. "Shh."

I swallow.

We face each other, holding hands, looking into each other's eyes. I step closer. I lean. My lips are close to hers. The air between us feels heavy, weighted by both our breaths.

It would take such a slight movement for my mouth to be against hers.

"Can I—"

Sojourner kisses me. Her lips are on mine, then our mouths open, our tongues touch. We wrap our arms around each other, my fingers find the nape of her neck, her hands slide across my shoulderblades.

A wolf whistle louder than a siren snaps us apart.

"Get a room, yo!"

"Nasty."

Two men, not much older than us, walk past way too close, almost bumping us.

"You want a real man, let me know."

Sojourner grabs my arm. "Jerks."

"I wasn't going to go after them," I say. "You don't have to pull me away. I avoid fights."

She laughs. "I was pulling *me* away. I was this close to giving them a beat down. Then you'd've had to back me up."

"True. But I know you don't like to fight outside the ring. I was relying on that."

She slips her hand back into mine and my heart speeds up again, like before sparring. We're walking towards Tompkins Square Park. "You're funny," she says, "and you taste good."

"I—"

"Shh. I don't want to think of reasons why we shouldn't. Let's find the darkest bench."

We do, under a busted light, and our mouths find each other's. We're panting. I'm filled with so much want. Sojourner's all I can smell or feel or taste. She slides her hand under my shirt, along the flat of my belly. I moan.

"Stop," she breathes. Her mouth is on mine, her hand doesn't move from my stomach. "We should stop."

"We should," I say, kissing her again, trying to slow.

She kisses me back. We speed up again. Kissing harder, my hands go to the back of her head. She pulls away again, looking at me, panting. She slides her hand up under my shirt to my left nipple. I gasp.

She kisses me again. "We have," she says in between kisses, "to,"—another kiss—"stop."

We don't stop.

She has one hand on my chest, the other just above the waistband of my trackpants.

"Fuck," I breathe.

"You swore," Sojourner says, laughing, sliding her hands out from under my shirt. "The first time since I told you not to."

"God, Sojourner."

"Now blasphemy."

"All I've got are words I'm trying not to say."

She smiles and it makes me shiver as much as her hands on my skin. I want to ask her to come home with me, to spend the night in my room.

The parentals won't mind, or if they do, they'll act like they don't. We've talked about sex. They've given me books about it. They've made it clear that when I start having it they'd prefer I do it somewhere safe, like my bedroom, that *I think of my partner's pleasure, not just my own*—Sally's words—and that I use a condom.

"I've never," I begin.

"Kissed a girl?" Sojourner finishes for me.

"Jesus. Am I that terrible a kisser?"

She smiles. "Blasphemy. I was teasing." She leans forward, kisses me again. "We wouldn't be on this bench if I didn't like kissing you."

"Right," I say. "I'm actually pretty bloody good at it is what I think you mean to say. I've had a lot of practice."

"Modest."

"Very. I've kissed and kissed and kissed and kissed and never done anything more."

"Nothing more?"

I shake my head.

"You've never kissed a girl's neck?"

"Hilarious," I say, leaning forward to kiss hers, which leads to more kissing and more panting and more blood rushing. I pull away.

"Have you ever—"

I put my hand gently over her mouth. "You're being evil. Have you had sex?"

She nods.

"With that guy we ran into? Your ex?"

"Yes."

"So you're not one of those no-sex-before-marriage Christians?"

Sojourner sits up straight. "Che, did you listen to the sermons? You know when you were in church with me and there were people, including my mom, talking up front? You hear any of that?"

"Honestly? No. I was thinking about how close your thigh was to mine, about how wonderful it felt holding your hand, how close our mouths were every time I turned to look at you. I didn't hear a word."

She laughs. "Then you missed an excellent takedown of purity culture. Sex is not a sin. Sex is love. The sin is not in having sex, the sin is in having sex *without* love—that can happen within wedlock as well as without. I just quoted from the sermon you didn't listen to."

I'm staring at her again. She's said the words *sex* and *love*. My mouth has gone dry.

"You've really never had sex?"

"No."

"Ha! That's wild. Here's me, a nice Christian girl, and I'm not a virgin. Here's you, an atheist, and you are."

I'm about to unleash my rant about how being an atheist doesn't say anything about a person except that they don't believe in God, but I stop myself. "Are atheists supposed to be promiscuous? Bummer. I've failed."

"I think it's sweet. I think you're sweet."

"Sweet's not good, is it? How about *hot* instead? Can't you say you think I'm hot instead of sweet?"

"You want me to say you're hot?"

I nod. "*I think you're* hot and we've spent the last—" I look at my watch. "Fuck. More than an hour all over each other."

"You're hot, Che. You swear too much, you're going to hell, but your kisses are hot." She puts her hand on the band of my trackpants, then trails her fingers up. "Your stomach is hot. Your chest is hot. The line of your throat is hot." She presses her lips against mine again. "Kissing you is hot."

We kiss, hard and passionate, then she pulls away.

"But I have to get home. We have to get home."

She stands up. I pull my T-shirt down so it hangs over my groin. Sojourner smirks.

"Sojourner, come home with me."

"I love the way you say my name. No one else says it like that. I'm glad you don't call me Sid."

"Was that a yes?"

"That was an *I don't know*. You're an atheist. I don't know what dating you would mean. I need to go home and think and sleep and study—I have exams and a fight coming up, and yeah, I don't know what this is, but I like it. You're not like anyone else."

I shake my head, trying to clear it. "You neither."

She holds her hand out, strokes my cheek. I feel it all the way to my dick.

"Good night, Che."

I shake my head. "I'm walking you home. Again."

"Okay," Sojourner says, holding my hand, leaning into me. "I can live with that."

CHAPTER TWENTY-NINE

I can't sleep. My brain won't stop thinking about Sojourner, replaying our kisses in the park. The feel of her hand at my waistband. I masturbate. I still can't sleep.

I wash up and call Georgie.

Her hair's cut even shorter than last time. The sides are shaved. She looks happy. I tell her about Sojourner and Rosa. Mostly about Sojourner. Georgie tells me about her and Nazeem, unable to keep from grinning. She's glad I told Leilani about Rosa. She tells me to enjoy whatever it is I have with Sojourner, to stop worrying about whether it's a thing or not. She's right.

I finally get sleepy. I say goodbye, crawl into bed. I'm about to slide under when I hear giggling from Rosa's room.

I knock on her door. More giggling, and the sounds of hasty cleaning up.

Rosa opens the door and yawns. Seimone is under the covers pretending to be asleep, but her mouth keeps twitching. I forgot she was sleeping over.

"It's after three. Stop being loud."

"Sorry," Rosa says, letting off a peal of fake giggles. "Seimone was being too funny."

"Stop being funny, Seimone."

Seimone sits up, grinning. Her eyes glisten with the tears of her suppressed laughter. "I'll try."

"Goodnight, girls," I say as Rosa heads back to bed and crawls in.

"Goodnight, Che," they chorus, looking exactly like two innocent friends having a sleepover.

I close the door and go to bed. I'm asleep within minutes.

When I wake up it's after nine. I lie in bed for a moment thinking about Sojourner's mouth.

I hear Rosa laugh. Genuine laughter, I can tell, laughter she doesn't want anyone to hear. Then her laughter cuts off. I pull on my trackpants and sprint downstairs.

Seimone is slumped forward on the island, her face on its side, her nose running, her eyes swollen shut. She's turning blue, not enough oxygen in her blood. Rosa stands next to her, staring, an auto-injector in her hand.

I grab it from her. The cap is already off. I stab Seimone's thigh through her pants, holding it down for a ten-count, hoping that's right, that I haven't hit a vein. I pull it out, drop it on the counter, rubbing her leg where I injected her.

Her eyes open a little. They're too swollen to open all the way. She gasps, then starts coughing. Her hands go to her chest.

We all watched the vid. We practised with a dummy injector. The McBrunights don't let Seimone spend time with people who don't how to use one.

Rosa's not laughing now—she's screaming.

Seimone needs medical help. I press 00, then realise where I am before I hit the final 0. I punch out 911.

"What is the nature of your emergency?"

"She's in anaphylaxis. I used the auto-injector. Yes. She's breathing."

Sally and David emerge from their study.

"What's . . . ?" Sally begins. She rushes to Seimone.

David enfolds Rosa in his arms.

I keep answering the operator's questions, confirm our address.

Sally's holding Seimone, telling her everything will be all right. Seimone nods. "I'm fine," she says. "It's like nothing happened."

She doesn't look fine. Her face is pinched, red, her eyes swollen, she's filmed with sweat. She smiles at Rosa.

David lets go of Rosa, pulls out his phone and calls the McBrunights. Rosa hugs Seimone. Seimone returns it with one arm.

My sister almost killed someone.

Rosa knew Seimone was allergic to peanuts. There's two glasses on the island filled with a gross-looking smoothie and the blender's in the sink. Rosa must have put peanut butter in it. She said she wouldn't kill anyone *unless she could get away with it.*

Rosa stood there and watched Seimone losing consciousness from an allergic reaction. She stood there with the injector in her hand, and she laughed.

After the ambulance is gone—Seimone and Sally with it—Rosa bursts into tears and rushes up to her room. David goes after her.

I text Leilani: —Seimone was talking. Her colour already looks normal.

My heart's beating too fast. I walk over to the windows, look down at the avenue. I can hear sirens. Someone else's emergency. Seimone's ambulance didn't turn on its siren.

"Rosa wants you, Che," David says. "She's pretty upset."

He hugs me. "Thanks for what you did. We're proud of you. Thank God for auto-injectors, eh?"

I nod. I can't believe what Rosa did. I look at the blender in the sink. The remaining sludge in it is brown.

I don't want to talk to Rosa. But David is waiting for me to go up to my sister's room and comfort her.

"She needs you," he says.

How can he not know?

I climb the stairs. What am I going to say?

"SHE DIDN'T DIE," ROSA says as I close the door behind me. My phone is set to record in my pocket. "I was about to use the injector."

She's sitting cross-legged on her bed, no trace of tears on her cheeks. I sit on her desk chair, turning it to face her.

"It's not my fault." She sounds as if she's saying she didn't eat the last biscuit. Not as if an eleven-year-old girl almost died.

The anger that flares in me is so intense I have to close my eyes and put my hands behind my back.

I wish Rosa were dead.

More than I've ever wished it. If she were gone, Seimone wouldn't have almost died. Who knows what else the world would be saved from.

My hands are shaking. I concentrate on slowing my breathing, on not letting anger control me.

If I open my mouth everything I've felt about Rosa—that she's broken, that she's evil, that she's the fucking devil—will come spewing out.

I can tell the parentals now. This is it. They know what happened. I can sit down with Sally and David and tell them everything Rosa has done and make them listen.

"It wasn't an accident," Rosa says.

"Of course it wasn't! Why did you do it?"

"It's a secret. I'm not allowed to tell. I promised."

"A secret?"

"Seimone's fine," Rosa says. "She said so. It's like nothing happened."

My heart's beating too fast. I don't dare open my eyes.

"Seimone told me she's almost died twice. But when she was little. She doesn't remember."

If I open my mouth I'll scream. When I'm calm I'll start from the beginning, ask her what happened. Then I'll tell Sally and David.

"What happened?"

"There was peanut butter in our smoothie."

"How did it get in there?"

Rosa shrugs. "I was about to stab her with the injector thingie."

I open my eyes. Rosa looks unconcerned. "You were just standing there."

"You snatched it when I was about to stab her with it."

"Don't smile."

She bites her lip. "I was going to save her."

"But you didn't."

"Because you took it."

"Don't lie, Rosa. You were just standing there. Why didn't you help her? You could have helped her. You watched the vid. We all did. You practised with it."

"I was *about* to. I told you."

"You laughed!"

I can feel my voice getting louder. I have to be calm.

"It was funny."

My hands turn into fists. For a fraction of a second I can see my right cross crushing Rosa's nose. I blink, force my fingers open. I try to think of how she was when she was a baby. Her little fingers curling around my thumb.

"She was coughing at first. But then her face went red and she was clutching at her throat and her lips were swelling. Really fast. Like they were balloons. I didn't know you could swell up that fast. I wanted to see. Then her eyes started to bulge. Did you see that? They were bugging out of her face. When you came downstairs she was turning blue. Blue! That plus her bulging eyes and her lips. It was funny, so I laughed. I can laugh and help her at the same time."

I close my eyes again. Focus on my breathing.

"You're going red now. That's kind of funny too."

I open them. "It's not funny. You knew you shouldn't laugh. You put your hands over your mouth so no one would hear it."

"I know you're not supposed to laugh when someone's swelling up. I was trying to be normal."

"By letting her die."

"I didn't want Seimone to die. She's my friend. She *didn't* die."

"No thanks to you."

"I was about to stick her with the injector. You stopped me!"

"Stop lying."

"I'm not," Rosa says. "You know I like seeing new things."

My hands are fists again. What can I say to that? What if I shake her? Will that get through to her? Could I rattle empathy into her brain?

"Death is interesting."

"Death is *not* interesting. When someone's in trouble, you help them. You want to pass for normal? Helping is what normal people do!"

"I was *trying* to. I keep telling you. But what if in helping someone I get hurt? Should I still help?"

"How was helping Seimone going to hurt you?"

"She was kind of thrashing around at first. She could have hit me. That's why I waited."

Calm, I have to be calm.

"It would have been interesting if she'd died. I've never seen anyone die. I wonder if it's like a guinea pig?"

"She's your friend. She's *not* a guinea pig," I say. "Wouldn't you miss her?

"Yes. Seimone is very useful. She's teaching me to be like a normal girl. I'd miss her. I could try to be friends with Maya."

"Maya doesn't like you."

"I'd make her like me. I'm good at that. I decided Seimone would like me. I looked up all the things she liked. Ask me anything about Korean pop music."

"That's not how friendship works."

"It's how it works for me." The smile creeps back onto her face. "I'm glad I can tell you these things, Che. I like being able to tell you what I think."

I hate hearing it.

"Was this your chance to kill without being caught? Is that what you were thinking?"

"Oh, no. I don't want Seimone to die. She's my friend."

You keep saying that. Saying it doesn't make it true.

"You have to promise me that if something like this ever happens again you'll do what you can to help. You won't stand there and watch."

Rosa shakes her head. "I *did* try to help. But *you* won't believe me. I think I've made enough promises. I've kept them all. I said I wouldn't kill anyone and I haven't. That's enough promises."

I stare at her.

"I definitely want to drive an ambulance when I grow up," Rosa says. "Emergencies are exciting."

CHAPTER THIRTY

I march to the parentals' office and knock hard on the door.

My hands are sweating. My heart's beating as fast as it does when I spar.

"Come in," David calls out.

I open the door, step into their study. David's in front of the computer, typing intently. He doesn't look up.

"Have you heard from Sally?"

He types some more, then swivels on the chair towards me, nodding. "They checked Seimone, said she was fine. Thanks to you, Che. We're proud of you."

He stands up, hugs me awkwardly with one arm, then sits again.

"They have to keep her under observation for a few more hours. Her own doctor will be checking her as well."

My phone pings in my pocket. I switch it to silent without looking.

"Did you want something else?" David's swivelling the chair back towards the computer while looking at me.

"Yeah."

I sit down on the couch, next to the window. Then I stand up again, stand by the window.

"What's wrong?" David asks, but he's looking at his screen, reading, not focused on me. He starts typing again.

"My sister is a monster," I say. I feel leaden, as if I've left my own body.

"Uh huh," David says, typing.

"My sister is a monster," I repeat, louder this time.

"What did you say?"

"She's . . ." I trail off. "She put peanut butter in that smoothie they made. I think she tried to kill Seimone."

David's not looking at his computer now.

"Rosa. She's not neurotypical. I know you don't want to hear it. She has antisocial personality disorder."

I tell him about Apinya's guinea pig, about the passport. I tell him more of the awful things Rosa says.

He's leaning forward on his chair, watching me as intently as Rosa does. He doesn't blink. I keep talking and he doesn't interrupt me.

"She only cares about getting what she wants. I don't know how to stop her and some day she's going to kill someone. I don't know what to do . . ."

My throat aches. My brain. My heart, too. My eyes burn. I can't get my mouth around any more words. I'm crying. I wipe at my eyes.

I'm furious. With Rosa, with my malfunctioning eyes, with David, with Sally.

I scream. Tears stream down my face. I'm shaking and screaming.

Then David is holding me, hugging me. He *there-there*s at me. It works.

We're sitting on the couch, David looking at me, frowning. I feel empty. He hasn't said anything. I have no idea what he's thinking.

David pours me water, hands me the glass.

A dust mote drifts into the glass, then floats on the surface. Dead skin, probably, but I gulp down the water. Swallowing hurts.

"When . . ." David finally says, then looks down at his fingernails. The cuticles are ragged. When did they get like that? David always keeps his hands immaculate. It's one of the many vanities Sally teases him about.

"When what?"

"How long have you thought," he says, pausing again, "this about Rosa?"

Fuck, I think. *He doesn't believe me.*

I sink back, wipe my eyes. My throat burns. I've laid it out. I'm not sure I have any more words.

"You're tired," David says. "We can talk about this later."

I shake my head. We have to talk about it *now*. We talk about it now or . . . I don't know . . . or I'll scream again and not stop screaming until we deal with the problem of Rosa.

"You don't believe me." My voice isn't the croak I expect.

"Of course I do." His voice sounds sure. "I always believe you, Che."

"You don't always listen."

He opens up his hands as if to say *that's fair*. "How long have you thought something was wrong with her?"

"Longer than I've been trying to get you to listen. But it was the guinea pig that freaked me out, and now this. She almost killed Seimone! Do you believe me?"

David moves his head briefly. A short nod. I think. But it could be a shake.

"I started a journal, wrote down every weird thing she did. To see if I was imagining it. Then she started confiding in me. She knew that I knew."

This one-sided conversation is making me tired.

"Remember when she was killing insects? When you took her to the doctor? Back then I made her promise not to kill. So she stopped. Until she figured out a loophole: Apinya and her guinea pig, and now Seimone's allergy. Rosa was laughing, David. Both times. *Laughing*."

David's looking at me the way a disinterested scientist would. Is he in shock?

"I know this is hard to take in. I didn't want to believe it either."

He hugs me again, one-armed. I'm glad.

"Do you believe me?"

His head moves again. It's ambiguous.

"When's Sally coming home?"

"Lisimaya was pretty upset. She'll stay with her as long as she's needed."

I nod. "Right. I guess we can talk about it more when Sally gets back."

"Maybe tomorrow," David says, but his tone says *maybe never*.

"You don't believe me, do you?"

I'm crying again. What a waste of time.

"I believe you," he says. "I know about Rosa. I've known for a long time."

All the breath goes out of me. "Sally? Does Sally know?" The hope in me is so big it burns.

He shakes his head. The movement is clear this time.

"Not at all?"

"We talk about Rosa. But Sally's never said anything that makes me think she suspects anything worse than Rosa being socially awkward." He shakes his head again. "She's said a lot that makes me think she doesn't *want* to know."

"But you believe me."

"I believe you. Rosa isn't normal."

This dizziness I'm feeling is relief. *David knows.*

"I try to talk about it with Sally. But she won't listen. She talks about how young Rosa is. You've heard her."

I have.

"Then she changes the subject. So I watch Rosa. I talk to her. I've been doing what you've been doing."

When? I want to ask him. *How did I not see any of it?* "You've been talking with Rosa about how she is?"

David nods. *How did I not know?*

"We have to tell Sally."

"You can try," David says. "You *have* tried. Did she listen?"

"But Rosa almost killed Seimone."

"She *almost* let her die. You've said it yourself: Rosa keeps promises. She's never killed anything bigger than—"

"A guinea pig."

"Right."

"I think we need to tell Sally."

"Go right ahead."

"She needs to know."

"I think Sally *does* know. She won't admit it to herself. She doesn't want to believe there's anything wrong with Rosa. She . . ."

"What?"

"She wanted a daughter. She hoped you would be a girl. She loves you, Che, but she always wanted a daughter. Then Rosa came along and wasn't what she expected. Sally loves you more than Rosa. You're more like her than Rosa is, but she can't admit that to herself. She can't admit that Rosa is the way Rosa is. I think mostly she can't because Rosa's a girl. In Sally's mind men are violent—like I was. Women aren't."

"She hates that I box."

David nods. "It reminds her of how I used to be. I've tried to talk to Sally about Rosa, Che. She doesn't even want to *think* about it. Sally talks about *everything*."

It's true. Sally is a relentless communicator about everything *except* Rosa.

"She's not ready. She can't believe the evidence in front of her own eyes."

I didn't think I was ready, or that I've ever been ready to deal with what Rosa is, yet somehow I do.

"Why does Sally get this time? I've dealt with it on my own. She's decades older than I am."

"You were born old," David says.

I have the strongest desire to punch him.

"Have you told the McBrunights about Rosa?"

David shakes his head.

I shouldn't be surprised, but I am. "Seimone's not safe. Maya's not safe. Leilani's not safe. Rosa's said she wishes Maya and Leilani were dead. They need to know."

"She won't kill anyone."

"How can you be sure?"

"Because she knows what the consequences are. She's not stupid."

"No, she's not. But she is impulsive."

"Not the way she used to be. Rosa's improving."

"Do you believe that?"

"Yes. Also, telling anyone could be disastrous, Che. It could destroy our family."

His phone rings. "It's Sally."

I pull out my phone. Loads of messages, but the battery's low. I realise I've been recording this whole time. I turn it off and check the messages.

From Leilani:

—This was Rosa, wasn't it? Seimone's saying she wanted to see what would happen. That she made Rosa promise to use the auto-injector. Mom is furious. Sally and Dad are trying to calm her down. Seimone won't stop crying. She would never have done this before she met Rosa.

"Well," I say, when David finishes talking to Sally, "Leilani says Seimone claims it was her idea." I read out the text.

"Sally said the same thing."

I stand up, walk to the window. David knew. Rosa knew that David knew. Neither of them told me. They've both been lying to me for years.

I need to not be here.

"I'm going for a run."

I open the door. Rosa is standing there. She doesn't pretend she hasn't been listening.

She looks from David to me, then back again.

"I told you I didn't do anything wrong. It was Seimone's idea. She wanted to see what would happen."

"Why didn't you say that?" I ask.

"She made me promise not to tell. But now you know. I didn't touch the peanut butter, Seimone did. She's never tasted it, you see. Not that she remembers. We watched the video three more times so I wouldn't mess up injecting her. I think Seimone was hoping nothing would happen. She doesn't like being allergic. I'm glad I'm not."

"But you didn't *use* the auto-injector!" I meant to say it, not yell it. David puts his hand up.

"I told you: I was *about* to, but then you grabbed it from me. I didn't get a chance."

I look at David. He's watching Rosa.

"We're still friends. You saw, Che. Seimone hugged me. She texted too." Rosa holds out her phone. "Seimone realises it was a silly thing to do. I told her that *before* she did it. I can show you the text. She understands how serious her allergy is now. She's learned her lesson."

There it is: the Rosa smile.

"Seimone is my very best friend. I'd do anything for her."

"Then you won't let anything like this happen to her again, will you?" David says.

Rosa shakes her head.

"Do you promise?"

"I promise, David. If someone is in trouble I will help them. Just like you do."

She's arranged her face into an expression of sincerity.

"We both heard you make that promise," I say, which is when it hits me again: *David knows.* I don't have to have these conversations with Rosa alone anymore. I don't have to deal with her by myself ever again.

David's phone rings. While he takes the call I stare at Rosa, not knowing what to say. How long has David known about her?

"He won't let you tell the McBrunights. Not because of Sally, but because it will ruin their business. Then they'll be truly skint."

David's on the phone. He hasn't heard.

"How long has David known about you?"

"Known what?" she asks innocently.

"That you're not like him. That you're—"

"I'm exactly like David," she says. "None of us are normal. Our whole family. You, me, David, Sally. Like Sally says, we're different."

"Seimone's asking for you, Rosa," David says.

Rosa holds her hand out for the phone. David slips it into his pocket.

"Seimone's home. She wants you to stay the night with her. She doesn't want to be alone."

"Don't she and her twin share a room?" I ask.

"Not anymore," Rosa says. "I'm going upstairs to pack."

"You're okay with that?" I ask David. I can't believe David's okay with that.

David nods. "We'll both be there. The McBrunights will be there. We'll be checking on both Seimone and Rosa. Come too? I'm sure Leilani will be pleased to see you."

I shake my head.

"She wasn't trying to kill Seimone, Che."

"This time."

"I don't think Seimone's in danger from Rosa. Not physically."

"I wish I believed that."

"You heard her. Seimone's her best friend. Having a best friend is useful to Rosa. She's talked to you about how she finds us useful?"

I nod.

"We're both watching her. We know how she is. It's going to be okay, Che."

David hugs me and I let the relief wash over me. Having him on my side is huge, even though all I want is to lie down, close my eyes, and stop thinking about what happened, stop picturing Seimone's face turning blue.

I walk them to the door. Rosa has her backpack on. She's smiling like a little girl who's having a sleepover with her best friend. She races ahead to the lift to press the button. I lean against the door. "See you later," I say, as if we were a normal family.

David turns to me. "It'll be okay. We're both making sure she keeps her promises."

CHAPTER THIRTY-ONE

I check my phone. Texts from Leilani, Georgie and Sojourner.
Sojourner.
The phone switches off before I can read it. No juice. I plug it into the charger on the kitchen island, bouncing back and forth, waiting for my stupid phone to come to life.

I want to see Sojourner. This time yesterday we were in the park kissing.

The blender is still in the sink. I can't stand seeing it. I turn my back, look at the phone. It's still dead.

Seimone could have died right here.

I don't believe it was Seimone's idea. Christ. Rosa has wormed her way deep for Seimone to risk dying to please her.

I pull the blender out of the sink, tip the contents into the bin, stick it in the dishwasher. I wash my hands even though none of that peanut mess has gotten on me. Then I check the phone again.

It's alive.

Sojourner's text is —Whatcha doin?

—Thinking bout you.

—Wanna go for a run?

—Wanna come over to my place? Everyone's out.

—My moms are out too.

—You at your place now?

—Yeah.

—Walk along ninth. I'll meet you.

—I'm walking.

—Me also. Walking towards you.

I lock the apartment door and bypass the lift for the stairs.

—So romantic, Che. I'll swoon.

—Because I'm hot.

—Gag.

I don't walk. I run along Ninth dodging foot traffic, darting across the avenues against the lights, not pausing until I see Sojourner crossing through the park. I stop, feeling like an idiot for having run because I want to see her so bad. At the streetlight she smiles, raises her hand.

I speed up. She does too. Then we're standing in front of each other grinning like idiots.

We kiss. I'm not thinking about anything but the feel of her mouth against mine. She pulls away. "My place? Moms won't be home till after eleven. You wouldn't have to leave for ages."

"Mine won't be back till tomorrow."

"Oh," Sojourner says, taking my hand. We walk Manhattan west to my place. Our hands fit together like our fingers are meant to be entwined. Sojourner walks faster, I keep pace. She pulls her hand away and half runs.

Then she is running, laughing. My heart expands. I chase her, dodging a woman walking two chihuahuas, jumping the leash. I narrowly miss bumping into a couple holding hands and swinging them as if they're littlies. Sojourner's ahead of me, still laughing. If there weren't so many people out, walking slowly, taking up most of the footpath, I'd catch her.

She stops outside my apartment building. "What kept you?"

"Annoying people," I say, pulling her to me and kissing her again. I taste salt. I taste her.

I pull away to unlock the door to the lobby and nod hello to the doorman, but I'm not looking at him, I'm looking at Sojourner. We're holding hands again. I pull her into the lift and punch the button for our floor. We're kissing again, holding each other, bodies pressed tight together.

The lift doors open. We race each other to the apartment. I let go of her hand to pull out the keys, fumbling them out of my pocket into the keyhole, looking at Sojourner. I drop them. She kisses me. We press up against the door. Her hands are on my shoulders, down my back, under my shirt, my hands against her waist, pulling her tight against me. I can feel her breasts against my chest.

"Inside," she says between kisses.

"Right," I say, making myself let go of her.

My heart's beating in my ears, in my fingertips. My breathing's too shallow, too fast.

"Keys."

I bend for them. Make myself look at them, pick out the right one, insert it into the lock, unlock the door. We stumble in, shut the door behind us. I lock it. Slide the keys into my pocket.

Sojourner bursts out laughing again.

She's so beautiful. I don't know what to say. I touch her cheekbone. She takes my hand in hers, kisses my fingertips.

I groan.

The smile on her face is everything.

"Upstairs."

She nods. We take the stairs two at a time, bumping into each other, tumbling through the door to my room. I shut it, don't turn the light on. The blinds are open, and light floods in from the street.

We stand there, looking at each other, looking at my bed. My double bed. I've had double beds since I was twelve but there's never been anyone in any of them but me.

I want to touch her again but I don't.

What should I say? Are we going to have sex? We need to discuss it first. I don't want to push it. *Christ*, I realise. I don't have any condoms. So that's that then. Weirdly, the realisation that we aren't going to have sex makes me feel more relaxed.

"Nice room." She's looking at the Ali poster, at his knuckles.

Her left hand forms a fist. She holds hers up to his.

I look at her fist, then at Ali's. "You need more scars."

"Give me time." She does an Ali shuffle.

I whistle. "Almost as fast as the great man."

"Almost?" She swats at me.

"Almost." I bend to kiss each knuckle of her fist, peering up at her. "You taste good."

"Like sweat."

"Like *your* sweat."

"You taste good too." She steps closer, takes my bottom lip into her mouth.

I groan again. I can't help it.

"I can stay. I'll text my moms that I'll stay the night."

I swallow. "I want you to stay the night." *I want you*, I don't say. "But . . ."

"But?"

"I, um, I don't have any, um, protection." Jesus Christ, how old am I? I can say *condom* out loud.

"Sure you do," Sojourner says, waving her hand at my wraps, neatly rolled up and in a pile on the chair next to my desk.

"Funny."

"It's alright. I have condoms."

"Oh." She has condoms. We can have sex if we want to. My heart speeds up. Tachycardia. The thought of having sex is going to give me a heart attack.

She smiles, kisses me lightly on the cheek, puts her hands flat against my chest to push me towards the bed, till I'm sitting on it, lying back on it, and Sojourner's on top of me.

She's all I can smell, she's all I can see. I'm harder than I've ever been. My heart is beating faster than it has ever beaten.

"We don't," she says, kissing my nose, "have to," kissing my chin, "do anything," kissing my mouth, "we don't want."

"I want to," I breathe. "You're beautiful. You're so, God, Sojourner. I could worship you. I could—"

"Be the most blasphemous person alive," she says, but she isn't mad.

She's kissing me; I'm kissing her.

We're pulling each other's clothes off. Her breasts, I'm touching Sojourner's breasts. She's touching my stomach, a finger along the line of my obliques, her hand brushes past my dick.

"Oh."

We're falling over each other, moving too fast, not fast enough.

Then we're on our knees, facing each other. She's all sinew and muscle. Her shoulders look carved. I can see the line of each muscle of her rotator cuff.

I run my fingers along her bottom lip, her chin, her neck, over her breasts, along her abs, tentatively I touch between her legs.

I look up. Sojourner nods, then guides my fingers to where she wants them, whispers to me what to do. Her words against my ear make me dizzy, make heat spread over me as if my blood's burning.

We move in time with her hips, with the movement of my hand against her. My dick throbs. My head and my heart too.

We press closer together, breathing faster, kissing. I speed up in time with Sojourner, faster and faster, pressing harder when she tells me to, then faster, harder, faster, faster, then—

She presses her thighs tight against my hand, lets out a low moan.

"Stop," she whispers. "Stop."

We fall onto the bed, dripping sweat. My hand's a little numb. I shake it.

Sojourner grins at me. "Mmmm."

We lie there, her hand on my belly, her head on my shoulder. I listen to her breathe. Outside sirens blare and I realise there haven't been any since I went to meet Sojourner. Or, rather, I haven't heard them.

She leans up on her elbows to kiss me. "Salty," she says, rolling off the bed.

For a moment I'm scared she's leaving. Instead she digs in her track-pants pocket and hands a small foil packet to me.

"Your turn."

"We don't have to," I begin, nervous I won't put it on right, that I won't last long enough.

I stare at the foil in my hand. I've watched vids on how to do this. You're supposed to check the expiry date. I do. It expires when I turn twenty.

"I just bought them," Sojourner says.

"Right." I feel like an idiot.

I pinch with one hand, roll it over my dick with the other, slowly, determined not to mess it up. I read somewhere that a condom could tear if you go too fast or roll it the wrong way.

Sojourner giggles.

I look at her.

"You're concentrating all intent like this." She narrows her eyes, wrinkles her nose and forehead. "Like in class when Dido corrects you and you're all, *I will follow her moves exactly*. You get the same expression—like there's nothing else in the world."

She leans in to kiss me. "It's adorable."

"Adorable?"

"Hot. It's really hot." She moves in closer. "Really, really hot."

"IS THIS A THING?" I ask.

It isn't dawn yet. Sojourner lies on her side, her back to me. My arms are around her.

"It's a thing."

"What kind of a thing? A you're-my-girlfriend-now kind of a thing?"

"A pretty big thing." She laughs.

"What changed your mind? I mean, I'm still not a Christian."

"I can't lie. I wish you were. But . . ."

"But?"

"I like you. I like this. It doesn't matter how long it lasts."

It matters to me. I want this to last forever.

"I'm not being cool about this, am I? I want to be your boyfriend. I really like you, Sojourner. I've never felt like this before." I can't bring myself to say *love*, not yet, but that's what I'm feeling.

"You've never had sex before."

"Shhhh. You know it's not that. Though that was great. Don't get me wrong." I press closer to her, feel myself go hard against her arse.

"Mmmm."

"Since it was my first time, I need more practice. With you."

"With me."

"Because I'm your boyfriend?"

"Because you're my boyfriend."

I kiss her. Sojourner kisses me. We put in more practice.

I wake with sunlight in my eyes. I didn't pull down the blinds. Sojourner is lying next to me. I haven't thought about Rosa in hours.

I'M GOING TO MAKE Sojourner a fry-up of eggs and bacon and tomatoes and onions, not letting her help. She leans across the island to kiss me as I chop the tomatoes.

"Good morning," David says, emerging from the study.

We spring apart and I knock some tomato to the floor. "Fuck."

"Swearing," Sojourner says.

"Good morning, Sid," David says as if it's perfectly normal for her to be eating breakfast here, which makes it perfectly abnormal.

I scrape up the tomato from the floor and dump it in the bin.

"Want some coffee?"

We both nod. I start the onions frying. Then the bacon.

"Where are Sally and Rosa?"

"They're with Lisi and Gene. They're taking the two girls to a counsellor."

I wonder whose doing that was. "Good," I say.

"Yes. They need to understand the seriousness of what they did."

Sojourner looks at me but doesn't ask what he's talking about. I wonder why David wasn't going to the counselling session as well. To stay here so we can talk more? I want to know why he kept his knowledge about Rosa a secret for so long.

I crack the eggs into a second pan. One of the yolks breaks. "Scrambled okay?"

"Sure."

I flip the bacon again, push the eggs and the tomato and onion mixture around their separate pans. I'm starving. I turn the flames down a fraction. I don't want to burn the bacon. David hands us coffee. Sojourner takes hers with a lot of milk and sugar. David doesn't approve but he keeps it to himself.

I serve, handing Sojourner her plate heaped high. I know her appetite's like mine. "Forks!" I grab two and hand one to her.

We hoe in.

"This is great," Sojourner says, between mouthfuls.

I wish David would disappear into the study.

"Do all boxers eat as fast as you two?" he asks.

"I teach this morning," Sojourner says, "so I gotta go soon."

"Normally she eats as slowly as Rosa."

I wish I hadn't mentioned Rosa.

"What do you teach?" David asks.

"This morning? Self-defence, then kickboxing."

She finishes, grabs our plates and rinses them. I jump up to take them from her and put them in the dishwasher. "I'll walk with you."

Sojourner smiles. "Thanks for the coffee, David."

"WHAT DID YOUR SISTER do?"

"She . . ." I'm not sure how to explain Rosa almost killing her supposed best friend. Do I tell the story that Rosa and Seimone are swearing is true? Or do I tell her what I'm pretty sure happened? "She made trouble and dragged her friend Seimone into it."

Sojourner laughs. "So detailed."

"Explaining Rosa is complicated. She's not like other kids."

"She's cute. A bit vain and attention-seeking, but she's only a kid."

I weigh up telling Sojourner the truth. I've told Leilani. Sojourner's my girlfriend now. We're walking down Lafayette hand in hand. We've had sex. We've talked about religion and what we want to do with our lives. I've met her moms. She's met my family. I should tell her.

Not now. I want to hold on to this feeling, not talk about Rosa.

"Tell me more about what you believe. You say you're Christian but you're okay with sex before marriage, with homosexuality, with—"

"I believe that Jesus was the Son of God and He came to help us. To help everyone, but especially the most disenfranchised, the poorest, the most discriminated against. My Jesus was about feeding the hungry, throwing the money-lenders out of the temple. My Jesus believed passionately in social justice, economic justice, every kind of justice. He wanted to make the world a better place."

"Do you believe in evil?"

Sojourner nods.

"Do you believe that some people are evil? That they're beyond saving?"

"No one's beyond saving but some people are . . . They get pretty close."

"I don't believe in evil. Not like that. I think evil people can be explained by the morphology of their brains, their genes, their environment. Really, by the interaction of those three things."

Sojourner is staring at me. "That's very, um, detailed. You've thought about this a lot?"

"Yup. What about hell? Do you believe in hell?"

"I believe many people are living in hell right now. There are many awful things in the world. Including right here in America. Cops killing my people and not even getting a slap on the wrist. So many people inflicting pain on others. How could hell be any worse?"

When I tell Sojourner the truth, will she think I'm living in hell with my devil sister tormenting me? Am I?

"I guess," Sojourner says, "the idea of a hell and a heaven in the afterlife is a way to comfort us that those who do wrong in this life will be punished and those who do good are rewarded. But I doubt they really exist."

"So you don't believe that the Bible is the literal word of God?"

"I think it's a record of His words imperfectly recorded by humans. In the case of the New Testament, some of them generations after the death of Jesus. I believe there's truth in the Bible. Some of it metaphorical, some of it literal."

Sojourner's version of Christianity isn't like any version I've come across. I realise I've only talked with conservative Christians.

"Have you heard of Liberation Theology?"

I have, but I don't know anything about it.

"Look it up. That's what I believe. What do you believe? Is your God science?"

"No gods for me. I believe in a lot of what you're saying. Social and economic justice, helping other people whenever we can. Mostly I believe in empathy. Without empathy this world is doomed."

Sojourner nods. "How about love? Do you believe in love?"

I squeeze her hand. "Love and empathy? I believe in them absolutely."

I turn to kiss her and whisper in her ear, "Also sex. Big belief in sex right now."

CHAPTER THIRTY-TWO

When I get home I knock on the study door. There's so much I have to ask David about Rosa. He calls me in.

He's on the phone. His brow is all ridges and his mouth a tight line. It's the look he has when he's trying not to lose his temper. I'm tempted to leave it for later. I do not want to see David lose his temper.

"I understand," he repeats.

I look at my phone, because it feels rude to listen. I reply to Georgie, but don't tell her exactly what happened. I don't think I can sum up what Rosa did to Seimone in a few texts. Nazeem got an A+ on an essay about why this generation of Aussie teens don't drink as much as previous generations. I congratulate him. I text Leilani to get her version of what's happening with Rosa and Seimone. No reply. I wonder if she's at the counselling session as well.

I text Sojourner. ─I miss you already.

I don't care how sappy that is. I do miss her. I won't get to see her for hours.

"What did you want, Che?" David asks. Though I have no idea how what I want could be a mystery.

"Is this a bad time?"

"Yes. But I can make time for you. You know that."

I don't know that.

"I want to talk more about Rosa."

David nods.

I want to know why he didn't tell me he knew. I want to know if David has a plan.

"What do we do about Rosa?"

"We do what we have been doing. We let her know when what she's done is unacceptable. I spend a lot of time reminding her that if she can't pass as normal her life will be miserable."

"I've been recording our conversations."

David stares. "Yours and Rosa's?"

I nod.

"If we played them to a psychiatrist, if they could listen to her casually talking about not caring, about how she finds it interesting when people are in pain, that she enjoys messing with them—they'd see what she is straight away."

"They will. But then what?"

I don't know.

"We have a practical problem. How do we minimise the harm Rosa does? We can't cure her. There is no cure. All we can do is containment."

"So we give up?"

"I didn't say that. It could be worse. I've seen it be a lot worse."

"Your brother or Papa?"

"Both of them. That's how I knew what Rosa was. I've lived with this before."

"They're worse than Rosa?"

"Why do you think I've kept this family as far from them as I could? I didn't want Saul or Papa anywhere near Rosa."

I have a moment of dizziness. We are talking about Rosa, about psychopathy, about this family.

"I've read some studies that say empathy can be taught."

"It's too late for Rosa."

I stare at David. "How can you be sure? There must be a psychiatrist or therapist or someone who can help her."

"How does Rosa respond to people trying to change her? Remember the last few times we took her to doctors?"

I do.

"She gamed them," David says. "She figured out what they wanted her to say, then said it until they said she didn't have to go back anymore."

I should feel happy hearing my own thoughts voiced by David. I'm not. "You think there's no hope?"

"I didn't say that. We're teaching her how to be normal. We've been doing that for years. Rosa doesn't think the way most people do, but she knows what could happen if other people realise that. She's become good at acting."

"Too good," I say.

David shakes his head. He's leaning forward, his office chair tilting with him, his elbows resting on his knees. "Sometimes pretending to be something you're not can change you. The pretence can become real."

"You believe that?"

"I know it. When I first met Sally I was out of control. I did some terrible things back then."

I know this. It's part of family lore. I know he ran a high-stakes poker game at his fancy private school, that he wiped out several of the richest students. That's not what got him expelled. Breaking another student's jaw did that.

"I wanted to impress Sally, be her crazy wild man. I thought she liked that side of me. But it scared her. Back then I was terrified she was going to leave me."

He shrugs briefly, almost apologetically, as if I don't know how much he loves her.

"I started consciously being more like her. I went to anger management classes like she wanted me to. You've never seen my temper, Che. That's why. I modelled myself on Sally. Did what she did, said what she said. I stopped getting into fights. It was the hardest thing I've ever done. I have so much rage. It burns in me and the urge to let it go, to raze everything—sometimes I have to run to get away from it. I can't stay in the same room, the same city, the same country as it."

"Doesn't it travel with you?"

David shakes his head, then nods. "Not when I'm with Sally. She's shown me how to outrun it. I changed. The anger burns less intensely now. How many times have you seen me lose my temper?"

I haven't. "I've seen you *not* losing your temper. Your face tightens. I can see you fighting it."

"It's a struggle."

"Rosa doesn't have a temper. Not since she was little." I try to imagine Rosa changing. I can't. "You aren't Rosa. You care what people think. You cared what Sally thought. *That's* why you changed. Rosa doesn't care—you should hear some of the things she's said to me. I'll play them for you."

David straightens up on the chair, pushing it back a little, all his intensity gone.

"No need. I've heard what she says. Our job is to make it clear to Rosa that passing as normal is her only choice. She knows being diagnosed reduces her chances of getting away with anything. Maybe acting normal *will* change her. I changed."

I want to believe him. "We're not professionals. These are big decisions we're making. Shouldn't we at least get advice from someone who knows more than we do? If we take her to someone who's worked with young . . ." I pause at the label. I haven't called her a psychopath in front of David yet.

"What's a formal diagnosis going to achieve, Che?"

"A professional will help us understand our choices."

"What do you think will happen to Rosa once she's labelled? She hasn't broken any laws. She's ten years old. If we get her tested, what will those tests prove? Say they confirm what you think—then what?"

"She's a *psychopath*. Isn't it our duty to protect people from her?"

"You can't call a ten-year-old a psychopath. How do you think people will treat her once they know? What school will take her? Will she have to go to a school for other disturbed children? What will she learn from kids like her?"

I don't know.

"The best we can do is to keep her under control and make her aware of the consequences of doing what she wants to do. Containment is our only option."

But we haven't contained her, have we? We've let the virus that is Rosa contaminate Apinya and now Seimone.

THAT AFTERNOON AT THE gym Sojourner kisses me when she sees me and slides her hand into mine. We really are a thing. Thoughts of Rosa and my fucked-up relatives slide away.

Jaime laughs. "Resolved your religious differences, did you?"

"We good," Sojourner says.

"Very," I say.

Jaime makes vomiting noises.

We work out together and spar together. There are long moments when I don't think about my sister.

The three of us walk home. I'm having dinner with them and Sojourner's moms.

"Hey, thanks for inviting Elon the other night," Jaime says. "We been hanging. Elon's cool."

Elon is pretty much definitionally cool.

"You know Leilani dumped Veronica, right?"

I shake my head. "Again?"

"For real this time. Veronica's drama-ing everywhere. Cut her wrists."

I stare.

"Not very convincing, you know? More like a graze. But she's weeping over Elon and they've known each other since they were gooing and gah-ing. She's family. Elon's gotta hold her up."

"Poor Elon."

"Truth."

"Don't look at me," Sojourner says. "I don't know Elon. Bring him to church, Jaime."

Jaime snort-laughs. I've learned that it's a running joke that Jaime will never go to church.

"There's a protest on this Sunday. Me and Elon are fixing the world the direct way."

"That right?"

Before they can argue I ask, "Your moms know we're together, right?"

I'm a bit nervous about this dinner.

"Of course they know," Jaime says. "Sid tells them everything. No secrets in that home."

"You say that like it's a bad thing," Sojourner says.

"I never thought I'd miss the crazy Catholic everything's-a-secret, children-should-be-told-nothing chaos that is living with my parents. But you guys totally overshare."

"We don't!"

"Girl, your mom talks about the colour and texture of her poop!"

"She's sick. It's one of the signs of how she's doing."

"Too much," Jaime says, shaking her hands out. "And your moms are way too noisy when they're going at it. Least when my olds were together they had the decency not to do it anymore. Or if they did they were quieter than a mouse."

"Low bar. Mice round here are noisy."

"Whatever. I do not need to know. Olds shouldn't be at it, anyways. Nasty. Your mom does not need to be in my business asking me about whether I'm using protection and whether I'm—what did she say?—oh, yeah, I remember, *getting pleasured right*. Oh. My. God. She was going to tell me about my clitoris. So embarrassing."

Sojourner laughs. I'm torn between wondering how Jaime manages not to blaspheme in front of Sojourner's moms and laughter at how much her moms are like my parentals.

"Wait. Does this mean they're going to give me the third degree on whether I, um, *pleasure* you right or not?"

Now Jaime's laughing too. Both of them are egging each other on to louder and louder bursts of laughter.

"They'll probably ask you to draw a map to demonstrate that you know where the clitoris is."

Jaime is struggling to walk, she's laughing so hard.

"Oh, look," I say, waving my phone around. "My parents. They say I have to come home, right now."

Sojourner grabs my phone. "Nuh uh uh." She holds it out to Jaime. "Do you see any such message?"

Jaime shakes her head. "I do not see any such message."

I clutch my stomach. "I think I have sudden-onset nausea." I turn and take a few steps in the opposite direction.

Sojourner grabs my arm, Jaime the other.

"Not so fast, Mister. There's no escape from interrogation by the moms."

"Lesbians are the worst," Jaime says. "No shame, no boundaries. They'll probably want to make sure your dick's the right size too."

Sojourner snorts and mock punches Jaime. "Too far!"

"She's kidding, right?" I'm pretty sure she's kidding. "Right?"

They crack up laughing again.

We meet Diandra and Elisabeta at a Venezuelan restaurant. Elisabeta's mother was from Venezuela. I eat arepas for the first time. I consume six to make sure the last one is as good as the first. The moms don't say a single word about my penis. We don't even talk about sex. We talk about politics, injustice, a demonstration they went to, Sojourner's upcoming fight, what winter's like in Sydney and whether a drinking age of twenty-one is stupid.

Sojourner and I spend almost an hour saying goodnight, each last kiss leading to yet another one.

I don't tell her what Rosa did.

I don't think about what Rosa did.

IT'S PAST MIDNIGHT WHEN I get home. Sally is there. She and David are sitting at the island drinking wine together. They know I was out with Sojourner and Jaime and Sojourner's moms, but I haven't gone into any details about me and Sojourner yet.

Sally puts her glass down and pulls me into a hug. "What a day— night and day—whatever it is. Are you okay?"

"Yeah. You?"

She answers by hugging me again. "I'm not sure. I can't believe they would be so reckless. Seimone could have died!"

I return the hug and open the fridge. It's almost empty. No ham or cheese. I can't see any proteins. I open the crisper and grab the last apple. It won't go far. "No ham?"

"Neither of us got a chance to shop," David says. "You're welcome to do it tomorrow."

"Sure," I say, wondering how I'll pay for it. "Is my credit card working again?"

"I'll give you cash."

I slide onto a stool and pour myself a glass of water.

"Seimone believes it now," Sally says. "That peanuts can kill her."

If only Seimone believed Rosa can kill her.

"How are Lisimaya and Gene?"

"Shocked. I think the therapy was a good idea. I was just telling David it was a shame he couldn't be there."

David doesn't look like he thinks it's a shame.

"Someone has to keep working. We're not far from launch."

"Ten months? Hardly close. You can give yourself a few hours off."

David waves Sally's objections away. "I need to work."

"What did the counsellor say?" I ask.

"He was very practical. He made them both talk about what they thought they were doing. What outcomes they expected. If they thought about what would happen if it went wrong. If," Sally pauses, "if Seimone died."

I bet Rosa thought about it. "What did they say?"

"They hadn't thought that far, of course. They assumed their scheme would work."

"To be fair," David says, "it did. Seimone's alive."

"True. But as the counsellor pointed out, irrelevant. You can't base your decisions on the expectation of the best possible outcome. Especially if the worst outcome is death!"

"How did they react to the counsellor making them think through what could have happened?"

"Seimone was beside herself. She kept saying she didn't want to die. Rosa was distraught."

I bet. Rosa probably modelled her tears on Seimone's. Not that she isn't capable of manufacturing them without mirroring these days.

"Seimone's taking it hard. That's why Rosa's there, comforting her."

Whispering poison in her ears.

"I wanted Rosa to come home, but Seimone was almost hysterical at the idea. She's spending another night over there."

"Is that wise?" I ask before I can stop myself. Behind Sally, David shakes his head.

"I think so," Sally says. "Seimone's learned her lesson. Rosa too. They won't try anything like that again."

No, I think. *She'll try something different.*

"You think they've both learned, just like that?"

"Seimone almost dying was a huge shock."

Not to Rosa. "Will they be getting more counselling?"

Sally nods. "The counsellor wants to talk to them more about how they should speak up when they think the other is going to do something she shouldn't. Rosa should never have let things go that far. She should have told Seimone testing her allergy was wrong."

"She sure should have."

Sally cuts me a look, recognising my sarcasm.

In my pocket my phone buzzes.

—We need to talk about this, Leilani texts me. —Figure out what to do.

"I'm knackered," I say.

Our goodnights are more overwrought than usual. Sally hugs me twice.

"I can't help thinking about what would have happened if you hadn't given her the adrenaline in time. Poor Rosa froze. Thank you, Che."

David shudders. I bite my tongue.

Up in my room Leilani and I arrange to meet for breakfast.

I crawl into bed and lie there staring at the car lights moving across the ceiling. I wish Sojourner were with me.

At least I can be sure that whatever Rosa is plotting next, it won't happen soon. She got away with almost killing Seimone—that'll satisfy her for a while.

CHAPTER THIRTY-THREE

I'm woken the next morning by Rosa knocking on my door. It's grey outside, and not much light filters in.

"Che!"

"Just a minute," I say, wishing she'd go away.

I get dressed and open the door. "When did you get home?"

"I don't want you to violate my rights anymore," Rosa says, marching in and climbing onto my bed where she takes up a cross-legged position, resting the back of her hands on her knees like she's going to meditate.

I stare at her. "You what? Who's sitting on whose bed, Rosa?"

"You record our conversations."

It's not what I expected her to say. I sit down on the floor.

"How did you know?"

"I heard you tell David." She's looking at me the way she looks at an ant before she squishes it.

"From behind a closed door. Super ethical, Rosa."

"I didn't hide that I'd been listening."

"No, you didn't sneak away in time. I opened the door before you were ready."

"You shouldn't talk so loudly if you don't want to be overheard. You always say you don't lie, Che, but recording conversations without asking for permission—that's lying. You acted like we were having normal conversations, but you were studying me as if I was a bug. You're a liar."

"No, I'm not." I have a sickening feeling she's right. "If you'd asked me if I was recording I'd've told you. Am I denying it now?"

"Only because you know I know. You're as sneaky as I am, Che. You're like me. You're just better at pretending you're not."

"I'm nothing like you, Rosa."

"You're my brother. Of course you're like me. There's no one who's as much like me as you are."

"Have I ever threatened to kill your friends?"

"I've never done that."

"You said you'd push Soj—Sid down a flight of stairs."

"No, I didn't."

"*Yes*, you did. You said you wanted Leilani and Maya dead."

"I never said I'd kill them. I promised I wouldn't." Rosa has never looked more smug. "You lie to yourself, Che. I know exactly who I am. I like me. You'd be a lot happier if you liked yourself, Che."

I feel like screaming.

"What would you say if you discovered I'd been recording our conversations? Would you think that was creepy?"

"Of course. But it's not the same, because I'm *not* like you, Rosa. I don't *want* to be like you. I've never made anyone kill their pet. I've never tried to kill my best friend. I don't lie and steal and cheat. I'm not you."

"I *didn't* kill the guinea pig. I *didn't* try to kill Seimone. You don't listen. I'll never kill Seimone. She's my best friend. I need her. I don't want you to record our conversations anymore. It's creepy, Che. Just because I'm different doesn't make it okay."

"You're not merely different. Different isn't dangerous, Rosa."

"You shouldn't be telling Leilani lies about me either. She told Seimone that I kill pets. I told Seimone you're jealous because you're not smart like me. She knows you play chess like a baby. She feels sorry for you."

"I'm glad I'm not like you."

Rosa smirks. "Dumb people are always happy to be dumb. I'm different from ninety-nine percent of the population. My kind of different is better."

Is she referring to one of the estimates of how many psychopaths there are, or of how many geniuses?

"Did you know that there are people like me who keep blogs? I've learned a lot. They talk about how to pass for normal. A few of them say you should change your name and leave your family behind as soon as you can. Family only gets in the way."

I imagine her doing that. I *wish* she would do that.

"The comments are full of arguments. Lots of psychopaths . . ." She pauses, and smiles to acknowledge that she knows what I think she is. "Lots of *us* think family is the best disguise because everyone thinks psychopaths are loners. They never suspect someone with a family, who loves them, could be a monster."

"I don't think you're a monster," I say. She's right. I do lie.

"David doesn't want you to tell the McBrunights about me because he doesn't want them to pull out of their business. It's about money, Che, not Sally. You can't trust David. Why do you think he never talked to you about me? He's always known."

"Why, Rosa?" I'm fascinated to hear her conspiracy theory. She gives everyone motives as heinous as her own. "Why would he do that?"

"He needs us to be a happy, normal family so we don't scare investors away. David hates being broke. He hates having to have a normal job. Why do you think we've moved so often? Why do you think he's working so hard?"

"David always works hard."

Rosa smiles. "He always makes it look like he's working hard. More people are like me than you think. One percent? Researchers must have pulled that number out of the air. Almost everyone is like me."

"You think that, Rosa, because you can't imagine what it's like to be anyone else. The only way you could understand that most people in the world give a damn would be if you gave a damn."

Rosa shrugs. "You'll see. We're making dinner tomorrow night, me and Seimone. It's going to be a family dinner to bring us closer together."

I can't wait.

I GET TO THE cafe a few minutes late because of Rosa. Leilani is sitting with Maya at a table in the corner. She has her arm around her sister, and is leaning into her, speaking to her in between sips of coffee. There's an intimacy there, a palpable sense of their mutual love.

Maya looks small. There are shadows under her eyes. I think she's lost weight.

She looks haunted. They both look haunted.

Because of Rosa.

I sometimes wonder if Rosa is an alien virus. Everyone she touches is infected with the same inhuman DNA: she turns us grey. I'm sure I was a different person before she was born. A happier person. When the mothership lands we'll be too broken to repel the invasion.

Leilani sees me, gives a half wave. So does Maya. I walk over.

"We need a plan," Leilani says before I've sat down.

We do. "Is this our war committee?"

Maya's lips curve. It's almost a smile. "Can we put camouflage paint on?"

"Sure."

"The main thing is to keep Rosa away from Seimone and Maya." Leilani isn't smiling. "I can protect Maya, but I don't know how to get through to Seimone. She's completely under Rosa's thumb. Did Seimone tell you she and Rosa are making us dinner tomorrow night?"

Maya's almost-smile disappears.

Leilani nods. "Clearly the two of them think poisoning us is the next step."

"Hilarious."

"Seimone keeps repeating that Rosa is her best friend in all the world and that the whole thing was her idea. No matter what I tell her about Rosa."

Maya looks at her hands.

"It couldn't have been Seimone's idea," Leilani says. "She wears gloves everywhere. She's *terrified* of peanuts."

I'm starving. "Is it okay if I order food? I haven't eaten yet." This was supposed to be a breakfast meeting.

Leilani nods. I order the big breakfast. She and Maya both order the fruit and granola.

"I keep warning Seimone about Rosa," Leilani says. "I warned her before you told me anything. I haven't flat out said *Rosa's a psychopath*, but I told her about the guinea pig, about the horrible things she says. Seimone didn't believe me. She said I was jealous. *I love you*, she said. *Maya too. But Rosa is my best friend. She understands me.*"

"Ugh." I can imagine Rosa saying *you understand me* to Seimone the same way she says it to me.

"Maya sleeps in my room now."

"Good. Are you and Seimone still not talking?"

Maya droops. "She's not talking to me. Rosa does. I wish she wouldn't."

"Make sure you're never alone with her—Seimone doesn't count. Call me if you're worried Rosa is going to do something. You have my number?"

Maya nods.

"I can't believe she wanted to kill Seimone," Leilani says. "They're friends. Why would she want to kill her?"

"I'm not sure she did," I say. "The auto-injector was in her hand. The cap was off."

"She *was* going to inject her then. That's what Rosa says. That she froze."

"She didn't freeze. She was laughing."

Maya slumps, which makes her look even smaller.

"I don't think Rosa meant to kill her. I think she was fascinated by Seimone's face turning blue. She wanted to see what would happen. That's why she made Seimone eat peanuts. I think Seimone was willing and that Rosa doesn't want her to die."

"Rosa can make her do anything," Leilani says.

"She can make Seimone believe it was her own idea."

Our food arrives. My big breakfast is truly big: four sausages, many rashers of bacon, scrambled eggs, mushrooms and onion. I hoe in. Maya pushes her spoon through her granola, mixing the yoghurt and berries together, not bringing any of it to her mouth.

"You really think she's a psychopath?" Leilani asks between spoonfuls.

It's the second time she's asked me. I get it. We should be cautious. But I've been living with this for years. I've been certain for years. "So does David."

"What? I thought they didn't believe you."

"I didn't know! We talked after it happened. David admitted he knows what she is. That he's been trying to control her too."

Leilani stares. "Then why didn't he tell Mom and Dad?"

"Sally's in denial." As I say it, I realise it doesn't make any sense. Why *isn't* David warning people? Most of all the McBrunights? He said it would destroy our family, but he can't truly believe that, can he? "He doesn't want to upset her," I finish weakly.

"That's bullshit! Seimone could have died. Fuck Sally."

I flinch. "She . . ." I begin, but nothing David said justifies keeping Rosa secret. "Rosa says he's afraid your parents will pull out of their new business."

"I'm telling Mom and Dad what you've told me. Your dad will *have* to back me up. Why would I make this up?"

"He might not. They could lose everything."

"I don't care."

"Tell your parents. I'll go with you if you want. I'm sick of not telling people. Secrets are bullshit. Did I tell you Rosa hinted about pushing Soj—Sid down a flight of stairs?"

Leilani's eyebrows go up.

"I don't think Rosa would do it. I don't think she could. Sid's a trained fighter. Rosa says shit like that all the time—to mess with me."

"Callousness," Leilani says.

"You looked up the checklist?"

"Of course. I read it, thinking about Rosa, and it was check, check, check."

"Callousness, disinhibition, fearlessness and charisma."

"Obviously I have the charisma, but I wouldn't mind the fearlessness," Leilani says. "Imagine never being stressed or anxious."

"Too big a cost." I know Leilani's joking, but I can't help myself. "We worry *because* we care. Besides, fearlessness goes with disinhibition. If Rosa wants something she takes it. She doesn't think about consequences, because she doesn't care. Except now she does. The peanut thing was planned. You have to think about consequences in order to plan."

Maya shudders. She hasn't eaten anything. My plate is empty.

"Rosa doesn't learn to be good; she learns to be better at being bad."

Leilani hasn't touched her phone. Leilani is *always* on her phone.

"How do you live with her?" she asks. "My stomach would be acid, waiting for her to do something. Ten years you've been dealing with this?"

"Well, I . . ." No one's ever come close to understanding what it's like living with Rosa. Not Georgie. Maybe David? But we haven't talked about that yet. I don't know how I live with it. I'm not sure I *am* living with it. "The worst is the poison she whispers in my ears. Her twisted view of the world."

Leilani squeezes my hand. "I'm seeing my therapist tomorrow. I'll tell her everything. She'll know what to do. I'm telling Mom and Dad too, whether David backs me up or not. You will."

"Thanks." I mean it. I wish I could let her know how much.

"Do you love Rosa?" Leilani asks.

"Yeah. That's the worst part. She's my little sister. I held her when she was a baby. I've always looked after her."

Maya slides from her seat, slips around the table and gives me a hug. She means it. Something Rosa has never done. It's all I can do to keep from crying.

CHAPTER THIRTY-FOUR

Rosa and Seimone don't make us dinner.

Leilani tells her parents everything I told her. David doesn't back her up. I accuse David of lying. David tells me he's disappointed. He told me we couldn't tell the McBrunights. He won't say anything else. Sally can't believe I'd say something like that about Rosa—especially to the McBrunights. She seems to have forgotten I've told her exactly the same thing.

Rosa smirks.

Leilani and I text back and forth.

We were expecting explosions. Instead, we meet at the McBrunights' to discuss what Sally calls a *misunderstanding*, and Gene calls a *situation*—like grown-ups. Even those of us who are not grown up.

I take a sip of water from the glass in front of me. There are four water jugs and a spread of cheese, meats, salads, dips and breads in the middle of the table.

We shouldn't be seated like this, with the McBrunights on one side of the table and the Taylors and Kleins on the other, because that's not the faultline. Rosa, Seimone and the adults should be on one side; Leilani, me and Maya on the other.

Gene has blueish shadows under his eyes. He smiles and pats Lisimaya's shoulder. She returns the smile, but not brightly. She doesn't look as strained—her makeup is perfect—but she's painted over the top of her exhaustion.

I doubt anyone has slept much since Seimone almost died. Except Rosa and David—nothing can keep them from sleep. The circles under Sally's eyes look like bruises. Maya suppresses yawns. Leilani too. She isn't looking at her phone. My phone burns in my pocket. I have the recording of Rosa not promising that she won't kill Maya ready to play.

Rosa and Seimone exchange glances and wave their hands at each other in pretend sign language.

"Shall we start?" Sally asks.

"I don't know," Leilani says. "Are any of you going to listen to what we have to say?"

Gene turns to her. "C'mon, Leilani. Can we at least *try* to keep this civilised?"

Leilani rolls her eyes.

No one's touched the spread. I pick up a piece of celery filled with something pink and take a bite. The crunch is as loud as a gunshot. Everyone looks at me.

"Sorry," I mumble, putting the celery on my plate.

"Che can't not eat," David says. "It's a boxing thing."

"The food's there to be eaten," Lisimaya says, gesturing at the spread. No one makes a move to eat it.

"Why don't you start, Leilani?" Sally says. "We promise to listen."

"Rosa is . . ." Leilani looks at Rosa, who's arranging her face into a picture of innocence: opening her eyes wide, glancing down, her bottom lip on the verge of a pout.

"I—we," Leilani says, glancing at me, "we think Rosa has antisocial personality disorder."

"I do not!" Rosa says. Seimone shakes her head.

"It means she likes to manipulate people, and she doesn't care what happens to them."

"I do too!"

"She manipulated Seimone into eating peanut butter and—"

"No, she didn't!" Seimone objects. "That was my idea!"

"Let Leilani finish," Lisimaya says.

"I keep telling you—" Seimone says.

"Leilani speaks first," Gene says. "You'll get your turn."

"You, Che," Leilani says, "tell them about the guinea pig."

I do. Rosa protests her innocence.

"Why didn't you tell us this at the time?" Sally asks.

"Because you never believe anything I say about Rosa."

"Because you lie," Rosa says.

"You'll have your turn, Rosa."

"There's something wrong with Rosa," I say, keeping my voice low and calm. "Seimone could have died. Listen to this recording I made of a conversation with Rosa."

"You recorded your sister?" Sally asks, her voice rising.

I nod. "Because I needed evidence."

I press play before anyone else can say anything.

Rosa: Maya's mean. It would be a lot easier if she was dead. Seimone wishes she was dead.

Me: Jesus, Rosa, you can't kill Maya.

[Silence]

Me: If you kill Maya you'll be locked up.

[Silence]

Me: You're clever. But even the smartest killers get caught. Read up on them.

Rosa: I have. Those are the ones who were caught. There are lots of unsolved murders.

[Silence]

Me: You want to live in this world with as few restrictions on you as possible, yes?

[Silence]

Me: If you kill Maya, what do you think will happen? You're different. You already have to work hard to hide that from people, and even then some of them don't want to be near you.

Rosa: Like Maya. I'm getting better at being the same as everyone else, though. You saw me at the party. I talked to everyone and they liked me. They told Sally and David how talented I am.

"SHE'S TEASING YOU," SALLY insists as Lisimaya hugs herself. "She's ten years old. She's not going to kill anyone."

"I would never," Rosa says.

"It is disturbing," Lisimaya says. "Does she say things like that often?"

I nod. "That's how she thinks."

"No, it's not!" Rosa says. "I was pretending. You know I like acting."

"Has she ever been violent?" Lisimaya wants to know.

"Does killing insects count? She steals."

I tell them about the passport, then about the things she did as a smaller kid. As I speak, none of it sounds that bad.

Gene hasn't said anything. David hasn't said anything.

"She's malevolent," Leilani says.

"*You're* malevolent," Rosa says, stumbling over the word as if she doesn't know what it means.

Seimone nods. "It's true, Lei-Lei, you've been mean to Rosa since she got here. Maya too. I'm allowed to have my own friends, you know. Just because we're twins we don't have to like the same things."

"They're both seeing James," Lisimaya says. "If Rosa is what you say she is, James would notice, don't you think? He spent years working with disturbed children."

"He's only seen her once," Leilani says. "Why did you lie, David?"

"Are you asking why I don't agree my daughter's dangerous? Because she isn't."

I shake my head.

"She's *not*, Che. Yes, she has difficulty connecting to people. She always has. Yes, she says inappropriate things. Very inappropriate. She's learning about inside and outside voices and her impulse control isn't great. Yes, she likes to get to you, Che. Little sisters do."

Are Gene and Lisimaya buying this?

"As you know, she was diagnosed with developmental disabilities when she was younger," David says, looking at his two oldest friends. "But she's been improving. My God, you should have seen her three years ago! Rosa used to struggle to make friends. Now she has two. She and Apinya are still in contact. So whatever happened to Apinya's guinea pig—"

"I didn't—"

"Let me finish, Rosa," David says. Rosa's bottom lip sticks out. "They're still friends."

I thought David had agreed Rosa *was* dangerous. Hadn't he?

"She's not normal," Leilani says.

"I agree. Rosa's not normal. She's at least five years ahead in mathematics. Even further ahead as a chess player. Two or more years behind socially. Apparently those often go hand-in-hand. I don't agree with your diagnosis." He cuts a look at me. "Neither has any professional who's examined her. There have been many. I know Che *wants* to be a doctor, but he isn't one yet."

I can feel the burn on my cheeks. "No one's ever examined her to see if she has antisocial personality disorder."

Sally glares.

"David, why didn't you tell my parents any of this? Don't you think they should have known she's not normal before letting her near the twins?"

All the adults speak at once, but Lisimaya cuts through the noise. "They did, Leilani. We've known about Rosa for years."

"Then why didn't you tell *us*?" Leilani demands.

"Because we didn't want you to judge her," Lisimaya says. "Rosa has enough trouble fitting in. I think we erred."

"Seimone stopped talking to Maya because Rosa made—"

"No, she didn't," Seimone says. "You make me sound like a baby, Lei-Lei. I'm *not* a baby. Maya knows why I stopped talking to her."

"Can you tell us why?" Gene asks gently.

"Because Maya called Rosa an evil robot."

"Did you, Maya?"

Maya nods. Gene suppresses a laugh. No one else is amused.

"I want you two to talk to each other again," Lisimaya says. "Can you promise me that? Maya?"

Maya nods again.

"Seimone?"

"Not unless she stops being mean to Rosa."

"What about Rosa being mean to me?" It's the first time Maya's spoken.

"Rosa," David says, before anyone else can speak. "Will you stop being mean to Maya?"

"I wasn't—"

"Rosa?"

Rosa nods.

"Do you promise?"

"I promise," Rosa says, drawing the word *promise* out a fraction of a second too long, so that it almost sounds sarcastic.

"Will you stop messing with your brother?" David gestures at my phone. "What you said is not funny. Don't ever joke about death."

Rosa looks chagrined. "I didn't mean it. I didn't think Che'd take me seriously."

"Seimone, will you talk to your sister now?" Lisimaya asks.

"I promise," Seimone says, pronouncing it exactly as Rosa did.

THE FAMILY WALKS HOME together. I can't call us *my* family. It doesn't feel like they have anything to do with me. Yet here we are. I have bits and pieces of both of them: David's hair and nose, Sally's eyes. But right now it feels like we have nothing else in common.

Rosa's half smiling. I can see she counts tonight as a victory. She's right. It is.

"You said you believed me," I say to David. We're less than a block from the McBrunights, but I can't hold it in.

"I do," he says. "I also told you I have to keep this family together."

"How could you?" Sally says, turning to me. A vein twitches on her forehead. "How could you say that about your own sister? How could you *record* her?"

Rosa giggles. Sally turns on her. "It's not funny, Rosa."

Rosa's giggles stop instantly.

"This is not a game. Why do you think your brother thinks such ill of you? Because you don't take anything seriously, Rosa. I know it's hard. I know you struggle. I know you'd prefer everything were numbers. But it isn't. You need to try to fit in better. You need to stop laughing when it's not funny. You need to stop saying scary stuff like that. That you want Maya dead! Why would you say that?"

Rosa's face is as expressionless as David's. "I'm sorry."

"You should be, Rosa. Wanting people dead is never funny! You can't talk like that."

David puts his hand on Sally's shoulder. She shakes it off.

"How did we get here? Thinking the worst of each other? Spying? How is this us?"

I don't know who she's asking. She's not looking at any of us.

David puts his arm around her. This time Sally lets him, resting her head on his shoulder. I think she might be crying.

They cross the street to the park. Rosa and I follow. We walk the rest of the way home in silence. Rosa's face is blank.

More than anything, I wish I was with Sojourner.

PART FOUR
I Want to Go Home

CHAPTER THIRTY-FIVE

—It's so cold today, Georgie texts. —I'm wearing mittens!
—Boiling here.

Summer's finally arrived. I'm in shorts at the gym waiting for Sojourner to show up for our sparring session. I'm sprawled on the bench in front of the change rooms, guzzling water and two protein bars, and catching up with Georgie.

—You'd love it. The clothes are every style you can imagine. Every colour. Pastels, neons, candy colours.

—You're paying attention to clothes now? You know what pastels are all of a sudden? NYC has changed you.

I don't tell her I'm quoting Leilani.

—I saw these people in short red jumpsuits skating down the bike lane on old-fashioned roller skates. One of them had her hair in rollers.

This I had noticed. Everyone had. The skater in front had a vintage boom box balanced on his shoulder, blasting music as old as the roller skates.

—So cool. One day I'll see shit like that. Is the little devil still away?
—She gets back tonight.

I thumb through the photos Rosa's sent from dance camp and send Georgie today's one of Rosa posed in a Bo Peep costume with Seimone in her ballet gear.

—Cute. Had we learned to do selfies at ten?
—Kids these days.
—So no dead animals?
—Funny. Not that I know of. How's your major?

Georgie's major project for textiles is a ball gown. While she texts me about it, including images of the latest calico dummy, I run through my list.

1. *Keep Rosa under control.*
2. *I want to spar.*
3. *I want a girlfriend.*
4. *I want to go home.*

1. Rosa hasn't done anything scary since Seimone almost died and we had the family conference. She's stopped talking to me. Not *talking* talking. She's pretending she's normal. She hasn't snuck into my room again. She hasn't said who she wishes is dead. She hasn't said a single thing that makes the hair on my arms stand on end.

If Rosa doesn't make any trouble for the next ten years will I believe she's changed?

David is more optimistic than I am. But David says different things about her in public than in private. He's forgiven me for telling the McBrunights. I'm not sure I've forgiven him. He reiterates that our family's survival is at stake. That all a label for Rosa will do is destroy her life and our family. He sees the darkness in her, but he won't admit it to anyone but me.

There are millions of people like Rosa around the world, he says, *who live their lives without killing anyone. Rosa's smart. She wants to live a normal life. Look at how well she's been behaving.*

James the therapist doesn't diagnose Rosa with anything. He doesn't think Rosa and Seimone's friendship is unhealthy.

He's wrong. But at least a professional is talking to her. She'll slip up and he'll see. Between David and James, it feels like she's less my responsibility than she was.

Seimone is talking to Maya again, but not like they used to. Maya continues to sleep in Leilani's room. Rosa and Seimone continue to be thick as thieves, inventing their own hand signals. Holding up different arrays of fingers, tapping their elbows, waving their hands around and laughing their arses off whenever anyone asks them about their secret language.

Leilani and Maya believe me. Before, I only had Georgie. I could never bring myself to tell her how terrorised I felt, how Rosa consumed almost every minute of my life. Being able to talk about Rosa with Leilani has changed everything. I feel like I've been breathing with one lung for years and now I have two.

2. I've sparred. My boxing is a thousand times better than it was before I sparred. The parentals don't like it. But they're not stopping me.

3. I have a girlfriend. Sojourner is everything. I don't get to see her as often as I'd like, which would be every minute of every day. She has two jobs, she fights, she teaches Sunday school. If I didn't box too, I'd see her at most twice a week.

4. I don't want to go home to Sydney. It's starting to feel like home here.

Because of Sojourner and Leilani and Maya and even Elon and Jaime. But Sojourner is the biggest part of my happiness. She's more than everything.

When she walks into the gym, her hair pulled back, her bag slung over her shoulder, my heart beats faster. I smile, stand up, draw her into my arms. Her bag slides to the floor. We kiss.

"Get a room," Meathead snarls, but we ignore him.

Sojourner kisses me again, then disappears into the change room. I'm smiling as I text Georgie.

—Sparring now. Your project looks amazing.

We grab pizza on the way home. It's our ritual now. Sojourner pays. She knows my parents are having what they call *cashflow problems* and that I'm afraid to overuse Papa's credit card even though he said it was okay. Mostly because Papa loves writing *I told you so* to David as many times as he can.

Usually I walk Sojourner home before going back to my place, but not tonight. Tonight her moms are at a church conference in Charleston in South Carolina. It'll be just me and Sojourner in her tiny flat until morning. When I'll have to go home and see Rosa for the first time in two weeks. I wish her moms were away for a week so I could put off seeing Rosa longer. A month would be even better. When I'm with Sojourner I don't think about Rosa.

I'm not thinking about her as we fall into Sojourner's room, peeling off our clothes and landing tangled together on her bed.

WE SLEEP IN. I wake to a phone full of missed calls and urgent texts and Sojourner doing her equivalent of swearing her head off, which switches back and forth between *gosh* and *oh no*. She's going to be late for the self-defence class she's teaching over the holidays.

—Can you look after Rosa and the twins this am? Take them to their tennis lesson?

Suzette, the au pair, is sick. Leilani's busy with Neophyte. The McBrunights don't fly in from Tokyo until tonight, and the parentals are in meetings all day, which leaves me, because the McBrunights' staff have more important jobs to do than babysit.

Maya greets me at the McBrunights' door. "They're coming to tennis too."

Maya has on a white tennis shirt and shorts and flip-flops. I assume her tennis shoes are in her enormous bag, which is by the door.

"Rosa doesn't play tennis." As far as I know she's never held a tennis racquet.

"Neither does Seimone. But now they're coming to *my* tennis school to get beginner's lessons."

In a week Maya goes away to tennis camp in Florida. No one's admitting that the timing of the two different camps gives Maya as much time without Seimone and Rosa as possible.

"She's never been interested in tennis. She says it's stupid. Tennis is not stupid."

I nod, though I have no opinion. Other than boxing I'm not much into sports.

"It's Rosa's doing," Maya says. "You know what she said? *Rich people play tennis.* Then Seimone says, *I'm a rich person*, and Rosa says, *I'm going to be a rich person.*"

I devoutly hope not.

"She's the worst."

We sit down on the couch furthest from the door.

"Where are they?"

Maya directs her gaze to the gallery above, where the girls' bedrooms are.

"How long do we have to get to your lesson?" I stretch out on the couch, look up at blue sky and white clouds beyond the insane skylight. I don't feel like scrolling through a million texts. I think about last night, about Sojourner.

"An hour," Maya says. "But I want to warm up first. If we take the L we'll be there in twenty minutes. I told them we should go as soon as you get here. They know you're here."

—Come downstairs, I text Rosa. —We're ready to go.

"I wish they weren't coming," Maya says. "Seimone hates tennis. I wish their camp lasted all summer long."

I can't help agreeing.

"They're going to make us late."

"Not yet." I wouldn't put it past them.

"They ruin everything," Maya says.

"They're not going to pull anything. If they make us late or do anything else they know I'll tell your parents."

Maya nods, but she doesn't look convinced.

—Thinking of you, I text Sojourner. I wish she was here.

The lift chimes. Seimone and Rosa step out wearing matching outfits: red shirts and blue skirts, red and blue runners, red and blue ribbons in their braids. They even have matching red and blue backpacks. As if they're trying to say *we are the twins now*.

"Hello, Che," they chorus. "Hello, Maya."

Maya doesn't say anything.

Seimone's hair is almost as long as Rosa's. I wonder when she started growing it. They look like tiny members of a psychopathic cheerleading cult.

"Can we choose how to walk there?" Seimone asks. "Tennis is Maya's thing, so we should get to choose."

That sounds like Rosa logic to me. Who cares how we walk there? Maya gives an exact replica of Leilani's minimal eye roll.

"We're walking to the First Avenue L stop, not the whole way," I say. "We're not walking on tiptoe or balancing chairs."

"Funny," Seimone says.

Rosa stares. "We meant that we want to pick the route."

I wonder if she'll ever understand sarcasm.

Maya's already at the door, shouldering her bag.

"I can carry that if you'd like, Maya."

"Coach says—"

"Lugging your bag around will toughen you up. You told me. I'm not sure about your coach's logic."

Maya pokes her tongue out at me. "She's great. So *nyer!*"

"Let's go across on Ninth," Rosa says.

"Fine."

Outside the sun is shining, and even though it's a weekday plenty of people are ambling, looking like they have no particular place to go. There are birds in the trees, sparrows. Sojourner says there are hawks too, but I've never seen them.

As we walk, Rosa and Seimone dart around Maya and me. Then they switch again and then again. Their hands flutter in their sign language.

"Quit pushing," Maya says.

"We're not pushing. We're dancing," Rosa says. "We have to practise fluid movements."

"We're gliding," Seimone says, but to Rosa, not Maya.

"No, you're not. You're bumping me. Che, tell them to quit it."

"Save the gliding for the tennis courts."

They switch positions again. I see Seimone hold four fingers up, with her thumb to the base of her little finger. They both giggle, bouncing from one foot to the other, as we wait for the lights to change.

—This blows, I text Leilani. —Maya's miserable. Rosa and Seimone are insufferable.

We cross. I've decided it's easier to keep an eye on Maya than to watch for transgressions from Rosa and Seimone. Maya walks fast, sticking to my side.

—Insufferable? Leilani responds. —When did you decide to relocate to a ye olde British kids' book?

Maya mutters something that sounds like *I hate them.*

I pat her shoulder awkwardly, hoping she remembers I'm on her side.

"Let's stop at the dog run," Rosa says. "I want to watch the dogs."

She's somehow managed to keep her fake dog alive. Email alerts on its status go to me and the parentals. She probably thinks there's a chance the parentals will get her a real one.

"We'll be late," Maya says. "There's no time to watch dogs."

"Straight through the park, girls."

"Yes, Che," Seimone and Rosa say simultaneously in singsong voices, then giggle. I'd like to ban them from giggling.

I know there's no chance I'll run into Sojourner—she's teaching—but I still look around. The park is where I first saw her outside the gym, it's where we had our first real kiss.

I'm pretty sure it's too early for me to be nostalgic about how we got together. I'm not going to ask Leilani or Georgie, and certainly not Jason. Especially as his response to my having a girlfriend was —Gettin laid at last. Orsum. Was worried yer dick wld fall off. Sometimes I worry he means that shit.

Maya switches her bag from her left shoulder to her right.

"Will you let me carry it for a bit? I won't tell your coach."

"It's okay," Maya says. "It's not as heavy as it looks."

It looks very heavy. "Any time you want a break."

More giggles from the red-and-blue twins.

"We could play chess," Seimone says. Rosa nods. They change places again. This time I see Seimone bump into Maya.

"Stop that. Don't bump Maya. There will be no stops for anything. There will be no dog-watching and no chess-playing and no bumping into Maya."

We're out the other side of the park and crossing Avenue A.

"Yes, Che," they sing, and skip slowly and profoundly annoyingly. They're humming, too, adding to the annoyance.

—Would it be wrong if I killed them both?

Leilani's response is immediate. —Isn't that a Rosa kind of question?

—I'm suitably shamed.

I trip, almost dropping my phone.

"Shouldn't walk and text," Rosa says.

"It's against the law," says her less-evil twin.

I can't see what I tripped over, but I suspect it was one of their skipping feet. I put my phone in my pocket. I need to pay attention.

Maya shifts her bag again.

"Let me take it."

She shakes her head. Her fingers are white where she's holding it.

"Not too many blocks now."

We stand waiting for the lights to change. Beside me, Maya shifts her bag to the other shoulder. I don't offer. I'll wait for her to shift it one more time, then I'll insist. On the other side of her, Seimone and Rosa are bouncing up and down on their toes.

A huge semitrailer rattles past, blowing a horn loudly. It's brilliantly festooned in a red, green and yellow exhortation for a beer I've never heard of. The sun is as intense as I've seen it since we arrived. This busy, crowded avenue is all bright colours and glorious contrasts. I can't remember why I thought New York City was ugly. Any city Sojourner is in can't help but be gorgeous.

Something moves wrongly beside me. Maya's bag spins, the shoulder strap twisting around her arm and pulling her off balance. I grab at her as she flies past me into the road. A bike slams into her. Her head hits the road with a sound that makes my stomach roil.

"Maya!"

Seimone is crying hysterically.

"Why did you push her?" Rosa screams, tears streaming down her face. She's pointing.

"What the fuck?" a man says. "Why would you do that?" He has his phone out.

I can't see who he's talking about. Rosa and Seimone cling to each other.

Maya isn't moving. She's breathing, though, and her eyes are open.

I crouch beside her, not sure if I should take her hand. Beside her head is a freshly chewed wad of chewing gum. Her ruby heart necklace sparkles. One of her pupils is huge.

"You'll be okay," I tell her, hoping I'm not lying. I touch the back of her hand gently.

"It hurts," she says. "I want Lei-Lei."

I slide my phone out of my pocket. *911*, I remember, punching it in. This is the second time.

Behind me people are yelling, and the girls' sobs are even louder. Then I hear sirens. Loud. So loud.

The 911 operator tells me help's already on the way. I text Leilani that Maya is hurt.

"I'm getting Leilani, Maya. She'll be here soon."

Someone puts their hand on my shoulder.

"Sir?"

I turn. Ambos. I step back onto the footpath. They crouch down beside Maya. I'm relieved she's getting help. I want to ask if she's going to be okay, but they can't know that yet.

"Che!" Maya calls out.

"I'm right here." I'm not sure she can hear me.

"Why did you push her?" Rosa screams again.

I realise she's pointing at me.

CHAPTER THIRTY-SIX

The police keep me waiting in a small room. I already told them what I saw, as we stood on the footpath watching the ambos assess Maya. I'm not sure what happened. It didn't occur to me that Maya was pushed. She lost balance. I thought maybe she tripped or someone bumped her heavy bag, pulling her off the kerb.

The police don't ask me if I pushed Maya. They write down everything I say.

A police officer waits with me. She doesn't speak much except to tell me David's on his way.

There are four chairs and a table and water in a paper cup and nothing else. I reach for my phone. It isn't in my pocket. The last time I had it was when I was beside Maya, when I texted Leilani. Did I drop it then? Or in the cop car on the way here?

I keep reaching for it, then remembering it isn't there halfway through the movement towards my pocket.

I want to stand up and walk around, but it's a small room.

"Don't do that, kid," the cop says.

I'm about to say *do what?* when I realise that my legs are doing a seated Ali shuffle.

"I'm not great at sitting still."

"Learn, kid."

I focus on keeping my legs from moving. It makes me want to tap my fingers instead. I settle for stretching out my arms and shoulders.

I don't know how much later David walks in and draws me into a hug. I can feel tears burning, but I don't cry. The police officer gets up and leaves us.

I fall into a chair. David takes the one beside it.

"How is Maya?"

"The hospital's assessing her. She's conscious. It can't be too bad."

It looked really bad.

"Where's Sally?"

"At the hospital. Rosa too. Gene and Lisi are still in the air. Danny called a lawyer for you. She'll be here soon. She said they shouldn't have brought you here. She'll sort everything out."

I don't know who Danny is. Two police officers come in and introduce themselves. I can't be sure they're talking to me, because they keep looking at David, not me. They both have hearty handshakes. I don't catch their names.

It feels like this has nothing to do with me.

One of the cops is tall and the other one is short. For a moment I think they're the same cops who came the night Rosa went missing. But this time it's the man who's tall. I'm not able to focus on what they're saying. Maybe none of this is about me?

My feet are moving as quietly as I can manage. I haven't had to sit this long since we flew here.

"My son won't be answering questions until our lawyer gets here."

"I won't?"

"You won't." David is firm.

I take a sip of water. It tastes oily.

The two cops talk more with David, then they leave.

I notice that the floor is covered with that fake tile stuff. I can't remember what it's called, but in the corner of the room it's started to curl up, like old wallpaper. I guess real tiles are too expensive.

The lawyer comes in with another police officer. Her hair is in a silver bob, but not the same kind of silver as the shop assistant at Spool. It grows out of the lawyer's head like that. She tells me her name and we shake hands. The police officer tells me I'm free to go home, but I'm not to go out of town because there may be further questions.

I ask about my phone. The police say they'll search the car I was brought in.

My legs are itching to run.

WE DON'T GO TO the hospital. David says that would cause a scene, because Rosa and Seimone are saying I pushed Maya.

"I didn't push her."

"I know." David reaches across the taxi to squeeze my hand.

At home I sit at the kitchen island. The lawyer is opposite me. David's already said her name several times but I can't remember it.

She doesn't mind when I get up and walk around.

David makes coffee. I take a sip, but it tastes like soap. I put it down and look out the window, but all I can see is Maya lying on the road.

The lawyer says something. I'm not sure what.

I walk back to the island and sit down. There's an ant on the counter. Do they have ants in New York City? If it were Sydney I'd believe it. Little black ants are everywhere back home. I look closer. It's a small black grain of something. Coffee? Cocoa? Dirt? I can't tell.

"Che?"

"Yes?"

"You need to answer Ilene's questions."

I nod and stand up again. My legs twitch when I sit.

My lawyer—*Ilene*—is sipping coffee as if it were the most normal thing in the world to be sitting here asking me about an eleven-year-old girl being hit by a bicycle. Maybe for her it *is* normal.

Ilene explains that charges may not be pressed. They've only started looking, but so far CCTV footage doesn't show anything. There aren't cameras on that corner, and the traffic cameras were pointing at the cars, not pedestrians. But they haven't checked the surrounding shops.

That's something I learn: there aren't CCTV cameras everywhere in New York City. Then I remember Rosa told me that. And Rosa decided what streets we should take on the way to the subway.

Rosa engineered this. Did she mean to hurt Maya this badly? Did she mean to blame me?

The lawyer says the police have interviewed five witnesses. Seimone and Rosa and a man all say I pushed Maya. Two women say it was one of the girls. They're both adamant it wasn't me. One of the women says it was Seimone. The other one can't be sure which girl it was.

Maya doesn't know what happened. She doesn't know who pushed her, only that she was. She's talking, but she has concussion, three broken ribs, two broken vertebrae, and her left leg is broken in two places and will need surgery. Her spine is fine. She'll be able to walk.

The cyclist doesn't know what happened either. He came out of it with a broken leg, lots of gravel rash, and a destroyed bike. It's as well it was his own lightweight racing bike, and not one of the heavy blue Citi Bikes. It's not good for him that he wasn't in the bike lane.

"The police might not press charges," Ilene says. "No one died, and you're minors. Can you tell me what happened?" She's turned the stool so she's facing me. "In as much detail as you can."

"Not really. I didn't see. We were about to cross the road, then Maya was on the road. I thought she tripped." *Had* I thought that? I'm not sure I was thinking about what happened. I was thinking about how to help her. "I didn't push her. I didn't realise she was pushed."

"What did you say?" David asks.

I'm on the other side of the room.

"Sorry," I say, walking closer. "I said I didn't push her."

"Could you sit down, Che?" David says.

I sit at the island again. My legs vibrate, but there's nothing I can do to stop them.

"Who do you think pushed Maya?" Ilene asks.

"Rosa."

David's lips thin. The anger vanishes from his face before Ilene looks at him.

"Yet Rosa thinks *you* pushed Maya."

"She's setting me up. It's what she does."

As I tell Ilene about Rosa, I wonder why Rosa's blaming me. What does it get her?

"Do you have proof that this is something she would do?" Ilene asks.

I tell her about the recordings I made, the notes I have on Rosa.

Ilene looks briefly unsettled. "Can you give me access?"

I walk upstairs and get my laptop. I unlock the protected folders and copy them to the USB drive she hands me. She now has everything. David hasn't said a word.

After the lawyer leaves he hugs me.

"It's going to be alright," he says. "Ilene needs to know about Rosa. You did right."

"I did?" He hadn't looked like he thought that.

"I have a tonne of phone calls to make. Are you going to be okay?" He disappears into the study before I reply.

I check my tablet. A million texts. I use it to call Leilani. She's still at the hospital.

"I'm sorry."

"It's not your fault."

I'm not sure about that. I should have kept myself between Maya and the girls at all times. Not let them mess about so much. I should have known they were planning something. *Were* they planning something? Or was it Rosa seizing an opportunity?

"How is she?"

"She's doing okay. She's talking. Doesn't remember much. She has concussion. She's banged up. Lots of broken bones. Her left leg is bad."

"Is she in pain?"

I'm not sure Leilani hears me. She sounds like a robotic version of herself. As if she's slid into the uncanny valley and is telling me about some stranger. I feel like I'm right there with her.

"She knows who she is, who the president is, blah blah blah. She swears it couldn't be you. She thinks it was from the other side—that Rosa did it. But she's foggy."

"Can I see her?"

"Immediate family only. But she asked for you. And her tennis bag." Leilani makes a sound that I guess is a forced laugh. "Her rackets were totalled. She doesn't know Seimone and Rosa are saying you pushed her. She refused to see Seimone." Leilani's voice quavers, sounding human again. "I'm scared, Che. I'm scared Seimone pushed her."

I CALL SOJOURNER. SHE doesn't answer. We weren't going to see each other tonight. Sojourner's studying for her first-aid exam.

I need to see her. But Ilene said I should stay at home until the situation is clearer.

—Can I see you? I text. —It's important.

No response. I start to look at my texts, then realise I don't have the heart to respond. No one knows what's going on. How can I joke with Nazeem or Georgie or Jason right now?

When Rosa and Sally return I'm sitting at the kitchen island eating cereal because there's nothing else. David's in the study.

Rosa is wearing the red and blue outfit. I'm not sure why I thought she'd have changed. This is the first time she's been home since the accident.

No, not *accident*.

Sally is holding Rosa's hand. Sally's face is red and blotchy, like she's been weeping. I'm sure Rosa has cried too, but there are no signs of it. She takes one look at me, then looks away, marches up the stairs and slams the door to her bedroom.

"It's been a long day," Sally says. "The McBrunights are at the hospital."

She hugs me, but it's brief. There's no weight behind it, there's almost no Sally behind it.

"I'm going to lie down. I'm buggered," she says. "I'll get David to check on her."

I nod, but she's already walked away.

I check my tablet again. There's a text from Sojourner. —Okay. I need a break.

I'm about to ask her to come here when I realise I need to get away too. Even if it's only for a few minutes.

I ignore what Ilene told me. —How about the park? Near the dog run. —5 mins.

—Ok. I don't have my phone.

—See you soon.

I leave a note on the island saying I'll be back in half an hour, grab a jacket, and close the door quietly behind me. I doubt they'll notice I'm gone.

THE PARK IS MUCH quieter than it is during the day. It can't be far off ten o'clock.

A few dogs are running back and forth in the dog run, leaping on their owners, who look exhausted. I walk past the entrance, wishing I'd been more specific about where to meet. I make the circuit back to the entrance. Should I hover closer to the direction she's coming from?

"Che!"

Sojourner's in trackpants, T-shirt and a hoodie. I run to her and hold her. She hugs me. I don't want to let go.

"What's wrong?"

I don't know where to start.

I kiss her. The taste of her is so amazing that for a brief moment I can almost forget what's happened. Sojourner pulls away first.

"What is it, Che?"

"There was an accident. Maya's in the hospital."

Sojourner pulls away from me. "Is she going to be alright?"

"She's conscious. Broke a lot of bones. Concussion. They think she'll be okay. She doesn't remember what happened."

I kiss her again.

"I was there. Rosa and Seimone too."

"That's awful."

I nod. How do I tell her the worst of it?

"I had to see you."

She takes my hand and leads me to a bench. She knows there's more. It must be all over my face.

"I thought it was an accident. That she tripped or something. Her bag was too heavy. I should have carried it."

"It wasn't an accident?" Sojourner looks confused.

"They don't think it was an accident."

"They?"

"The police. I don't know what happened. We were standing waiting for the lights, then Maya was on the road. A bike hit her. A bike! Bastard should've been in the bike lane. Though I guess a car would've been worse. She'd be dead. I didn't see what happened. I couldn't stop it."

Sojourner's arms are around me. "It's not your fault, Che."

"I know. But the witnesses are saying different things. They're saying Rosa pushed her, or Seimone."

"No." The shock makes her flinch. "That can't be right."

"Rosa and Seimone say *I* pushed Maya. A witness agrees. I didn't push her."

"Of course you didn't." Sojourner sounds utterly certain. "But why would your sister say that? Why would Seimone?"

"You know how I told you Rosa likes to make trouble? This is the kind of trouble she makes. She's not normal."

Sojourner stares.

"She's always been like this. Always. I try to stop her, but she always wins."

I'm crying. Sojourner's holding me. The feel of her skin against my skin is enough to make me feel better. I don't know how long we hold each other.

"MAYA'S DEAD."

I hear the words but they don't stick. I'm still holding my keys. David holds the door open and pulls me inside.

"What?"

"Maya's dead." David's face doesn't change. He's in shock.

I can hear Rosa sobbing upstairs. Sally must be comforting her. I wonder when Rosa learned to sob like that.

"She's dead?"

"From a cerebral haemorrhage."

I run through everything I know about bleeding inside the brain. I wonder where the bleeding was. She landed on her back, hit her head hard. Was it her brain stem? That's really bad.

Of course it's bad. Maya's *dead*. Does it matter where the bleeding was?

I could have saved her. I could have taken her bag. I could have made sure I was always between Maya and my sister and Seimone. I could have refused to look after Rosa and Seimone, stuck them with one of the McBrunights' staff.

I could have smothered Rosa before she was old enough to hurt anyone.

I know Rosa pushed her.

Rosa is a murderer, like she's always wanted.

I hate my sister.

CHAPTER THIRTY-SEVEN

In the morning the police interview me at the station, my lawyer and a parent accompanying me. Rosa and Seimone are interviewed, too, but at home. They each have their own lawyers.

Sally stays with Rosa, David with me.

David and I are shown into a room that looks exactly like the one they took me to after the accident. Or the not-accident. The fake tiles aren't pulling up in the corner, so I know it's not the same room, and it has a weird damp smell the other room didn't have.

Ilene doesn't come in with us. "Don't talk to anyone until I return. Paperwork," she says vaguely.

I was awake most of the night, thinking about what the witnesses said, how they agree Maya was pushed even if they can't agree on who pushed her.

I text Leilani from my tablet that I'm thinking of her. I *am* thinking about her, worrying about her, but it feels like a lie.

The girls tripped me. On our way to the station, when they were switching back and forth, they deliberately tripped me.

I think.

I wasn't sure then, so I can't be sure now, can I? Except now I am. They tripped me. I know they did.

Maya is dead.

I can't take it in. I haven't seen Leilani. When I see Leilani I'll know. I wish yet again for my phone.

"I didn't push her," I tell David. Is it the third or fourth time I've said that? Why am I so hazy?

"Yes," David says. "I know you didn't. Yes," he says before I can say it, "I know Rosa would. But I don't know that she did."

I can't quite parse what he said. It's like one of those annoying logic puzzles Rosa loves. *If A is on a train . . .*

"You think it was Seimone?"

"I don't know. None of us do."

For once David almost looks tired. There's faint blue under his eyes. They're a little bloodshot, too.

Ilene comes in. She pats my shoulder, which is more than David has done. She runs me through my story yet again, taking notes in a little black notebook, and apologises for asking me the same questions.

My eyes burn. My legs won't stop twitching, but I'm pretty sure I'm not allowed to get up and walk around the tiny room.

David checks his phone, sends texts, but I'm sure he's listening.

"Those recordings of yours?"

I wait for Ilene to say more.

"Your sister isn't like most ten-year-olds, is she?"

It's hard not to laugh. "No, she's not. How many have you listened to?"

"Just a few."

It's clear she hasn't gotten to the truly awful conversations yet. There hasn't been much time.

"Are they going to let me go?"

"I'm working on that," the lawyer says.

David leaves the room.

Ilene pats my shoulder again. "It's going to be okay."

I remember saying the same thing to Maya.

David returns with water and a packet of chips. I'm not hungry. I'm always hungry.

At some point I fall asleep with my head on the desk.

When I wake Sally is in David's place and Ilene is gone.

I wipe the drool from my mouth and try to focus. Sally looks older. So many lines on her face. So much grey in her blonde hair. I never noticed any of that before.

Her head's bowed.

"What's going on?" I ask. "What did Rosa say?"

"She still says you did it." Sally doesn't look up. "Seimone does too."

"You don't believe them, do you?"

"Of course not."

It would be much easier to believe she means it if she'd look at me.

Sally looks at her hands, twisting her wedding ring around her finger.

"I would never push Maya. I like Maya! Leilani's my best friend here. Why would I kill her sister?"

"I don't think you killed her, Che." Sally keeps rotating the ring.

It doesn't feel like she believes me.

"Then why won't you look at me?"

"I'm tired, Che. I'm gutted."

"Rosa did it. You know what she's like. Did you ever think about taking me to a specialist? It was always Rosa. This is Rosa too."

Sally looks up. Her eyes are red, and the skin under them looks loose. She reaches across and touches my cheek. "Yes. Rosa's the liar and you're the truth-teller. We know that. That's our family. I'm the one who holds us together and David's the wild one."

"Mum?" I don't understand what Sally's saying.

"You've never called me *Mum* before."

Ilene comes in to explain that Rosa, me and Seimone are all going to be assessed by a psychiatrist.

"Does that always happen?" I ask.

Ilene shakes her head. "They also want you to have a brain scan, which is definitely not usual. The McBrunights' lawyer requested it. The McBrunights will be covering the expense."

"They want a scan of my brain? What about Rosa's?"

"Rosa's too," Ilene says. "As well as Seimone's."

"Why?" I ask. Maybe what we said to them about Rosa got through. They want to see if she's what Leilani and I said she is.

"They haven't explained why. You don't have to agree."

Sally asks Ilene something, but I don't hear because I'm trying not to laugh. Finally Rosa's getting that brain scan.

"That's great," I say. "What kind of scan? MRI?"

Ilene looks down at her notebook and flips a few pages. "Yes. They'll be MRI scans. You don't have to do it if you don't want," she repeats. "It's a highly unusual request. It may complicate things."

"I'll do it." I want to see how the morphology of our brains differs. I want to see exactly what makes Rosa the way she is. "Everyone will see Rosa's not normal."

"I wouldn't get your hopes up," Ilene says. "These kind of assessments are often inconclusive and contradictory."

"Rosa said yes, too, you know," Sally says, looking up, meeting my eyes. "She's not scared of a scan. You're obsessed, Che. While she adores you."

"Even when she's saying I pushed Maya?"

"She's trying to understand why."

"I thought you said you believed me?"

"I do," Sally says. "You're persuasive. You've always been able to get people to like you."

"Huh? What are you talking about?"

Her hands are over her eyes. I'm pretty sure she's crying.

"You're too much like David," she murmurs.

"David?" I repeat.

Sally stands up. "I love you, Che." She wipes her eyes, moving to the door.

I can't speak.

She walks out.

I stare after her.

"I'm sorry," Ilene says. I wonder how much she understands of what just happened. I wonder how much I understand.

THEY LET ME GO home. Ilene explains that the police would like us to stay in the city and that no charges are being pressed. We've heard this several times. She'll let us know as soon as the scans and assessments are scheduled. I wonder how long that will take and what will happen to Rosa when they realise what she is.

Sally walks home with me. Or rather, beside me. The sun's still up. I don't know what time it is and I don't want to ask, but it must be late. The shadows are long and the restaurants are full.

"I'm sorry," Sally says.

She's not looking at me. Her eyes are on the footpath, which is pocked with old chewing gum.

I don't say anything. When I get home I'm going to use my tablet to text Sojourner. I've never wanted to see anyone as much as I want to see her.

"Do you notice how bad this city smells?" Sally says. "Far smellier than Bangkok."

"I doubt that," I say. "No durian here."

She keeps talking as if I haven't said anything. "The heat opens up the asphalt and lets out the stench of everything that's ever spilled on it, mostly urine and vomit and stuff that's gone off."

I'm not sure what to say. All I can smell is the incense from the secondhand shop we're passing. Sally's setting a fast pace, but I wish it was faster. I wish I could run.

"I hate this city," Sally says.

I'm not sure she's saying any of this to me.

"I never wanted to come here. It was David's idea. Everything is always David's idea."

If I'd known that when it mattered, I would have argued even harder not to move here. But now? Sojourner is here. Now it doesn't matter. Now I'm afraid of having to leave.

MY PHONE IS ON the kitchen island as if it were there all along. Did the cops return it? Did Rosa? Does it matter?

I look at texts from Sojourner. There's one from last night that didn't show up on my tablet.

—Stay strong.

Then from this morning:

—Rosa says you were arrested. I'm sorry about Maya. About you.

When did Rosa talk to Sojourner? What else did she say?

—No one's been arrested. Can I see you?

When did Rosa talk to Sojourner? What else did she say?

There are no texts from Leilani.

—I'm sorry. As I text her, my eyes burn and my throat tightens. But I'm not ready to cry, not yet.

—I miss you. I text Sojourner.

I slip the phone into my pocket. I've missed the weight of it.

"Are you hungry?" Sally asks.

It used to be a superfluous question, but not anymore. I haven't felt hungry since Maya was hurt, and now she's dead.

"Sure."

Sally opens the pantry door, stares at it, then pulls out a box of spiral pasta and a bottle of pre-made arrabiata sauce. David will be horrified.

I put a saucepan of water on to boil and add salt.

"Thanks, Che."

I've never heard Sally sound so flat. This is what grief does, I guess. No one I've ever cared about has died. I'm not even sure I believe Maya's dead.

I want to give Sally a hug, but she's not looking at me.

I sit on a stool and watch her stir the pasta sauce. My stomach is full of lead.

ROSA AND DAVID JOIN us for the pasta. The four of us sit on stools around the island almost as if we're a family.

David isn't horrified by the sauce being out of a bottle or by the absence of parmesan.

Rosa doesn't speak or look at me. She pushes the pasta around her bowl, making sure each spiral is drenched in sauce. Neither Sally nor David notices that she's not eating. I don't believe she's too sad to eat.

I put a forkful of pasta into my mouth and chew. It doesn't taste like anything, and when I swallow I almost gag. I put my fork down.

I don't ask Rosa what she said to Sojourner. She'd lie.

The parentals talk to each other as if we aren't there, which they so often do, but this time it's desultory. Their affectionate touches and professions of love seem mechanical.

I check my phone.

—Miss you too. I can't tonight or tomorrow. Sojourner texts. —But soon. Mom's having a rough time. You okay?

—I guess. Sorry about your mom.

No reply from Leilani. I didn't expect one. I can't imagine how she's coping.

"Do you think it'll be okay if I go to the gym?"

"I don't know," Sally says. It sounds like *I don't care.* "Keep your phone on."

I run the whole way, my feet pounding the footpath. It's like my body has let go of everything it knew about running and decided to attack the ground as hard as it can.

When I get to the gym my feet are throbbing and my left calf cramping.

It doesn't stop me from working out as hard as I can. No one I know is there and I'm relieved. I don't know how I could talk to them.

Not for a second do I stop thinking about Maya. She's dead. My brain keeps swirling to that. Maya's dead.

WHEN I GET HOME Rosa is in my room. Of course she is. Though this time she's sitting at my desk, not on my bed.

"Sally's asleep," she says. "David's in the study."

"I thought you weren't talking to me?"

"Of course I am. You're my brother."

I lie back on the bed and close my eyes. "Please leave."

"What are you doing, Che?"

"Ignoring you, Rosa. What are you doing?"

I'm not going to let her get to me.

"Praying for you. Sojourner thinks it will help."

"Why are you talking to Sojourner?" I sit up.

"I thought she'd be worried, so I called her and told her what happened."

"No, you called her and lied. I *wasn't* arrested."

Rosa shrugs as if to say, *You will be.* "She's praying for you. She told me to tell you that she'll pray for you every day. I told her you don't believe in God. She said she knows that, but she's praying anyway. I told her I believed in God. That I felt His presence when I was at church. That's His with a capital H. You write it that way so people can tell you're talking about God and not some regular man. Though I don't see why God would be a man. Sojourner says I can go with her to church again this Sunday. But only if David and Sally tell her it's okay."

I don't say anything. Why would I let Rosa know I feel sick? It's a hard enough battle to keep what I'm feeling from my face. Does Sojourner believe I'm a killer now? I lean forward, stretching my hamstrings. They burn.

"I don't believe in God," Rosa tells me as if this is news. "Whether God's a man or a woman or neither like Elon. Jaime doesn't either. She confessed to me. She says she doesn't *not* believe, but she's not sure. She doesn't want Sojourner to know. She says it's hard when your whole family is religious and you just aren't. Did you know Jaime lives with Sojourner and her moms? It's so she can stay at the same school. Her family used to live in the same block, but then the building was sold and turned into fancy apartments and now they live almost two hours away. They don't have much money."

I know this.

"But that's okay. Neither do we. Just ask David. He's in the study trying to make money appear out of nothing."

She's getting to me.

"Do you like your lawyer? I like mine. She says nothing bad will happen to me because I didn't do anything, and even if I did I'm too young. I wonder who's paying her. I doubt it's the McBrunights anymore."

"Why did you kill Maya? Why, Rosa?"

"I didn't. It was Seimone. She didn't mean to kill her. It was an accident."

I don't believe her.

"She wanted to give her a fright. Seimone's upset."

Upset?

"Maya dying is the last thing I wanted. Seimone pushed too hard. I told her not to. Seimone wanted to punish Maya. I keep telling Seimone that it's better to punish people without violence. Violence is too obvious."

I stare at Rosa.

"It's what you always say, Che. People go to jail if they're violent. Unless they're boxing. Seimone doesn't want to go to jail."

"You make my head hurt."

"I miss you," she says. "We've hardly talked since I came back from camp and I have so much to tell you. Before that we weren't talking. I miss talking to you, Che. It's not the same with Seimone. I can't tell her *everything*."

I don't miss hearing *everything*. I lie down again and close my eyes. Maybe she'll go away.

"It's better when you're my friend. It's better when you're not so sad."

"I'm sorry for your suffering," I murmur, not caring if she can hear or not.

"That was sarcasm, wasn't it?" Rosa says. "You see? I *do* know what it is."

CHAPTER THIRTY-EIGHT

I don't fall asleep until after seven-thirty in the morning, then at nine I'm woken by David knocking on my door, telling me my lawyer is here. I shower and dress as quickly as I can.

Downstairs Sally, David and Ilene are sitting at the island, drinking coffee. Only David looks like he slept.

Ilene greets me with a brief touch to my shoulder. "Did you sleep?" she asks. I know I look bad.

"A bit."

I sit on the stool next to her, accepting the coffee David offers me. Ilene's little black notebook is on the island.

"The scans and assessment are at noon," she says. "For both of you."

"So soon?"

She nods and gives us the name and address of the private clinic. "The McBrunights have managed to expedite everything."

"Money, eh?" David says. "Don't those machines cost millions?"

"Anything else?" I ask. "Have the police said anything?"

"Nothing new. They're continuing their investigation," Ilene says. "I've finished going through everything you gave me."

"Going through what?" Sally wants to know.

"The conversations Che's been taping with Rosa," David says.

Sally looks like she's going to say something, but David takes her hand in his.

"The conversations are odd, yes," Ilene says, "but they don't prove Rosa wanted to hurt Maya."

"What about the conversation where she said she wanted to hurt Maya?" I say, trying to keep the sarcastic edge out of my voice.

"Rosa doesn't say that though, does she? She says she wishes Maya were dead. We all wish people were dead from time to time. Rosa's a child. Children wish people dead more often than we do. My daughter wished me dead loudly yesterday when I wasn't home in time for dinner. What's clear to me from the recordings is that Rosa likes making your life as difficult as she can. I'm not going to say she's a typical little sister, because some of what she says is awful, but she's not as extreme as some siblings. It will be easy to portray this as ordinary sibling rivalry."

"What about my notes?"

"Honestly, Che, they're a lot of speculation, and," she pauses, "some of what you've written about your own thinking is, well, disturbing. If charges are pressed I don't think any of this will help you."

"Like what? What have I written that's disturbing?"

"That you've been spying on your sister," Sally interjects, "is disturbing, Che. How do you not understand that?"

"That's not what I was referring to," Ilene says. "It's what you've written about learning to control your temper, not giving in to your desire to hurt people, how helpful boxing has been for redirecting your anger." She opens her notebook and reads aloud, "*My rage burns in me. The urge to unleash it, to raze everything and everyone. Especially Rosa. I wish I could kill her. Sometimes I can't keep it inside me. Without boxing I don't know what I'd be.*"

"What the fuck? I never wrote that. I've never even *thought* that."

"Then why is it in the notes you gave me?" Ilene's face hasn't changed. She looks as professional as she did before she read those violent words out loud. She's not judging me, she's telling me what will support my case and what won't.

It's on the tip of my tongue to say that Rosa put them there. But after what Sally just said?

I know it was Rosa. I think about what I found written in my journal: *Set it on fire, watch it burn.* That was Rosa, telling me she knew about the recordings *before* she overheard David and me. She added those extra notes. She set it on fire. Now she's watching me burn.

Christ.

The only one who can back me up is David and he's not saying anything. He knows what Rosa is. Why isn't he saying it must have been Rosa adding that bullshit?

"Rosa," I say, because it's true. "She must have done it."

"Really?" Sally says. "Rosa's writing in your journal now?"

Which is when I realise I've heard those words before. David said his anger burned in him. David told me he had to outrun the urge to raze everything. David's the one with a temper. He's known about Rosa all along, but he's never done anything. He was insistent we not tell Sally. Sally thinks I'm like David. David was wild in his youth. *How wild?*

Thrill-seeking and risk-taking are on the psychopath checklist. David's charismatic, charming. Sally called me charming. It wasn't a compliment.

David's the one setting me on fire, watching me burn.

That's what Sally was talking about—me being like David. That's her fear, not me being like Rosa. David is her psychopath like Rosa is mine.

How did I miss it?

You're not smart, Che. How many times has Rosa said that to me?

My father's like Rosa.

Super-citizen David doesn't care about any of the people he helps, he doesn't care about making the world a better place. He only cares about himself.

We're his disguise.

Like Rosa said, some psychopaths have a loving family to hide what they are.

Rosa warned me. She said David was like her. She told me so many things about David. True things. I didn't listen. I didn't believe her.

"Are you okay, Che?" Ilene asks.

"Not Rosa," I whisper.

"Che?" Ilene repeats.

David doesn't smile, but I can see he knows I know. He's watching to see if I'm going to tell Ilene. Sally is looking at her hands. A tear hits the counter.

How does Sally live with him? She says she saved him. None of the stories of wild David made me think he's like Rosa.

Sally knows, and she's watched Rosa and me, terrified we'll be like him. But she lives with him, she believes she's changed him, she *loves* him.

But David doesn't love Sally. He needs her because she's essential to this bullshit life. That's why he keeps her by him, makes her believe that he's changed and that Rosa is normal.

But me?

I know what Rosa is, so I have to go. He's decided I'm expendable. Did he put Rosa up to this? Did they plan it together?

"*Jesus,*" I whisper.

Nothing about my family is what I thought.

I should have gone home. The aunts always said they'd have me. I should have left Rosa to her fate, flown home, hung out with Jason, Georgie, Nazeem.

There's no saving Rosa. There's only going down in her wake.

I close my eyes. All I can see are Rosa's and David's smiles. How did I never see how alike they are?

"Che's always been jealous of Rosa," David tells Ilene. "He wanted to stay an only child. He was convinced there was something wrong with Rosa almost from the moment she was born."

"That's bullshit," I say. "You know I doted on Rosa. I did everything I could to protect her."

Sally is weeping.

"It was you, wasn't it?" I stare at David.

He stares back. "What? You're saying I pushed Maya now? I wasn't even there."

He holds his hands open as if to demonstrate to Ilene what a lost cause I am.

"You can see, can't you, Che?" Ilene is somehow pretending that we haven't said anything. "These notes and recordings don't prove anything about Rosa."

"I didn't push Maya. I didn't write those notes about my temper. I don't *have* a temper."

Ilene pats my arm.

"The scans will prove that it's Rosa, not me!"

"We'll see," Ilene says. "I have to go."

She gets up. I have no idea what she's thinking. She's probably had worse clients from worse families.

David and Sally say goodbye.

It occurs to me that even after the scans show Rosa is the psychopath, not me, I'm still screwed. My father's the monster who's been teaching her how to be a good little psychopath. Of course he was never going to admit to anyone else that he knows what Rosa is. He couldn't let anyone suspect what *he* is.

For me this is the end of family.

I ache to see Sojourner.

"We need to talk," David says after Ilene's gone.

"What are we going to talk about exactly? I know what you are now."

"What am I, Che?"

"A fucking monster."

I walk away. I can feel David glowering behind me. I'm not scared, but I have a feeling I should be.

"This is your only chance, Che," David says. "Walk away now and I tell you nothing."

"Don't forget your appoint—" Sally calls out. The rest is lost as I slam the door and sprint down the stairs, fighting the urge to scream.

I TEXT SOJOURNER. —I MISS you.

I don't go to the gym. I can't. I'm hurt and angry and I can barely see. I would probably destroy a bag. Or more likely my hands.

I jog to the East River, wanting to sprint, but there's too much traffic, too many people. I don't care about the rising heat, the sticky, polluted air, I have to push myself hard and fast.

When I get to the river I take off south, driving with my arms, springing from my toes. I need to run like this until everything I'm feeling is run out of my body.

Too soon I'm breathing hard, feeling the burn in my lungs and legs. I lose rhythm. Little black dots appear in front of my eyes.

I stop. It's that or fall over. The path spins. I'm in the middle of it, bent over, hands on thighs, blinking rapidly as if that will clear my vision. I need to sit. Long moments pass before I can see again. I straighten, make my way to a bench, grip the back to turn myself and sit.

Have I drunk any water today? Just coffee. That's it: I'm dehydrated. I don't remember the last time I ate, either. Mystery solved. My heart's beating too hard, my head feels wrong. There's a bubbler a few metres away. I pull myself to it and drink deeply. I'm still wobbly. I need food. I'm not hungry.

I check my phone. Sally's texted me a reminder and the address of the clinic. I have to get across town.

I get there ten minutes late, dripping with sweat and still dizzy. The Dawson Medical Center has a doorman. He checks my ID before letting me into the building. Once inside I have to go through a metal detector monitored by men with guns. On the other side a receptionist checks my ID again and tells me what floor to go to.

I wonder if this is normal for a medical centre in New York City.

I step out of the lift into a waiting room that looks like the lobby of an expensive hotel. Ilene is sitting on a leather couch with a man I don't know. Behind them is a view of the Hudson River.

"Hi, Che," she says rising. "This is Al Vandermeer. One of the McBrunights' lawyers."

We shake. I'm relieved the parentals aren't there. I have no idea what to say to David.

"Are you alright?" Ilene asks.

I say that I am and sit breathing deeply for a ten count. I wonder if the McBrunights' lawyer is here to verify that we didn't send impostors? There are four doors but no receptionist area. There's no basket of magazines either. It doesn't look like a waiting room.

On the glass table in front of us there's a jug of water and glasses. I pour myself one and drain it.

"Rosa's already getting her scan. Your mother is with her," Ilene tells me. "You'll see the psychiatrist first and then have the scan."

"Seimone too?"

"Hers was done earlier."

"Were you here?"

I check my phone. Another text from Georgie. —Are you okay? I saw about Leilani's sister.

How did she see that? Then I remember Leilani's fame.

—Things have been rough. Tell you more soon.

As I press send, a text from Sojourner arrives. —I miss you too. Mom's at the hospital. More tests. Mama had to work.

—She okay?

—She's weak. Been having more bad days than good lately. It's boring here. Hate sitting around waiting.

—I'm sorry. Wish I was there to keep you company.

A man with a tablet comes out of one of the doors. "Che Taylor? Welcome. Your paperwork is already filled out," he says. "If you'll follow me Dr. Gupta will see you now."

—I gotta go. I slide my phone into my pocket. I'm not ready but I follow him to the doctor's office. The psychiatrist's office.

It looks like a regular doctor's office. Nothing seems to be made of gold. Though the couch is the same as the ones in the waiting room. The shelves are full of textbooks, the DSM.

The doctor stands and shakes my hand, introduces herself, indicates an armchair opposite hers. She's in a tailored suit much like Ilene's, but brown, not grey. She smiles, says there are no right or wrong answers, tells me to take my time.

The air between us wavers. I don't know if it's because I haven't eaten in—a day? two days? three? how long is it since the accident?—or because she's asking questions from the psychopath checklist—the checklist I've been reading about for so long—but it feels like I've stepped into someone else's dream.

"Are you unwell, Che?" Dr. Gupta asks.

I say I'm fine.

I'm not fine.

But I must be in better shape than Leilani. How is she coping? How *can* she cope? We haven't spoken since Maya died. I wish there was something I could do.

"Do you find it difficult to keep still?"

My feet are shifting under my seat, not quite an Ali shuffle, more of a slight gesture in that direction.

I nod.

What is that question testing for? Disinhibition? Fearlessness? Physical restlessness isn't a symptom of psychopathy. David can sit still for hours, as can Rosa. Has Dr. Gupta already seen Rosa?

While Dr. Gupta asks about whether I was in trouble as a child, I worry about the MRI. I'll have to stay still for at least ten minutes. Maybe longer. What if I can't do it? What if they can't get a decent scan of my brain?

THE MAGNETIC RESONANCE IMAGING machine is luminous white under the fluorescent lights. I'm wearing a cotton hospital gown and the room is cold. I'm feeling dizzy enough that I'm glad to lie down on the bed that will slide inside the machine. They've explained that the machine is basically a giant camera, that a cradle will extend over my head like an astronaut's helmet, that it will be noisy, but that it won't hurt me, so there's no need to be afraid.

I know this. I'm not afraid. Because I'm not claustrophobic and I'm not a psychopath. Rosa wouldn't have been afraid either, because she is a psychopath.

I put on the headphones offered. It's classical music. I wonder if that's what Rosa listened to.

A mirror above my head lets me see the technician in the room. Neither Sally nor David are there. I said I didn't want them. It isn't true. I want Sally. I would like my mum to hug me.

The bed slides into the machine and makes a humming noise almost like a bird, then a series of loud crashes. The music is doing little to drown it out. Thirty minutes I'll have to be in here, they told me. I'm not sure I can do it. My right leg twitches. My neck feels tight. I want to move my head.

I close my eyes and breathe as Natalie taught me, filling my lungs, letting the air out slowly, being conscious of my muscles and of them letting go. I start with the lumbrical muscles of my foot, then the bed is sliding out of the machine, and I'm blinking as I sit up.

Somehow I fell asleep.

CHAPTER THIRTY-NINE

Ilene is waiting for me. The other lawyer's gone and there's no sign of the parentals or Rosa.

"Your parents have taken your sister home," Ilene says. "The results of your scans are being fast-tracked. We'll know about your sister's brain by four. We have to be back here so they can explain the results."

I nod, which makes me feel dizzy again.

"Are you alright?"

"I haven't eaten. Low blood sugar, I think."

"Let me get you lunch," Ilene says.

We walk into a burger place around the corner. The thick smell of meat frying should make me hungry, but it doesn't.

I order a cheeseburger and fries. Ilene gets a mushroom burger with bacon.

While we wait I sip my glass of water.

"Are the McBrunights paying you?" I ask, because I know my parents aren't.

She nods.

"Isn't that a conflict of interest or something?"

"You're my client, not the McBrunights. They're paying, but I'm not reporting to them. Nor will I. But I understand if you're uncomfortable with the arrangement and would like a different lawyer."

"No, it's fine. I just wondered."

"Are you getting any counselling, Che? I know your sister and Seimone are. But what about you?"

I shake my head. "I'm okay."

"It was a traumatic experience. It's going to be with you for a long time. Trust me on that. You'll be better off if you get help now. I've already suggested it to your parents."

I nod, wondering what traumatic experience Ilene's had.

She looks at her watch. I pull my phone out. Almost three.

The burgers arrive. Ilene digs right in. There's blood dripping from my cheeseburger through the bun and onto the plate. There wasn't any blood when Maya went flying, but I still can't eat it.

"You're not hungry?"

"I should be."

I pick up the burger and take a bite, hoping the taste will ignite my appetite. It has the texture of meat and bread, but it tastes like cardboard. I put the burger down to concentrate on chewing and swallowing. Ilene's burger is half-finished.

I make myself take another bite. It's no better than the first, but at least it stops me from feeling shaky.

Ilene's on her last bite when she gets a call. "I have to take this." She goes outside.

I text Leilani again. —Wish there was something I could do. I'm sorry.

For Maya's death, for not protecting her from Rosa, for not warning them straight away, for so many things.

—I miss you. It's true. I miss Leilani almost as much as Sojourner.

"That was the medical centre," Ilene says when she comes back in. "Dr. Gupta's ready to talk to you about your results."

WHEN WE GET BACK to the Dawson Medical Center Ilene and I are shown into a conference room. Dr. Gupta is there. So are Gene, Lisimaya and Seimone, as well as Sally and Rosa and the McBrunights' lawyer, and a woman in a suit I assume is Rosa's lawyer.

"Why is everyone here?" I ask. "Where's David?"

"He's on his way," Sally says.

"We thought it would be better for everyone to look at the results together," Gene says.

"I didn't agree to that," Ilene says. "What about patient–doctor confidentiality?"

"I've given my consent," Sally says in a small voice. "As their parent. David has agreed too."

"You don't have to agree, Che. You can keep this private."

I want to see Rosa's scan.

"I agree," I say.

Seimone's scan is, of course, normal. She may be under Rosa's sway, but Rosa doesn't have the power to alter the structure of her brain. Dr. Gupta points out the activity in her orbital cortex.

She presses a button on the computer and the next scan appears side by side with Seimone's on the whiteboard.

I can't help but gasp. Rosa's brain is as I've always known it would be. While Dr. Gupta explains to the others what we're looking at I'm staring at Rosa's darkness. There's almost no activity in the orbital cortex, in the amygdala. It's a typical brain scan for someone with antisocial personality disorder. There are no lights on in the parts of her brain that feel empathy, that love, that have a conscience.

"And this is Rosa's scan," Dr. Gupta says, pressing a button so that a third scan appears. "This one has even less activity in the amygdala."

"Whose is . . ." I trail off.

The middle scan is mine. It has to be. It's larger than Rosa's or Seimone's.

"I don't understand," I say. "There's been a mistake."

Dr. Gupta shakes her head. "No mistake, Che. But these scans don't mean you or your sister have antisocial personality disorder."

"It does, though, doesn't it?" Gene's shouting. Everyone's asking questions. The lawyers jump in, trying to calm things down. Dr. Gupta patiently tells them all the things I've learned about what makes us who we are. She says we're not just our brain morphology. It's so weird hearing someone else say it that I stop listening.

I stare at the darkness in my brain.

Dr. Gupta explains our checklist results. Rosa scored much higher than Seimone or I did.

I don't feel vindicated. My brain is full of darkness, too.

I'm not who I thought I was.

I almost laugh.

But it's not funny. I'm not a monster.

Have I been deluding myself? Do I feel what I think I feel? Do I have empathy? How can a brain with such darkness feel what I feel?

"You're sure there's no mistake about my scan?"

"You're not your brain," Dr. Gupta says.

I stare at her. I know that's not true.

"You're not *only* your brain," she amends.

Gene and Lisimaya and the lawyers keep arguing. Sally hasn't said a word.

The darkness in my scan isn't going anywhere, no matter how I hard I stare.

Rosa takes my hand in hers. I've been so mesmerised by my scan I don't know how she's responded to her diagnosis.

"You're just like me," she says.

• • •

THE MCBRUNIGHTS WANT US to sign a document their lawyers are drawing up to guarantee we won't go near them or their children again. In return they'll fly us home to Sydney.

Rosa says she won't sign. Seimone is her best friend. Seimone doesn't say a word.

Ilene buys us time to think about it.

I go to the gym because I can't deal with any of it.

I train hard, but I have little energy. I text Sojourner to ask about her mom. I would love to see her, if only for a few minutes.

I can't stop thinking about my brain.

Jaime shows up to spar. She nods at me, but doesn't move over to talk.

I go to her. "Hey," I say. "How's Sojourner doing? Any news about her mom? I know they were at the hospital today."

"I'm fine. Thanks for asking."

"Sorry. I . . . I miss her. It's been . . ." I trail off.

"Fucked up," Jaime says. "What happened is totally fucked up. We're freaked out. Veronica's a basket case. Leilani's kinda shut down. She hooked up with Veronica, then told her she never wants to see her again. She won't talk to Elon. Her kid sister died, was maybe killed—" Jaime stops, clearly remembering I'm one of the people who might have killed her. "What happened, Che?"

"I don't know," I say.

Jaime's look is both sceptical and cutting. I flinch.

"Maya," I begin, then have to pause. Saying her name hurts. "Maya was beside me. She was carrying her tennis bag. It was really big, heavy. I asked if she wanted me to carry it, but she wouldn't let me. We were waiting for the lights to change, then she was . . . she went flying. I thought someone bumped her bag, but they're saying . . ."

"You didn't push her," Jaime says. It's a statement, not a question. I'm relieved. "Leilani thinks your little sister's a psycho. It's fucked. The whole thing is fucked."

I nod. I don't tell her that Rosa *is* a psychopath. I don't tell her my father's one too. That I . . . I don't tell her about the brain scans.

I spar against a new guy. He's not as good as he thinks he is.

I decide to show him how not-good he is. Dido doesn't have to yell at me to throw a punch. I throw all of them. Fast and hard, but not as precise as they should be.

I want to kill him.

Dido shouts something I don't hear. I've got this guy in the corner, alternating between destroying his kidneys and his head. His blocks and parries are rubbish. I'm hitting him as hard as I can. It feels amazing.

"Dial it back, Che." Dido pulls at my shoulders, stepping between us. "Are you listening to me? This is not a championship bout. Stop going so hard."

I start the rotation that leads to a right cross and check the movement just in time.

Woah. I almost punched Dido.

Was that the dark space in my brain? Am I turning into David?

"Shit," I say, stepping back, blinking. "Sorry. I'm sorry."

"Are you okay, Nate?" she asks the guy I was pounding on.

The guy says that he is. Dido undoes his headgear, checks his face. "Your nose is bleeding. Go get cleaned up and put some ice on it. I'll check you in five."

The guy nods. Dido turns to me.

"You better be sorry," she says, taking my head in her hands, looking straight into my eyes. I've never seen her like this. "Do not bring your anger into this ring. Do not bring your anger into this gym. Do you hear me, Che? You're here to spar, not commit murder."

I nod, breathing hard. She's right. I was angry. I was out of control.

"I hear you. I'm sorry, Dido. I'm really sorry."

She lets go and steps back, shaking her head.

I'm scared that I'm David. But I'm not. I *didn't* hit Dido.

I crack my neck in both directions. Dido is not David. That guy is not David. Neither of them are my enemy.

"Are you okay?"

I nod.

"You better go apologise to Nate. You were out of line."

I nod.

"You pull any shit like that again, Che, you are out of this gym. You hear me?"

"Yes, Dido. I'm sorry."

Jaime sees the whole thing. I wonder what she'll tell Sojourner.

When I take my gloves off my knuckles are red and starting to purple.

I sit on the mat watching the other bouts, telling myself I'm not like David. If I was, I'd've been on the verge of punching someone every day. But I haven't—not once in seventeen years.

My phone buzzes. It's Ilene. They've found footage. Seimone pushed Maya.

WHEN I COME OUT from my shower Leilani is sitting on the bench outside the change room, tapping away on her phone. She must have asked Jaime where I was. She's wearing a vivid blue suit with red piping and a matching hat. She's made up and looks amazing. She doesn't normally wear this much makeup.

It's because of her that I notice what's she's wearing and know what piping is.

"Hi, Leilani."

She looks at me. The makeup doesn't hide her grief.

I feel the rush of words—the explanation—everything I want to say about David, about what I've learned about his and Sally's relationship, about my fucked-up family. But I don't know where to begin.

I'm so sorry, I don't say, because the words have stopped meaning anything. How the fuck is my sorrow going to change anything?

My backpack is slung over my shoulder and the T-shirt I'm wearing is frayed. My trackpants are thin at the knees. I look like I've rended my clothes. If it'd help I would.

"I can't text what I want to say, so I had to come find you."

I nod.

"Will you walk with me? I have an art gallery opening, but I don't need to be on time."

I can't believe she's going to an opening so soon after . . .

We walk past the boxing rings and I think of the first time I saw Sojourner fighting. Right there in the one closest to the entrance. She looked so beautiful. I think I fell for her then before we'd said a word, which is ridiculous.

Out on Houston Street it's all horns and blaring music from slow-moving cars.

"They found footage," Leilani says. "Did they tell you?"

"Yes."

"Maya said it wasn't you. She said she was pushed from the other side. She was afraid it was Seimone."

"I'm sorry," I say.

"I could use a drink," Leilani says. "But dressed like this I'm too recognisable."

We go into a cafe on Clinton Street. It's Cuban, painted in the colours of the flag; the blue matches Leilani's suit.

"The olds won't let me see you. They're stupid. They want to give me and Seimone bodyguards. They want me to *start behaving like a teenager, not a proto-adult*." She mimics Gene perfectly. "Even though they're the ones who brought your family into our lives."

I flush. "Your parents are making us leave."

"I know about the scans, Che," Leilani says at the same time. "I don't believe you're like Rosa. You can't be like Rosa."

She wants me to prove it to her. I babble about environment, about the differences between me and Rosa.

"I think it's your dad," Leilani says. "I think he's like Rosa. They both make the hairs on my arms stand on end. If they did a scan of his chest they'd find a black hole. I've seen the way Rosa looks at him, but he's too smart to return her little conspiratorial glances."

I'm staring at her.

"What?"

"Why didn't you say anything?"

She gives her efficient half shrug. "I wasn't sure. I didn't know if it was just because I don't like him."

"I didn't realise until today. I'm such an idiot. I thought he loved me."

"Che," Leilani says.

"He is like Rosa. I think my whole fucking family is."

"Not Sally," Leilani says.

"No. But my uncle, my papa. Fuck, Leilani. I'm one of the fucking Borgias."

Leilani explodes with her awful snort-laugh. "I always thought *my* olds were the Borgias!"

Then I'm laughing too, because Leilani's laugh is like nothing in the world and it's too much. What else can we do?

We calm down as the coffee is placed in front of us. The waiter grins, wanting to join in the fun we're obviously having.

I take a sip. The coffee's very strong and very sweet. Exactly what I need. There's cake too, but neither of us touches it.

"I don't have to live with them," Leilani says. "I can afford to move out, so I'm going to. I can't pretend to give a shit about them anymore. I was only staying for the twins. Now Maya's . . . I could take Seimone with me."

"How is Seimone?" It's a stupid question. How could she be?

"She's not speaking."

"To you?"

Leilani shakes her head. "To anyone. Not since Maya died. I don't think she's even talking to Rosa."

I doubt that. Rosa won't let Seimone go that easily. I reach across the table to squeeze Leilani's hand. I'm weighed down by Rosa being my sister, and David my father.

"Seimone won't be arrested."

"Of course not. Even if she wasn't a minor. No one can prove Seimone meant to kill Maya. She didn't! If the bike hadn't been there . . . Maya wouldn't just be alive, she probably wouldn't have worse than bruises."

"Rosa says it was an accident."

"From the psycho child's mouth, so it must be true. On this I believe her. If the plan was to kill Maya, then it was a shitty plan. I guess Rosa got lucky."

"It's so fucked."

"Yeah. Seimone's therapy is going to be daily from now on. That's the olds' solution to everything. Throw money at it. God, Che. I can't deal with them anymore. I have to be there for Seimone, but I *can't* be there. I can't stay in that mausoleum. I don't want to lose both my sisters."

"There's hope for Seimone," I say. "At least her brain's wired right."

Leilani snorts. "You're not like them, Che. You have the right instincts. Watch David. He doesn't. Do you think he'd squeeze my hand like that? Have been texting me to see if I'm okay?"

I shake my head. He's a lot better at it than Rosa, but it's still learned. He's never as quick to hug Rosa or me as Sally is. I always put it down to him being a man.

"You have friends. I see how often you text with them. I see you around Elon and Jaime and Veronica. I know what our friendship feels like. It's real. Not the weird approximation that's all Rosa and David can manage.

"I slept with Veronica. You know I dumped her again? I went to her place last night because I wanted someone to hold me. But it was worse than being alone. Everything she says and does is wrong."

I wonder if I'll feel the same way about Sojourner. I won't.

"I told her to fuck off. Forever. Does that make me like Rosa?"

She's joking. I manage half a smile. "Never. You're as far from Rosa as it's possible to be. Did I ever tell you that when I first met you I was worried you were like her?"

"Because I was mean?"

"Uh huh. But you were too nice to Maya, and Rosa creeped you out, and—"

"And what?"

"You seemed, I dunno, vulnerable? Your face shows everything you're thinking. Not like Rosa's."

"Or David's. Hey, at least we've learned to avoid anyone who's good at poker."

"Hah. Definitely noted. I realised you weren't like her pretty fast."

"So much for my cool exterior. I was a bit of a bitch that day. Sorry about that."

"You were funny. I liked you straight away."

Leilani puts her empty coffee cup down and signals for another. "I don't know what's going to happen."

"Me neither." My throat hurts again with the weight of those tears I can't let loose.

"It hurts. Maya's absence. I can feel it all over my body," Leilani whispers. Her eyes are wet. "I don't know how to get through this."

I nod and try to blink away my own tears. Maya's dead and even though I didn't push her it's my fault.

"The funeral's tomorrow," she says. "I'm sorry."

She doesn't have to explain that we're not invited, but I wish I could go. I wish I could say goodbye. I want to tell Leilani that Maya was a great kid, but she'll be hearing that all day tomorrow. It will hurt.

"It's okay," I say instead. None of this is okay. "I keep wishing," I begin. "I wish it had been Rosa instead."

"Me too. I hate her." There's no fury in her words.

I'm not sure Rosa's death would make much difference, because David would still be here.

"Did you know that they're completely skint?" I say before remembering *skint* is Rosa's word. "Your parents bankrolled us."

"Everything?"

"Pretty much. They're even paying for our lawyers. How fucked up is that?"

"Very. I wonder what your parents have over mine?"

"What do you mean?"

"I've never seen them do anything like what they've done for your family. Like, ever. They do charity on a big scale: end malaria, save the starving children, not bail out old college friends. What's in it for the olds? Nothing that I can see."

"They've known each other forever . . ." I trail off. "Whatever it is, they've decided we're even now. They're turning the tap off."

"I'm sorry. You have to get away from your family, Che. They're even more fucked up than mine. Do you have somewhere to go?"

"I have aunts. Sally's sisters. I'll be okay." I don't want to leave New York. I can't leave Sojourner.

"If you need help, let me know."

I nod. But asking Leilani for help after my sister killed hers? I can't.

"We both have to get away," she says. "Promise me you will? You don't owe Rosa anything."

I reach across the table to squeeze her hand again, and that hurts too.

CHAPTER FORTY

When I get home Sally is sitting on the couch drinking wine. David must be in the office.

"How are you?" Sally asks. She puts down her wine and hugs me hard. "I'm sorry. About everything. So much of this is my fault. But I'm going to fix it."

"How?" I say when I should have said, *No, it isn't.* But I'm not sure how true that is.

Sally takes another sip of wine. The bottle on the coffee table is more than half empty.

"Ilene told me," I say. "About Seimone."

"Yes." Sally's eyes are wet. "It's awful. Poor Seimone."

Rosa marches downstairs, her chin up. She's wearing her white dress with the blue sash and holding her Shirley Temple handbag.

"Are you ready?" she asks Sally.

Sally nods, takes the last sip of her wine, rinses the glass and puts it in the dishwasher.

"Ready to what?" I ask. "It's late. Where are you going?"

Sally looks at Rosa. Rosa shakes her head.

"She's not talking to you, Che. I'm sorry. We'll tell you when we get back."

Sally gives me a quick hug. "We're fixing things. I promise."

"What does that mean?"

"It means things will get better." She kisses my forehead. "There's stew on the stove if you're hungry. It's out of a tin, but it's not bad."

"I ate already," I lie.

Then they're out the door.

I pull my phone out to text Leilani. There's one from Sojourner:

—I can see you now.

It's from twenty minutes ago.

—Yes! Now? I text back.

I text Leilani what just happened. —No idea what Rosa's up to.

No response. I hope the art gallery thing is distracting her. I'm more anxious for Sojourner to respond. I'm watching the phone the way I watch a sparring partner in the ring. I almost drop it when it buzzes.

—Meet me outside my place in ten.

I run.

SOJOURNER SLIPS OUT OF her apartment building less than a minute after I get there. She must have watched for me from their kitchen window. She leans against the door, her hands behind her back. She looks leaner than I remember. Her big fight. It must be soon.

"Cutting?" I ask.

"Yeah. I'm so hungry all I can think about is food. Fight's in two days."

I should have known that.

"Do you feel ready?"

She pushes off from the door and walks towards the river. I match her stride but make sure I don't walk too close. The air is still and hot. Sweat runs down my back.

"I think so. Mostly I'm thinking about the burger Bruno's gonna hand me after the weigh-in."

Sojourner looks good—her muscles etched, every fibre visible. I'd like to see her fight. It's over on the other side of the Hudson River in New Jersey. Not far by train.

On the other side of the Sixth Street bridge, she doesn't break into a run like she did last time. She walks closer to the river and leans on the railing. A cool breeze wafts over us, giving a momentary respite from the heat. My T-shirt is sticking to me. Sojourner's face shines.

"I missed you." My hands are on the railing but not close enough to hers. The wood's starting to roughen. I can feel little splinters.

"I missed you too." She makes no move to touch me. "Rosa has been texting me all sorts of stuff, Che. She says you killed Maya. But I heard from Jaime that it was Seimone. That Rosa made her do it. What's going on? You said Rosa was trouble, but this? This isn't just *trouble.*"

I want so badly to feel Sojourner's arms around me.

"Rosa says you lie, but she's the one who keeps lying. What's wrong with her? She lays it on too thick. She's . . . I don't have a word for it, but it's like she's acting, trying to sell me something. She doesn't talk or act like a little kid."

I want to hug her. I want to touch her, but she hasn't moved. Her hands are centimetres from mine.

"What's wrong with your sister, Che? Jaime says she's a psycho. That that's what Leilani says."

I can hear the water slapping into rocks below. Here the traffic is a low rumble. I can't hear individual horns. I can't hear sirens.

"She is. Psychiatrists call it antisocial personality disorder. It means she lacks empathy, that she doesn't care about anyone else, that she doesn't follow rules."

"She told me you'd say that about her."

"Well, it's not just me anymore. She was diagnosed today."

"That's good, right? Her being diagnosed? She told me *you* were the one with that disorder."

Now is the moment where I should tell her about my own scans.

"She said your whole family is like that. Your dad, your uncle, your grandfather. All of you cold, uncaring, cruel."

"That part's true. But it's Rosa who's like them, not me." I can't tell her about my brain. I can't tell anyone.

"I know."

"You know?" I whisper.

"Of course," she says, but she doesn't move any closer to me. "From the first time I met you I could tell you care. You're nothing but feelings, Che. You can't keep them off your face. There's a lightness to you that . . ." She turns to smile at me. "It's part of why I like you so much."

I almost say, *You do?* I want to kiss her.

"You never seemed cold. Your sister is scary. I didn't see it at first, but talking to her?" Sojourner shivers. "Rosa's bad news. You should see her at Bible class. She memorised lots of passages. But she didn't *feel* it. Rosa wanted to know the Bible better than the other kids so she could win. She could have been memorising anything. She's got no conscience, Che. *That's* what's wrong with her. *Nothing in all creation is hidden from God's sight. Everything is uncovered and laid bare.* A conscience means you want to make things right with God. Because God will see. Rosa doesn't fear God, she doesn't fear anyone."

I've never thought of it in religious terms, but she's right. "Do you think she's evil?"

"That's a big question, Che. I believe everyone can be saved. Even Rosa. Does doing evil mean you are evil? Sometimes, yeah, I think so. I'm glad you're not like her."

"I'm really not, Sojourner. I can love. I love y—"

"Stop." She puts her hand up. It reminds me of David and for a fraction of a second I want to push it away. "Why didn't you tell me, Che? Why didn't you warn me?"

I tried to tell you, I almost say.

But even as I think it I know it's not true. I was scared that if she knew she wouldn't want anything to do with me. Even if she believed me, which I didn't know she would.

"Why, Che? Why didn't you trust me enough to tell me?"

She's looking at me, waiting for an answer.

I don't have one. She's right. I betrayed her.

"I'm sorry." It's all I can say.

"You're sorry?" She shakes her head to show how little my sorrow is worth. "Your whole family is like Rosa?" For a moment I think she's about to swear. "How is that even possible?"

I'm pretty sure it's a rhetorical question, that she doesn't want me to explain the interaction between DNA, brain morphology and environment. I think about making a joke about it not being my fault I'm related to demons, but it wouldn't be funny.

"It's too much, Che. Not telling me this is too much, and your family is too much. What if your sister decided to push me under a bus?"

It was a bicycle. I don't correct her, though. Or tell her Rosa talked about pushing her down a flight of stairs.

"Or your father or your uncle or your grandfather. I got my own family problems. My mom is really sick, Che. She's almost died more times than I can count. She has to be in the wheelchair all the time now."

"I'm sorry. Diandra's amazing." It occurs to me that their building doesn't have a lift and they're on the fifth floor. Has Sojourner been carrying her up and down those stairs this whole time? What about the wheelchair?

"She is." Sojourner breathes deep, trying to hold herself together. She's not looking at me. "She likes you too. But she agrees with me about this. You know I've been praying on it? My moms too. Trust is everything, Che. Your family is—I don't have words for what your family is. I know bad can run in families, but I never heard of anything like yours. How can I have a relationship with you when I can't trust you? How can I have children with you?"

She thought about having children with me? I imagine us ten years from now, living together, with our children.

She's right. That can't happen. Not for me, not with anyone. The risk of my children being like Rosa, like David. I can't bring more demons into the world.

I always thought I'd have kids.

"I would keep my family away from you," I say, knowing how pathetic that sounds.

"But you haven't, have you, Che? You didn't even warn me. Do you warn anyone? If Rosa is what you say she is, how can you not warn people? Your father? Have you ever warned anyone about him? It's your duty to protect people. Even if you haven't found Jesus. You have to do good in this world."

I want to tell her that I didn't know about David. But it doesn't matter, does it? Sojourner's right. Not warning her about Rosa was unforgiveable. But I didn't know *how* to warn her. I still don't.

"I told Rosa not to contact me. It was weird saying that to a kid, but I can't deal with her. I can't help her."

"Has she tried to contact you since you said that?"

"I blocked her number."

"Wise."

"I'm not going to take your calls either, Che."

I flinch.

She turns to me, takes my face in her hands. My heart speeds up. Maybe she'll change her mind.

"I care about you, but I can't be with you, Che. It's too much. It will always be too much."

Her lips are against mine. I lean into the kiss, wanting more, but she's already pulled away.

"Goodbye, Che. God bless you."

Sojourner turns and runs. I don't follow her.

WHEN I GET HOME Sally and Rosa aren't there. My heart is broken over Sojourner. It hurts to breathe.

I wish I was a psychopath so I wouldn't hurt, so I wouldn't care. Right now I wish I had no feelings. If I had no feelings I might be able to survive this. Maya's dead, Sojourner's gone. I have nothing.

Why can't I stop feeling? Be like David? Why aren't I like him? What saved me?

My genes. Not from David's side, from Sally's. My Taylor genes saved me. It strikes me how appropriate it is that I have Sally's last name and Rosa is a Klein like David. It's almost like they knew.

I laugh. My loving family: a psychopath father and sister; a delusional mother.

What does that make me?

I don't know.

All I know is that I'm not a psychopath.

I cry. My brain and heart are both broken.

I have never cried as much as I have since we came to New York City.

I FALL ASLEEP AROUND dawn. If they come in before then, I don't hear them. When Sally wakes me it's after nine. She sits beside me on the bed as I wipe sleep from my eyes. She looks terrible.

"When's the last time you slept?"

Sally waves the question away. "Rosa confessed."

"She what? But there's footage of Seimone pushing Maya."

What's Sally talking about?

"Seimone only pushed her sister because Rosa bullied her into it. That's where we went last night—to the police to tell them."

"Why didn't you tell me?"

"Because Rosa said she wouldn't go through with it if I told you." Sally pats my arm. "I couldn't risk her changing her mind. Lisi and Gene needed to know the truth."

I nod. Though I'm pretty sure they already knew why Seimone did what she did.

"What are they going to do to Rosa? They haven't arrested her, have they? She's a minor. Ilene said—"

Sally's shaking her head. "The McBrunights aren't pressing charges. They just want us to leave the country."

"The McBrunights were there?"

"No. Their lawyers."

"So you signed that contract?"

"No, Rosa would only confess if they didn't make us sign any contracts. She had them put that in writing."

"Was that her lawyer's idea?"

"Oh, Che, it was awful." Sally's eyes fill with tears. "I didn't know Rosa was going to tell them about David."

"She told them David's a psychopath?"

"Rosa said killing Maya was David's idea. She recorded a conversation with him. Several. He told her if she killed someone it would get it out of her system and she wouldn't have to do it again. He said no one would believe a kid like her was a killer. She just had to make it look like an accident."

"That's recorded?"

Sally wipes at her eyes, nods. It doesn't stop her tears. "I thought he'd changed, Che. I believed in him."

"Where *is* David? Did they arrest him? That's gotta be conspiracy or something, doesn't it?"

"He's gone."

"What do you mean, gone?"

"David ran."

I get out of bed and run downstairs. I open the door to their study. No David.

I go into their bedroom. He's not there either. But when I open the wardrobe there are empty hangers. One of the drawers has been cleared out. David really is gone.

"HE'S ALWAYS BEEN READY to disappear if he needs to," Sally tells me.

She's made coffee. I sit at the island and sip it.

"He didn't know I knew about his escape kit. But I did. I never thought he'd use it. I thought it was a leftover from the old days."

"Escape kit?" Rosa told me about that. I didn't believe her.

"It has passports, cash in different currencies. He updates it every time passport technology changes. As long as I've known him he's been ready to run."

"Can't they catch him? Track his phone?"

"You don't think he took his phone, do you? David's not stupid. He's gone."

"When did he go?" He wasn't at the medical centre. I haven't seen him since Ilene was here yesterday morning.

Sally's crying too hard to hear me.

I'm not shocked. I'm not sure what I am. I wonder what Sojourner would say. Then I remember I can't tell her any of this—she's blocked my number. I'll never get to tell her anything again.

"It doesn't make sense."

I hug Sally, and stroke her hair, and wonder why David would tell Rosa to kill someone. It doesn't make any sense. David wanted camouflage. All Rosa causing Maya's death has done is destroy his cover.

CHAPTER FORTY-ONE

Rosa comes downstairs and pulls herself onto a stool. "What's for breakfast?"

"No idea," I say. I'm not hungry.

"You have to stop crying, Sally," Rosa says. "It's annoying."

Sally looks like the merest breeze will break her; Rosa looks like she's never missed a night's sleep in her life.

Rosa smiles. She's all dimples.

"You look a lot like David, you know that, Rosa? Especially when you smile."

"Good. That means everyone's going to be in love with me the way they always are with David. I bet he ran away with Suzette. Did you know she quit?"

Sally flinches. I don't tell her that Suzette is the au pair. I don't ask Rosa if it's true.

I turn my attention to my coffee. Sally continues to weep into hers.

"Everyone knows everything now, Che," Rosa says. "No more lies. You should be happy." She pulls her legs up underneath her on the stool, balancing precariously, and I'm hit by a memory of Rosa sitting like that as a small child.

"He killed someone when he was young." Sally's looking at her coffee, not us. Her tears have slowed.

I want to ask how she knows that. Did she see? Why would David tell her about committing murder if she wasn't a witness?

"He said he'd never do it again. He said it was an accident."

He lied.

Rosa's expression says as much.

Sally doesn't respond and I realise I didn't speak out loud. I wonder if he's killed more than once.

"David never did it again. When he felt wild he did other things. Legal things. He sublimated. He's not what he was when I met him. I thought that part of him was gone. I loved him, Che. I still love him. I thought he'd *changed*."

"Where did he run?"

"I don't know. He didn't even tell me he was going."

Sally sounds heartbroken. I have a horrible feeling she's more broken up over David leaving than anything else. Not Maya's death. Not Rosa's evil. Not her children's brain morphology.

"Rosa?"

Rosa shakes her head. "He left his phone behind and took the emergency kit. He took Sally's jewellery too. He didn't say goodbye, and I was his favourite."

Sally doesn't look at either of us.

"I'm not like him, Sally. I know you think the brain scan means I am, but I scored low on the psychopath checklist."

Rosa giggles. I'm not endearing myself to my mother by declaring I am not like the love of her life.

"I'm not like him either," Rosa says to me. "I'm much smarter."

"I didn't think what David was could be inherited." Sally's tears have stopped.

"Does that mean you wish we weren't born?" I ask.

"Of course she does, silly. She's only ever wanted to be with David. She thinks having kids was a mistake."

Sally doesn't contradict Rosa.

"You wish I wasn't born, don't you, Che?"

"Not all the time." Since we're being honest I can say that. Rosa smirks.

"Didn't meeting Papa and Saul make you think twice about having kids?" I can't resist asking.

Sally's mouth moves up in what could be an attempt at a smile. "Lots of good people have awful relatives."

"Not *that* awful. Besides, David wasn't a good person."

"*Isn't* a good person. He's not dead. He killed more than once, you know," Rosa tells Sally. "But not for ages now. Not since I was born."

"What do you mean?" Sally's staring at Rosa. "What did he tell you?"

"Many things."

"Who did he kill?"

Rosa shrugs as if it doesn't matter. "He didn't tell me names."

"Did he tell you why he killed?" Sally asks. "Or how many people he's killed?"

"He's not a serial killer, Sally. You don't have to worry about that. It was only a few times."

"How many times is a few?" I ask.

Sally's face is grey. I wonder how many conversations like this she's had with Rosa. This could be her first. Though who knows what Rosa said to her to get her to the police station for that confession.

"Three," Rosa says. "I'm pretty sure it was only three."

"Dear God," Sally says.

"David didn't do it because he likes killing. He was annoyed."

"I'm so reassured," I say.

Sally looks like she might throw up. I wonder how much she actually knows about the man she loves so much.

"Sarcasm," Rosa says. "I don't have a temper and I've never wanted to kill anyone. See? I'm not like David."

"What about Seimone and the peanut butter?"

Rosa rolls her eyes. "How many times do I have to tell you that was Seimone's idea?"

"I'll never believe that, Rosa. Tell me how you made her believe it was her idea—then I'll believe you. Now what?" I ask Sally.

"Now?" she repeats. "I don't know."

"We could stay here," Rosa says. "We don't *have* to go anymore. I fixed that."

"No, we can't," Sally says. "Gene and Lisimaya want us gone."

"But they can't *make* us go anymore. It was a six-month lease," Rosa says. "Besides, Seimone needs me."

Sally shakes her head in disbelief.

The urge to tell her *I told you so* is overwhelming. At last she can see what Rosa is, but all I feel is empty.

"Seimone does not need you, Rosa," Sally says. "You've ruined her life. You made her kill her sister."

"I did not. It was an accident. I've never killed anyone. I promised Che I wouldn't. I keep my promises. It's my favourite game."

"Then why did you tell the police that you and Seimone meant to kill Maya?"

"To get rid of David. I didn't want him to get annoyed and kill me. He's been too annoyed with me lately. It's scary." Rosa doesn't sound scared.

Sally's hands are over her face. I should feel for her. I will later, but not now. She lost David, but he's a monster. I've lost Sojourner, who's the most amazing person I've ever met.

"I want to stay here," Rosa says. "We could at least stay until the lease runs out, couldn't we?"

"So we go home," I say. "Then what?"

Sally gulps, stemming the flood of tears. "One of my sisters will take me in. I'll start over." She pauses, as if remembering she has two children. "*We'll* start over."

"I'm not like him," I say again, but I can see she doesn't believe me. She thinks we're both like David. She thinks she fell in love with a monster and gave birth to monsters.

I NEED A SHOWER. I need sleep. I need a different brain. If only a shower and sleep could change my brain morphology.

Sally says something about making breakfast, but there's nothing in the fridge, and only a half-empty box of muesli. "I meant to shop," she says, trailing off. "I should do that."

Instead, she goes into the study and closes the door.

I should eat. I wonder when I'll feel hungry again.

Rosa pours half of the remaining muesli into a bowl and eats it dry. "Sally's not herself," she says.

I wonder if Sally's ever been herself. David and Sally always shared so many opinions, ideas. Most of the time they sounded the same. It hasn't occurred to me how very alike they were. No, how very alike they *seemed*. The only difference was his temper.

Sally thought she'd changed David, but he changed her. All these years of being his wife, David was shaping her into the perfect disguise for him. What must she be feeling now?

I don't know my own mother. I will never know who she was before David. Then I realise I will never know *me* before Rosa.

Rosa pulls out her phone. "Seimone says her parents are going to pay for our flight home. But that's it. They don't want to have anything to do with us again. Seimone's distraught. Her heart's going to break without me."

"I doubt that, Rosa. She'll be like Apinya. She'll wake up and realise what you did to her."

"Apinya's still my friend. We talk all the time."

"Show me. Call Apinya right now and show me what good friends you are."

"She's asleep right now."

"Where's your tablet? Show me the list of calls so I can see how often you talk to your dear, dear friend Apinya."

Rosa shrugs, not caring that I've caught her in a lie. "Seimone is my best friend in the universe. We're much closer than I ever was to Apinya. She'll never forget me."

That I believe. I'm going to miss Leilani. I should go to her. I wish I could go to Sojourner. I close my eyes.

"I'll be back here living with Seimone soon. You'll see."

She's delusional. "Gene and Lisimaya wish you were dead."

"It will be much better with David gone," Rosa says. "It will be just you and me."

"What about Sally?"

"Sally doesn't count. Only you and I do."

"I can't think of anything worse. Unless it's David returning. I hope I never see him again. Where do you think he went?"

Rosa shrugs. "Far away."

"It's a pity he didn't take you with him," I say. "You being his favourite and all."

"I'm not a killer like David. David was the ticking bomb, not me. But now he's gone."

"Because you got rid of him." As I say it, I realise that Rosa also got rid of Sojourner. She was never going to push her down the stairs, just away from me. I will never forgive her.

"I told you I'm clever. We're the same, you and me," she says. I can hear the crunch of muesli between her teeth. "We have the same brains."

"If that were true I'd be clever too, wouldn't I? But you always say I'm not." If I was clever I'd have run away from this family, from Rosa, years ago. I'd have known what David is.

"Compared to me, you're not, but you're more clever than most people. Because we have the same brain."

"No, Rosa, we don't."

"I thought you didn't lie, Che. We've both seen those scans."

"I am not my brain. The doctor said my scan doesn't mean I'm like you."

"*The doctor said*," Rosa mimics.

"There's environment, DNA. We're not merely the shape of our brain."

Rosa giggles. "That's the same too. We live together. We have the same parents."

"No. No, it's not. I'm seven years older than you. That changes everything. For the first twelve years of my life we lived in the same house in Sydney. I had stability. Most of your life has been on the move. Five different countries, a million different cities and homes and schools and tutors. It's been chaos. On top of that I looked after you. I was your third parent. I cared about you, Rosa. Looking after you—it changed me. You had David push you in the worst directions. I didn't. You—"

"I saved you," Rosa says. I've never seen her look so smug. "If looking after me is why you're not like me, then *I'm* why you're not a psychopath. If I'd never been born, you'd be me, Che. David would have taught you how to be a good little psycho. You're a nice guy *because* of me. Why aren't you thanking me?"

This time Rosa doesn't smile, she laughs.

PACKING MY STUFF DOESN'T take long. There's no shipping crate this time. We're back to packing only what we can carry. I have one suitcase and one backpack.

What I want to take doesn't quite fit so I sacrifice books and my tattiest trackpants and T-shirts for my boxing gear. I'm sorry to be leaving the Ali poster. I look at his scarred knuckles, then at my own. They're bruised from my last sparring session. I wish there was a way to give the poster to Sojourner, but she told me not to contact her.

All I want to do is contact her.

I try to focus on going home. Georgie, Nazeem, Jason. They know I'm on my way. Jason is his oblivious self. —Cool. You can come to my next fight.

Georgie and Nazeem are all questions. I say I'll tell them when we get there.

But I'm not sure I can. I'm not sure I want to tell anyone about the dark spot in my brain. No police reports will follow us. The death of Leilani McBrunight's little sister was reported as an accident, and not widely. Leilani's only a big deal for a subset of the fashion world.

Folding up the soft shirts Leilani bought me, I feel the prickle of tears. Sojourner's not the only one I'm going to miss.

—Any instructions for packing the fancy clothes you bought me?

Instead of texting a reply, Leilani calls me.

"Do you have any tissue paper?"

"You've cut your hair!" Her hair is now shorter than mine—a buzz cut that's left her looking like a prisoner. "Is that a number two?"

Leilani nods. "It was too much, so—" She flicks her fingers. "Gone. You could use a haircut yourself."

It's true. My hair is falling forward into my eyes. I push it back. "Hasn't been time." Or money. Or the will. My hair isn't important.

"Tissue paper?"

"Nope."

"You have old T-shirts. Use them. Clean ones, though! Lay them flat in between the shirts. Make sure the tags of your T-shirts aren't in contact with the shirts. They'll be plastic." She shudders. "They can do nasty things to good fabric. Best to cut 'em off. Fold the shirts as little as possible. You want to avoid creasing. As soon as you land, hang them up on moulded hangers. Not wire ones!"

I salute her.

Leilani bows.

"Thanks," I say. "For the tips, for the clothes—for teaching me to appreciate them."

"You're welcome," she says as if she's in customer service. But I can see she means it.

"And teaching me this city."

"No problem."

"Also the searing wit."

"Always."

She looks away briefly.

"I'll miss you," I say.

Leilani smiles.

"Especially your laugh."

"Oh, shut up! I'll send you a laugh ringtone if you're not careful."

"Please! It's all I've ever wanted."

"But you'll see me again, Che. You're going to get away from Rosa, right?" She moves closer to her screen so she's all eyes. "Promise me?"

I nod. "I promise."

"When you're free I'll visit you wherever you are." It's a promise.

"I'd like that."

She makes a face to take the edge off. "I want to meet your friend Georgie."

"She wants to meet you too," I say. I try to think of something light to say; instead, I take a breath. "If you see Sojourner, tell her I love her."

Leilani shakes her head. "Not now. Maybe later. Jaime says it cost Sid to break up with you."

My throat tightens. It's been less than a day, and I've been on the verge of texting Sojourner almost every minute.

"I miss her so much," I whisper.

Leilani looks away. I shouldn't have said that. Losing Sojourner is nothing compared to Leilani losing Maya.

"I miss Maya too," I tell her.

"Is it ever going to stop hurting?" There's no attempt to hide her pain. Her face is pinched with it.

"It has to," I say. But I'm not sure I believe it.

CHAPTER FORTY-TWO

"There aren't enough buttons."

Rosa sits between Sally in the window seat and me on the aisle. We're not in business class. Rosa is unhappy.

Back in cattle class I can smell the baked-in sweat of the thousands of people who've sat here before us. But the air is the same: recirculated, tasting like recycled plastic and devoid of any moisture. My tongue already sticks to the roof of my mouth.

"It's not like they can't afford to send us first class. They're being mean. Did you at least ask them for business class?" Rosa asks Sally.

Our mother doesn't answer. Her cheek is pressed to the window, her eyes are on the clouds. She's said little since she and Rosa and I had our first honest conversation. It's not like talking takes away the ache of a broken heart and a ruptured soul. Talking to Rosa only increases it.

I wish I could tell Sally that my heart is broken too. But I don't think she believes I have a heart.

I think about my list. I got everything I wanted: a girlfriend, sparring, and now we're going home to Sydney. I got everything except number one on my list: *Keep Rosa under control.* I will never have that. I should tell Rosa about my list. It would be a perfect way to explain dramatic irony to her.

"Sally," Rosa says. "When we're in Sydney, can I have a dog? I didn't kill my pretend dog."

Sally doesn't respond.

"I bet if you asked the McBrunights they would have bought us business-class seats. The cost of that would be like nothing to them. They could buy us a whole plane if they wanted to. They *should* buy us a plane. I saved Seimone from the electric chair and they haven't even thanked me."

"New York doesn't have the death penalty," I tell her. "If they did, they wouldn't use the electric chair, and they certainly wouldn't execute a little rich girl. Besides, the police were never going to press charges."

"I still saved her. That's why she gave me this." Rosa pulls a necklace from under her shirt; a ruby heart dangles from a gold chain. "Seimone gave me Maya's. She says we're twins now."

The nausea hits me in a wave. I put my hand over my mouth and haul myself out of my seat and down the aisle and into the toilet. Vomit burns up my oesophagus and through my mouth and into the bowl. I taste acid, lettuce, bread and cheese. Then the wave hits again and again. I vomit until there's nothing left to come up but bile.

When I turn to wash my hands and face, the now-red whites of my eyes stare at me from the mirror. Subconjunctival haemorrhage. It looks awful, but broken blood vessels are nothing. They're the opposite of Rosa, who is so much worse than she looks.

I fill a tiny paper cup with water, rinsing and spitting, shocked again every time I see my eyes.

When I sit down Rosa is drinking a Coke. Something Sally would never allow. She looks at my eyes and laughs. "You've got devil eyes."

"When did you steal that necklace?" Maya was wearing it when she died.

"I didn't have to steal it. I just had to ask. Seimone loves me best."

She swings her legs back and forth, stopping short of kicking the seat in front of her. That's not an interesting kind of trouble to make. It's too easy. She'll think of something else.

I know with certainty she's going to make more trouble. Rosa's scared Sojourner away, destroyed Sally, gotten rid of David, and broken me. I'm sure the rush of that makes her want to do it again, do it worse.

I can't help thinking about something Rosa said to me when she was four:

"*I can make you cry if I want.*"

I laughed. "*I've got a pretty high pain threshold, kid. But go ahead, punch me.*"

"*Not ouch pain, silly.*"

"*What kind of pain, then?*"

Rosa pointed at my heart.

She was right. She's always been right.

ACKNOWLEDGEMENTS

Tayari Jones gave me the initial idea for writing a young adult take on *The Bad Seed*, that wonderful 1954 book by William March, when she wrote about it on Twitter. She inspired me to reread the book, and to find out how much the research on psychopaths has changed. A lot, it turns out.

I was also inspired by watching my fantabulous niece, Lyra Larbalestier Bern, learn to laugh, walk, talk, and become a little empathetic loving person. Watching Lyra helped me imagine all the ways in which Rosa is nothing like her.

Nadine Champion, my boxing trainer, is one of the most amazing people I've ever met. She taught me everything I know about the fine art of pugilism and had a huge influence on this book. If it wasn't for her I would never have sparred and learnt so much about myself I didn't know.

Jill Grinberg has been my agent for more than ten years. I am thankful for that fact every day. Thank you. Thanks also to the wonderful team at Jill Grinberg Literary Management: Katelyn Detweiler, Cheryl Pientka and Denise St. Pierre.

Many thanks to everyone at Soho Press, especially Daniel Ehrenhaft and Meredith Barnes and Rachel Kowal. And at Allen and Unwin, especially Jodie Webster, Hilary Reynolds and Clare Keighery. I'm so glad to have such wonderful homes in my two countries of the USA and Australia.

Thank you to Lili Wilkinson and Anna Grace Hopkins for sending me down the path of reading about empathy.

Thank you to my first readers: Jack Heath, Alaya Dawn Johnson, Daniel José Older, Meg Reid, Tim Sinclair, Scott Westerfeld and Sean Williams. My sincere apologies for how shit that draft was. It's much better now. I promise.

Extra special thanks to Scott Westerfeld, Jill Grinberg, Meg Reid and Alaya Dawn Johnson, who for their sins, read multiple drafts. (They're listed in order of how many drafts they read.)

Jill Grinberg and Denise St. Pierre provided exceptional emergency notes. I owe you both.

Thanks to Coe Booth, Jessie Devine, Sarah Dollard, Emily Jenkins, Alaya Dawn Johnson, Bronwyn King, Gemma Kyle, Jan Larbalestier, Jason Reynolds and Lili Wilkinson for your comments on later drafts. Invaluable. Especially those continuity catches, Lili and Sarah! So glad they didn't make it through. Coe, Emily and Alaya saved this book by pointing to even more places to cut. Sometimes it's hard to see the trees because of the damn forest. Jessie Devine provided extremely useful notes on my writing of Elon. Any mis-gendering that remains is my fault.

The McBrunights' family name is a mash-up of the names of several Minnesota Lynx players who were on the 2013 WNBA championship winning team. Their win was an amazing team effort, so there was a lot of speculation about who would be named MVP. Richard Cohen, a well-known basketball blogger, tweeted that it should go to the whole team and mashed their names together. I told him I was going to put those names in my next book, and I did. Janine (Mc)Carville, Rebecca (Brun)son, Monica Wr(ight) = McBrunight. Maya is named for Maya Moore and Seimone for Seimone Augustus. It's pronounced the same as *Simone*. Lisimaya is a combination of Maya and Lindsay Whalen. (Okay, Lisi for Lindsay is a stretch but it sounds better.) Leilani is named for one of my favourite basketball players, Leilani Mitchell. No, she wasn't on that team. I just love her.

As always I'm grateful to my loving and very functional family of Jan Larbalestier, John Bern, Niki Bern, Lyra Larbalestier Bern and Scott Westerfeld.

ABOUT THE AUTHOR

Justine Larbalestier is the author of *Razorhurst*, which received four starred reviews, and of the prize-winning *Liar*. She also edited the collection *Zombies vs. Unicorns* with Holly Black.

Justine lives in both Sydney and New York City—(though not at the same time). She is a proud Australian-American.

justinelarbalestier.com
@justinelavaworm